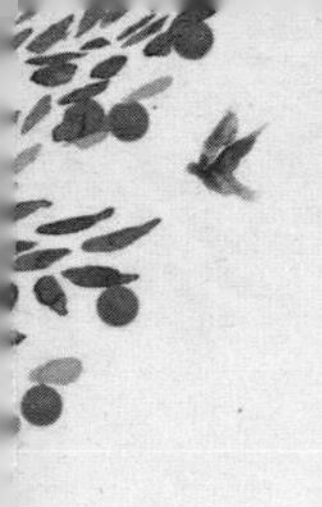

Shelly walked around the side of the house for a last look at the garden before she returned to the square. It had clearly been beautiful once. Under the jumble of weeds and brambles, she could envisage a whole lot of magic waiting to be uncovered. In her imagination, the entire property felt as if it were holding its breath as it waited for someone to come and rescue it from its neglect. As the light finally faded, she felt at one with Casa Maria. Almost as if the spirits within the house were beckoning to her. Shelly had always believed that things happened for a reason. Now she felt certain that Casa Maria had come into her life to serve a very important purpose.

By Emma Hannigan

Keeping Mum
The Pink Ladies Club
Miss Conceived
Designer Genes
Driving Home for Christmas
Perfect Wives
The Summer Guest
The Heart of Winter
The Secrets We Share
The Perfect Gift
The Wedding Promise

The Wedding Weekend (e-short)

Talk to the Headscarf

Emma Hannigan is the author of eleven bestselling novels and a bestselling memoir charting her journey through cancer. Emma lives in Bray, Ireland, with her husband, two children, two cats and a dog.

For love, laughter, tears and joy, read Emma Hannigan . . .

'A glorious read . . . A wonderfully uplifting novel about women's friendship by a writer who understands exactly how women think'
Cathy Kelly

'Hannigan's novel, much like the vivacious author herself, is brimming with hope, joy and inspiration'
Sunday Independent

'A moving tale celebrating the bonds between women, Emma Hannigan beautifully captures the difficult and wondrous thing that is loving and learning to let go . . . just a little. An excellent read'
Irish Tatler

'Emotional and heartbreaking . . . A fast-paced story with endearingly warm characters – you'll savour this touching tale'
Candis magazine, Book of the Month

'This fast-paced and endearing novel is about friendship between women, accepting yourself and trusting your own judgement'
Belfast Telegraph

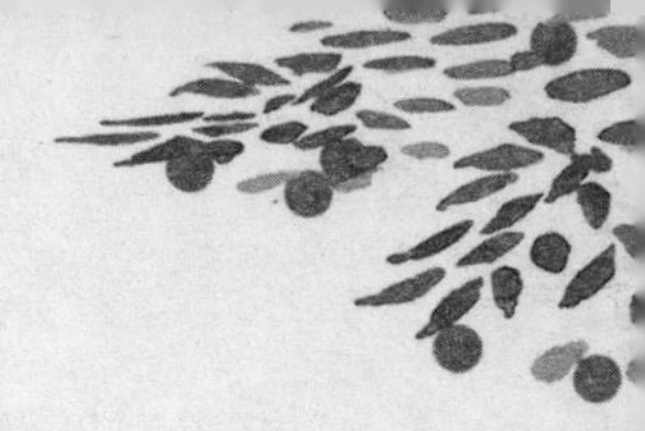

More praise for Emma Hannigan:

'Restores our faith in human nature and makes us feel warm inside'
Writing Magazine

'Moving, imaginative and believable, this emotional novel is the perfect read for a rainy day'
Reveal magazine

'This is her best novel yet. Her heart and soul was poured into every word of this story and it just radiates from the pages . . . a wonderful, heartfelt, emotive book'
Shaz's Book Blog

'Savour a novel from an author who knows what makes people tick'
Irish Independent

'I didn't just like it, I really LOVED it . . . Grab this book, curl up on the couch and prepare to have a few lump in your throat moments too'
Celeste Loves Books

'The author deals with some hard-hitting and sensitive issues, giving the story a depth that I really did not expect . . . Emma Hannigan is a gifted storyteller'
Random Things Through My Letterbox

'An inspirational novel . . . Warm, lovingly written and full of hope'
Bleach House Library

'This was a feel-good read great for the cold winter nights ahead . . . This is yet another winner for me from Emma Hannigan . . . She has become a firm favourite of mine'
Rea Book Reviews

Emma Hannigan

The Wedding Promise

First published in Great Britain in 2017
by HEADLINE REVIEW
An imprint of HEADLINE PUBLISHING GROUP

First published in paperback in Great Britain in 2017
by HEADLINE REVIEW
An imprint of HEADLINE PUBLISHING GROUP

1

Cataloguing in Publication Data is available from the British Library

ISBN 978 1 4722 3015 7

Typeset in Palatino by Palimpsest Book Production Ltd, Falkirk, Stirlingshire

Printed and bound in Great Britain by Clays Ltd, St Ives plc

Headline's policy is to use papers that are natural, renewable and recyclable products and made from wood grown in well-managed forests and other controlled sources. The logging and manufacturing processes are expected to conform to the environmental regulations of the country of origin.

HEADLINE PUBLISHING GROUP
An Hachette UK Company
Carmelite House
50 Victoria Embankment
London EC4Y 0DZ

www.headline.co.uk
www.hachette.co.uk

In loving memory of my beloved aunt Mitzi.

Prologue

A SWEET, HEADY CITRUS SCENT WAFTED ON THE balmy breeze as he pushed open the large rusty gates. They creaked and groaned as if complaining about being used, as if they were letting him know that it had been a long, long time since they'd been opened.

Inside, the ground was rough and weeds grew freely, but he could see the contours of what once must have been a charming and verdant garden. He followed his nose towards the source of that fragrance, and as he rounded a corner, he saw the house. Although it was tired and forgotten-looking, the delicious aroma emanating from the laden orange trees drew him closer. His eyes took in the facade, the tall windows, the sturdy wooden front door, and he smiled. As he stood there, barely able to catch his breath, something in his heart shifted, as if in recognition – as if, strangely, it was home.

Gerry looked around at the neglected tangle of the grounds and shook his head. He was crazy to even be here, to be contemplating this, but fate had guided him this far, so what was the point of turning back now? He didn't know what had made him stop dead at the sight of this place in the estate agent's window, but he knew now, looking at it, that it was just meant to be. Simple as that. As simple and as complicated as that. He had no idea how the suggestion would be received, but as far as he was concerned, it was already a done deal. He could see the future, and it was beautiful.

Chapter 1

SHELLY DILLON HAD ALWAYS IMAGINED A WHOLE new chapter unfolding in her life once she turned fifty. She and Gerry had been married with Jake on the way before her twenty-first birthday. By the age of twenty-five, their daughter, Leila, had completed their family and they'd bought their first home. In today's world, they'd be regarded as mere babies themselves, yet they'd taken it all in their stride. She'd no regrets whatsoever about how things had panned out for them, and had always felt blessed to have her children while she was young enough to enjoy them.

Having said that, in the tough times – and there were many as she raised two confident, boisterous kids – she'd comforted herself that her and Gerry's sacrifices would be worthwhile and that they'd have plenty of time to share an entire second half to their lives once they had an empty nest.

'We'll grow up as the children grow and then we'll have all the time in the world together,' Gerry often said when money was tight or one of the children was in trouble at school.

They had all sorts of plans to explore the world in a far more upmarket way than they had with two children in tow. The benchmark she'd had in her mind for this second phase of life was fifty.

Now, as she stood in the beautifully decorated marquee that her children had ordered at their Dublin suburban home, she still felt utterly blessed but more than a little edgy. The future was here. Fifty was now and she was oddly nervous of what was about to unfold. She took a deep breath and swallowed the fluttery feeling in her tummy. She knew she was doing that thing she shouldn't do – over-thinking instead of just doing and being . . .

'The Stokeses are here!' Gerry said gleefully, beckoning to her to come and join them. Shelly went over to hug their old friends, who they didn't see enough of since they'd moved to the UK.

Shelly had known the party was happening tonight, but Jake and Leila had insisted on doing everything. Along with Fee, Jake's girlfriend, and Matthew, Leila's boyfriend, they'd taken it in hand, insisting that all Shelly needed to do was show up. Nothing more.

'Could I at least give you a list of people to invite?' Shelly had asked anxiously. 'I'd be so upset if you unintentionally forgot someone.'

'We won't,' Leila insisted. 'But if it makes you feel better, you can submit your list to my work email and I'll merge it with our one.'

'Thank you, madam,' Shelly said with a smirk.

It was genuinely endearing that they'd gone to so much trouble. The marquee had been erected while she was enjoying a romantic long lunch with Gerry. They got home, and it was all done. Inside, the little touches, such as bunches of her favourite sweet peas in tiny glass vases on each table, brought a tear to her eye. She'd been feeling rather teary all day, in fact, and now that the guests were arriving in their hordes, she was having a hard time holding it together. She had never expected so many people to turn up just for a birthday party.

The Stokeses turned away, calling hellos to other friends they hadn't seen in some time, and for a moment, it was just Gerry next to her, as always.

'How are you coping, love?' he asked as he circled his arm around her waist and kissed her lightly. A camera bulb flashed in her face, making her jump.

'Oh, this is Jen, the photographer,' Gerry said with a smile. 'She's here for the night to mingle and capture some moments of this very special occasion. It's my little surprise gift for you, along with this.' He handed her an envelope, watching her intently as she opened it. Inside was a piece of card bearing one simple sentence: *You are going on a family holiday for four in St Lucia, leaving on Friday.*

Shelly gasped and looked up at her husband. He was grinning widely, delighted by her reaction.

'Oh Gerry! This is wonderful. Are Jake and Leila joining us?'

He nodded vigorously.

'But what about Matthew and Fee? Didn't they want to bring them along?'

'It wasn't possible for everyone to get the time off, so we decided it would be lovely for us to have a week as a family of four. One last hurrah before either or both of them are married off.'

'Why, is there an announcement on the way?' Shelly joked.

'Not that I know of,' Gerry said, 'but Jake would want to get his finger out sooner rather than later if you ask me. He's almost thirty and isn't getting any younger.'

'I agree,' said Shelly. 'But times have changed, love, and

I guess it's up to him and Fee to do things at their own pace. Thank you for this, darling. It'll be such a treat to have our little family together with no outside distractions.'

'This is merely a taste of what lies ahead for you and me,' Gerry said. 'We always said we'd start doing what *we* want when you hit fifty.'

'Yes, we did,' she said, kissing him as she fought back emotional tears.

As more guests arrived Shelly mingled and sipped champagne while a wonderful jazz band struck up and kept them entertained. Before long the marquee was buzzing and the champagne was flowing, and everyone looked very happy. The atmosphere was one of sheer jubilation.

Jake took to the small stage to welcome the guests.

'Good evening, folks,' he called out. 'I'm here to call you all to your tables; the delicious food you've been smelling for the last while is now ready to be served.'

People found seats at the pretty round tables, which were adorned with pale pink tablecloths and crisply wrapped matching chairs, complete with oversized bows at the backs. Jake wasn't a man for interior decorating, but he could see that Leila had really pulled out all the stops with the decor. The marquee looked stylish and welcoming – just like their mother.

'Okay, thank you. Now I don't want to hold you back from the celebrations, but I do just want to say a quick but heartfelt thank you to everyone for joining us this evening. It's an incredible turnout, which I think is testimony to the high esteem in which this woman is held – my mother, Shelly.'

The marquee erupted in applause and Shelly felt her face getting hot as every head in the room turned to look at her. She waved awkwardly, then felt for Gerry's hand. He stood beside her, beaming at everyone. She loved and admired his confidence; he could stand up in any room, in front of any amount of people, and feel at home.

'And of course,' Jake went on, 'that esteem also extends to our wonderful father, Gerry.'

More applause, and Gerry took a theatrical bow, making Shelly laugh.

'Leila and I are very lucky to have these two people as our parents,' he said, as Leila went up to stand beside him. 'We wanted to show them tonight how much we love and cherish them, and we thank you for helping us to do that. I don't know how much we'll see them from now on, though,' he added with a grin. 'These two have been banging on about their fabulous fifties since they were half that age, so I'm fully expecting them to abandon us now and run off into the sunset.'

Leila laughed as the room erupted again into applause and cheers.

Jake raised his glass, and there was a cacophony of scraping chairs as the guests all rose and did the same.

'To Shelly and Gerry,' he called out.

'To Shelly and Gerry,' they all roared back.

Shelly clinked her glass against Gerry's and laid her head on his shoulder.

'I'm mortified,' she whispered into his ear. 'But also overwhelmed.'

'Don't be silly,' Gerry whispered back. 'This is fantastic. I'm going to enjoy every second. You won't be turning fifty again, my love, so forget embarrassment and let your hair down.'

'You crazy old fool,' Shelly murmured as she kissed him.

'Ahem, do you two need to get a room?' Leila was standing next to them with Jake, her arms folded as though she was dealing with two naughty children.

Shelly laughed. 'All in good time,' she said with a wink.

'Mum!' Leila and Jake said together, which made her laugh even more.

Jen, the photographer, interrupted them gently.

'I'm sorry to butt in, guys, but could you all turn to face me. You look stunning standing there; I want to get one of the family together.'

They stood and posed as Jen's camera clicked and flashed.

'Thanks,' she said, moving on to look for more moments to capture.

'Dad gave me my gift,' Shelly said, smiling at Leila and Jake. 'I couldn't be happier. I can't believe we're going to get time out together. It's wonderful.'

'I can't wait,' Leila said. 'A bit of down time in St Lucia is exactly what I need.'

'Mum,' Jake said, 'this isn't a holiday of a lifetime, I'm afraid, just a small thing for you.' He held out a carefully wrapped parcel and Shelly took it, turning it round.

'An unusual shape,' she said.

'Go on, open it,' Jake replied.

She pulled back the wrapping; inside was an exquisite hand-carved wooden lily, one of her favourite flowers.

'That's beautiful,' she breathed. 'Is it one of your own?'

Jake nodded. 'A one-off, made for a unique woman.'

Shelly kissed him, blinking to hold back the tears. 'I adore it. In fact I think it's the most beautiful thing you've made. It's really good, Jake. You're getting better and better.'

'All right, lovebirds,' Leila said. 'Why don't you two wander around the tables as the starter is being served? That way you can be certain you've spoken to everyone, then you can kick back and relax for the rest of the evening.'

Shelly did as she was bid, even though she felt a little bit like an ageing bride.

The first table was made up of their oldest friends, all of whom picked up on her mild discomfort.

'Bet you didn't see yourself doing this kind of gig over thirty years on!' Sue said.

'Except this time we aren't in royal-blue taffeta bridesmaid dresses,' said Jane.

'And I'm not in a pouffy little Bo Peep number with a veil the length of a football pitch,' Shelly said. 'It's so special to have you all here, even if we have toned things down in the fashion stakes!'

By the time she arrived at the last table, Gerry was already there, and was perched next to his oldest friend, Jim.

'Jim, thank you so much for coming,' Shelly said, swooping down to kiss him.

'I wouldn't have missed it,' Jim said, taking her hand. 'What a fantastic night. You lot do parties in style, that's for sure.'

'Well I can claim no credit,' Shelly said. 'It was all Jake and Leila's doing. I didn't get a look-in on the preparations.'

'They've done you proud,' Jim said. 'I'm just sorry Martha's not here to share it with us. The four of us would have been dancing till dawn.'

Shelly laughed, but her heart broke a little at the mention of Martha. Jim's wife had died eighteen months ago, and their lives had been left emptier without her. Before, they were the perfect foursome and regularly got together for dinners and parties. Now, although Jim was still invited to everything and still a fixture in their lives, it just wasn't the same without Martha beside him, her dry wit setting the night on fire. Shelly missed her terribly.

'I wish she was here, Jim, with all my heart,' she said, squeezing his hand.

Jim looked momentarily grief-stricken, but quickly regained his composure.

'This isn't the time for looking back; it's all about looking forward when you turn fifty. Isn't that right, Gerry boy?'

Gerry laughed. 'Absolutely. I've only got eyes for the future now. Yesterday is over, as they say. I've got lots I want to do next.'

'That's the spirit,' Jim said, raising his glass. 'I'll drink to that. And what about you, Shelly? I'd have thought you'd have found something to replace the café by now. You can't exist without a few projects on the go.'

Shelly and Martha had set up a small café in the village about eight years ago, and they had both adored it. They'd baked their own bread and cakes, served the best coffee they could find, and on Friday and Saturday nights did a wine and one-pot-wonder night that had become the meeting point for all their regulars and friends. Those had been happy times, and the truth was that Shelly hadn't yet had the heart to replace them with something new.

'You're right, Jim,' she said. 'I should be looking for something else. I'm sure the right thing will turn up and I can pour my energy into it. It would be nice, in fact; I really miss the café.'

'Maybe something will turn up sooner than you think,' Gerry said enigmatically.

'Oh,' Shelly said, 'is that your way of telling me something?'

Gerry laughed. 'No. I'm just saying fate has a funny way of working sometimes. Maybe your moment is on its way.'

Shelly looked at him sideways, wondering what had made him say that. But before she could press him further, the main course was announced and they made their way back to their seats.

The rest of the night went by in a flash. Shelly wasn't sober going to bed, but she certainly wasn't drunk either. She'd held back on drinking too much, terrified of missing anything. But apart from that, she was still a little unnerved and very emotional. She knew fifty was the new forty and that she was in a fortunate position in so many ways. They were financially secure, their family was grown up, and both she and Gerry were in perfect health. She had no reason whatsoever to feel anxious. But there was a little voice inside her head whispering that she ought to strike while the iron was hot and plan some new and slightly wild adventures. It would be a waste just to roll on as before. He probably didn't know it, but when Jim had made those remarks about a new project, he was hitting the nail on the head. She wanted to do something, but she just couldn't figure out what.

She turned over in bed and draped her arm over her sleeping husband. It had been an unforgettable night. And, as Gerry had pointed out, this family holiday would probably be their last one as a group of four. She planned to savour each moment of it, while also having a little think about what they could do next. She made herself a promise: as soon as they returned from St Lucia, she would take up a new hobby and do something fresh and new that got her right out of her comfort zone. Maybe they could take up art classes together, or go on a wine appreciation holiday? The possibilities were endless! With a smile on her face, she sighed and closed her eyes, happy in the knowledge that she was about to jump into the next phase of life with both feet.

Chapter 2

SHELLY SHOUTED UP THE STAIRS TO LEILA. 'WHERE are you? I know your father is the pilot, but it wouldn't look good if he has to hold the plane for us.'

'I'm coming,' Leila yelled back, with a little too much aggression for Shelly's liking.

As her daughter came thundering down the stairs with a puss on her face and bustled past her and straight out the front door, Shelly had to bite her tongue. Why was Leila behaving like a crotchety teenager? At twenty-six she ought to have come out of this type of moodiness. Sighing, Shelly knew it was futile to argue. Leila had never been a morning person, and clearly that hadn't changed. She lived with her boyfriend Matthew now and had only stayed over so they could share a taxi to the airport this morning.

Shelly didn't fancy sitting beside a silently seething madam all the way from Dublin to St Lucia, so she said nothing. But she had noticed the fact that she'd been walking on eggshells around Leila a lot lately.

Not for the first time, she wondered if Matthew was having to put up with these kinds of moods. Perhaps they were only for her benefit, and Leila was charming elsewhere. She'd been like that as a teenager. A total tyrant at home, and then Shelly would have her friends' mothers congratulating her on her charming daughter and praising Leila to the heavens. She used to fret about it and wonder why Leila couldn't at least be civil to her.

'Try to let it go over your head,' Gerry would say. 'Wouldn't it be worse if she was rude and obnoxious in public? Play along, let the other mothers think we've bagged ourselves an angel!'

Shelly always thought of that when Leila crossed the line over the years. But she'd assumed they'd gone past this kind of carry-on by now. Maybe Leila was exhausted after the party. It had taken a lot of organisation, and judging by how smoothly it had gone, she had shouldered the pressure.

All the same, Shelly had fresh respect for Matthew. He was one of life's calm and placid souls; the perfect yin to Leila's yang. The first time Leila had brought him home, Gerry had whispered to her in the kitchen that he felt sorry for the poor fellow.

'Why, what's wrong with him?' Shelly had asked innocently.

'I'm worried that he's too nice for Leila. She'll massacre him and he'll probably let her.'

'Well, isn't it better than seeing your only daughter with a thug or a bully?'

As the weeks turned to months, they'd all become very fond of Matthew, and Gerry had realised that he was the perfect man for his often explosive daughter.

'Did you call Matthew this morning?' Shelly ventured as they sat in the taxi on the way to the airport.

'He called me,' Leila said, pulling a fold-up brush from her handbag. 'He's such a worrywart. He was on about those hideous compression stockings he got from the chemist. I'm *not* wearing those on the plane. Apparently he's worried about deep vein thrombosis.'

'He's very thoughtful, Leila. You need to appreciate him more.'

'I know,' Leila said with a sigh.

'He's a lovely person, and you can be moody sometimes,' Shelly said.

'I'm not that bad,' Leila said defensively.

'Well, I'm not saying you're Attila the Hun, but you can be hard to be around at times. You can make a person feel small when you've got the hump.'

To Shelly's astonishment, tears sprang into Leila's eyes and she bit her lip to fight them back.

'I'm sorry, Mum,' she said.

'Oh God, Leila, don't cry. I don't mean you're awful, sweetheart. I'm just reminding you to be nice to Matthew, that's all.'

Leila covered her face with her hands. 'Mum, I need to tell you something. I'll burst if I don't.'

Shelly's heart plummeted. Leila looked so upset, what could be the matter?

'Is everything all right?' she said gently.

Leila started to sob. Shelly pulled her close and stroked her hair.

'What is it, love?'

'It's good, really. Well, we're happy,' Leila said. She looked up at Shelly, lip quivering. 'I'm having a baby.'

'Oh, Leila!' Shelly gasped, then she too began to cry. 'That's wonderful news.' Relief flooded her. No wonder the poor girl was all over the place at the moment. Her pregnancy hormones were clearly having a big effect on her.

'How far gone are you?' she asked as they both calmed down.

'Nine weeks,' Leila said with a watery smile. 'It wasn't exactly planned, but Matthew is as excited as I am.'

'That's fabulous, love. Wait until your father hears! He'll be over the moon. Oh, I can't believe it.' Shelly grabbed her daughter in another tight hug. 'You must be wrung out after doing so much work for my party. I feel really guilty. I wish you'd let me help more.'

'Don't be silly, Mum. It was my idea to do your party and I loved being able to give back. You've been such a rock for Jake and me. It was the least we could do for you. Sitting there feeling guilty will ruin the entire effect, so please don't.'

'Okay, love,' Shelly said, patting her hand and trying to hide her concern.

'I haven't told Jake or Dad either, so I'll drop my bomb when I see them. If I'm on fizzy water in St Lucia, Jake will guess anyway. I wanted to tell you all together, though. Sorry about that.'

'Don't apologise for a second. And it's not a bomb by any stretch of the imagination,' Shelly said. 'It's Jake's niece or nephew and our grandchild! Now isn't that wonderful!'

'Do you think I should put on the hideous stockings? Matthew made me promise I would.'

'It won't do any harm, and if you made a promise, you should stick to it.'

'Yeah,' she sighed. 'I'm not great at doing what I'm told, and there are *so* many rules with this pregnancy lark.'

'Wait until we get to the members' lounge. You can go into the bathroom there and pop them on,' Shelly said.

* * *

By the time they'd checked in and made their way to the lounge, Leila was looking genuinely nervous.

'Do you think Dad will be cross with me?' she asked Shelly, suddenly sounding like a little girl once more.

'Why?' Shelly was puzzled.

'We're not married and we don't have any plans to be.'

'Oh for goodness' sake, nobody cares about that any more. Your father and I don't, at least. As long as you're happy and Matthew is with you, isn't that all we need to focus on? Now, your brother and father should be here,' Shelly said excitedly. 'If we hurry, we'll be able to have a coffee with them before we all board.'

They were used to the luxurious surroundings of the Gold Circle lounge, not to mention the admiration of the other passengers when Gerry walked in. Dressed in his navy and gold uniform, he never failed to turn heads. But Shelly had noticed that since Jake had qualified, those stares had increased tenfold. Now she watched as father and son strode towards them, laughing together. Seeing the effect they were having on the Gold Circle lounge, she wanted to giggle. Many of her friends had commented that Jake was a good mix of both his parents. He'd inherited Gerry's height and dark features and her cheekbones and flawless skin. And while Gerry's hair was now greying, he still held himself erect and walked with confidence. The eyes of every female in the room scanned the two men unabashedly.

'Hey, goon,' Leila said, punching Jake on the top of his arm.

'Hey, squirt,' Jake said.

'We got you both coffees,' Shelly said as the two men

pulled out chairs and sat down to join them. 'The holiday starts here.'

'Why, is there brandy in it?' Gerry said, looking suspiciously into his cup.

'Don't be daft,' Shelly said, swatting his arm. 'Just an Americano, pure and simple.'

She glanced over at Leila, who was looking ill with nerves now, and inclined her head towards Jake and Gerry meaningfully.

Leila cleared her throat. 'Er, I've got some news to share now that we're all together.'

Jake and Gerry looked at her, then at Shelly, then back at Leila.

'Well, spit it out,' Jake said.

'Matthew and I . . .' Leila hesitated. 'It's just . . . we . . . well . . . we're going to have a baby.'

There was a beat of silence, then Jake jumped up and went around to her seat.

'No way!' he said, hugging her. 'That's mind-blowing. I'm going to be an uncle!' He stooped to kiss Shelly. 'And you're going to be a granny.' He grinned.

'I couldn't be more delighted,' said Shelly.

'Damn, I can't stay for long. I'm flying to New York shortly,' he said, looking at his watch. 'Sorry to rush off, especially after your news, Leila.'

'Okay, love,' Shelly said. 'Are you still able to join us tomorrow?' she asked hopefully.

'Yup, unless something goes badly awry, I'm all set. I can't wait to have a few days' holiday.'

Since qualifying as a pilot and working his way swiftly to long-haul flights, Jake had had literally no time off.

'Dad and I are so proud of you,' Shelly said, patting his

jacket. 'You've worked like a Trojan to get to where you are. It wasn't easy in your father's time and it's even harder now. The competition is fierce. You're fabulous.'

'Thanks, Mum,' he said, rubbing his face roughly as if trying to feel more awake. 'I'm sure I'll be delighted about the fact I've practically no life when my bank balance begins to bulge.'

'You *do* have a life,' Shelly said, straightening his collar. 'And a wonderful girlfriend who is the envy of all the women who lay eyes on you.'

'Yeah,' he said with a tired smile. 'I'm living the dream. Lord only knows how Fee has stuck by me with the hours I've had to put in lately.'

'Well, you did the same for her while she was at medical school,' Shelly pointed out.

Jake was still living at home, as was Fee with her own parents. Shelly had thought he'd have flown the nest by now, but she'd managed to remain philosophical about the situation.

'Right, better go. I'm so happy for you, Leila,' he said, giving her a final kiss. 'See you all tomorrow.'

When he'd left, Leila looked over at Gerry, who still hadn't said anything.

'Dad?' she ventured. 'Is this okay with you?'

Gerry's face broke into a wide smile. 'Leila, my darling, you've made me so happy,' he said, getting up and going over to hug her. 'I can't believe it! Isn't it the best news, love?' he said, turning to Shelly. She nodded emphatically. 'I'll be sleeping with a granny now!' he quipped.

'You aren't annoyed or disappointed in me?' Leila asked.

He turned to her, surprised. 'Of course not. If you'd told

me this when you were still at school and the father was that dreadful spotty article who dressed like an undertaker and spoke in grunts, then I'd be worried.' He laughed. 'But you and Matthew are made for each other.'

'See,' Shelly said with a warm smile, 'I told you Dad wouldn't be upset. She's been fretting about telling us.'

'Ah, you poor love. You should know us better than that,' he said, kissing the top of Leila's head. 'I'm glad in a way. You've been like a tiger with a sore paw for the last while. I was beginning to think you'd turned into one of those dreadful high-maintenance vipers the cabin crew have to give frozen smiles to.'

'Sorry I've been such a cow,' Leila said as tears rolled down her cheeks.

'Hey,' Shelly said, hugging her. 'No need for that. We've noticed you're not quite your usual sunny self, that's all. It'll even out once you settle down.'

Leila nodded but still looked miserable, and Shelly had never felt more protective.

They had a few more minutes together before it was time to board. Then Gerry kissed them both goodbye and went off to take his place in the cockpit.

The flight was smooth enough, bar a little turbulence, and Leila slept a good bit. Shelly felt as if she'd never stop smiling. She thought of all the lovely things she and Gerry could do with their grandchild. Would it be a boy or a girl?

'Will you find out the sex of the baby?' she asked Leila as they enjoyed the in-flight meal.

'No, I don't think so. We both want a surprise, I think.'

'Lovely.' Shelly nodded.

Leila took her hand. 'Thanks, Mum. You're already being an amazing granny.'

By the time they'd landed and been transferred to the hotel, it was dinner time. Shelly and Gerry told Leila they'd knock on her door in twenty minutes, then went on to their room along the corridor to freshen up.

'There's just enough time for us to have a little cuddle,' Gerry said suggestively. 'Now that we're about to become a granny and grandad, we need to make sure we don't leave our youth behind!'

Afterwards, they lay in each other's arms, talking about the future and what a wonderful difference this child was going to make to their lives.

'It's the next chapter,' Gerry said cheerfully. 'I've often thought about how it might feel to be a grandad, but I never dreamed it would happen so soon.'

'Me neither,' Shelly said. 'I stupidly assumed Jake and Fee would have a child first purely because they're older.'

'They'll all find their feet when they're ready,' Gerry said. 'For now, I think it's absolutely marvellous that Leila and Matthew are forging ahead and making themselves happy.'

Shelly eventually stepped into the shower, then pulled on a brightly coloured silk maxi dress and silver sandals.

'I'm looking forward to a bit of sun on my skin tomorrow,' she said. 'I'm sick of slapping on fake tan. The weather in Ireland has been abysmal lately.'

'A few days on the beach will do us all the world of good,' Gerry said as he went to shower. 'In fact I'm going to make it my business to ensure we all have more regular bursts of sun going forward.'

'Well I've no objection to that,' Shelly said.

She was putting on lip gloss when there was a knock on the door. She went over to open it.

'I don't think I'll come for dinner, if you don't mind,' Leila said. 'I'm wrecked and I'd prefer something light to eat in my room. I'd only be a moan if I came down with you.'

'Oh,' Shelly said, feeling disappointed. 'Would you not come and have a starter with us? I hate the thought of you in your room alone.'

'I'd prefer it, Mum, honestly. I'll order some room service and relax. You and Dad enjoy the first night together.'

Shelly and Gerry meandered to the restaurant and enjoyed a delicious meal of fresh fish followed by delectably sweet exotic fruit salad. Afterwards, they sat in a swinging seat overlooking the beach and shared a glass of champagne. With the sound of the ocean lapping against the shore and the blanket of twinkling stars above, it couldn't have been more perfect.

'I do love you, you know,' Gerry said as he took her hand.

'I love you too,' she smiled.

'We're lucky,' he sighed. 'So many couples we know haven't made it.'

'I know,' she said, resting her head on his shoulder. 'I keep thinking of poor Jim.'

'Me too,' said Gerry. 'It's been almost two years and he's still quite lost without her. Cancer is such a bloody horrible disease.'

'We should make an effort to go away somewhere with him,' Shelly said. 'They were together as long as we've been. We shared so much as a foursome and I'd hate Jim to think that he can't see us any more because Martha is gone.'

'I don't think he does. We've included him as often as possible, but you're right, we could book a weekend somewhere, maybe next month or even August. The three of us.'

They fell into a comfortable silence as they sipped their champagne.

'I could sit here like this forever with you,' said Gerry. He leaned over and kissed her. Shelly's heart still skipped a beat when he did that. Sighing, she savoured the moment. She was looking forward to many more like it.

'It's not so bad being kissed by a grandad,' she said as he chuckled. It was wonderful to have a new direction in life mapped out. Thanks to Leila, she now knew that her fresh start would kick off with becoming a grandmother.

Next morning, as he enjoyed the in-flight movie, Jake made a decision: he was going to find a house as soon as he got back to Dublin. He had a good deposit saved and his dad had told him in no uncertain terms that he'd be happy to help him out when the time came. It had been on his mind so much lately – every time he had to kiss Fee goodnight and drop her to her door. He hated that that was how their evenings ended. He was crazy about Fee, and there was no point waiting for some perfect time in the future. Their time was now, and they needed to live it.

He loosened his tie and stretched out as best he could, smiling to himself. Yes, it was the right decision, he could feel it. Fee and he should live together sooner rather than later. It might ease the slight tensions he'd felt between them lately. They weren't fighting or anything like that, but there was a constant struggle to find time for each other in the face of work and general life commitments.

Jake also knew that Fee was finding living with her parents more and more difficult. Hearing his little sister's news had given him the final kick he needed. If Leila and Matthew could manage to live with one another *and* make a baby, he really ought to get sorted too.

Fair enough, Leila's job at the bank wasn't quite as stressful as his, but she'd still got herself together. Matthew was pretty stretched too, setting up his car repair shop and garage, but all his hard work was definitely paying off now, and his was quickly becoming the go-to place for high-class motors.

By the time he'd gone through the airport and found a taxi to bring him to the resort, Jake was hot and fed up. The road was not much more than a dirt track lined with potholes, and the taxi had no air conditioning. The kamikaze way the local driver flung the car around corners and challenged the craters in the road made him quite grateful to be alive when they finally stopped.

He paid the driver and waved him off, and said a little prayer that they might never meet again. He could almost taste the cool beer he was hankering after. The receptionist gave him the key to his room and pointed him in the right direction.

As he stepped inside, he breathed deeply. It was gorgeous. Simple, but beautifully decorated and very clean. He went through the sliding glass doors and stood looking out from the balcony, drinking in the view. The glittering azure Caribbean Ocean was stunning against the pale powder sand beach. Calico umbrellas ran in a perfect row, dotted on each side by plush-looking loungers. Eager to catch the last rays of sunshine before dinner, he pulled on a pair of swim shorts and flip-flops and made his way to the beach.

His family waved enthusiastically as he trudged through the baking sand to where they were sitting. He stooped to hug them hello.

'Beer?' his dad said, and raised his hand in the air. A waiter skipped barefoot across the hot sand to take the order.

'Wow, that was quick,' Jake grinned. 'Do those guys hide in the dunes and jump out as soon as you lift a finger?'

'The service here is second to none,' Shelly said. 'I feel like I've been here a week already. It's so relaxing.'

Their drinks arrived within minutes and they all clinked glasses.

'This is like holidays when we were kids,' Leila said with a grin.

Time flew and the sun started to dip lower as they chatted about the fiftieth party and future plans. When it finally disappeared below the horizon, they all gathered their things and made their way back to their rooms.

'Want to meet in the bar for a sneaky pint?' Jake asked his dad.

'You're on,' Gerry said with a gleeful wink. 'See you in ten minutes? Quick shower and we'll run.'

'Perfect,' Gerry said as Jake banged him on the back.

When Jake walked into the bar fifteen minutes later, Gerry was already waiting for him. They ordered beers and sat at a table overlooking the sea.

The barman delivered their drinks.

'Wow, that's delicious,' said Gerry. 'There's nothing quite like a bottle of very cold beer in heat like this. I could happily spend a month here.'

'Me too,' said Jake. 'Although I need to channel all my cash into my new abode.'

'Oh really? Have you bought somewhere?'

'Not yet, but the time has come. I need to put down roots at some point. Fee and I are finding it hard to see one another while working so much, so it's the obvious solution.'

'Are you going to make an honest woman of her?' Gerry asked with a grin. 'You know your mother and I adore her, don't you? I'm aware it's not really the way of the modern world, but I think Deirdre and Dermot would appreciate it if you could show some solid commitment towards her. From what I know of them, they're rather more old-fashioned than we are.'

'I'll think about it,' Jake said. 'Of course it's on the cards. I don't see myself being with anyone other than Fee. But marriage isn't something I'm jumping up and down at the thought of just yet. I'm trying to take one step at a time.'

'I get that, son, but in my experience there are windows of opportunity in our lives,' Gerry said. 'Don't drag it out and miss yours. Go for it while you're both young and hungry for life. Succeed and move onwards and upwards together. You don't want Fee getting sour at being made to wait around. Most women are more interested in being married than we men realise.'

'I don't think Fee falls into that category, Dad.'

'Have you asked her?'

'What, to marry me?'

'No, whether or not marriage is on her radar?' Gerry said.

'No. We've talked about getting a place together, but nothing else. Fee knows I love her,' he said, yawning.

'Take a leaf out of your sister's book,' Gerry said. 'Do things together and it'll make you stronger as a couple.'

'I hear you, Dad. Thanks,' Jake said.

When the girls joined them, the conversation turned to babies.

'I'm so happy,' Leila said with shining eyes. 'I've been so sick these past few weeks, but I'm starting to feel excited now. Matthew is utterly besotted. He lies beside me on the sofa and chats to the baby.'

'He'll make a wonderful father,' Gerry said with a smile. 'I'm delighted you both have such fabulous partners. After all, that's what matters most.' He leaned over to kiss Shelly as both Jake and Leila made fake puking noises.

Shelly laughed. 'Come on,' she said. 'A toast to our wonderful partners, present and absent, and to all of us being happy together for a long time to come.'

'Hear, hear,' Gerry said as they clinked glasses.

Chapter 3

THE JUNE SUN WAS ENOUGH TO MAKE THE hospital feel like a sauna. The smell of antiseptic never mixed well with heat. Fee had finished an emergency appendectomy that wasn't on her list and was headed straight for a scheduled surgery on an elderly patient's leg when her mobile rang.

'Hi, Jake,' she said, blowing an escaped strand of hair from her eyes. Pulling the disposable cap from her head, she binned her apron too.

'Hey, sweetie,' he said. 'How are things going, *Ms Davis*?' He paused. 'I still need time to get used to you being a proper surgeon.'

'Believe me, I'm right in the zone. Talk about running from Billy to Jack. It's like *M*A*S*H* in here today. How's the Caribbean? I'm so envious,' she said with a sigh.

'Oh, it's lashing rain, cold and miserable,' he said.

'Really?'

'No, it's divine, I'm afraid. I wish you were here, though.'

'So do I. You've no idea how much I wish I was there. How's everyone?'

'Good,' he said evenly. 'Leila seems to be settling down. She's stopped puking and is only acting like a crazy lady sporadically as opposed to all the time.'

'Poor Leila, being pregnant can't be easy in the heat. You

know she rang me last night to tell me? She was really emotional. At first I thought she was ringing to say that she and Matthew had split up! Make sure you look after her, won't you?'

'Ah, I'm sure she'll manage. I'm not great at being with Leila when she's acting all schizo. It's like when we were kids. I'm trying to give her a wide berth, excuse the pun.'

'You're her big brother, Jake, and I'm sure she's not being a schizo, as you so horribly put it.'

'Are you due a night off any time this century?' he asked, clearly wanting to change the subject. His sister and girl-friend being close friends wasn't always a good thing. It meant two against one more often than not. 'I'm back on Saturday just after seven, all going well.'

'I'm supposed to be off for the weekend, as it happens. Apparently that's one of the perks of being a surgeon. We only have to work one weekend a month. It goes on rotation.'

'Will you book somewhere nice for us then?'

'Yeah . . .' she said, feeling suspicious. 'What are you up to? I thought we were saving every cent to try and put a deposit down. Why don't we go to the pasta place in town?'

'No, we've both been working our asses off lately. Book somewhere nice and we'll have a treat. We're celebrating your new job.'

Fee hadn't time to interrogate him any further as she arrived outside the operating theatre. The anaesthetist approached and waved at her.

'I have to go into surgery. I'll book something. Enjoy your holiday. I love you, but I hate you quite a lot too.'

* * *

By the time she'd finished work and got home that evening, Fee wasn't able to speak, let alone think about booking restaurants. She was bone tired.

Her parents, Deirdre and Dermot, were only a few years older than Shelly and Gerry, but they acted as if they were from a different time altogether. They lived quietly and routinely, eating the same dinners for the past forty years and carrying out the same rituals. They'd met Jake's parents at special occasions and always had pleasant exchanges, but Fee knew they would never be bosom buddies.

Her parents' preferred holiday involved a large tour bus with organised evening entertainment and a strictly planned agenda. Dermot was recently retired from a snack food company, where he'd worked his way up to a managerial position. Deirdre had worked as a bookkeeper until Fee was born and had never gone back once she'd had her.

'Hello, dear, your dinner's in the top oven keeping warm for you.'

'Thanks, Mum. If you didn't have it sitting there for me, I doubt I'd bother,' Fee said, smiling gratefully.

'You should never go without meals. Think of the people in Africa who would love a dinner and can't have it,' said Deirdre.

'Yes, you're right,' Fee said. She knew her mother had a point, but she was finding it hard enough to stay awake, let alone exercise her social conscience.

'It's time for our cocoa unless I'm mistaken, Deirdre,' her dad said as he appeared in the kitchen.

'Hello, Dad, how are you this evening?' Fee asked.

'Hello, Fiona dear.'

Her parents were firm on the fact that they had chosen Fiona as her name and were sticking to it. Nicknames or terms of endearment weren't in their comfort zone. 'Dear' or, at a stretch, 'pet' was the beginning and end of their frippery.

'I'm heating the milk now, Dermot,' Deirdre said. 'I'll bring it in to you. Would you like a chocolate biscuit or a plain one?'

He stood and pondered for a second. Fee stifled a giggle.

'You'd swear Mum had just asked you how to solve world peace in one sentence.'

Dermot appeared unperturbed by her statement.

'The type of biscuit I eat now could determine the quality of my sleep, Fiona. There are nights when I lie awake because the chocolate has made me hyper.'

'Go for a plain one in that case,' she said, giving up on any kind of frivolity. 'Or don't have one at all. Biscuits aren't exactly good for you. Have a piece of fruit instead.'

'Oh no. That'd play havoc with my stomach,' Dermot said with a very serious expression on his face. 'Besides, we still have in excess of thirty boxes of assorted biscuits left over from the factory.'

'Just because they're there doesn't mean you have to eat them all,' Fee said. 'Why don't you take them to a nursing home, or to the charity shop?'

'Why would we do that?' Deirdre asked. 'I've checked the best-before date on them, and going by my calculations, we're well on target to consume them all in time.'

'Thank God for that,' Fee said. 'I'll sleep better tonight now.'

'Don't be sarcastic, Fiona,' her father said. 'It's not becoming of a lady. I know you're tired after your day at the hospital, but that's no excuse to be disparaging about our biscuits.'

'Yes, and a little bit of what you fancy never did anyone any harm,' Deirdre said, looking at Fee as if she'd just committed a mortal sin. 'Now go back inside like a good man, Dermot. She's only pulling your leg.'

'I'm very sorry, Dad,' Fee said. 'I won't mention the biscuits again. Consider me well and truly told.'

Fee thought of Jake and his family over in the Caribbean. Gerry and Shelly were so different from her own parents. They chatted and laughed and enjoyed a glass of wine. Leila was always great fun too, and although he was pretty quiet, Matthew never failed to make an effort with her.

Her parents would walk over hot coals for her and she knew that they loved her in their own way, but she had definitely reached saturation point with her living arrangements.

'You never said hello to Marvin,' her mother said as she washed Fee's now empty plate.

'His cover is on and I haven't heard him tweet, so I didn't think of it,' Fee said. The budgie adoration was beyond her. In fact, she worried that the ageing bird harboured disease, especially seeing as he was stationed on the counter and her mother let him fly around the kitchen each day.

She lifted the cover and peeked in. Marvin's head shot around and he stared at her with his creepy little beady eyes. 'I think he hates me,' she said, thinking that the feeling was mutual.

'He wouldn't know the meaning of the word,' Deirdre said. 'He's the best boy, aren't you, Marvin?' She tugged at the cover and proceeded to make chirping noises at the bird. In fairness, he cheeped back, and he obviously made Deirdre feel great. But Fee just didn't get it and never would.

'Will you join us for cocoa?' Deirdre asked.

'Thanks, Mum, but I'm going to bed. Night, Dad,' she called in. 'Night, Marvin,' she added, making her mother beam with delight. 'Night, Mum. Sleep well. I'll be gone really early in the morning, so I'll see you around this time tomorrow, okay?'

'Right you are, Fiona. Sleep well now. Oh, I meant to ask you, have you heard from your young man?'

Fee grinned. They always referred to Jake as that.

'Yes, he's in the Caribbean with his family. He'll be back on Saturday and he's taking me out for a meal.'

'That's good to hear,' Dermot said. 'Make sure he pays and walks you home afterwards. The things I've read in the papers about women being attacked would stop anyone from stepping foot in Dublin city.'

'Don't worry, Dad, we'll take a taxi and I'll be quite safe. Jake always pays his way, too.'

'He's a good lad really,' Deirdre said grudgingly. 'Although in our day he'd have made an honest woman of you by now. You're leaving things terribly late, Fiona. Your ovaries won't keep churning out eggs forever.'

'That's enough of that sort of talk,' Dermot said. 'I don't need to hear that kind of thing.'

When her mother made comments like that, Fee always felt both undermined and a disappointment. Her parents only ever seemed to want her to get married and produce grandchildren. The fact that she'd slogged her guts out to become a surgeon didn't seem to cut the mustard with them. She knew they were proud of her. At least, lots of their friends and neighbours told them repeatedly that they ought to be. But as far as they were concerned, their daughter should be settling down and doing what they'd done.

They were more excited about Jake becoming a pilot than about her graduation.

'Now he's dependable,' her father had said, as they'd stood huddled in a corner at the graduation party.

To give him his due, Gerry hadn't let them get away with it.

'We're very proud of our son, of course. But I'd say you two should be on cloud nine with Fee's news. She's incredible! I've told Jake to hold on to her with both hands. She's a credit to you both.'

Her parents had tittered and nodded, but that was as far as they went. Fee knew deep down that they would be more comfortable with her if she lived in a two-up, two-down house with her husband, children and budgie.

Knowing she'd never sleep with the cloying smell of hospital clinging to her, Fee stood under the shower and closed her eyes. The heat of the water mixed with the cleansing bubbles of her body wash eased her anxious mind. She knew it was time to move out and get her own place. She'd broach the subject with Jake at dinner this Saturday.

Damn, she hadn't booked anywhere. Pulling on an oversized T-shirt, she climbed into bed and scrolled through her phone, choosing one of their favourite haunts, where they hadn't been in ages. As she pressed call, she fully expected to get an answer machine. To her delight, a bubbly-sounding girl answered and took the booking.

Smiling, Fee texted Jake to say it was all sorted.

Excellent! Missing u & can't wait to c u on Sat x

She plugged her phone in to charge and flicked off her bedside light. Even though she was totally wrecked, sleep evaded her. As she stared at the ceiling, she wondered where she and Jake could find somewhere to live. Maybe they could get a flat somewhere off the motorway so it was convenient for the airport and the hospital? Once the idea took hold of her, she could barely contain herself.

She'd try to make it to the shops on Saturday and buy something new to wear to dinner, too. It was a long time since she'd spent any money on herself.

Feeling excited, she snuggled into the covers and closed her eyes.

Chapter 4

THE WEEK SEEMED TO FLY BY. PERHAPS IT WAS THE sun and the wholesome sea air, but Leila felt she'd turned a corner by the time she and her mum flew home to Dublin.

'I enjoyed every second of that,' Shelly said as they settled in their seats for the return journey.

'Me too,' said Leila. 'It was kind of nice to have a surprise holiday with just the four of us. Who knows when that'll happen again?'

'I know, it was just like old times,' Shelly said, patting her hand.

'Except back then I wasn't up the duff and Jake didn't leave dressed in a uniform with the entire female population of the airport drooling in his wake.'

'True!' Shelly laughed. 'What is it with women and uniforms?' She shook her head.

Leila raised an eyebrow. 'Well, you fell for it.'

'Touché! I hope Fee manages to get him to put a ring on her finger soon. She must notice all the female attention he gets.'

'She's a strong character,' Leila said. 'I don't think there are many people, either male or female, who would argue with her. She'll make an amazing surgeon. I can't imagine anyone else as my sister-in-law, now that you mention it.'

* * *

It was late by the time they dragged their bags into the house. Leila's back was aching and she needed to lie down. She'd decided to stay for one more night before returning to their flat. Matthew was away working and planned on returning the following day, so it was better for Leila to be at home.

'Why am I so wrecked?' she moaned to Shelly.

'You're growing a person in there. It's hard work. It'll be worth it in the end, though. Nothing compares to holding your child in your arms. You'll see. Now make the most of having your mum minding you. Go up to bed and I'll bring you a nice cup of tea.'

'Thanks, Mum,' Leila said, hugging her.

Upstairs, she sank into her old bed. Much as she loved Matthew and their home together, she couldn't help enjoying being at home. She sighed and rubbed her belly. She felt truly excited about the future. Matthew's business was on the up and up, and her own job was permanent and pensionable, as her careers guidance teacher in school had said over and over again like a mantra. She'd need to tell her boss that she was expecting, but from talking to friends over the years, she knew the bank had favourable packages for maternity leave.

Her parents had been brilliant, too. They were both excited at the prospect of being grandparents. Shelly was already concerned about Matthew becoming a dad without his parents' involvement – they were of the absentee variety – and Leila knew that both she and Gerry would do everything possible to make him feel one of the family and give a helping hand whenever it was needed.

She tried to do some deep breathing with her eyes shut. She needed to try and de-stress as much as possible.

According to the books she'd read, babies could feel their mothers' emotions. If she could try to keep her stress levels to a minimum, it would have a positive effect on her baby.

The door pushed open gently and Shelly came into the room carrying a mug of tea.

'Here you go, love. You might be too tired now, but sure, if you want it, it's here.' She placed the mug on the bedside table. 'My baby having a baby,' she said, smiling down at Leila. 'It still hasn't sunk in properly.'

Leila smiled tiredly. 'Let's just hope I'm half as good a parent as you and Dad.'

Shelly left and went back downstairs. She tidied around the kitchen, then checked the clock and decided to give Gerry a call. He was in LA. She dialled his number, perched on a high stool at the kitchen island.

'Hello, my darling,' he said the moment he answered. 'I was just thinking about you.'

'Oh were you now,' Shelly teased. 'I hope they were good thoughts.'

'Only ever,' he replied. 'And how are you? Home safely?'

'Yes, and Leila is upstairs. She's going to sleep here tonight.'

'I'm glad to hear that. You can keep each other company.'

'It was such a wonderful holiday, Gerry. I can't thank you enough for organising it.'

'I'm so glad you enjoyed it. I think we need lots more breaks like that. Life's too short for all this hard work. I want us to get out and about more, see places, enjoy ourselves and relax.'

'Well I'm with you one hundred per cent on that one,' Shelly said. 'We should start enjoying life a bit more. In fact, if we're looking to make a plan, I'd love to go back to Spain. Remember the amazing holidays we used to have before we got married and later when the children were little? I loved the villages high above Malaga. Let's go back there and explore. This time we won't have Jake and Leila complaining that they're missing time at the pool with the other English-speaking kids.'

'We're like synchronised clocks at this point, my darling,' he chuckled.

'What do you mean?' she asked, puzzled.

'I was thinking along the same lines. You'll have to be patient, though. All will soon be revealed. But suffice to say you're going to love what I have in mind.'

'I'm intrigued. You can't leave me hanging, Gerry. What have you booked?'

'All in good time, my love! Now, you need to sleep and I'm going to relax before having an early night. I'm actually pretty tired and I don't want to feel under par tomorrow. I'm not retired just yet, sadly.'

'Don't you dare hang up!' she said. 'Where are we going? What's happening?'

'*Te quiero,*' he said, making exaggerated kissing noises down the phone.

She giggled. 'I love you too, but come on, you have to give me a hint.'

'I just did. Think back for a second. Remember the promise I made to you at our wedding?' She could hear the smile in his voice, so she played along with the game. 'Night, my love. Sleep well.'

'Gerry, you do drive me nuts when you start being cryptic,' she said with a light-hearted laugh. Sleep tight when you get to bed later.'

'I'll sleep like a baby. I love you, my darling.'

'I love you more,' she said with a smile.

Half an hour later, Shelly turned out the lights on her way to bed. The house felt peaceful. She really liked it when Leila stayed over. She'd make some scones tomorrow, before Leila woke up, and they could enjoy a leisurely breakfast. Right now, though, she was looking forward to curling up in her own bed and having a good night's sleep.

There was a sound, in her dreams, or was it coming from somewhere else? Shrill and persistent. Her foggy brain struggled to place it and make sense of it. Suddenly it came to her: the doorbell. Shelly sat up, feeling confused. She looked at the digital alarm clock. She wasn't losing her marbles, it was only four o'clock in the morning. Who on earth was at the door? Her heart started beating faster as she pulled on a dressing gown. An image of Jake flashed into her head, then Fee, then Matthew. Who the hell would come knocking at this hour of the night?

As she walked down the stairs, the blue flashing light from the driveway shone through the tempered glass panels on either side of the front door. Fear gripped her. The hairs on the back of her neck stood up as she ran the last few steps, unlocked the safety chain and yanked the door open.

Outside stood three people she didn't know, and Jim.

'Jim,' she breathed. 'What is it?'

'Shelly,' Jim said, and she could see the strain in his face. 'We need to come in and talk to you.'

Numb with fear, Shelly stood to the side and waved the three officers, two men and one woman, into the hall. As Jim stepped in behind them, he took her hand.

'Come to the kitchen, please,' Shelly said, closing the

front door. She glanced upstairs, hoping the noise hadn't woken Leila.

They all stood in the kitchen, facing each other. Shelly desperately wanted them to tell her why they had come, but at the same time she never wanted them to utter a word. She knew it couldn't be good news.

'My name is Aoife.' The female officer looked her directly in the eye. 'I think you should sit down, Mrs Dillon. I'm terribly sorry, but I have some bad news.'

'I'm happy standing,' Shelly said, unsure of why she was suddenly being so difficult. She hovered above a chair, clutching its back. 'Sorry, I don't know what's come over me. I'm feeling quite unnerved.'

'That's okay,' Aoife said gently. 'Mrs Dillon, we asked your friend Jim to be here with us because we have to give you some very difficult news. It's your husband . . . Gerry . . .'

The words became jumbled after she heard Gerry's name. Shelly's focus wandered and she felt as if she were having an out-of-body experience. Jim never let go of her hand, but she felt she had drifted far away from him and from the kitchen, where the policewoman just kept talking and talking and destroying her world. Shelly's mind wandered to their wedding day. The sun was warming her face as they'd stood in the courtyard of the church and celebrated with their loved ones. She could smell the roses beyond the church porch. She could see her husband-to-be, waiting patiently for her at the altar. She'd been glowing with happiness, alight with it . . .

'Mrs Dillon, did you hear what my colleague just told you?' one of the men said. 'We're very sorry, but your husband Gerry has died.'

Shelly focused on the man. He had a moustache, even though he was young, baby-faced even. Why would a person with such unblemished skin grow that dreadful facial hair?

'Mrs Dillon,' Aoife said, 'Gerry had a heart attack.'

'But he didn't have trouble with his heart,' Shelly said immediately. As soon as the words were out, she smiled and waved her hand in front of her face. 'Silly remark . . . Of course he had trouble, if he had a heart attack.'

'Shelly, please sit down,' Jim said. 'I'm so very sorry.' She could see he was struggling not to cry and she felt sorry for him.

She tried to take a step towards the chair, but her legs crumpled beneath her. Jim caught her and one of the men helped him to sit her down. She sagged in the chair, like a rag doll. Such was the force of emotion, she felt as if her insides would combust with grief. Her heart and head pounded as she tried to come to terms with what was happening. Aoife crouched by her lap, patting her knee and telling her she was sorry.

The rocking happened naturally. It helped. It was something to do. It was oddly comforting.

'Mum?'

Their heads turned quickly at the sound of Leila's voice. She stood in the doorway looking bleary-eyed and confused.

'Leila,' Shelly said faintly, her heart bursting all over again. Her beautiful pregnant daughter, about to have her life ruined. It was more than she could bear.

Leila looked around at the faces watching her. Her eyes met Jim's. 'What's going on?' she asked. 'Jim, please tell me.'

'It's your father,' Shelly said, before Jim could utter a word. She felt like the voice was coming from somewhere else, not from inside her. 'He's had a heart attack.'

'Will he be okay?' Leila asked, looking into her mother's eyes, beseeching her to say yes.

A sob caught in Shelly's throat and she rose to embrace her daughter. Jim moved as if to catch her again, but adrenaline was surging through her now. The desire to protect her children was stronger than the initial shock, pushing aside the grief. That was good; she couldn't breathe through the grief, it was going to consume her. She focused on Leila, on rubbing her back, stroking her face, on being her mother.

'I'm so sorry, but he's gone, darling. Dad is dead.'

Those three words rang through Shelly's head for days afterwards. While she called poor Jake, while she spoke to the undertakers, while she arranged for Gerry's body to be brought back from the hotel room in LA and while they endured the funeral and the burial. And now, as she struggled to come to terms with how on earth she was going to manage without him, those words echoed around the empty house: *Dad is dead . . . My husband is dead. My world is dead.*

Chapter 5

JAKE WAS STRUGGLING WITHOUT HIS BELOVED dad. Even now, six months to the day after Gerry's sudden death, he felt as if he were drowning in grief. Each morning he woke and remembered, and the heaviness of the reality settled on him immediately. With December just three weeks away, the thought of Christmas without Gerry was nearly crushing him, and he knew Leila and Shelly felt exactly the same. If he could go to sleep and wake up in January, that would suit him just fine.

The funeral had been what many would consider a good one. There'd been a massive attendance. Everyone from old schoolmates to Gerry's colleagues from the airline had turned out in droves to say farewell. The church had been packed to capacity, and that had offered some comfort. It had made Jake proud to see how many people had felt a special connection to his dad. But what he remembered most clearly was how many of the congregation had placed a hand on his shoulder and said they understood his pain.

He'd no doubt that they had all felt intense grief at losing their own fathers, but he simply couldn't imagine that any of them were anywhere near as close as he and Gerry had been. They couldn't have been. He and his dad were like two peas in a pod. They were carbon copies of one another. When he'd gone to the careers advice lady in school, he already knew what he wanted to be. Gerry had told him from the time he could walk that he would follow in his footsteps. It was what Jake had lived for, had worked for, always.

'You have the makings of a great pilot,' Gerry would say. 'Look at how you aced that test! Becoming a pilot will be no bother to you, son.'

'It's a tough choice,' the careers guidance teacher had said with a smile. 'It takes dedication and a lot of nerve. That's before the exams and flight time training.'

'Oh, I know,' Jake had nodded. 'I've grown up around the whole thing and my dad thinks I can do it.'

'I wish you the best of luck,' she'd said.

It had irked him that she clearly didn't believe he had what it took to get through the training. He'd voiced his concern the next day when his dad got home.

'Ah, she doesn't know you like I do,' Gerry had said. 'She's right about one thing, though. It's not an easy career path to follow. But you'll fly it, excuse the pun!'

Instantly his dad had given him the boost he'd needed to channel his belief into his abilities. If he happened to be slipping in a subject at school, Gerry would sit him down and ask how he could help.

'You know you can't make it as a pilot unless you raise those grades. I can give you a hand, or we can get you some grinds. You're doing well, but I know you can do better.'

That, Jake mused, was his dad all over. He was always there to reassure him he could do anything he set his mind to. Lately, though, since Gerry had died, Jake was beginning to question his career for the first time in his life. He couldn't admit it to anyone, but privately he was filled with self-doubt, a feeling he'd never experienced before, and he didn't like it. Perhaps it was purely grief that was making him feel reluctant about flying, a side effect of the shock and the sadness. Obviously being at the airport and on flights made his mind wander to memories of his dad. But there was a nagging feeling in the back of his brain that the sheen had worn off being a pilot big-time.

The alarm on his phone buzzed, making him jump. Damn, he needed to get to the bank. As he showered and dressed, he couldn't help thinking that today was going to be very difficult. Gerry normally accompanied him to anything serious like this. Most grown male adults would probably snigger at the thought of him taking his daddy along to important meetings, but that was the way they were.

If he was honest, Jake would happily stay put with his mum for the foreseeable future. He enjoyed living with her and being fed royally, and it was good to have someone there who knew how he was feeling. But then he thought of Fee, and that spurred him on. He knew he needed to move on with her, to get back the momentum they had lost the day Gerry died. And if he was going to get down on one knee and propose, he had to make sure they'd have somewhere decent to live.

It was one of the last conversations he'd had with Gerry – about proposing to Fee. He wanted to honour his father's advice. A part of him found it impossible to think of celebrating an engagement, a wedding day without his dad. At moments, it made him positively not want to do it all. But then he remembered Gerry at the bar in St Lucia, how sure he had been that Jake and Fee were meant for each other. And he thought about Fee, her wonderful patience and support over the last awful six months. Her unwavering ability to put him and their future life together first, to keep it in focus, always ready to work hard for it. Thinking about all that, he knew he had to pick up the thread that had been broken that day six months ago. He needed to live his life with Fee, even if living felt like a betrayal right now. He had to believe those feelings would change and get his life back on track. A new year was approaching, and it needed to signal a fresh start for him.

He pulled a comb through his dark hair and added a slick of gel. He still thought of his father as being dark, even though he'd turned into a very dapper silver fox in recent years. His hazel eyes and sallow skin had made his pale hair gleam.

'Aren't you going to do the Grecian 2000 thing, Dad?' Jake had teased.

'I considered it,' Gerry said, 'for about ten seconds. Imagine the hassle of trying to stay dark. Nah, I'll leave it to you now, son.'

Jake wasn't sure how long his own locks would last, let alone stay dark, considering the stress he'd been under for so many months now.

He looked at himself in the mirror and felt an intense hit of missing Gerry. 'Come with me today, Dad,' he said to his reflection.

He ran down the stairs, clipping his watch onto his wrist as he went. He swallowed hard, hoping to banish the lump of emotion that was sitting in his throat, making him want to curl into a ball on the floor and howl like a girl.

'All set, love?' Shelly asked as he joined her in the kitchen. 'I'm more than happy to accompany you this morning. Leila said she'd go with you too. She probably knows the people you're meeting.'

'Thanks, Mum, but I'll be fine on my own.'

'Really?' She looked misty-eyed. 'I suspect you would've taken your dad if he were still alive. I know I'm a poor second choice, but the offer is there if you'd rather not be alone.'

'Oh Mum,' he said, pulling her into a bear hug. 'You're not a poor anything. You're right, though, Dad would probably have come with me. But I think I'd like to start as I mean to go on. I need to step up and be a man now. My own man. Besides, I have several other things to do before I go to work. I'll be heading straight to the airport this afternoon.'

'All right, love,' she said, patting his arm. 'I'm here if you change your mind. I can meet you for a coffee after your appointment if you like?'

'I'll be fine. I'll call you later, okay?'

As he sat in traffic, Jake checked that his tie was straight and made sure he looked presentable. His stomach growled; he hadn't had any breakfast, but he was feeling too worked up to eat. The meeting should be fairly straightforward. He had pretty much sorted the details, so today was literally the final step. Leila had been amazing. It had opened his eyes to how well she was thought of at the bank. He'd always secretly thought that she'd settled for an easier job than his, but once he saw the amount of paperwork that was required, he took his hat off to her. He'd enjoyed the process of sorting the mortgage with her. It had put them on a new adult level together as brother and sister.

He glanced at the clock on his dashboard. He had another very important matter to attend to before his appointment at the bank. Sweat beading his forehead, he took a planned detour. He longed for today to be over and done with.

Within fifteen minutes he was back on the road again. His hands were clammy and his heart was racing as he pulled up at the bank. Mercifully, the meeting with the official went according to plan, and as he signed the final pile of forms and shook hands, the woman paused and smiled.

'Good luck with your new home, Jake. We were all so sad to hear of your father's passing. Leila is such a well-respected member of staff here, and we all met your father when he used to come in to see her. I'm sure he would be very proud of you.'

Perhaps it was because she was a stranger, or maybe it was because he wasn't expecting such heartfelt words, but tears began to well up in Jake's eyes.

'Thanks,' he whispered. 'I miss him so badly. I wish he could've been around today. I'm doing all sorts of life-changing things, and I know he would've loved to share these moments with me.'

'I'd say he *is* with you. I'd say he's standing right next to you, in fact,' she said. 'I lost my mother when I was twelve. Some days I can actually *feel* her spirit with me.'

'Really?' he said, looking around. 'How do you *do* that? I'd like to be able to feel Dad around me. Is there some secret to channelling spirits?'

'It'll come. It happens at all sorts of times in life. When it happens, you'll know. Don't forget to talk to him, too. Tell him what's in here,' she said, patting her chest.

All of a sudden, it was as if she realised she was being too familiar. She stood up straighter and held out her hand. 'I'm sorry for your troubles. But I wish you the very best in your new home. Once you sign for the house the estate agent will give you the relevant paperwork and you can draw down the mortgage money.'

He took her hand and looked into her eyes.

'You've been more help than you'll ever know,' he said sincerely.

As he walked out to his car, Jake spoke to his father. 'Thanks for helping me get my own home,' he said. 'I'll probably need the girls to take over now. I'm not the best with that kind of thing, as you know. I should probably leave it to Fee and Mum and Leila, right?'

A passer-by stared at him as if he was unhinged. He honestly didn't care. It was nice to chat to his dad again, even if it was a one-way conversation.

Knowing he'd be out of the country for ten days on a long-haul route, Jake wanted to get as much organised with the house as he could, so he drove directly to the leafy suburb of Blackrock, to the estate agent's office. Clutching his paperwork from the bank, he grabbed a takeaway coffee from the café next door and walked in ready to close the deal.

'Ah, Mr Dillon,' the receptionist said when he explained why he was there. 'I'm afraid Sean isn't here today. Is there something I could help you with?'

'I'm here to close the deal on number twenty Furzedale Close,' he said.

'Right. Well in that case you do need to see Sean. But unfortunately we have a training day today and we only have a skeleton staff to keep things ticking over. I did send you an email to notify you, but clearly you didn't receive it. All I can do is offer my apologies for that oversight.'

'No, I didn't get any email,' he said, feeling incredibly irritated.

'I'll take your number and have Sean call you first thing in the morning. Unless you'd like to make an appointment for tomorrow afternoon?'

'No, I won't be here. I'm a pilot and I'm about to head off on a ten-day run. It'll have to wait until I get back.'

'I'm ever so sorry,' she said. 'We literally only have these days a couple of times a year as it causes such inconvenience. As I said, I thought I'd notified all our final-stages customers by email. My sincere apologies.'

'Right,' he said impatiently. This really wasn't part of the plan. He'd wanted to get things finalised and get going on drawing down the mortgage. He didn't want any obstacles throwing themselves in his way and making him question his decision.

Thanking the girl, he left and headed back to his car. As he checked his inbox and scrolled to the junk mail, he realised there *had* been an email. It was from somebody called Claire, explaining quite clearly that Sean wasn't available today. Damn.

He sat back and opened the glove box to make sure everything was as it should be, then took a deep breath. It was time to swing by the hospital and see Fee. He turned the car into the traffic.

'Stay with me, Dad,' he said. 'Stay with me, please.'

Between the drive across the busy city and having to jostle for a parking space, Jake was stressed to the hilt by the time he made it to the hospital foyer. He sent a text to Fee saying he was there and could she come and meet him for five minutes.

She appeared from the coffee shop and rushed towards him.

'Hey! This is a wonderful surprise,' she said, kissing him. 'Brilliant timing, too. I'm on my lunch break.'

She walked him back into the café, chatting away, not seeming to realise that his mouth was too dry to speak. It was now or never. Literally. There and then, in the middle of the mayhem, he dropped to one knee.

'Jake!' she gasped, her hands shooting to her mouth. All of a sudden, the bustling area came to a halt.

'Hey! Look, he's proposing!' a woman shouted.

'Fiona, will you marry me?' Jake said loudly and confidently.

'Oh bloody hell,' Fee said, bursting out laughing. 'Did you have to do it when I'm standing here in my horrible blue scrubs with medical shoes on?'

'I'm on my knees here, in case you haven't noticed,' he said pleadingly.

'And we're all waiting for you to answer,' a man from the crowd yelled, making everyone around them laugh.

'Yes!' Fee said, pulling him up to his feet. 'Yes, of course I'll marry you.'

As they kissed, applause echoed down the corridors of the hospital. Friends and acquaintances and even passing patients came to pat their backs, shake their hands and wish them well.

'Well this day is turning out a lot better than I'd ever dreamed,' Fee said, her eyes shining with love.

'To add to the occasion,' Jake whispered, 'I've bought us a house. Well, I've got all the right pieces of paper and I just need to sign off on it when I return. But it's pretty much a done deal.'

'No way!' Fee said. 'I thought we were going to look at the ones in Furzdale Close again?'

'We'll be looking at number twenty in minute detail on a regular basis for the foreseeable future,' he said with a grin.

'You didn't?'

'I did,' he said, nodding.

'Jake Dillon, you never cease to astound me,' she said, cupping his face in her hands. 'I'm off duty at eight. Please tell me you've wangled the night off so we can celebrate?'

'I wish I had,' he said. 'But I was so intent on buying the house and proposing, I didn't get that far!'

'Ah well, two out of three ain't bad,' she joked. 'We'll celebrate when you get back.'

'I'd like that,' he said, kissing her again.

As he drove out of the hospital, Jake felt a rush of pride. Fee was incredible. He was going to be married to an incredible woman, and their life was going to be wonderful.

He was so caught up in thoughts of his future with Fee, he only got the now-familiar heebie-jeebies as he turned onto the motorway that led to the airport. The thought of going through all the protocols and preparing for the flight gave him a tight feeling in the pit of his stomach. He hated that he felt this way, but didn't know how to make it stop.

He tried to shake it off by concentrating on Fee and how delighted she was to be engaged. He replayed his crazy proposal in his mind and laughed at himself. But underneath his attempts to be normal, he was feeling anything but. If his dad were here now, he'd probably be ashamed of him, ashamed of his nervousness and his dread. And that thought made Jake feel sick to his stomach.

Chapter 6

AFTER JAKE HAD LEFT, SHELLY WENT THROUGH the motions of housework and vacuuming, though she didn't know why she bothered. With Jake gone for ten days, there was absolutely no one to care if the house was tidy or a tip. She was just doing it to have something to do, which made her feel weak, like a failure. There were probably so many things she could be doing today, but she couldn't be bothered with anything. Doing the housework was just a way of hiding the fact that she had no life to live, and what was worse, she didn't even care. If Gerry's key wasn't going to turn in the door today, then it was all pointless. That was her life now – pointless, purposeless, tedious.

Her black thoughts were interrupted by the doorbell. She went to answer it, imagining it would be Leila. She wasn't expecting anyone.

The young woman standing on the doorstep looked vaguely familiar. Shelly racked her brains, wondering where she'd seen her before.

'Hello, Mrs Dillon,' the woman said. She was twisting a large envelope in her hands. 'I'm so sorry to intrude unannounced. I'm Jen, the photographer your husband hired to take pictures at your birthday party?'

The penny finally dropped. Shelly remembered Jen

clicking away at the party, getting them all to pose together. The memory of it hit her with a cold jolt and she had to work hard to compose herself.

'Oh yes, of course. Come on in, please,' she said, stepping aside.

Jen followed her into the living room, where they both sat down.

'I was so terribly shocked and saddened to hear of Gerry's death,' Jen said, looking awkward. 'He was such a warm and charming man.'

'He was,' Shelly said, sounding desolate. 'It's been a harsh few months.'

'I can only imagine.' Jen's voice was full of sympathy. 'Look, you might not be ready, but . . . I have the photos. From that night. I've thought about coming over so often, but I just couldn't bring myself to intrude on your grief. But I noticed today that it had been six months, and, well, I thought . . . maybe . . .'

Shelly blinked and swallowed to dislodge the hard lump in her throat. The photographs. She had completely forgotten.

'I understand,' she said, smiling at the young woman. 'I totally forgot about the pictures. It's a lovely surprise, thank you. Please don't feel you're upsetting me.'

Jen looked relieved and put the envelope down on the coffee table. 'Okay. The thing is, your husband paid for an album to be made, and I'd like to do that. I hope that in time it might bring solace to you and your children. He asked for the medium pack, which comprises eighteen photos. So if you could choose your favourite eighteen from these and email me the numbers that are on the back of them, I'll make it up for you to his specification.'

'Oh, of course,' Shelly said, feeling a bit dazed. 'What a lovely idea! Gerry was incredibly thoughtful.'

Jen smiled. 'I don't normally print out all the pictures like this, but considering your circumstances, I thought you might cherish them.'

'That's very kind of you, Jen. We have a few pictures from a holiday we took as a family just before he died, but I'm sure these will be treasured by all of us. Thank you.'

Jen stood up to leave and Shelly saw her to the door, promising to make her selection as soon as possible. When she closed the front door behind the photographer, her smile lasted approximately ten seconds. Her hands began to quiver, then her entire body became engulfed in shaking sobs.

With trembling, clumsy fingers, she edged the envelope open and pulled out the fat bunch of photographs.

The very first one made her drop to her knees on the carpet as she felt her heart breaking a little bit more. The picture showed Gerry hugging her around her waist as she looked delightedly at him. He was grinning like a naughty schoolboy, his eyebrows raised in mirth. She had an instant flashback to that very moment, and him telling her that he'd hired Jen to take pictures as an extra surprise.

Propping her back against the side of the staircase, she slowly went through the stack of pictures, wallowing in the painful deliciousness of the memories each one evoked. Wonderfully, Gerry was in many of them. No wonder Jen had been so generous about printing them off. If he wasn't forefront, he was mingling in the background, laughing and chatting and clearly having a ball. Either way, it was a divine memento of a very special evening. She had no idea how she would narrow them down to only eighteen pictures, but one thing was for certain: the album certainly wouldn't centre around her as Gerry would have intended. It would be a final homage to her darling husband.

'Little did you know you were giving me a priceless gift for my birthday, Gerry darling,' she whispered sadly.

As she clutched the pictures to her chest, further tears engulfed her. She'd learned to give in to the grief. To simply allow it to take hold and cry it out. There was no point fighting it.

Nothing was the same without him. Nothing. Shelly felt as if she were living in a shadow that would never shift and let the light in again. She felt utterly desolate, but most of all she felt cheated. This was supposed to be their time. It was going to be the next wonderful step in their life's adventure.

Anger washed over her. She threw the pile of pictures across the hall, then balled her fists and screamed like a woman possessed. For what felt like the hundredth time since Gerry's death, she wondered what on earth she'd done in a previous life to deserve this hideous pain. Why was she being punished so horribly?

When her sobbing eventually subsided, she scraped herself up off the floor and gathered the strewn pictures, frantically hoping she hadn't damaged any. Mercifully, they were all intact. She pushed them back into the safety of the padded envelope and brought them to the kitchen. She'd need Jake and Leila's advice on which ones to pick for the finished album.

She flicked the kettle on and stood staring into space as it heated. It was early afternoon, and although she rarely did so, she reached into the cupboard and found a bottle of gin. Pouring a large measure, she busied herself adding ice, tonic and cucumber. There was no reason why she'd need to drive for the rest of the day. Nobody was expected, and nobody would even care that she was drowning her sorrows. She raised the glass to her lips and drank, wincing at the bite of the alcohol as it slid down her throat.

But as she sipped her drink, she suddenly felt immeasurably low. What a cliché she'd become: a middle-aged grieving widow, drinking in the afternoon. She'd been many things in her life, but she'd always hoped she hadn't been a cliché. She and Gerry had tried to live honestly; that was what made them who they were. Now here she was, acting a part that held no comfort for her. She was being wilfully stupid. The answer to her pain wasn't at the bottom of a gin bottle. It wasn't even in the glossy photographs Gerry had commissioned, she now realised. Her mind raced, going over the past six months, accusing her, taunting her. It was like a wave of realisation cascading over her, and there was no hiding from it, even if she'd wanted to.

She knew in her heart of hearts that the only way the desolation would ever lift was if she commanded it to go. Pouring her half-finished drink down the sink, she grabbed a warm coat from the coat rack in the hall and ventured outside. Fresh air might level her better than gin. One thing was crystal clear now, even amidst the blur of grief: she needed to make some changes, and fast. She couldn't allow her life to continue the way it was. She had two children, and a grandchild on the way, and she did not have the luxury of drowning. It was a very seductive idea, but she had to resist it. She couldn't give in and let down the people she loved most.

As she walked, the rain started to come down in sheets.

The stinging chilliness seemed fitting. She cast her mind back to her birthday party. Gerry had been such a jovial and kind-hearted man. It would devastate him to see her in such pain. She knew he'd hate her to wallow, struggling to find anything good in the world. She dug her hands into her coat pockets and wished with all her heart that she could force herself out of this rut. Get out of it and leave it behind.

Squeezing her eyes shut, she prayed to Gerry to help her turn the corner.

Chapter 7

THE GOOD NEWS SPREAD LIKE WILDFIRE. FEE KNEW she was beaming like a fool as she strode towards theatre. Aware that her massive cheesy grin was entirely inappropriate for a nervous patient who was about to be sliced and diced, she tried to secure a poker face.

'Hello, Mrs Devon. I see you're nice and relaxed. You'll have a sore throat afterwards, but removing your tonsils should help with your constant infections,' she said soothingly.

As she ploughed on with the operation, Fee kept getting little rushes of excitement. She'd need to plan the wedding. She'd need a dress and all sorts of other things. She'd grown up in a no-frills house, where nothing was done needlessly and everything was accounted for. Although her parents were faultlessly loving, there'd never been much fun.

Once she'd wrapped up Mrs Devon's surgery, she decided to call home to deliver her good news.

'That's good news, Fiona.' Her mother still shouted into the phone as if it were a megaphone. 'Your father and I are pleased about it and are prepared to give you our blessing. Your young man called to speak to us this morning. He asked both of us for your hand in marriage. We thought that was thoroughly modern of him, including me in the conversation.'

Fee cradled her phone to her ear and her heart swelled to bursting point. *Well done, hun.* Jake always thought of everything. Even her prickly parents couldn't fault him.

At the end of her shift, her good friend Norah came towards her grinning widely.

'Right, you, time to toast your bagging of a hot pilot!'

Fee tried to protest, saying she was exhausted, but Norah was not a woman you could say no to. She called to other colleagues to help, and in the end it turned into a hilarious tug of war as Fee's theatre team, along with a gaggle of other nurses and doctors, dragged her bodily to the nearest pub and thrust her into a raucous celebration.

She phoned Jake and shouted above the din that he was missing the first of many engagement parties.

'I love you more than words can say,' she said before hanging up.

Norah was a theatre nurse, and an excellent one at that. Fee had always loved having a laugh with her – Norah did a good line in gallows humour on the tough days – but lately they'd begun taking lunch together and talking at a different level. Fee knew that Norah was anxious to meet 'the one', and she really appreciated that her friend could put aside her own feelings to celebrate with her so wholeheartedly.

Norah raised her glass and grinned. 'How is it we both wear the same outrageously unattractive scrubs to work, with the same ugly hairdo encased in a hideous hairnet, yet you end up with a rock on your finger and I don't get so much as a hug?'

'I saw Janey hugging you earlier,' Fee teased. Janey was the theatre's general helper. Nobody knew how old she was, but she'd been at the hospital since the year dot. Fee guessed she was somewhere in her mid sixties, but couldn't be sure. She was like a mother to everyone, whether they needed another one or not.

'Janey hugs lamp posts, bless her,' Norah sighed. 'Go on then, show me your ring properly.'

'That sounds decidedly rude,' Fee said, and they both dissolved into giggles.

'Are you doing the big white wedding thing, or will you scuttle away and get married on a beach with beautiful locals decorating your photos and making you look like you've got fabulously exotic friends?'

'I've never really sat down and thought about my wedding,' Fee admitted. 'I've been so busy forging a career, I didn't really stop to think about the rest. But now that it's upon me, well, I think I want a gown, and a large function room full of stupidly happy onlookers.'

'Apart from me,' Norah said, elbowing her and winking. 'I'll be the miserable one being measured for the shelf I'll be left on for evermore.'

'In that case, why don't you go the whole hog and ruin the family photos too? Will you be my bridesmaid?'

'Seriously?' Norah said, her expression changing instantly from grim to glee.

'Seriously,' Fee said, laughing at the look on her friend's face. She was enjoying this new-found position of being able to give people a role in her wedding.

'You won't make me wear a figure-hugging satin sheath that shows every inch of my flab and intestines?' Norah warned. 'Nor do I want to wear a big fat gypsy wedding ball gown that'll scar my hips or light up on the dance floor.'

'I can promise that neither of those designs will be forced

upon you,' Fee said solemnly. 'But, you cheeky mare, if you love me and want to be my bridesmaid, you'll take a deep breath and agree to wear whatever I decide.'

Norah finished her drink in two gulps. 'Right, you're on. But keep in mind that I might just manage to crawl off my shelf and become entangled in the loins of a dashing man. Revenge can be a dish served with scratchy lace and pouffy skirts that make one's hips look devilishly wide.'

'I'll keep that in mind,' Fee said, grinning at her. 'And I've no doubt that your Prince Charming is waiting around a corner.'

'Well I wish he'd appear,' Norah said. 'Still, aren't bridesmaids meant to get lots of male attention? Things could be looking up, my friend! You wouldn't like to have your wedding in the next couple of weeks, would you?'

Fee raised an eyebrow. 'No. Why? What's the rush?'

'I need a date for the hospital fund-raiser ball,' Norah sighed.

'My wedding isn't a matchmaking service,' Fee said with a laugh. 'Jake and I haven't even had a chance to talk yet, let alone make any plans. So I reckon you'd better get active on Tinder.'

Norah grabbed her in a hug as they both laughed.

Fee's mobile started ringing, and she was thrilled to see Leila's name pop up on the screen.

'Leila!' she shouted. 'We're going to be sisters-in-law!'

'I know,' Leila squealed. 'Where are you? It sounds like you're at a festival.'

'Not far off it,' Fee said. 'A few of the staff insisted I go for drinks. Jake's missing it all.'

'We've plenty of time to organise a proper party,' Leila

said. 'I'm so happy for you guys. I couldn't ask for a better sister-in-law. Mum is beside herself too.'

'Aw, brilliant,' Fee said, as guilt flooded her. She hadn't called Shelly yet, when that should have been her first priority. 'I'll pop outside now and give her a call.'

'She'd love that,' Leila said. 'I'll leave you to it. Give me a shout tomorrow or whenever you're free. I can't wait to see your ring. Do you like it? Jake should've told me and I would've steered him towards those ones we were drooling over last summer in the window on Grafton Street!'

'Don't worry, he did a superb job. It's a fine rock and that's okay by me. While I have you, would you do me the honour of being my maid of honour?'

'Really?' Leila sounded all choked up. 'Oh sorry, baby hormones,' she blubbed. 'I'd love to. And if you could wait until I have a waist again, that'd be fabulous.'

'Lord,' Fee said. 'I have Norah here wanting it to be instant and now you petitioning for a postponement. You're on Team Fee now,' she said, grinning over at Norah. 'You're both going to have to be obedient from here on.' Norah pulled a face and made her laugh. 'Anyway, Leila, you're due next month, and we won't be racing down the aisle for a while. I reckon you'll be back to your slim and slight self in plenty of time.'

After finishing her chat with Leila, Fee told Norah she needed to ring Jake's mum, then pushed her way out to the beer garden so she could call her without a raucous backing track. Grateful for the overhead outdoor heaters, she huddled directly beneath one in an effort to keep warm.

They had a lovely chat, and Shelly was warm and welcoming, only choking on her words when she told Fee that she knew this was exactly what Gerry would've wanted.

'Oh thank you, Shelly,' Fee said, her own voice cracking a little. 'That means so much to me. I know this is meant to be a happy time, but I miss him. I can't begin to imagine how bittersweet it must be for you.'

'You're a kind and thoughtful girl,' Shelly said, sighing deeply. 'Now we all need to pull together and try to enjoy this lovely time. What with Leila's baby on the way, Christmas approaching and a wedding to look forward to, we'll be okay.'

'I'll need lots of help with planning,' Fee said. 'Mum isn't exactly up on fashion the way you are. I'd love you to be involved in choosing my dress.'

'I'd like nothing more,' Shelly said, sounding delighted. 'You know me and a good project, I'll be in my element.'

'I'm very glad to hear it,' Fee said with a smile. 'I'm feeling a bit daunted by all we'll have to think about!'

'Don't worry a bit,' Shelly said. 'We'll have fun doing it. Oh, and by the way, I took delivery of a pile of photographs from my fiftieth earlier on today. I have to pick eighteen of the best ones for an album. So maybe you'll help me with that?'

'Oh Shelly,' Fee said. 'You poor thing. Are you okay? That's a massive thing to have to do without Gerry.'

'I'm okay now, love. Your news has come on the perfect day. I asked Gerry to help me earlier on. I was struggling to cope . . . one of those bleak moments. This shows he was listening!'

Fee hung up feeling a little overwhelmed by emotion. Not wanting to be a killjoy, she stayed a while longer before thanking her colleagues for the impromptu celebration and flagging down a taxi.

Her parents were in bed when she got home. She hesitated, wanting to knock on their door to have a quick chat, but knowing they wouldn't take kindly to being woken, she tiptoed into her own room.

As she lay in bed, she held her left hand aloft, admiring her beautiful ring. She couldn't wait to start planning the rest of her life. She was a lucky girl. She never missed those appreciative glances women gave Jake. He was a gorgeous-looking man and could charm the worms out of the soil if he put his mind to it. But most of all, Fee adored the fact that he was as ambitious and forward-thinking as she was. They wanted the same things in life and were prepared to work as hard as it took to get them. They were a dream team. She knew that together they'd achieve everything they wanted.

Her thoughts turned to the house. She couldn't believe Jake had taken the plunge and gone to close the deal. They'd looked at Furzedale Close a few weeks back. Jake had asked a hundred and one questions about insulation and other man stuff, while Fee had tried to imagine what colour sofa they could put in the living room. She was certain it was the right starter home for them.

The thought of having their own home was a dream come true. She needed to talk to Jake about money. She didn't have a huge amount of spare cash right now, but she was sure her earning power would increase from here on in.

As she closed her eyes, Fee thought about wedding dresses and bridesmaid dresses. It was all so romantic. She could barely believe it was happening to her.

Chapter 8

LEILA WAS GETTING PRETTY FED UP WITH BEING pregnant. It was the final week of November, and her last day at work. There was a plan afoot to go to the pub for lunch.

'There are fifteen of us now,' Maeve said, as she passed Leila's desk. 'I'll grab my coat and we'll go, okay?'

Leila nodded, hoping against hope she could hold it together for the afternoon. She kept bursting into tears, and it was so embarrassing. Earlier this morning, Fee had called to see if she'd like to go for coffee tomorrow, and she'd burst into uncontrollable sobs.

'Hey, what's wrong?' Fee had asked. 'Is everything all right with Bump?'

'Oh God,' Leila had groaned, 'I feel like I'm not in control of any part of my body at this point. Please tell me I'm going to be more normal soon.'

'Well, I'm obviously not a mother, but my medical experience tells me that the way you're feeling right now is pretty normal.'

'I'm in with my gynae tomorrow, so I'm sure he'll tell me I'm okay.'

She suspected Fee was laughing at her, which made her feel even worse. But of course to svelte, newly engaged, non-pregnant women, the spectacle of a sobbing, big-bellied whale was probably a bit amusing and unfathomable.

As they walked across the road to the pub, Maeve linked her arm. The wind was icy and they were both relieved to get inside, making straight for the blazing open fire.

To Leila's surprise, Maeve and the rest of the department had decorated a section of the pub with pink-and-blue bunting, and there was a pile of gifts on the table.

Inevitably, she promptly burst into tears.

'This is all I do lately,' she said apologetically. 'Thank you all so much for being so thoughtful!'

Matthew appeared, and threw his eyes to heaven. 'She's blubbing again, I see.'

Everyone laughed and Leila swatted his arm.

'Did you know about this?' she asked, sweeping her arm around the decorations and gifts.

'I might have had a little clue,' he said, kissing her. 'Now you all see what I'm having to put up with. And me a grease monkey. I've no idea how to tap into my feminine side.'

They all laughed again, smiling warmly at him. Leila watched as he chatted and thanked people. He was one of those people who managed to connect with everyone. He was much quieter and less outgoing than she was, but she didn't know of anyone who disliked him. Now that she thought of it, he was a bit like her dad – warm and charming and universally liked. It was a nice thought, like parts of Gerry would come down to the baby from both sides.

Platters of food arrived, and although she was hungry, Leila couldn't manage more than a small triangle sandwich and a single chicken wing.

'I'm on fire with heartburn,' she whispered to Matthew.

'I'll grab you a bottle of Gaviscon,' he said, and slipped

out to the chemist. Within minutes she'd taken a spoonful and was feeling better.

'I've to go back to the garage,' Matthew said. 'Enjoy your time with your friends and I'll see you later on.'

The atmosphere in the pub was great and Leila even made a little speech about how grateful she was to everyone and how much she'd miss them while she was on maternity leave.

'You'll come and visit with the baby, won't you?' Maeve asked as the others nodded.

'Try and stop me!'

By the end of the afternoon, Leila was wiped out. She texted Matthew while she was on the bus and asked him to bring in a takeaway. When he arrived home, she was out for the count on the sofa.

'What are you doing lying here in the dark with no heat on?' he asked with a grin. 'Are you exhausted after your party?'

She nodded and stretched and yawned as Matthew flew about, making the flat more comfortable. He pulled the curtains, turned on the table lamp, lit the fire and found plates and cutlery.

'I got you some of that fizzy grape stuff so you can pretend to have a glass of wine with me.'

'Thanks, love,' she said, accepting the glass. 'I don't know what I'd do without you.'

He opened a bottle of red wine and poured a glass for himself, and Leila looked at it longingly.. 'Ah, you'll be back to your old self in no time, flying around, bossing me about. I believe Jake is home tonight,' he said, changing the subject. 'He called earlier to say your mother was on to him about meeting up tomorrow morning with the solicitor.'

Leila fished her phone out of her bag and realised it was on silent and that she had six missed calls.

'Shoot,' she said. 'Both Mum and Jake were looking for me. What's all this about a solicitor?'

'Er . . .' Matthew hesitated. 'It's about your father's will.'

'Oh,' Leila said, fighting the urge to cry yet again.

'Sorry, love,' Matthew said, wrapping his arm around her. 'I know you're feeling sensitive at the moment, but Shelly and Jake are going to hear the will being read tomorrow morning at nine. Do you think you can manage it? Your mum really wants you there if you can. In fact, I doubt it would be legal for them to read it without you.'

Leila nodded. Her heart hit her toes. She had been dreading this day. She knew her father had left a will, but it hadn't occurred to her that she'd need to be there for the reading.

'Your mother kindly said I could come along if you want me. Not if you want me,' he corrected, 'more if you *need* me.'

'Okay,' she said. 'Thanks, love. I'll probably ask Jake to pick me up if that's all right with you.'

'Sure,' he said as he got up to plate their takeaway. 'I ordered you a mild curry. You said you enjoyed it last time. I noticed you barely ate at lunchtime.'

'I'm not feeling the best,' she admitted. 'But what can I expect? I've less than a month to go. I really hope this baby comes before Christmas.'

'It'll be worth it in the end,' Matthew said. 'He or she will be the best Christmas present ever.'

Leila laughed. 'If I'd a euro for every time you've said that, I'd be loaded right now!'

As they enjoyed their dinner, Matthew broached the subject of going away the following week.

'I need to visit one of the suppliers in Italy. He's been asking me to come since September, and if I leave it any later, it'll be too near Christmas. I'll only be away for two nights.'

'Of course,' Leila said. She knew it was utterly stupid and very selfish of her, but she wanted to shout at him and say he wasn't to leave her, even for one second. What if she had the baby in the middle of the night, all by herself, in the flat?

The nightmares were beginning to freak her out. Last night she'd woken, lathered in sweat, having gone through the most lifelike dream that the baby had been born with three arms. It was so vivid, it had taken a few seconds to adjust to the fact that it hadn't actually happened.

'Maybe you could stay with Shelly while I'm gone?' Matthew said.

'Maybe,' she said, trying to sound nonchalant. 'Don't you worry. I'll be fine.'

She couldn't eat much. She needed to go to the loo, and in all honesty, all she wanted to do was sleep. Knowing it wouldn't be fair to leave Matthew sitting staring at the television on his own all evening, she suggested he go and meet the lads at the local.

'I'm no company at the moment, so you may as well.'

'They're actually down at the snooker club tonight,' Matthew said. 'I could drop over there for a bit. I don't want to drink tonight anyway. I've a good few jobs to do in the morning.'

'Fair enough,' Leila said. 'I am *so* longing for a gin and tonic . . . As soon as this baby is born, that's what I'll have!'

'I'll make sure to bring you one as quickly as I can.

There's a pub across from the hospital. I'll run over and ask for a takeaway!'

She kissed him goodbye and rang Shelly.

'What's the story, Mum? Matthew tells me the solicitor wants to see us.'

'Yes, it's time for us to hear your father's will,' Shelly said, sounding tentative 'I don't want to upset you, but can you come, do you think?'

'Of course,' Leila said, sounding far more convinced than she felt. She hated the thought of hearing her father's last wishes. All these final things were awful and unthinkable, but they had to be done.

'Jake has offered to drive, so we'll pick you up in the morning at eight.'

'See you then, Mum.'

As was now par for the course, Leila had a frustratingly awkward night's sleep. No matter how many pillows she tucked under, beside and behind her bump, she couldn't get comfortable.

She lay watching the light change as night turned to day, wishing she could get a few hours, but knowing it was too late now. Her phone on the bedside table said 6.30 a.m. She'd have to get up soon anyway to be ready to go at eight.

She listened to Matthew going about his morning rituals, then the sound of his feet padding up the stairs. He came into the room with a tray bearing tea and toast with marmalade and bent to kiss her.

'Good luck this morning. If you're upset, text me and I'll get one of the staff to cover for me.' The look of concern in his eyes touched her. She stroked his face and thanked him for being so good.

Chapter 9

ONCE MATTHEW HAD LEFT FOR WORK, LEILA busied herself getting ready. By the time Jake's car pulled up outside, she was showered, dressed in her favourite maternity dress and fortified by a strong coffee. She was ready and not ready, but either way, it was time.

As she walked towards the car, she could see Shelly looking pale and anxious in the passenger seat. Leila knew the best policy was to chat away so her mother was nicely distracted. She filled her in on all the little gifts her colleagues had given her and how lovely the party had been. Before long, they'd arrived at the solicitor's office.

'At least we're not a feuding family,' Shelly pointed out as they walked in the door.

The secretary greeted them and showed them straight in to see Mark Willett.

'Hello, folks,' he said, standing to shake their hands. 'Take a seat, please.' He was sympathetic, and commented on how wonderful Gerry's funeral had been.

'A great send-off for a great man,' he said, pausing momentarily before carrying on. 'If you're all ready, we'll get down to business.'

He looked at them, and they each nodded silently.

'Okay, Mum?' Jake said quietly as he took Shelly's hand in his. Leila reached over and took her other hand.

As expected, Gerry had left all his affairs in neat and unquestionable order. He was a very organised man, and it was no different when it came to his final wishes. He and Shelly had prepared wills some years ago, at Mark's insistence. Mark was a man who liked to cross every t and dot every i, which was exactly why Gerry had chosen him as their solicitor. He had ensured that they had both considered the possibility of sudden death, and Shelly was now very glad he had done so.

He read through the preliminaries, then turned to Leila. As he read out that Gerry had left his daughter three hundred and fifty thousand euros – enough to buy her own home – Leila burst into tears (again) and leaned against Shelly.

'He'll be there to look after you and Matthew and the baby after all,' Jake said kindly.

Mark then turned to Jake. He was to receive the same amount, with Gerry's hope that he would use it to buy a home of his own too.

Jake shook his head in disbelief. 'I'd swear he orchestrated that mess-up with my mortgage before I went away,' he said.

'How do you mean?' Leila asked.

'Ah, I was hoping to sign off on my house. But when I got to the estate agent's, there was a mix-up. The person I needed to deal with wasn't available, so I had to leave it until now. It looks like I won't need to draw down that mortgage money after all.'

'Yup, that was your father,' Shelly said. 'I think you're right. He interfered with things so you wouldn't have a big mortgage weighing you down.' She stroked Jake's face, then turned to Leila and kissed her cheek. 'I'm happy for you both,' she said. 'We always wanted to leave you both with a decent legacy when we were gone.'

'No money could ever replace having him around,' Jake said sadly.

'I know, love,' Shelly said. 'But the house you're buying would've taken a large chunk of your and Fee's wages. This way, you can have a lovely quality of life with your father's blessing, generosity and grace. You and Fee can concentrate on planning your wedding knowing you don't have massive debts weighing you down.'

'Let's take it one step at a time, Mum,' he said, patting her hand.

'I can't believe Matthew and I will be able to buy a house too,' Leila said in awe. 'Ever since we found out about the baby, we've been scouring for a suitable place. Something bigger than Matthew's poky one-bedroom flat. But even with my best negotiating, it was looking as if we'd be damn lucky to get anything bigger taking our wages into consideration. I can't believe Dad has done this for us.'

'You and Matthew deserve it,' Shelly said. 'This is a good day, we should go and—'

'Er, sorry, we're far from finished,' Mark said, interrupting politely. 'This is for you, Shelly.' He slid a piece of paper across the desk. It looked like an estate agent's brochure.

'What's all this?' Jake asked, gazing at it. 'It looks like some tumbledown Spanish hacienda.'

'That's exactly what it is,' Mark said, raising an eyebrow. 'The details are all in this folder. You'll need to take it home and read it. But here are the deeds and the legal papers. It's in your name, Shelly.' He reached into a file and pulled out a large brown envelope. 'The letter in here explains it.

As a matter of fact, Gerry only finalised the details two months before he died.'

'I don't understand,' Shelly said in shock.

'He was planning to retire early,' Mark said, peering over his glasses. 'I assume he told you that?'

'Yes, of course,' Shelly said defensively. 'Well, we'd had a brief chat about it. I'd said I wanted us to enjoy our remaining time together . . .' She trailed off and began to cry. Both Jake and Leila moved to embrace her. Mark waited patiently for Shelly to calm down before he continued.

'He had plans for that retirement,' he said. 'A project. I had him browbeaten into coming in here every year to update his documents, and maybe he had some sort of sixth sense about what was going to happen to him, because he came in early this year, which is why everything is so perfectly up to date. He said he wanted his affairs in order and that I should hold a copy of the deeds, et cetera. This time, he included that letter with the paperwork.'

'Open it,' Jake urged. 'Knowing Dad, he had it all worked out.'

Shelly hesitated.

'Clearly you may prefer to wait and open it in private,' Mark interjected. 'But in the event that you have any questions, it might be wise to do it now. I can step out of the room if you wish.'

'No. Not at all, Mark. But thank you for offering,' Shelly said. 'You stay right where you are. It seems you knew more about what Gerry was up to than I did,' she added sadly.

Mark looked at her over the top of his glasses. 'I think,' he said gently, 'it was intended as a surprise rather than a secret, if that helps at all.'

'Yes,' she said, blinking. 'It does help. Thank you.' She took out the letter with shaking hands – even seeing his sloping handwriting was enough to wring her heart – and read it out loud.

My darling Shelly,

If you are reading this now, clearly I'm not with you any longer. I agreed with Mark that I would update the will, etc. yearly as we progressed. If the worst has happened, please know that it was never my intention to leave you. I cannot imagine my life without you, so I hope you are not struggling too much without me. (Well, okay, a small part of me hopes you miss me like crazy!)

Even though it was incredibly sad, Shelly, Jake and Leila laughed out loud at that part.

I hope you know that you were my world and my everything. From the first moment we met, I knew I would never find another woman like you. I held onto you with both hands, never wanting to lose you. I never took our marriage for granted and I know I was lucky to love and be loved by you.

As my retirement approaches, I'm constantly thinking about how we might live out our latter years together. Recently I revisited Rondilla, the picturesque little Spanish town where we first fell in love. Remember the promise I made to you on our wedding day? I vowed that we would go back there some day and relive the magical moments we spent there during our first flush of love.

As I wandered, I happened upon Casa Maria. This property was once a grand and beautiful home, but it has been neglected and left in a derelict state for decades.

My grand idea was that you and I would spend time bringing it back to its former glory. I thought this would be a project we could take on together, so we would leave a lasting legacy that our children, and eventually their children, could use and love. When we were married, we made solemn vows to one another in front of our families and friends. I am proud to think we've managed to keep them for all these years. But this promise was ours. It was between you and I and it has always stuck in my mind. Lately I have felt compelled to honour it.

I'm sorry to leave you with all the work, but if you are grieving even half as much as I would be without you, then perhaps this project will take your mind off things. I believe Casa Maria deserves to shine once more. So perhaps you could mend your broken heart as you simultaneously breathe new life into this enchanted place.

The first moment that I stood in the hallway of Casa Maria, I felt welcome. The atmosphere is beguiling and I hope you will share my enthusiasm for this charming old building. Use your keen eye and your wonderful attention to detail, and of course your amazing energy. Create a home that is filled with love and laughter, rather than the sad and dilapidated place that exists at the moment.

I will always be with you in your heart. I will watch over you, and please know that all I want is for you to learn how to live without me. I know it's probably odd of me to write this, but I don't want you to be alone for the rest of your days, Shelly. So if love comes knocking, let it in. Be happy, if you can. Life is too short to be miserable. Honour my death by living.

In the words of A. A. Milne: Promise me you'll always remember: you're braver than you believe, and stronger than you seem, and smarter than you think. *And you're loved more than you know.*

Your adoring husband,
Gerry

There wasn't a dry eye in the room as Shelly stumbled through the final lines. As she folded the letter and put it back in the envelope, she looked from Leila to Jake, unable to speak.

'I wasn't expecting this,' Jake said finally. 'Dad certainly gets the last word, eh?'

'Yes, either him or Christopher Robin,' Leila laughed through her tears.

The atmosphere was strained as they got back into the car to drive home. Gerry had certainly left them plenty of food for thought.

'I can't fathom any of this,' Shelly said. 'He gave me no hint . . .' She paused for a moment as a light bulb went off in her head. 'Oh my goodness, he *did* give me a hint,' she said. 'We were talking on the phone and he said there was something he was planning but he couldn't tell me yet. And that other time, in St Lucia, he said, "I'm going to make it my business to ensure we all have more regular bursts of sun going forward." I'd no clue what he was talking about then, but it must have been this. He must have already bought this Casa Maria place.'

She felt a wave of relief wash over her. Gerry hadn't locked her out of his plans, she wasn't the last to know – he was just relishing the prospect of delivering his bombshell in person, when he was ready. The realisation that he hadn't kept secrets from her was delicious. She'd felt like a fool in front of Mark, being so in the dark, but Gerry *had* mentioned it to her – and knowing him, he was probably planning some elaborate way of finally telling her. She smiled to herself. What a man.

'Tell you what,' Jake said suddenly, interrupting her

thoughts. 'Let's go somewhere for a coffee and a chat. That's a lot to take on board. I could do with talking it over.'

He drove them to a place nearby and they walked towards the welcoming glow of light and the smell of fresh-baked bread. Once inside, Jake took their orders and went up to the counter. Christmas music played in the background and already there were hordes of shoppers bustling about with bulging bags.

'I can't get my head around Christmas this year,' Leila admitted. 'I've bought a pair of socks for Matthew and a bracelet for Fee and that's it.'

'That's more than I've done,' Shelly said. 'I've been so busy trying to get up in the morning and act normal that I haven't managed to get into any kind of Christmas spirit.'

'Maybe we'll skip it this year?' Leila suggested hopefully.

'No,' Shelly said with a determined sigh. 'We need to buck up and start getting on with living. Your dad would be furious with us if we succumbed and became miserable. He adored birthdays and Christmas and any chance for a bit of a celebration. We can't become the family who doesn't bother. Besides, your baby will be joining us soon, and we owe it to him or her to create a world full of magic and hope.'

'I wish I could have a glass of wine,' Leila said, sounding far more peevish than she'd intended.

'I'm sure it won't kill you to have a small one later on,' Jake said as he placed a loaded tray down on the table.

'No way, Jake,' she said. 'If the baby was born with an extra eye in the middle of its forehead, I'd blame myself.'

'It's not as if you're necking a bottle of tequila every hour on the hour,' he scoffed.

'I need to think of my child now,' she said. 'You don't understand that notion. All you ever have to think about is yourself.'

'Yeah, and a few hundred passengers every time I go to work,' he shot back.

'*Please*,' Shelly said, putting her hand over her eyes. 'Don't bicker. You're not toddlers.'

'Sorry, Mum,' Leila said. She glanced over at her brother. 'Sorry, Jake. I'll put my claws away and gorge on one of those delicious-looking Danish pastries instead. Well done, Jake, that's a fabulous array of naughty things for breakfast.'

As Leila bit into the Danish, Jake handed Shelly a large mug of coffee.

'How are you coping after those revelations?'

'Well,' she sighed. 'I'm trying to remember what Mark pointed out . . . that this . . . this Casa Maria thing was meant to be a surprise rather than a shock or a secret. But still, what was your father thinking?'

'Maybe it's a really beautiful place that will provide comfort for you,' Jake said, without enough certainty in his voice to convince anyone.

'Let's take a look at it again,' Leila said. 'I'm on maternity leave now, remember, so once the baby is born there's nothing to stop us going down to Spain and taking this project on. It could be fun.'

Shelly took a big gulp of coffee as she pulled the brochure out, along with the paperwork.

The picture on the front showed a rather blurry image of a hacienda that must have been a delight at some point. The pale stone walls were partially covered in bougainvillaea and the oversized dark wood front door looked inviting. The paths and driveway leading to the door were all overgrown with weeds and what looked like some sort of green creeper.

Inside the booklet were equally dark and sketchy pictures of reception rooms, a massive kitchen and a stunning hallway with an imposing wooden staircase that wound its way up towards several bedrooms.

'Each room looks more dilapidated than the next,' Jake said as they all examined the photos.

'It looks like a mammoth task,' Shelly said doubtfully.

'Forget about it for the moment,' Jake said. 'Leave it for a year or two. Wait until you feel you might be in a state of mind to face going down there.'

'Actually, Jake's right for once, Mum,' Leila said. 'There's nothing to say that you have to even look at it. If you hate the thought, it could always be put up for sale.'

'Are you miffed with Dad that he left you that old pile?' Jake asked.

'It was a gorgeous idea,' Shelly said wistfully. 'I think he was a dote to buy it with the plan that he and I would go down there and make it beautiful once more . . .'

'It's so romantic,' Leila said. 'He really adored you, Mum.'

'Yes,' Shelly said, her thoughts turning back to the letter again. One phrase had leapt out at her: *honour my death by living*. It was such a beautiful and generous sentiment. She loved him for letting her go like that; it took courage and great love. And here she was, not letting him go at all and living a half-life in his long shadow, unable to move on in any direction. She was letting him down, she felt that with a sudden force that surprised her. She was letting Gerry down.

She looked at her two children, who were embarking on their own lives now, filled with promise. She didn't want them to think of her as an item on their to-do list – *mind Mum*. She felt a shot of anger dart through her at her own weakness, followed by one of pure determination, like something had lit a fire inside her. In a flash, there was a clarity that she hadn't had for the past six months.

'Do you know what?' she said, putting down her coffee cup firmly. 'I'm going to go to Spain and look at this place. Sooner rather than later, as a matter of fact.'

'Really?' Leila said, looking from Shelly to Jake. 'Are you sure?'

'I'm totally sure,' Shelly said. 'I need shaking up a bit and I need to get out of this rut of half existing.'

'When are you thinking of going?' Jake asked. 'After Christmas?'

'No, Leila is due then,' Shelly said. 'I'm going tomorrow. How's that for a decision!'

Chapter 10

FEE WAS BOWLED OVER BY THE NEWS THAT GERRY had left Jake enough money to pay for a house.

'Wow,' she said, lacing her arms around his waist. 'That's pretty amazing.' She bit her lip and stood back from him, looking into his eyes. 'Hun, do you think we should do something separately? That money was meant for you. Perhaps we should get the house at Furzedale Close in both our names, with the mortgage we'd agreed upon, and you should use your money to buy a second property as an investment.'

'Why?' Jake asked, looking puzzled. 'Dad knew we were headed for marriage. He even told me I should make an honest woman of you. The money is for both of us, Fee. What's the point in getting this amazing help and being burdened with debt anyway?'

'I know, but . . . I feel guilty that you're paying for it all.'

'We'll be married soon,' Jake said. 'In fact, I reckon we should set a date. Give us all something to look forward to. Mum is struggling without Dad. She'd love to go out shopping with you and the girls.'

'When are you thinking?' Fee asked. She'd been wanting to broach the subject, but was afraid it was a bit soon.

'How about the summer?'

'Next summer? Summer coming?' Fee asked in delight.

'Yeah, there's no point in having a really long engagement. How about we find some kind of boutique hotel and have the people we see most of, keep it small and personal.'

'How small is *small*?' Fee asked, looking worried.

'Oh, great.' Jake grinned. 'You've already invited half the hospital, haven't you?'

'No!' Fee said. 'But I have been thinking that I'd like a great big party. It doesn't have to be expensive, but I'd like it to be fun.'

'How many are you thinking?'

'Maybe sixty or so for a sit-down lunch, and then invite everyone we can to an evening party?'

Jake seemed pretty happy with her ideas, so Fee allowed herself to start feeling really excited. Once Christmas was over, she'd give Leila a few weeks to have her baby and settle, and then they could go gung-ho into preparations.

'What about a venue?' she asked. 'I was thinking of that place in Kildare. The one that used to be a flour mill and they've turned it into a cookery school and wedding venue. It's gorgeous.'

Jake held up his hands, looking as if he were ready to be shot. 'I surrender. You can take care of it!' He pulled her into his arms and kissed her. 'And the best part is that I have the money to pay for it.'

As they hugged, Fee felt oddly anxious. She wasn't sure about this new-found wealth that Jake had come into. They weren't on any kind of even footing any more. Jake would buy the house and still have money over – how could she ever catch up with that level of wealth? Saving any sort of decent amount would take years for her. She disliked this new sense of imbalance between them, like she was lagging behind in a race, never destined to win.

She vowed she would take on more hours and build up her own little nest egg. She wanted to be certain she could pay for the things she wanted personally. Her own wedding dress, the bridesmaid dresses and all the trimmings that men wouldn't think of would come out of her pay packet alone. She would make sure of that.

She couldn't have Jake thinking she was useless, nor could she bear to feel like a kept woman. She'd studied so hard and worked her way up the career ladder in order to make a difference and in order to *feel* different from her own mother. Guilt washed over her as she thought of Deirdre. Her hands had spent more time in bleach than Fee would like to think about. She had earned a little extra money by cleaning houses while Fee was at school. But Deirdre had never known luxury, nor had she expected much from life. While Fee loved her dearly, she didn't want to end up like her.

Up until today, she and Jake had had a dream of working their way up to owning a detached home with electric gates and a big garden, a space to call their own, separate from everyone else. They'd fantasised about driving matching flashy cars and going on holidays to resorts that only the well-to-do could afford. A part of her worried that it made her shallow to think like that, but after all her years living frugally as a student, she was hungry for something completely different.

She and Jake had shared that hunger and drive; they were living it together. Now, though, she was suddenly on a different rung of the ladder to Jake, and she had a horrible feeling she'd never catch up with him.

Something else was bothering her, too. Yes, Jake seemed happy to share his wealth with her for now, but how might he feel in the future? What if things didn't work out between them and she was left out in the cold? What if he began to resent her free ride and fell out of love with her?

All of a sudden, Fee was riddled with doubt about everything she'd thought was perfect in her life.

Chapter 11

SHELLY COULDN'T CONCENTRATE ON THE BOOK she was reading. She'd gone over the same two pages half a dozen times before giving up. She was waiting for the taxi to come and take her to the airport. For the fiftieth time that morning, she picked up the A4 brown envelope Mark had given her yesterday.

There were so many things she found difficult without Gerry. The worst part, however, was not having him here to share stuff with. She still thought, after all these months, that he'd walk back in the door at any moment. She still reached for her phone to text him. Right now, she'd exchange her last moments on earth to see him.

What were you thinking, Gerry? she wondered as she balanced her glasses on her nose and stared at the images of Casa Maria once more.

Her decision to go to Spain immediately had been so certain yesterday. She had booked the flights as soon as she'd come home from the café, in a flurry of clarity and determination. Both the kids had been so encouraging. Bless him, Jake had even offered to go with her.

Leila was pragmatic. 'Go and suss this place out, and that way you can make a decision on whether or not you want to keep it.'

The taxi appeared and the driver beeped the horn. Shelly

rushed out and put her bag on the back seat, then got in beside it.

It was all a little surreal as she pulled up at the airport and made her way to check-in. Not sure she could cope with the familiarity of the Gold Circle lounge, and hesitant about whether or not she was still entitled to be there now that Gerry was gone, she perched nervously on the edge of a plastic seat, waiting for her gate to come up on the screen.

As soon as it did, she walked purposefully to the correct area and waited silently to board. The familiar uniform as the pilot passed her made her stomach churn. The air hostesses were pleasant, but thankfully none of the staff were familiar to her, and clearly they didn't associate her with Gerry. She settled down for her flight, sighing with relief that nobody joined her row of seats. She gazed unseeing out of the window.

She had no accommodation booked and was hoping that one of the hotels or B&Bs in the village would have a spare room for the night. If the worst came to the worst, she'd get a taxi back to Marbella, where there were countless places to stay.

The flight and subsequent taxi ride from Malaga airport, past Marbella and on up into the rolling hills of Rondilla, seemed to pass in a flash. As they approached the village, the driver asked her for the exact address. She read it out loud and he climbed out of the car to ask a passing stooped and shrivelled little man. Much gesturing later, the driver got back into his seat.

'You certain is the right address?' he asked. 'That man say this place is kaput.'

'Yes, that's right,' she said with an even smile.

He trundled forward again, having to stop and pull to the very edge of the road when a small lorry approached. As vigorous horn-beeping and shouting ensued, Shelly stifled a giggle. She'd forgotten quite how explosive the Spaniards could be. In a flash the argument was over and the driver seemed to have totally forgotten it had even happened.

As he pulled to a halt, she craned her neck to catch a glimpse of Casa Maria.

'*Es aqui*,' he said pointing to a large set of metal gates. The flaking paint, thick cobwebs and rampant weeds made the place look more like a scene from a creepy Hallowe'en movie than a potential home.

Shelly paid the driver, and waited until he'd turned and driven away. Her heart sank as she realised there was a thick rusty chain securing the gate. She was about to walk towards the village when she realised the chain wasn't actually padlocked. Unravelling it, she managed to shove the gate open wide enough to pass inside, dragging her bag behind her.

The drive was tree-lined on either side and she could see what once would have been a lovely hedge. The ground was greened over, and dry and spongy to walk on. Clearly, December in Rondilla wasn't as wet as December in Ireland. She raised her head and sniffed the air – there was a faint but delectable smell of oranges. It made the air around her fragrant and her stomach rumble.

As she rounded the corner, Casa Maria came into sight, the blurry brochure images taking on sudden solid form before her. A gasp escaped her lips as her eyes darted from one end to the other, taking it all in. The large, heavy front door was centred sturdily between two magnificent bay windows. On the first floor she counted four large sash windows. The floor above that had four slightly smaller ones. The stone cladding was covered in creeper and some of the windows were totally obscured by the unruly growth. As she walked slowly towards the building, tears began to blur her vision.

'I can see why you thought I would love this,' she whispered as she gazed momentarily skywards. 'Oh Gerry, this is incredible.'

By the time she reached the front door, her heart was pounding. Fumbling in her bag, she found the single key that had come with the deeds. Like a prop from *Alice in Wonderland*, it was a large, carved metal key with a decorative hoop shape at the handle. It was almost the same length as her hand. Sliding it into the keyhole, she expected it to resist turning. Astonishingly, it rotated with ease, the sound of the clunking barrel echoing down the hall. Pushing the door open, she half expected bats or some kind of wild creatures to shoot out. Thankfully that didn't happen, and she peeped inside.

The first thing she saw was the mosaic flooring of the hallway. She dropped her bag and sank to her knees, running her fingers over the tiled pattern in terracotta and clotted cream shades, lifted by a striking royal-blue central colouring. Standing up, she gazed at the majestic wooden staircase. It must have been magnificent once upon a time, but now it looked savaged by woodworm, and many of the balusters were either missing or broken. The handrail had seen better days and cried out to be replaced with a glossy new version.

The dingy photos on the brochure did the place no justice. They most certainly didn't capture the warm feeling of welcome that Shelly was feeling – just as Gerry had described it. It was as if she'd instantly connected with this lonely shell of a house. In some weird way, it felt like home.

She longed to climb the stairs, but was conscious of the fact that she was alone. She wondered if the steps were rotten and unsafe. Against her better judgement, unable to stop herself, she ascended on tiptoes, pressing each step gingerly before putting her full weight upon it.

At the return, she put her hand on the intricate stained-glass window. The afternoon sun illuminated the banister, casting a myriad of colours onto the floor below. Walking up the final three steps, she saw that she could go either left or right. She chose to go left first, and pushed open a large panelled door using the round wooden handle.

The bedroom she entered must have belonged to a girl: the pale pink walls were adorned with cream cornices and yellowing, once white, woodwork. Going over to the window to look at the view, she felt slightly giddy as she stared across at the valley below. She returned to the landing and walked from room to room before going to the smaller, but equally beautiful staircase that took her to the remaining four bedrooms on the third floor. Yet again the balusters were damaged and in need of extensive repair.

With eight large bedrooms in total, this place would be ideal as either a boutique hotel or a wonderfully plush bed and breakfast.

As Shelly made her way back down the stairs, there were a million questions zooming around in her head. Why had Gerry bought this? Had he wanted them to run it as a little business, or had he seen them as lord and lady of the manor? She decided to try and free her mind of questions she could never answer. Instead, she forced herself to deal with the here and now.

There was still downstairs to explore. She returned to the front door. There appeared to be large reception rooms on either side. She walked into one, looked around, then crossed the hall and stood with her hands on her hips in the second.

Both rooms were vast and had the luxury of bay windows that overlooked the garden. If it were tidied up, the views would be fabulous. The walls were ragged with peeling paper, the floor coverings were dank and musty and encrusted with mould that had clearly been growing without interference for years. The ceilings seemed to be miles away as Shelly tilted her head to look at the intricate cornice work. Brown curling wires squirmed from the walls and ceiling, and she wondered if the fittings had been made from crystal. It took surprisingly little imagination for her to envisage how the room could look..

She walked back to the hallway and towards the rear of the house. The sizeable kitchen was like a scene from a movie. A huge cream stove took pride of place, with wooden cupboards huddling around it on both sides. The flagstone flooring had clearly been painted in an effort to add light, but the years of neglect had left it looking dull, chipped and sad. However, the view out back took her breath away. It was certainly overgrown, but it was obvious that someone with green fingers had once nurtured and loved this place. Beneath the criss-crossing briars lay rows of trees laden with fat citrus fruits. The whole scene called to her to come out and explore some more.

The key that rested in the back door turned as freely as the front one had. Stepping outside, she inhaled the sweet tangy air. To the right was a stone-walled mews. It needed even more love and attention than the main house, but Shelly could also see plenty of potential there. A single iron chair sat dejectedly to one side, two of its legs immersed in years of mud. She walked over and pulled it clear, placing it on even ground. Then, sitting down with a sigh, she tried to take everything in, thinking about Gerry showing her around and talking nineteen-to-the-dozen about her brand new project. He knew her well, she mused; it was exactly the kind of thing she would love to do – take on something neglected and make it beautiful again, especially here, in a place that was so special to them.

'Hola?'

She jumped at the sound of a woman's voice.

'Hola,' she replied loudly. *'Estoy aqui.'* She turned to see a tall, thin lady in her late thirties or early forties, with smoky skin, glossy black hair pulled back into a bun, and eyes as dark as shiny buttons. Wearing a sundress with a cardigan and a large baker's apron trussed tightly around her, she looked more than a little formidable.

'¿Por qué estás usted aquí ahora? ¿Cómo se llama usted?'

Shelly racked her brains to try and remember some of her pidgin Spanish, but came up blank.

'Me Shelly,' she said rather loudly, wondering why on earth she was shouting.

The woman stared, folding her arms. 'Why you here?' She tossed her head in the air in a slightly disgusted way.

'My husband bought me this house, but he died. So I came to look,' Shelly blurted out.

'¿Qué?' the lady said as she clearly tried to piece the

situation together in her head. Her expression softened immediately. 'Oh, I am so very sorry to hear this.'

'You live near here, I take it?' Shelly asked.

The lady smiled tentatively; it transformed her face and made her look very pretty. '*Hola, me llamo Valentina*,' she said, offering her hand to shake.

Shelly took it gratefully and asked if she minded speaking English.

'*Sí*, no problem, I learn it at the school,' she answered. 'So you are the owner of Casa Maria?'

'Yes, I suppose so,' Shelly replied. 'My husband bought it. It was supposed to be a surprise, but he died before he could tell me about it. I only found out about its existence the other day, so now I have come to see what I should do with it.'

To Shelly's astonishment, Valentina suddenly lunged forward and took her face in her hands affectionately, as if they were old friends.

'I think I know your husband,' she said quietly.

'Really?' Shelly was taken aback. 'How?'

'He came to see this place too, and he ate at my restaurant. He was a most charming man. Very warm. Me and Mama were happy that he live here. I'm so very sorry to hear that this will not be so.'

'Thank you for telling me that,' Shelly whispered. 'It makes me feel like he is here with me.'

There was a long silence. Shelly felt incredibly awkward as this stranger stood and stared at her unabashedly, clearly sizing her up. Not sure of what else to do, she invited her to have a look around. Mercifully, it seemed to be the best thing she could have said. Valentina certainly didn't need to be coaxed, and shot off inside for a good snoop. For the next twenty minutes there was a lot of gesticulating and tutting as she opened every cupboard and examined each room in detail.

By the time they reached the front door and the end of their tour, the natural light was beginning to fail.

'You need a place for the night?' Valentina asked.

'Yes, do you know of somewhere?'

'You can stay with us. We have a restaurant called Café del Sol in the square, with two rooms for letting. We live in the house over there.' She pointed to a small, dank-looking place with tiny slits of windows. But its grounds told a different story. Even from here, Shelly could see that it had a proper kitchen garden: vegetables in rows and large wooden boxes of herbs.

'Thank you so much,' she said, feeling suddenly exhausted and glad she didn't have to organise accommodation as well. 'My name is Shelly, by the way. My husband was Gerry. It's lovely to meet you.'

Valentina bowed rather formally, and Shelly had to stifle a giggle. This whole day was becoming stranger by the minute.

'There is one thing I must say to you,' Valentina said, suddenly very serious.

'Okay.' Shelly felt nervous about what was coming next.

'*Las naranjas* . . .' She pointed at the trees. 'May I . . . harvest some fruit?'

'Of course.' Shelly nodded fervently. 'There are lots more trees in the back garden. You should go there really.'

'*Vale*,' said Valentina happily. 'Because I take them for the past fifteen years and wasn't planning to stop now.' She grinned at Shelly, and the two of them burst out laughing.

By the time they had collected some oranges and walked along the road and down a very narrow steep street, it was dusk. When the beautiful cobbled square came into sight, Shelly stopped and stared, overcome by the familiar beauty of this place. In the centre stood the gorgeous fountain she now remembered seeing with Gerry so many years ago. Memories came flooding back as she turned this way and that, trying to take it all in. The ornate church looked just the same. Some of the houses had been turned into shops or cafés, but in general it was very similar to the way it had been back then.

Valentina smiled at her obvious delight and led her to the right of the church, where her restaurant stood. Tables and chairs were set up outside, but it was clear that there wouldn't be a rush of diners. There wasn't a soul in sight as Valentina ushered her inside the building and up the side stairs.

'Which room you like?' she asked.

'I don't mind,' Shelly said, feeling suddenly shy and very much alone.

Valentina pushed open a door and took her bag. The room was cosy and pretty, and the queen-sized bed looked inviting, with plump pillows and a woollen rug over the top of a marshmallow duvet.

'So, you are hungry?'

Shelly nodded. Valentina placed her bag on the bed and told her to come down when she was ready.

She perched on the bed and tried to take stock of all that had happened. Casa Maria was beguiling. She could still smell the sweet scent of oranges on her hands. Had Gerry noticed that very smell? Had he looked at the fruit and imagined them sharing glasses of Buck's Fizz as part of a decadent holiday breakfast together? What plans had he made for restoring the place? Had he thought of using it as a business or a plush holiday home? She wished she could text him or call him, even for five minutes.

Not wanting to be on her own any longer, Shelly descended the narrow staircase to the restaurant below and sat at a table for two. Valentina brought her a glass of sangria, then shouted into the kitchen at the back, instructing the chef to do something Shelly couldn't quite make out, before sitting in the chair opposite with her own drink. Moments later, a smaller, plumper and rather more shrivelled version of Valentina appeared.

'Ah, Mama, *aqui es Shelly.* Shelly, this is Carmen, my mama.'

'*Hola, Carmen,*' Shelly said, standing to shake her hand. The older woman muttered something and sat heavily on a chair that she'd yanked from a neighbouring table. Shelly tried to put aside her feelings of intimidation. Valentina filled a glass for her mother and placed it in front of her.

They clinked glasses and a veritable interview began.

Shelly had to stifle a giggle as the two local women pumped her shamelessly for information. All Carmen's questions were in Spanish, which Valentina translated. Ordinarily Shelly would find such intrusive questioning rude and inappropriate, but in the absence of another soul she knew, it somehow seemed okay. Plus Valentina had a lovely manner, warm and engaging, so Shelly was actually enjoying talking to her, even if it was a bit one-sided.

'So it was Gerry's idea to do this,' she concluded, having described the whole story in a level of detail that satisfied Valentina and a nodding Carmen.

'You have photo of Gerry?' Valentina asked.

Shelly picked up her mobile phone and scrolled to find a nice one. Holding it up, she showed it to her.

'*Sí*,' Valentina said, nodding and grabbing the phone to show her mother, who nodded too. 'This is the man I thought. As I said, very lovely man. A pleasure to deal with.'

'So he came to eat here?' Shelly said.

'*Sí*, and he stay here too,' Valentina said, handing the phone back. 'In fact, he stay in the very room you sleep in tonight.'

'Oh.' Shelly felt like the wind had been knocked out of her. Before she could control it, her eyes filled with tears.

'I'm so sorry . . .' she started to say, but Valentina waved her hand dismissively.

'No sorry,' she said softly. 'This is normal. You have lost a wonderful man. Of course you are sad. I didn't get to talk to him like this,' she gestured to the table between them, the sangrias on it, 'but I had a quick chat with him at breakfast and he say he love Casa Maria and can't wait to show it to his wife.'

As Shelly hid her tears in her napkin, Valentina simply waited in silence until the moment had passed. Shelly was very grateful for her kind understanding. Carmen patted her hand, then stood up and walked away into the kitchen.

'Now,' Valentina said, 'I cheer you up with some good food, okay?'

Shelly gave her a weak smile and nodded. She didn't think she could eat now, but there was no way she was going to refuse this kind hospitality.

Several plates of tapas arrived and were banged down loudly on the table by the chef. Then Valentina laid a basket of delicious-smelling breads down too and gestured for Shelly to help herself. As the smell of the bread enveloped her, Shelly remembered how hungry she was and forgot any thought of going to bed without eating. She tucked in, trying a spoon from each dish, savouring the different flavours.

Everything from the tiny black olives to the spittingly hot prawns *al pil pil* was delicious. Forgetting her inhibitions, Shelly mopped up the warm garlic-infused oil with the bread and sat back contentedly.

'Delicious,' she said, smiling at Valentina. '*Gracias.*'

'*De nada,*' Valentina said, glancing at her watch. 'I need to work now.'

Shelly looked around at the empty restaurant, wondering what had to be done. But a minute later the doors opened and a stream of people poured in. Clearly they were all locals and knew one another well. The sound of clanking glasses and animated chatter washed over her as she watched the lively goings-on around her.

She knew she ought to be sobbing her heart out. This exact scene was part of Gerry's plan. They were meant to be here as a couple, so that over time they would become accepted by the locals. But for now, Shelly was thoroughly enjoying the atmosphere. Another glass of sangria replaced her empty one as Valentina removed the empty tapas dishes as well.

Shelly fished in her purse for cash, but Valentina shook her finger.

'You pay when you go away,' she said emphatically over the noise. 'No hassle, Señora Shelly.'

By the time she'd finished her drink, the place was hopping. One long table was being sporadically thumped as a group playing cards became more animated by the second. Roars of laughter and rounds of applause made her smile, though her eyes were burning with tiredness. As she pushed her chair back to leave, Valentina appeared as if by magic.

'I sleep here tonight,' she said, pointing to a door near the kitchen. 'You need something, you call me, *sí*? Mama, she go home. She never come here really. But she was very interested to see who is taking over Casa Maria.'

'I see,' said Shelly.

'She remember lots of things about the house. Some of the villagers would know many things. The older people. It would be very good for tourists if Casa Maria is fixed. More reasons for the people to come from Marbella and the Costa.'

'I'll have to think carefully about what I do with it,' Shelly said, not wanting to give this lovely woman a false impression. Right now, she had no idea what her plans were.

'Anything will be better than the way it is now,' Valentina said with a shrug.

'Yes, I suppose it would be.'

'You call me if you need something, okay?' Valentina said.

'*Gracias,*' Shelly said sincerely as the other woman kissed both her cheeks.

In the privacy of her little room, Shelly peered out of the window at the ornate square below. Happily, the noise from the restaurant was only just audible. Pushing open a narrow panelled door, she was thrilled to find a perfectly proportioned bathroom. Earlier, she had assumed it was merely a wardrobe and that she'd have to wander the corridor looking for facilities. She pulled off her clothes and delighted in taking a shower.

Climbing into bed, she suddenly realised that she hadn't called the children. Too tired for a long conversation, she texted Jake and Leila saying she'd arrived safely and would speak to them tomorrow.

Leila replied immediately, reassuring her that she was fine and saying she was glad that things were going well. Jake texted a few moments later, saying he was proud of her and couldn't wait to hear all the news.

The small bedside light cast a soft glow around the room, making her feel incredibly safe despite the fact that she was in a strange place and all alone. She smiled to think of Gerry lying here, in this very bed, thinking of Casa Maria and of her. He was planning their future, and she loved him for that.

She fell asleep dry-eyed for the first time since Gerry's death. One part of her brain was urging caution, but the other part ventured off on a wild and happy journey, dreaming of all the wonderful things that could be done with Casa Maria.

Chapter 12

JAKE COULDN'T PUT HIS FINGER ON IT, BUT THERE was something odd about the way Fee was acting. They were out having dinner in a buzzy bistro in Dublin, but she seemed to be away with the fairies.

'Is there a problem with your fish?' he asked. 'You've barely touched it. I ordered the pan-fried potatoes for you and I'm eating them all.'

'Sorry,' she said, looking edgy. 'I had a late lunch and I guess I'm not as hungry as I thought I was.'

'How's work going?' he asked. 'Is it everything you thought it would be? Was it worth all the study and hard graft?'

'It's great, and I reckon it'll get better, too. Once I've been there a while, I hope to move on to some more complex surgeries.'

They chatted a bit about the wedding, and Fee looked animated momentarily as she talked about Norah and Leila being in her wedding party.

'What about you? Who are you going to ask to be your best man and groomsman?'

'I'm not really sure. Maybe Matthew for my best man? He's a decent bloke and he's going to be part of our family.'

'Is that who you really want, or are you trying to do the right thing?' Fee wondered.

'I could ask any number of people from work or school, but I don't know if I can be bothered with doing nights out and getting in a flap over it all. Matthew is quiet and decent. He won't get trolleyed and make a hideous speech at the wedding, and he won't want to do a stag weekend in Vegas either.'

'I see,' said Fee, raising her eyebrows. 'You make it sound like the thought of any sort of celebration fills you with dread.'

'I want to marry you, Fee. I want us to be together and live in our house and be happy. Since Dad died, I feel as if a lot of the bullshit in life is totally superfluous. That's all.'

'I understand,' Fee said, as she reached across the table to take his hand. 'But your father would've been the first one to tell us that we should enjoy the good times and have lots of fun.'

'True.' He paused, then looked at her. 'Actually, I've just had an idea. How about I ask Jim to be my best man?'

'Your boss Jim?' Fee asked. 'Why would you do that?'

'He's more than a boss to me. He was Dad's best friend, and since he lost Martha, he's been even closer to us. It would be the next best thing to having Dad with me.'

'You do whatever you want to do, Jake. I know who I'm having, so you have a think about it and do what you feel is right.'

Jake looked at his watch. It was after midnight. He was flying out at ten the following morning. He needed to stop drinking. Reluctantly he pushed his full glass of wine to the side and poured a large glass of water. Pilots had to jump through hoops to get jobs with his airline, and the monitoring was extremely stringent after that. It wasn't worth it to push the limits. Quite apart from the fact that he wouldn't consider putting other people's lives at risk, it could cost him his job if he were breathalysed.

'I've to go to the airport for eight in the morning,' he said, 'but why don't you stay over? We have the house to ourselves with Mum away.'

Fee agreed, but he could sense tension.

Back at his place, even though they made love, Jake couldn't shake the feeling that something was wrong.

'Okay, enough is enough,' he said finally, raising himself on one elbow to look down at her. 'Spit it out. What's wrong?'

'What do you mean?' she asked, her eyes shining in the darkness.

'You've been acting weirdly all evening. What've I done?'

'Nothing,' she said. 'I have a lot on my mind, that's all. It's a big step that we're about to take. The house, the wedding . . .'

'But it's all good, right?' he asked.

'Sure.'

He was distracted by the pinging of a text message. Thinking it could be work, he reached for his phone to check. It was Shelly, saying she was safe and sound and would call him tomorrow. He smiled. He was glad to see her being decisive again, like her old self.

By the time he'd fired off a quick text in return, Fee had curled up on her side with her eyes firmly closed. Taking the hint, he lay down and shut his eyes too. He fell asleep feeling as if Fee wasn't being straight with him.

Chapter 13

THE RAIN WAS COMING DOWN HARD AS LEILA stood at the door of the flat.

Matthew had gone to Italy that morning, Shelly was off in Spain, so she reckoned she'd use the spare time to get her Christmas shopping done. Dashing to her car, she headed for Dundrum shopping centre. Everything was under one roof there, so if she stuck to her list and worked methodically, she should get the bulk of it done in a matter of hours. Normally she loved any excuse to shop, but having a baby bump that felt as big as a boulder, she wanted it over and done with as quickly as possible.

When she got there, the place was thronged. Even though it was a weekday morning, it looked like the entire population of Dublin had had the same idea as her. By the time she found a parking spot, having driven around in circles so many times she felt ill, her patience was already wearing thin.

A cup of tea and a scone called out to her, so she sat down in a noisy café and waited. After a few minutes of being ignored and having the back of her chair bashed into, she realised the place was self-service. The second she stood up to join the queue, her seat was snapped up. She leaned against a high counter and tried to enjoy her snack, but in all honesty, she just felt utterly harassed. She took out her phone and wrote a jokey comment on Facebook, which immediately got seven likes. Obviously there were other people out there feeling her pain.

She envied the other shoppers, who were able to fit through narrow spaces and dash about with ease. Pressing on, she took out her list and forced herself to focus. By being bloody-minded about it, two hours later she had managed to get most of the things on her list. The heartburn that was raging through her gullet finished her off. She'd heard that was a sign of lots of hair when the baby was born. But that notion made her want to sob, too. Who wanted a hairy baby? Admitting defeat, she made her way back to the car park with her awkward pile of bags.

As she walked this way and that along the rows of vehicles, she began to feel more and more panicked. Where was her car? She'd driven around so many levels that she'd totally forgotten which one she'd finally found a space on. In a wild attempt to find it by chance, she pulled the keys from her handbag and pressed the unlock button. Each time she did so, she stood on her tippy-toes in the hope that she'd see her lights flashing as the alarm was deactivated.

What felt like hours later, having searched several levels of the car park to no avail, she went to the ticket machine and pressed the Help button.

'Hello,' a voice boomed out.

'I've lost my car,' she said. 'I'm pregnant and I feel like I'm going to fall down dead. I've been looking and looking but I can't remember where I parked.'

'What's your registration number?' said the voice.

'It's 131 D 4635, I think . . . no, it's 132 D . . . Oh gosh, I can't remember that either,' she said, her voice breaking.

'Wait there,' said the voice. 'I'm coming down to you.'

Feeling like a total idiot, she stood to the side as impatient people tried to pay for their tickets. Not one person stopped to ask if she was okay.

'I'm Fred,' said a burly young man in a tracksuit and hi-vis jacket. 'Come with me and we'll find your car.'

They made their way to an area with mobility scooters. Fred chose one, and she put her bags in the back of it and climbed in beside him. They took off, scanning each floor, row by row.

'There it is,' she shouted a few minutes later.

'Now that didn't take too long,' said Fred, looking pleased.

Leila fished in her purse, but all she could find was a fifty-euro note.

'Here, Happy Christmas, and thanks for being so lovely and not laughing or calling me thick.'

'I can't take that,' Fred said, eyeballing the note. 'It wouldn't be right. You keep it. I don't mind helping. It gets me out of the office. I love driving the mobility scooters and we're not usually allowed.'

'No, I insist,' she said, pushing the note into his hand. 'Have a few drinks and a bit of fun, seeing as I can't. Think of it as a favour. You're having the fun *for* me.'

A delighted Fred lifted her bags into the boot and waved very enthusiastically as she drove away.

Back at the flat, Leila dropped her bags in the hall and went wearily into the kitchen, flicking on the kettle. If she never went shopping again, it would be too soon. The whole outing had been a nightmare from start to finish. Fred was her saviour, even if he did think she was totally unhinged.

She checked her phone for messages from Matthew or

Shelly, but there was nothing. Feeling a bit lonely, she went on Facebook again and told everyone she was safely home and that bliss was a cup of tea and a sharing bag of Maltesers all to yourself. The likes and comments in reply made her feel a tiny bit less lonely. She also noted that Fee had been to Marco Pierre White's last night, a restaurant Leila had wanted to visit for ages. She felt a brief stab of jealousy at Fee and Jake's carefree life, then liked Fee's status to assuage her guilt.

Turning on the television, she sank into the couch and decided to give herself over to the warm embrace of afternoon TV.

At first, she thought it was the hot tea making her feel odd. But when the same sensation happened again a few moments later, Leila looked around the room. Nothing had moved, so it wasn't an earthquake or anything environmental.

The tea tasted off, like there were metal chippings or something weird in it. Maybe Matthew had been fiddling under the bonnet of a car and hadn't washed the cup properly? She pushed it away just as a full force spasm of pain hit her.

Grabbing the edge of the sofa, she waited for it to subside. When it did, she picked up her phone and wondered who she could call. It was probably those Braxton Hicks pains that they'd heard about in antenatal class. Matthew was obsessed with them and kept asking her if she'd had any.

Smiling to herself, she sent him a text. *Hey, hun! So the Braxton Hicks have started. Pity you missed them. I thought there'd been a nuclear explosion in the flat! God help me when the real thing starts. Now I know why men don't have babies. Love you x*

He didn't answer, so she guessed he was in a meeting with his phone switched off. She grinned as she thought of him. He'd want her to describe the pain exactly. He'd even suggested filming the birth, but naturally she'd shot him down immediately.

'I'm not having a camera shoved near my froufrou while I'm reeling in agony. Remember that awful video we had to watch at the antenatal classes? I would be mortified if there was one of those going around of me. No money could pay me to have that shown to random strangers. '

'But it would be amazing for the baby to have in years to come.'

'Would you want to look at your mother giving birth to you?'

'Er, probably not,' he conceded.

Matthew was such a teddy bear, she mused as she walked up the stairs. He'd make a great dad. She'd gone about halfway up when another pain hit, almost knocking her off her feet. She gripped the banister tightly and doubled over, breathing deeply. When it had passed, she sat on the step and waited for what felt like an age. Nothing else happened, so she stood up and went to the bathroom. A nice hot shower sounded good, along with the prospect of changing into something more comfortable.

As she stood under the delicious heat of the cascading water, she groaned out loud at the relief it gave to her aching back. Leaning her forehead against the tiles, she allowed the power shower to needle her spine gently. Eventually she turned it off and dragged herself out into the steaming bathroom. Wrapping an oversized towel around her warm skin, she padded into the bedroom. She'd been in the shower so long, her skin had turned slightly purplish red.

As soon as she sat on the bed, there was a sudden gush of warm water down below. Gasping in shock, she sat like a startled chicken, unable to figure out what she ought to do. The next pain was all the encouragement she needed to grab her mobile phone and scroll through her contacts for the hospital.

'Hello?' she said, gritting her teeth and trying to breathe through the pain as she'd been taught. 'It's Leila Dillon here, I think I'm in labour. My waters just broke and I'm . . . Agh . . .' As another, more intense pain ripped through her, she thought she might drop the phone. 'I . . . I'm here on my own. My partner and family are away. I don't know what to do . . .'

The lady on the other end of the phone was wonderfully calm and said she'd send an ambulance.

'Is there a neighbour or friend you can call?' she asked.

'Er, no,' Leila said, trying not to cry. 'But Fee . . . Fiona Davis is my brother's fiancée. If she's on duty, could you ask her to meet me?'

'The ambulance will be with you in a few minutes. Hang in there, love. You're doing a great job. I'll page Ms Davis for you right now.'

Leila hung up and pulled on a soft jersey maxi dress, then tried to grab the things she needed. She'd packed the bones of a hospital bag, figuring she still had oodles of time, but there were a few things missing.

Another shocker of a pain ripped through her, making her drop the bag.

She dialled Fee's number, but it went to voicemail.

'Fee! It's me. The baby's coming and everyone is away. Please come and meet me if you're at the hospital.'

Momentarily she considered calling her mum, longing

to hear her voice, but quickly decided against it. Shelly would only panic, and she couldn't get back from Spain in the next couple of hours so there was no point in alarming her. Jake was probably in mid-air, so she didn't want to worry him either.

Hesitating, she dialled Matthew's number. Again, she didn't want to freak him out when he was powerless to help, but she was terrified and needed to speak to him. This call too went to voicemail, so she left a ridiculously tearful message.

'Hi, Matthew. I don't mean to bother you, but I'm in labour.' Biting her lip, she tried in vain to control her emotions. 'There's an ambulance coming to take me from the flat. I'll be fine, so don't panic. I love you more than words can . . . Agh . . .' She had to hang up.

She made her way down the stairs to wait for the ambulance and tried to steady her nerves. With shaking hands, she called Fee again.

'Hey, Leila! I just got the page from reception at the maternity ward. I'm trying to pass my next surgery on to a colleague. I'll be at the ambulance entrance when you get here, okay?'

'Okay,' Leila said. Another pain hit, and she cried out. 'It's really bad, Fee. Is it meant to hurt this much?'

'I can't tell you because obviously I haven't had a baby yet, but I've seen women giving birth and it usually looks pretty damn sore if I'm truthful.'

'The ambulance is here,' Leila gasped in relief. 'I'm hanging up. See you at the hospital.'

'See you in a few,' Fee said calmly. 'Try not to panic.'

Leila had never imagined any single body could endure such intense pain. She felt as if she might die. More than that, death would be a superb option. At least the pain would go away.

She opened the front door, leaning against it as another contraction swept over her. There was a man and woman with the ambulance and they helped her into the back.

'It's not exactly plush, is it?' she said as they set off noisily. 'Agh . . .'

As she clenched her teeth, the woman asked if she could take a look under her dress. 'Judging by the way you're breathing and bearing down, I'd say you're not far off, love.'

Beyond caring who looked where, Leila nodded, fleetingly thinking she ought to be mortified she wasn't wearing any underwear.

'I can see your baby's head,' the paramedic said. 'If you can hold on for a few minutes . . .'

With that, a massive contraction hit and Leila pushed automatically.

'Good girl,' the woman said, swallowing her words. After that, her instructions were precise and clear, and Leila was grateful to have her there.

'Pant, Leila, there's a good girl. Take it easy. I know you want to push like your life depends on it, but I need you to pant as I deliver baby's head.'

As they pulled up outside the hospital, the baby's head emerged.

'Leila?' came a voice from outside the ambulance.

'Yes, it's me!' she shouted, sounding like a wild animal. 'That's my sister-in-law. She's a surgeon.'

The door flew open and Fee climbed in and rushed to her side just as the baby was born.

'Oh holy cow!' she said, tears rolling down her cheeks.

'Leila, you little beauty. Congratulations! I can't believe you've done it! Matthew is going to be over the moon.'

The paramedic laid the baby on Leila's chest.

'What is it?' she breathed, unable to fathom what had just happened.

'It's a little boy,' the woman said.

The doors of the ambulance flew open once more and the waiting staff looked in with delighted surprise. Thankfully, she was covered over with a blanket by now, but right at that moment in time, Leila didn't care who saw her. As she looked down at the perfect little baby in her arms, she couldn't have been happier.

'Babies wait for nobody, eh!' said Fee with a massive grin. She turned and spoke to one of the nurses. 'This is my sister-in-law, Leila. Can we find a nice quiet room for her, please?'

The nurse said she'd go back inside and see what she could sort out.

'Well done, Mum!' Fee said again, as she wiped tears from her own face. 'Let's take you and the baby inside so we can get you sorted.'

'Is he okay? He wasn't due for another three and a half weeks,' Leila said weakly.

'The obstetrician will check him over properly in a minute, but he looks marvellous. He's a good colour and he looks to be a fine weight, too.'

Another blanket was draped over her and the baby as the trolley was lowered and brought directly to the delivery suite. There, they cut the cord, delivered the afterbirth and gave the baby a full check. Once he was handed back, Leila felt slightly more human, though she was shivering so much her teeth were chattering.

'Why is my body shaking all over like this?' she asked.

'You've gone into shock, hun,' said Fee, who hadn't left her side. 'You had a really quick labour, and sometimes when that happens, your body takes a while to catch up.'

'I never got to thank the ambulance lady,' she said. 'She was so brilliant to me. I couldn't have done it without her.'

'Believe me,' Fee said, 'you'd have given birth at home if they hadn't arrived when they did. This little man had his own ideas!'

'He certainly did.' Leila gazed down at the little blanket-cocooned bundle in her arms. 'Wow,' she said as tears of joy, love, pride and a million other emotions rolled down her cheeks. 'He's just perfect, look at him!'

'He's a little trooper. Seven pounds, and he was only thirty-six weeks' gestation,' one of the delivery ward nurses said, handing her a black cordless phone. 'Your mobile phone won't work in here with all the equipment, so you can call your nearest and dearest on this. Is the daddy on the scene?' she asked, ticking off boxes on a chart.

'Yes,' said Leila. 'He'll be totally gutted to have missed this. He's away on business. Not only did he want to be here, he suggested filming it all.'

'Well, the Lord works in mysterious ways,' said the nurse with a giggle. 'Maybe that's why your little boy came while his daddy was out of town!'

'I can't believe Shelly and Jake are both away too,' Fee said. 'That's what we call Murphy's law, isn't it?' She cooed at the baby, already besotted. 'Will I dial Matthew's number for you?'

Leila nodded and held a hand out to her. 'Thank you for being here,' she said tearfully. 'Thank God I had someone from the family by my side.'

'Aw, thanks, sweetie,' Fee said. 'It means so much that you think of me as family already. I'm such a lucky girl to have you too. I won't lie, you're one of the reasons I can't wait to marry Jake.'

Matthew answered on the first ring, sounding utterly frantic.

'Hello? Are you okay? What's going on?'

'Hello, Daddy!' Leila said, as the baby made a little snuggly noise.

'The baby's here?' Matthew yelled. 'No way! I missed it. Did you film it? Is it a boy or a girl? Is everything okay? Are *you* okay? Oh darling, I'm so sorry I wasn't there with you!' He was clearly overcome with emotion.

'No I bloody didn't film it.' Leila laughed as the nurse who was pottering around beside her grinned. 'Besides, it was all kind of eventful,' she said, going into a swift description of what had just happened.

'I can't believe it, Leila. I'm so, so proud of you, darling. I cannot wait to meet him. I'm getting the first flight home.'

'Fee's here with me, so don't panic.'

'Thank God for that. Please thank her for me, and I'll be there as soon as is humanly possible.'

Leila hung up and grinned at Fee. 'He's a little bit excited,' she said, rolling her eyes. 'The poor man nearly lost his reason when he realised he'd missed it.'

'Aw, he's such a sweetheart, Leila. What my mother would call a keeper!'

'I know, he really is a dote. Your daddy is going to spoil you rotten, little man,' she said, kissing the baby's head.

'Will I dial Shelly's number for you?' Fee asked. 'I know you're probably starting to feel exhausted, but I think she'd want to know.'

'Of course,' Leila said, smiling. 'This is almost like doing a *Candid Camera* thing! Nobody will suspect what's just happened.'

The phone only rang twice before Shelly answered.

'Hi, Leila,' she said. 'How are things, love? Did you get your shopping done?'

'I got it started, Mum,' Leila said, and promptly burst into giggles.

'What are you up to? Don't tell me you went berserk and bought all sorts of expensive stuff!'

'No. I was interrupted by something a bit more dramatic.'

'What's happened?' Shelly said anxiously.

'I just had the baby,' Leila said, her eyes filling with tears again. 'It all happened so fast. It's a boy and he's perfect, Mum! He's gorgeous. I can't wait for you to meet him.'

'Oh darling!' Shelly said, sobbing too now. 'What happened? How come he was so early? Who's with you?'

She filled her mother in on the details and ended by saying there was no panic for her to return home. 'I don't want to ruin your holiday.'

'Ruin my holiday? I'm only passing time here. I'll be on the first available flight home. I'm so proud of you, sweetheart. Well done. Can you text me a selfie with the baby? What are you going to call him?'

'I'm not sure,' she said. 'I'll wait until Matthew comes and we'll narrow it down and choose a name. We thought we had another three weeks to decide.'

'Of course,' Shelly said. 'Congratulations, darling, and I'm so thrilled you had one member of the family with you at least.'

'Me too,' Leila said.

Once she'd said goodbye to Shelly, Leila phoned Jake and left a message on his voicemail.

'He'll be made up,' Fee said. 'I think this little man is going to be amazing for us all. It's been so sad and bleak since Gerry died. I think this is just what Jake needs. Being an uncle is a wonderful honour.'

'And you're his auntie,' said Leila.

'Steady on,' Fee said with a wink.

'In fact, I'd like you to be his godmother if you would,' Leila said, ignoring Fee's hesitation.

'Really?' Fee's eyes glowed with delight. 'I'd be honoured. You and me are going to have a very special bond, little man. I'm always going to remind you that I was the first person to hold you after your mum.'

By the time they wheeled her to a ward, Leila was elated. She'd never felt so incredibly blessed.

'I reckon Dad was with me,' she said to Fee.

'Oh, I've no doubt he was.'

Fee stayed and helped Leila dress the baby in his first outfit. She held him while Leila showered, and waited until she said she was honestly fine to get into bed and try to have a bit of sleep.

By that time it was dark outside. The nurses were anxious for visitors to leave as they prepared the ward for the night. The lights were dimmed, and Fee hugged Leila and told her how proud she was of her.

'Thanks, Fee. I'll never forget you coming in and being with me today. Give your godmother a wave,' she said, raising the sleeping baby's tiny hand.

Fee blew them a kiss and slipped out.

Chapter 14

AT THE AIRPORT THE NEXT MORNING, AS HE SIGNED in and waited to board his flight, Jake was paged by his boss. He immediately made his way to Jim's office, hoping there wasn't a problem with the schedule.

'Congratulations on your engagement,' Jim said, pumping his hand and slapping his back. 'Take a seat.'

'Thanks,' Jake said.

'Listen, I told your father a long time ago that I'd keep an eye on you.'

Jake nodded. 'I appreciate that, Jim.'

'So an opportunity has come up. Mark Breen is retiring. He's going to live in some cottage in the middle of nowhere with his wife.'

'Good for him,' Jake said. 'I like Mark. He's a gentleman.'

'For sure,' said Jim. 'But I'm going to be short a captain. I've considered this and mulled it over. I know it's unusual for someone as young as yourself to be considered for a captain's position, but you've more than proved your worth over the past few years. I'd like to offer you his job.'

'Really?' Jake said, unable to hide his smile. 'Wow. I'm honoured, Jim, thank you.'

'I know your father would've loved to be here to see you taking such a highly sought post here at the airline.

But if you believe in such things, I'd bet my last euro he's watching over you.'

'Can I take a couple of days to think it over?' Jake asked.

The smile faded from Jim's face. 'Am I hearing you right, son? You're actually hesitating about taking this promotion? You're about to marry an up-and-coming surgeon – I thought you guys were the power couple leading the way in the world.'

'Yeah.' Jake laughed. 'I suppose when you put it like that . . . I don't mean to sound ungrateful, Jim. I think I'm just . . .'

'Shocked and a bit blown away?' Jim supplied.

'Couldn't have put it better myself,' Jake said.

'Take a few days, kiddo. I'm being a little harsh on you. I think I was more excited about offering you the job than I'd given myself credit for. I know it would've made Gerry so proud, so I was caught up in that too. Come back to me at the end of the week and we'll get a new contract drawn up. There'll be a written test and the usual physical, but you can do both with your eyes shut.'

'Thanks, Jim.'

'You're welcome. How's Shelly doing? I haven't spoken to her in a while.'

'She's down in Spain, actually. Dad left her this hacienda and she's taking a look at it. Did he mention anything about it to you?' Jake asked.

'He did,' said Jim. 'I haven't seen it, but he was so excited about spending time there with Shelly. I'd totally forgotten about it . . . My heart goes out to your mother. We were a great foursome, me and Martha, your dad and Shelly. Who would've guessed things would work out like this?'

'I know. It's hard, isn't it?' Jake said. 'Anyway, I honestly appreciate you offering me this promotion. Imagine it, Captain Dillon.'

'Hey,' Jim raised his hands above his head, 'I'm just the messenger. The higher powers make the end decisions. They all agree you're the best man for the job. Good for you, Jake.'

Jake smiled and turned to leave, then turned back.

'Actually, while we're on the subject of mulling over big decisions, I've got one for you.'

Jim looked surprised. 'Really? I'm intrigued. What is it?'

'It's just . . . well, I've been thinking and I was wondering if you might do me the honour of agreeing to be my best man?'

'Me?' Jim looked taken aback. 'But I'm too much of an auld fella. Wouldn't you go for one of your pals?'

'I'd rather not,' Jake said. 'Nobody else knows me the way you do. Or my family, for that matter. I know Mum would be delighted, and I want you to be involved in the wedding. You're not just a family friend, you're *part* of our family.'

Jim looked really choked. 'If you honestly want me to, I'd be honoured.'

Jake smiled at him. 'Fantastic. Thank you so much. And I'll talk to you in a couple of days about the other thing.'

The two men shook hands and shared a quick hug, then Jake slung his hat on his head and left Jim's office, heading for the boarding gate. He was aware of a tight knot in his stomach.

Jim was right. This was a superb opportunity. So why wasn't he over the moon and feeling as if he'd just won the lottery? This was exactly the type of promotion he and Fee had fantasised about over the past few years. When she'd passed her exams and become a surgeon, he'd hugged her and vowed inwardly that he'd take the next step up the ladder of success alongside her as soon as he could.

Now it was about to happen, and all he felt was anxiety.

Maybe it was grief . . . Or maybe it was because he didn't need the money quite as desperately as before. Either way, he was certain of one thing – he didn't want anyone to know what Jim had just offered him. At least, not until he'd figured out what was going on in his head.

When he reached the aircraft, he entered the cockpit and issued instructions to the crew. He glanced towards the captain. That could be him in a short while. He could be the top man and head honcho. He ought to be ecstatic, but he knew that the buzz had left him. As he went through the motions of preparing for take-off, all he could think was: had his love of flying died with Gerry?

Chapter 15

SHELLY FELT AS IF THE CLOCK WAS TICKING BACK-wards as she waited impatiently for her taxi. Normally, red-eye flights were her idea of hell, but she couldn't wait to see Leila and the baby. She was still in shock that he'd arrived, and so suddenly too. Every time she thought of her daughter giving birth with strangers in the back of an ambulance, it filled her with horror.

She smiled as she thought of lovely Fee. She'd texted Shelly to reassure her as she left the hospital last night. She'd also sent a flutter of photographs of Leila and the baby. Thank goodness for her; it would only strengthen the bond between the two girls. She'd also assured Shelly that she was on duty first thing this morning and would look in on Leila and make sure she had what she needed.

For what felt like the thousandth time, Shelly zoomed in on the selfie Leila had texted a few hours previously. The baby was like a little angel, snuggled under her chin. Leila's eyes beamed with such intense love, and Shelly was immensely proud of her. What a wonderful achievement. It was so hard for her to fathom that her own little girl was a mum now. She gave a dry cough as she tried to stop her tears. She had moved up in status too. Would she be Granny or Nana or Grandma? None of the titles seemed to sit well with her. She'd see what panned out.

Maybe they could come up with a fun nickname instead? She shrugged one shoulder, knowing deep down that she wouldn't mind what the baby called her, so long as she could be part of his life.

At 4.30 on the dot, the lights of a taxi filled the dark square in Rondilla. Shelly had already settled up with Valentina and explained that she'd be back in a few weeks.

'Any time, Shelly,' Valentina had said cheerfully. 'Casa Maria will wait too. She has been patient for so many years now, a few more months will be just fine.'

Shelly pulled her cardigan tightly around her as she settled into the back of the taxi. The driver was polite, but made it clear he had no interest in chatting. Her head nodded heavily on her jerking neck until they pulled up at departures. With her bags in tow, she paid the driver and rushed to the ticket desk. As it wasn't high season, there was no queue, and before long she was checked through and ready to go.

Seeing the pilots strut past as they all began to board jolted her. She wondered if she would ever stop feeling raw and traumatised at the sight of a pilot's uniform. The churning in her stomach and aching loneliness inside was all-encompassing. Their first grandchild, and he wasn't here to see him. By the time they were due to take off, Shelly wanted to curl into a ball and cry.

Admonishing herself, she tried to think positive thoughts. She knew this little baby would give them all a reason to keep going. Fleetingly she wondered whether Leila might think of naming him after Gerry. Would she actually like that idea, or would it be too gut-wrenching every time she heard the name?

Breakfast followed by a read of an Irish newspaper helped steady her nerves and fill in the time.

By the time they landed, it was just after nine o'clock in the morning local time. She grabbed her bags and found a taxi. The driver made her grin like a fool as, in stark contrast to the Spanish driver, he wittered on about everything from the weather to the state of the local GAA pitch.

'So who are you visiting at the maternity hospital?' he asked, glancing at her in the rear-view mirror.

'My daughter and my first grandchild,' she said proudly.

'What flavour is the grandchild?'

'It's a boy.'

'Lovely,' he said with a nod. 'I've ten grandchildren myself. Six boys and four girls, and they're the light of my life. They never cease to entertain me.'

'I'm looking forward to getting to know him,' she said. 'My husband passed away suddenly just over six months ago, so we need this breath of fresh life.'

'Ah, I'm sorry to hear that,' he said as they pulled up outside the hospital. 'I hope you enjoy every minute with that young lad and your daughter.'

She paid him and pulled her bags into the lobby. Once she'd convinced the people on reception that she was indeed Leila's mother, and explained how she'd just returned from Spain, she was allowed in to see her. She could understand that they were strict about visitors so as not to disturb the new mums and tiny babies, but she was so excited about seeing them both, it almost tipped her over the edge when she couldn't get in instantly.

The ward was busy when she eventually found it. Several mums were attempting to feed, while others were chatting.

The sound of newborn babies mooching and crying made her heart swell.

'Mum!' Leila called out, waving frantically from the far end of the ward. Shelly rushed forward and dropped her bags on the floor at the foot of the bed. There in Leila's arms lay the most perfect little boy.

'Oh, look at his shock of dark hair! He's just sublime,' she said, perching beside her daughter and gazing down at the baby. Sensing her presence, he opened his eyes and stared.

'Hello, baba,' she whispered, stroking his velvety cheek. Leaning over, she kissed Leila.

'Here, hold him,' Leila said.

Shelly bent down and took him into her arms. Her breath caught in her throat at the beauty of him, the new-baby smell, the realness of this little person they'd been imagining for nine months. Her heart swelled and she was overcome by a thousand emotions at once.

'What do you think? Isn't he amazing?' Leila said.

'Oh he's more than that,' Shelly replied, staring intently into his baby-blue eyes. 'I cannot even express how wonderful he is. So are you. Well done, darling. I'm bursting with pride. Is Matthew here, did he make it back? I half expected to bump into him at the airport.'

'I think he'll make it into the *Guinness Book of Records* for fastest ever journey to Ireland,' Leila said with a laugh. 'He got here at two o'clock in the morning and refused to leave, so they let him sit in a chair and watch us sleep. He's gone to try and find a bit of breakfast and some coffee.'

'Did I hear my name being taken in vain?' Matthew said as he walked towards them with a takeaway coffee in hand.

'Hello, love,' Shelly said warmly, standing up to kiss him. 'Congratulations. He is just gorgeous. I'm completely smitten.'

Matthew kissed Leila and then stood next to Shelly and stared in awe at the baby.

'He's so perfect, isn't he?' he said. 'How on earth did you do that, Leila?'

'*We* did it, you great big goon,' she corrected him. 'In case it's escaped you, I didn't create him on my own.'

'No,' he agreed, 'but you grew him and then gave birth to him.'

'Yes, she did,' Shelly said. 'On her own, too.'

'I feel so bad about that,' Matthew said.

'So do I,' Shelly added. 'How typical is it? The one night we're all away.'

'It wasn't anyone's fault,' Leila said. 'I would've preferred not to do it in the back of an ambulance, but it'll be a good story to tell him when he's older.'

'Can I hold him again?' Matthew asked, looking a little nervous.

Shelly passed the baby over carefully. She had to put her hand to her mouth as she stifled a happy sob. She'd never seen a man as besotted with a baby in her life. It brought her right back to the day Leila was born, and how Gerry had looked at his brand-new daughter. As Matthew kissed his son's tiny face, he crooned and whispered to him. The baby opened his eyes and stared right at him.

'Have you any names?' Shelly asked.

'We had a few, didn't we?' Leila said, but Matthew seemed to be on another planet. 'Matthew?'

'Huh?'

'Names!' Leila giggled. 'Mum is asking if we have a name.'

'Yes! Of course he needs a name. How about Hercules? Or Zorro?'

Leila laughed. 'Or He-Man.' Then she looked serious. 'What would you think of Oliver, Ollie for short?' she said. 'Oliver Gerry.'

'I think Ollie suits you,' Matthew said, holding him up.

'It looks like that scene from *The Lion King*,' Leila teased. 'Is it okay with you if we use Gerry as his second name, Mum?'

'That's wonderful, darling,' Shelly said, her heart breaking. 'Your dad is looking down on us right now, smiling and saying what a fantastic mother you are already.'

'You reckon?' Leila said as she wiped away her tears.

'Oh I know he is.'

A nurse swept over. 'Hello, all. I've just come on duty. I believe this little fellow arrived in the ambulance yesterday.'

'Yes, and we both missed it,' Matthew said.

'Ah, you can spend the rest of your life making up for it!' the nurse laughed. 'I don't even need to ask if you're Leila's mum. You're a mirror image of one another! Are we all right here? Are those happy tears, dear?' she said, looking down at a weepy Leila.

Leila nodded. 'Yes and no. We're missing my lovely dad, who passed away six months ago, and Mum was just saying she thinks he's with us.'

'The older you get, the more you'll realise we mums are nearly always right,' the nurse said as she hugged Shelly. 'I'm sorry to hear about your husband. I hope this little man brings some fresh hope to your family.'

'He already has,' Shelly said.

'Leila, I wanted to say that you can go home today if you like.'

'Really?' Leila looked fleetingly delighted before a shadow of doubt crept across her face. 'I don't know if I'll manage. Shouldn't I stay here for a bit longer? Like maybe a couple of years?' She grinned through her tears.

'All new mums feel the same way,' the nurse said. 'But believe me, once you get the first night over with at home, you'll feel better.'

'We've nothing organised,' Matthew said. 'Miss Superstitious refused to let me set up a proper nursery at the flat.'

'You could stay at my house for a few days if you want,' Shelly ventured. 'No pressure. It's totally up to you both.'

'That could be a good plan,' Matthew said. 'What do you reckon, Leila?'

Leila nodded and Shelly felt a thrill of delight. Having her grandson under her own roof was an unexpected and wonderful treat.

'You won't go wrong with your mum there. Nothing like an experienced hand to reassure you.'

'It's a long time since I had a baby in my house.' Shelly sounded apprehensive.

'You'll be surprised at how quickly it all comes back to you,' the nurse said. She gave Leila a piece of paper with contact numbers in case she needed anything, and explained that the district nurse would call to do the PKU heel prick test, and that she would also weigh Ollie and answer any questions Leila might have.

'So will we pack your things and get out of here?' Matthew asked.

Leila nodded. 'I'll call a taxi and we'll all go home together. This is so exciting!'

Back at Shelly's house, Matthew made tea and waited until he was certain Leila was settled before heading over to the flat to get an overnight bag together.

'Should I go with him?' Shelly asked. 'Your father wouldn't have had the foggiest idea what to pack for me.'

'Nah, Matthew is brilliant at that sort of thing. He usually does the laundry and everything.'

'Really?' Shelly was shocked. She knew Matthew was very attentive, but she'd thought the arrangement was that Leila did the housework and he did the cooking.

Leila asked if she could go and have a shower. 'I'll give him a feed, and that way he'll be milk drunk and will be all right with you for a bit.'

Shelly couldn't believe how well Leila was doing with the breastfeeding. She was so relaxed and easy-going with Ollie.

'You're doing so well, darling. When Jake was born, I was like a basket case. I found breastfeeding impossible. After a couple of days of crying, your father went to the chemist and bought bottles. I never even tried it with you.'

'It doesn't suit everyone,' Leila said. 'The nurses at the hospital were delighted when I said I'd give it a shot. If it keeps going like this, I'll be thrilled. The thought of washing bottles and sterilising stuff doesn't appeal to me.'

As her daughter shuffled upstairs a short while later, Shelly relished the first precious moments alone with her grandson.

'Just look at him, Gerry,' she whispered, as she laid the baby on her lap and looked towards the ceiling. The joy of this new and precious life was doing battle with the ever-present grief. 'Oh how I wish you could be here with me, darling. I reckon you *are* here, though . . . you couldn't possibly be missing out on this moment.'

Stroking Ollie's downy head, she made a conscious decision to try and concentrate on the positives in life. Gerry wasn't coming home. He was never going to walk through the door again. All she could do was make the best of what she'd been given. This darling little boy was a gift, and she was going to appreciate every second she got to spend with him.

As she looked around the living room, something dawned on her. This place didn't feel like home any longer. Home was where she and Gerry had raised their family and shared so many wonderful times. The atmosphere had changed, and she didn't feel the same way about it any more.

Taking a deep breath, she realised that she needed to try and create a new life. She needed to start over. Whether or not she lived out her days alone, it didn't make sense for her to be here now. She'd been battled by Gerry's decision to buy Casa Maria, but as soon as she'd walked into it, she'd felt the magic. She longed to have him there to advise and help her, but there was no point in wishing for the impossible. She would have to embrace what she *did* have.

'Everything okay?' Leila asked as she walked into the room wearing fresh pyjamas and towel-drying her hair. 'Wow, that was the most amazing shower I've ever had. I would've paid a million euros for it.'

'You look a million times better, love,' Shelly said, smiling up at her daughter. 'Sit down and let me tell you all about Casa Maria.'

Leila sat on the sofa beside her and tucked her finger into Ollie's little hand while leaving him cocooned on Shelly's lap.

'Tell me everything,' she said, snuggling into her.

Shelly tried to remember all the details of the house, from the grand front entrance to the intricate cornice work of the ceilings and the beautiful stained-glass window at the turn of the stairs. She pulled out her phone and showed Leila the pictures she'd taken, but none of them really did it justice.

'The staircase is crying out to be repaired. I sympathised with it. There are noticeable gaps there, ones that make it look dejected and sad.'

'You're really taken with this place, aren't you?' Leila asked, studying Shelly closely. 'I don't know why, but I assumed you'd take one look at it and hate it. I figured you'd put it up for sale and that'd be that.'

'I didn't think I'd fall in love with it either. But there's something enticing and magical about the place. Besides, I think it's going to be the making of me.'

'How do you mean?' Leila asked.

'My old life with your father is gone. I need to stop wallowing and yearning for the past. I need to stop waiting for Gerry to walk in the door.'

'So what are you suggesting?'

'I'm thinking about going back to Spain and taking a few months to work on Casa Maria. I'm torn, though. I don't want to leave you with a new baby.'

'I have Matthew,' Leila said. 'Why don't you go to Spain for a few weeks and see how you go? I'm on maternity leave, so once I get into my stride, I could come and visit with Ollie.'

'Would you?' Shelly said, brightening. Then her face dropped again.

'What is it, Mum?'

Shelly gazed down lovingly at Ollie. 'I don't know if I can leave this little fellow.'

'I understand where you're coming from, Mum. But you need to do whatever it takes to keep yourself afloat right now. There's no right or wrong way to get through this grief. Don't make any concrete decisions. See how you feel and you know you have my support either way.'

'No matter what, I would still visit you lots,' Shelly said, 'and we can Skype every day so I can see Ollie.'

The two women looked at each other.

'It's a big decision,' Shelly said, her voice quiet and strained. 'And the timing is awful – right when my darling grandson arrives.'

Leila considered for a moment. 'It all depends,' she said slowly, 'on how strongly you feel about Casa Maria. I completely understand that you feel homeless now and want to go about changing that.'

Shelly nodded. 'That's exactly it,' she said, her voice catching. 'You've hit the nail on the head. Here I am, sitting in my house of thirty years, and I feel homeless. It's the most horrible feeling.'

Leila wrapped her arms around her mother. 'Then go,' she said into her ear. 'Go and find your own home. I know this one isn't the same without Dad. You owe it to yourself to give this a shot.'

Shelly nodded, and felt a weight lift from her shoulders. This was the right decision, she could feel it.

Chapter 16

FEE COULDN'T QUITE BELIEVE SHE WAS IN HER OWN living room. The furniture van had arrived that afternoon, and although the two lads were incredibly helpful and had assembled everything, the place was still a mess.

The smell of new carpet and paint was lovely, though. In comparison to her parents' dark and old-fashioned place, this was like stepping into a whole new world. She was really looking forward to making this house a home.

It was in a lovely area, close to all the amenities they both required, and it was what Fee considered to be a great starter home. There were two nice-sized bedrooms and a bathroom with a power shower upstairs. Downstairs had a compact hallway that led to the kitchen-cum-living area. There was the option of a sliding partition should they want to close off the kitchen.

Jake had wanted to trade up after Gerry's money came through, but Fee had insisted they stick to the original plan of a modest starter home. Yes, Jake could now afford more, but she could only cope with this if it stayed small and manageable. She was still struggling with her worries about the wide chasm between them money-wise, and a larger house would only have made those feelings worse.

'The living room is a lot smaller than I thought,' she said as they pushed the sofa and two chairs into place.

'The coffee table is a bit big, isn't it? Should we take it back and go for the smaller size?'

'I think it's grand.' Jake stood and looked at it for a split second, and then walked back into the kitchen.

'How do you get all the bloody plastic off the oven?' he called. 'I think this is a job for you. You can get your scalpel out and remove all the tiny annoying bits.'

'Why don't we order a takeaway for tonight?' Fee suggested. 'Cooking is the least of my worries right now. The main rooms need to be finished so we can sleep tonight and get up and go to work tomorrow. I can't take more than one day off.'

'I know, I know,' he said. 'I'm in with Jim first thing as well. I've to let him know whether or not I'm taking the promotion.'

'We've been through this,' Fee said, nudging the coffee table closer to the gas fire. 'It's a godsend, Jake. I'm hoping my pay packet will soon start reflecting the amount of hours I'm putting in. If you can up your game too, we'll be out of here and into a detached home with electric gates before we know it!'

Jake was already on the phone to the pizza place around the corner. Fee grinned. Men and food! They were rarely far apart.

She started to drag a large suitcase up the stairs. Jake followed and grabbed it.

'You're as stubborn as a mule. Don't go lifting things the same size as you. Ask me to do it. You have a man on call now, you know!'

All Fee had was one suitcase, containing her clothes and toiletries. Everything else was either here already or arriving on a delivery truck, newly purchased with Jake.

She'd never been a bottom-drawer-gatherer, much to her own regret now.

Still, as far as she was concerned, this, like her career, was merely the first step on a long ladder. She could feel it in her waters: they were going to end up living the dream. From the moment she'd met Jake, she'd felt an invisible attraction that had drawn her towards him. When they began to date and he expressed the same ambition to make it in life, she knew they were a match made in heaven.

The icing on the cake was his family. Sadness stabbed at her heart as she thought of Gerry. He'd been a wonderful man, and she knew she had him to thank for this entire house.

'I miss your dad,' she said. 'Do you think he'd approve of us being here?'

'You know he would,' Jake said, pulling her into his arms. 'I miss him too. He'd be so happy to know we're together at last. He gave me a talking-to when we were in the Caribbean before he died.'

'What did he say?' Fee asked with a sad smile.

'More or less that I needed to get my finger out and snap you up before someone else did. That we needed to get going and start living our lives together.'

The bed was assembled, but the duvet and the covers were sitting in packets on the floor. Passion took over, and they ended up christening the bed just as it was.

'Not bad,' Jake said afterwards.

'Me or the bed?' Fee asked with a smile.

'Both,' he said, making his way to the bathroom. The shower was like a power hose, and he relished the needling hot water.

'Need a towel and a bath mat?' Fee asked, bustling in and handing him both.

'The towel doesn't work,' he complained. 'It's all fluffy and doesn't dry me.'

'They all need washing,' Fee said. 'Some things aren't good when they're brand new.'

A ring at the doorbell made them both jump. 'Are you expecting anyone?' he asked.

'No,' she said, rushing to grab her clothes. 'It might be my parents, or maybe your mum.'

Pulling his jeans on, Jake grabbed a T-shirt from the pile he needed to put away in a drawer and ran down the stairs.

Norah was standing on the doorstep with a bottle of bubbly in her hand.

'I hope I'm not interrupting. I was chatting to Fee earlier and she said to drop by.'

'Of course, come in!' Jake said, calling up to Fee.

He accepted the bottle of champagne and insisted they open it immediately. Searching through the packing cases, he eventually found wine glasses.

'I know they're not flutes, but we're not that precise yet. At least they're not mugs!'

They clinked glasses and toasted the new house. Fee showed Norah around, while Jake stayed in the living room pulling bits of plastic from the furniture.

'Why is everything covered in sticky-back plastic?' he asked as the girls rejoined him. 'What do you think, Norah? Not too shabby, is it?'

'It's gorgeous. I'm so envious. If I compare this with the horrible dark kip I live in, it makes me want to weep.'

'You need to snare a rich old surgeon who'll be your

sugar daddy,' Jake joked. When the suggestion caused Norah to stare at him with a wobbly lip, he tried to back-track. 'Hey, I was only kidding. You should find a poor young sexy creature who doesn't mind living in your kip of a flat.'

Luckily Norah burst out laughing and the mood was restored. As they polished off the rest of the champagne, Jake tried to reassure her that there'd be loads of eligible pilots at the wedding.

'That'd be a better option than a cruddy old surgeon,' Fee said. 'Men in uniform are where it's at. And I don't mean bloodstained scrubs.'

'Who's going to be your best man?' Norah asked. 'Is it some dreamy guy who's been so busy working his way up the ranks that he's forgotten to fall in love? Take pity on me, Fee, and let me wear a couture dress so I look like some sort of irresistible goddess.'

'The best man isn't going to be your type, I'm afraid,' Jake said. 'It's Jim, my dad's best mate. He's certainly high up. He's also my direct boss. He's senior management and pretty minted, but he's leaning towards sugar daddy territory. Mind you,' he held his hands aloft, 'maybe you go for the distinguished type.'

'No offence, but I'd rather someone who was born in the same decade as me.'

The girls continued to chat, so Jake went back upstairs and used the opportunity to finish unpacking. He liked Norah and found her funny, and she wasn't bad looking. Not a patch on Fee, but he certainly preferred her to some of the girls his mates turned up with from time to time. It baffled him that she didn't have a boyfriend. He'd make a mental note to keep her in mind at work functions.

Another ring at the door sent him running.

'I was wondering where our pizza had got to,' he said as he paid and took the boxes.

'Sorry, mate, I don't know this estate. I've been driving around like a lunatic.'

Norah stayed and had a few slices before kissing them both and waving as she skipped off up the drive.

'I hope you didn't mind her calling over on our first night,' Fee said. 'She rang earlier and was all enthusiastic, so I said to drop in if she was passing. I didn't think she would.'

'It's cool,' Jake said as he flicked on the television. 'You're allowed to have friends to your own house, Fee!'

She hesitated as if she were going to say something else, but clearly changed her mind.

'Sorry to be a party pooper, but I've a really early start, so I'm going to hit the sack. I've to make up the bed too, unless you thought of doing it earlier while I was chatting to Norah?'

'No, sorry, hun,' he said.

She kissed him. 'This is it! Our first night in our own home, can you believe it?'

'I know, it's amazing,' he said, smiling.

Fee left him in the living room and took the stairs two at a time.

As she made the bed, she thought about her parents. They were smarting because she'd insisted she and Jake would live together before they got married.

'What if it all goes pear-shaped?' her mother had asked, worried. 'Then you'll have to move back here and you'll have let the world know you're damaged goods.'

'I'm not a delivery from Amazon, Mum,' Fee had snapped. 'Nobody thinks like that any more.'

'We do,' her father had piped up.

'Well I don't have a crystal ball, but I'm pretty sure that Jake and I are on the same page. I'm not entering into this relationship with a view to breaking up any time soon.'

Her parents had stood on the doorstep like two disapproving little shrews as she'd driven off this morning. She hoped for everyone's sake that things worked out. And not for the first time, she wished her parents were a little less rigid.

Once the bed was made, she climbed in and wriggled around to find a comfortable spot. New beds were like new towels, she thought; they weren't quite right. It would take some adjusting.

Her parents did drive her nuts, but at least they had always been supportive of her choices in the end, even when they disapproved. They weren't absolutely delighted with having a surgeon for a daughter, for example. They didn't understand why she couldn't settle down and be a contented mother and housewife. But then, Fee thought, maybe that was ultimately where her drive came from. She'd always wanted more than the 1950s image her parents had mapped out for her.

She smiled to remember how, as a small child, she'd caused her mother to kneel by the kitchen table passing rosary beads through her fingers at a rate of knots, reciting prayer after prayer for her daughter.

'What possessed you to cut the teddy bear's little tummy and pull out his stuffing?' Deirdre had asked. 'It's not normal for a five-year-old to do that!'

Fee had thought she was helping. She'd heard that a girl

in school called Rosie O'Shea had gone to hospital to have her appendix out. Apparently Rosie had been in a lot of danger, and had they not done the operation there and then, the consequences would have been very bad. So Fee had decided to save all her teddies before one of them died.

'But they're not real,' Deirdre had said in a shocked-beyond-belief voice. 'You've *ruined* them.'

Fee had gone to her room with no dinner and sat cross-legged on her bed. That was what her parents had wanted. She'd said sorry, but she'd held her hand behind her back and crossed her fingers. In reality, she wasn't a bit sorry. In fact, she'd decided there and then that she was going to move on from teddies and do proper operations on people to make them better, just like Rosie O'Shea.

When she'd seen Rosie's scar a few days later in the school cloakroom, Fee had known for certain that this was her calling. She was fascinated that someone could cut skin, take out sore or bad bits and sew it all back together.

She'd studied hard and pushed for what she wanted. Meeting Jake along the way had been the icing on the cake. They'd met at a mutual friend's party and Fee had noticed him the second he'd walked in.

All the other guys were doing shots and trying to out-drink one another.

'Don't you like lining up shots of cheap booze and proving your manliness?' she'd asked.

'It's not my thing just at the moment,' he'd responded. 'I'm in flight school, and it doesn't really bode well if the trainee pilots turn up stinking of booze looking like they haven't slept for days.'

'What made you want to be a pilot?' She had been instantly drawn in by his quiet confidence.

'My dad is one, and I guess it's in my blood.'

'Well my dad works in a factory, and I realised a long time ago that I don't want to do that.'

He'd stared at her, to see if she was joking.

'Don't you get along with your father?' he'd asked.

She had shrugged, feeling uncomfortable about what she'd said. 'I don't *not* get on with my parents, but they're set in their ways and I guess I'd like to branch out a bit.'

He'd nodded. 'Jake, by the way.' He held out his hand.

'I'm Fee.' They'd shaken hands rather formally, but she'd noticed that he held on to her hand for a moment longer than necessary.

He'd chatted about his family and how he loved what he was studying, describing the feeling he got when he was flying.

'It's like nothing I've ever experienced. It's out of this world. I get such a feeling of freedom, yet I feel like I belong.' He'd looked at her sheepishly. 'Sorry, I'm going on too much, right?'

'No, I understand. That's how I feel when I'm at the hospital. Medicine is so complex, but knowing that a day will come when I'll be in charge of making a patient better . . . it's awesome.'

He'd smiled at her then. 'I love the fact that you're so sure you'll make it. That you have that much confidence in your abilities and know that you're going to make a difference in your field.'

'I probably sound like a cocky little cow,' she'd said, blushing.

He'd held her gaze. She'd sipped her Coke and stared right back at him.

'Yet you don't apologise for thinking that way. So many people are quick to say sorry for this and sorry for that. We need more people like you and me in the world. People who believe and are willing to work to achieve their dreams.'

She'd never been what one would call forward with men. In fact, she'd never had any kind of long-term relationship before meeting Jake. Men showed her plenty of attention, but until that night, none had seemed worth the hassle. She was worried they might get in the way and complicate matters for her. But Jake was worth it. Jake would complement her ambition, and more than that, she knew he would encourage her to shoot for the moon.

That was five years ago, incredible as that now seemed, and she loved him more and more with each passing day. He'd delivered on all his promises. Not promises to her, mind you. Promises to himself. She loved that about him.

When he said he'd do something, he did it.

Her moment in the sunshine was happening right now. She'd studied, scraped and fought to become a surgeon, and now that it had become a reality, she wasn't going to take any of it for granted.

This, Fee thought with a happy sigh, is about as good as it gets!

Chapter 17

A GOOD NIGHT'S SLEEP IN HER OLD BED MADE ALL the difference to Leila, and she emerged the next morning looking fresher. Matthew headed off to work early, and Shelly was up early too, busying herself with baking scones and bread. Even though the café was long gone, she still found baking therapeutic, and it was a comfort to be back in her kitchen, listening to the radio and filling the house with delicious aromas.

'Morning, Mum,' Leila said as she walked into the kitchen. 'My God, that smell is making me hungry.'

Shelly smiled. 'It's all for us, although we might leave a little bit for Matthew. Come on, sit yourself down and I'll pour you a cup of tea.'

Leila sat down gratefully, enjoying the pampering. Shelly poured out a cup of steaming tea, put a plate of scones in the centre of the table, then lifted Ollie from Leila's arms.

'Come here to me, you gorgeous thing,' she said, beaming at him. 'You look like such a dote in the morning.'

Leila smiled at her mother's loving tone. It was clear that she was besotted with Ollie already. It was such a lovely feeling, the three generations together. It made her feel very contented in herself.

They chatted as they ate the delicious warm scones,

talking again about Shelly's plans for Casa Maria. Leila was eager to get over there to see it all for herself.

They gave Ollie a bath, then enjoyed staring at him snuggled in his pram. The breastfeeding was still going smoothly, and Shelly watched in admiration as Leila made it look easy. She wouldn't let herself think about not being here. She tried to be completely present in the moment, savouring every second.

At about midday, they heard a key turning in the front door, and both women looked up in surprise.

'Is Jake around?' Leila asked.

Shelly shook her head. 'No, I think he's on a long haul this week. Besides, he doesn't live here any more.'

Leila grinned. 'Sounds like you won't get rid of him that easily.'

But when the door to the kitchen was pushed open, it was Matthew who came in, looking very hassled and stressed.

'Oh good, you're both here,' he said.

Shelly and Leila exchanged a look.

'What is it?' Leila said quickly. 'Has something happened? Is it Jake? Tell me quickly, Matthew.'

He looked at her, astounded, then shook his head. 'No, no, nothing's wrong, love. Sorry, I probably look like a madman, but I haven't got bad news, honest.'

'Then what is it?' Leila demanded.

'Would you like me to leave you two alone?' Shelly asked, feeling awkward.

'No, I need to talk to both of you,' Matthew said.

Shelly wondered what was going on. She got out a cup and saucer for him and poured some tea, then put a scone on a plate in front of him. 'Sit down, then,' she said. 'Have a break while we chat.'

Matthew nodded and sat down heavily. As he began to spread jam on his scone, Leila couldn't contain herself any longer.

'For the love of God, Matthew,' she cried, 'stop with the scone and tell us what's going on. I'm dying of worry here.'

Matthew put down his knife carefully and looked up at them. 'Sorry,' he said again. 'I'm so distracted. Look, there's been an unexpected development in our house-hunting. I had organised the valuation of the flat, as you know, Leila, and the estate agent rang me an hour ago to say he's had a generous offer for it.'

'Hang on a minute,' Leila said, standing up. 'What do you mean, you've had an offer? I thought we were only discussing buying somewhere. I didn't really want us to be out on the street with a new baby a couple of weeks before Christmas.'

'I know, love,' Matthew said. 'It's just that it turns out he has a couple who've been waiting for one of the flats in our complex to come up. He mentioned our intention to move soon, and they leapt on it. The problem is, they want to close the deal pronto. They've offered an extra three thousand euros if we finalise it now – I mean, basically within twenty-four hours.'

'Oh bloody hell, why do so many things have to happen at the same time?' Leila said, throwing her hands up. 'I know this is what we want, but the timing is awful.'

'No it's not,' Shelly said. 'I'm sorry to weigh in here on your decision, but I think Matthew is right, Leila, it's too good an offer to refuse. Plus you can stay here. You're very welcome to have this place for as long as it takes to get sorted, especially given that I won't be here.'

Matthew smiled in relief. 'That's exactly what I came back to ask you, Shelly,' he said. 'I know it's a lot to ask, and we'll try to be out from under your feet as quickly as possible, I promise, but it would make sense to . . .' He stopped suddenly and frowned at Shelly. 'What do you mean, you won't be here?'

Shelly laughed. 'The timing is actually perfect, because I'm planning to head back to Spain very soon.'

Matthew looked surprised, and Shelly could almost hear him wondering how she could possibly leave her beautiful grandson. A wave of guilt washed over her.

'I know you're surprised that I'd do this now,' she said, glancing over at Ollie, 'but it's just that . . . well . . .'

'Mum's feeling lost here without Dad,' Leila said. 'It doesn't feel like home any more, so she wants to give Casa Maria a go.'

Matthew sat back in his chair. 'Wow, when did all this happen?'

'Yesterday,' Shelly said sheepishly.

He leaned forward and smiled, taking her hand in his large rough one. 'I'm delighted for you, Shelly,' he said warmly. 'This is a good idea. I've felt worried about you these past months. I think you're right to change tack.'

Shelly squeezed his hand and felt tears prick the back of her eyes. 'Thank you, Matthew,' she whispered. 'I feel terrible leaving now, leaving Ollie . . .'

'You won't be so far away,' Matthew said. 'And we'll come visit. Ollie will be bilingual before he's five. It'll be brilliant.'

Shelly wiped her tears away and laughed. She was so grateful to Matthew for making this easy for her.

'So you three can move in here immediately, and you

won't have to factor me into the equation, which is as it should be for a new family. I've just decided that I'm going to book a flight for the day after tomorrow.'

Leila looked happily at them both. 'Never a dull moment around here, is there?'

'So tell me all about Casa Maria,' said Matthew, returning his attention to his scone. 'I'm intrigued.'

Shelly described the village and the house, and how it felt being there.

'I don't have any firm plans, as I've just been telling Leila, but I know I can't be here right at this moment. It's too painful. I've made a lovely friend in the village called Valentina, and she owns a restaurant with some rooms above it. I rented there and it's gorgeous.'

'I could take Ollie there for a bit, too,' Leila told Matthew. 'I'm on maternity leave, so I may as well be in Spain as here.'

Shelly reached out and stroked Leila's face.

'I don't want to interfere with your new family,' she said. 'Talk to Matthew and think about what's best for the three of you. I'll be fine.'

'I think we've made enough decisions for today,' Matthew said. 'Let's see how we go. But I'm certainly dying to see it all for myself.'

That night as she lay in bed, Shelly felt loneliness enveloping her like a blanket of ice. It had been an emotional day; offering her house to Leila and Matthew had made her own decision very real. In one way, it unnerved her a bit, but as the tears came, she knew she couldn't deny that being in Spain was so much easier. Everywhere she looked here reminded her of what she no longer had. Casa

Maria represented what she could possibly have in the future.

Sighing, she stared at the man's watch on the bedside locker. The love she and Gerry had shared was gone now. She had no doubt in her mind that the best way she could begin to heal and move on with life was by starting afresh.

Chapter 18

JAKE CAME OUT OF HIS PLANNING MEETING AND headed directly for runway number six. He hadn't time to call Fee and let her know how it had gone; that he'd accepted the promotion and was now Captain Dillon. Though looking at his watch, it was probably too late to call her anyway. She'd be chopping and sewing up bodies by now.

He shuddered as he thought of her job. He always felt mildly traumatised after sitting in the hospital lobby waiting for her to come out. But Fee thrived on making people better. It was all about perspective, he guessed. She told him often enough that she would rather die than attempt to fly a plane. There was a time when that had made him laugh out loud because it seemed so silly. But lately, he was secretly beginning to agree with her. He wasn't scared or anything like that. But the buzz had definitely gone from it.

At first, he'd put it down to missing his father. He and Gerry had always had great chats about everything from new planes to the advances in aviation over the years. They had colleagues in common and there was a wonderful sense of camaraderie and belonging. His father had never hidden his pride when they met new airline staff. 'This is my son, Jake,' he'd say, smiling proudly. 'We're keeping it in the family, as you can see! The Dillons are flying high.'

Jake felt a stab of pain as he thought of his amazing dad, his chest puffed out as he slapped him on the back and walked with him towards whatever flights they were piloting.

His colleagues had been nothing but supportive since Gerry's death. They asked him all the time how he was doing. Many of them had even gone to the trouble of sharing photos of Gerry with him, some of which went back to Jake's childhood.

The one in his wallet that Jim had given him just now, after the meeting, made him want to curl up in a ball and cry. He'd never seen it before. It showed Gerry standing to the side as Jake sat in the cockpit with his short legs dangling from the chair. He must have been only five or six years old.

'Your old man knew you belonged in a cockpit before you did,' said Jim. 'I'm glad you're taking the promotion. Good luck to you. I know I speak on behalf of Gerry when I say I'm really proud of you today. You're the closest thing I ever had to a son, and in Gerry's absence, I'd like to shake your hand.'

'Thanks, Uncle Jim,' he said.

When they were kids, he and Leila had called Jim and his wife Uncle Jim and Auntie Martha. Once he'd started at the airline, they'd agreed it wouldn't be appropriate, but now that it was just the two them, Jake reverted to the affectionate title.

They'd hugged, and Jake had straightened his jacket before walking away to board his flight.

He was trying very hard to feel elated, because that was

exactly what he ought to be feeling. The promotion he'd just accepted was amazing. It had come earlier than he would have dared hope, which should have made it all the sweeter. But there was such a stench of loneliness and grief about his day-to-day life lately that he was finding it hard to muster any enthusiasm for anything.

Fee was his greatest cheerleader. He knew she was really proud of this promotion and the step up the ladder that it represented. It was right on track with their plan to take over the universe by the time they were forty! He had been fully committed to that plan, but now, today, he felt lost. Like he'd been on a motorway and had ended up on a side road without any clue as to how he'd got there. Their ambition was simple and straightforward, but suddenly it didn't hold any interest for him. These new thoughts scared him, but try as he might, they kept rising up to assault his peace of mind.

He settled himself in his seat and readied for take-off. He was sitting with his head in his hands when one of the air stewards knocked on the cockpit door.

'Yes?' Jake said, not meaning to sound quite as narky as he did.

'Would you mind signing this for Jim?' the steward said. 'I told him I'd get it done and sent out to him via one of the ground staff. You forgot it apparently.'

'Sure, thank you.'

Jake took the envelope and closed the door gently. He longed to delay, to pretend he'd didn't have time and take off with the unsigned form in his pocket. That way, the new job wouldn't be official yet. But he knew that was wholly unprofessional and likely to get the air steward into trouble, so he scrawled his signature at the bottom of the document, shoved it back in the envelope and handed it out through the door.

The flight to New York was uneventful, and Jake disembarked without interacting with any of the other crew members. He wasn't in the mood for hanging out, and although he was hungry, he didn't feel like having dinner with anyone.

The same hotel welcomed them each time, and Jake knew most of the staff by now. He checked in and ordered a steak sandwich and a glass of red wine.

'Actually, make it a bottle,' he said. Normally he wouldn't drink more than a glass when he had a long haul the next day. The rules and regulations were stringent, to say the least. He had to take a written test every few months and could be subjected to compulsory random breath tests at any time.

Tonight, though, he figured the wine was medicinal. He pulled off his jacket and yanked his tie free of his neck, unbuttoning his shirt as soon as he got into his room. Knowing he only had a few minutes before his food arrived, he opted for a quick refreshing shower and shrugged into the warm bathrobe he found carefully folded on a shelf in the bathroom.

There was nothing wrong with the food when it arrived, but he couldn't stomach more than half the steak and a couple of chips from the small trendy metal bucket that all the restaurants had taken to serving food in these days.

The wine, on the other hand, was just what the doctor ordered. He guzzled the first glass and poured more immediately. Downing that speedily, he glanced at his watch, working out how many hours he had until it was time to take off again. He'd be fine, he reckoned. He'd been breath-tested a few days ago, which meant the chances of it happening again were slim to none.

Before he knew it, he was finishing the last glass in the bottle and crawling into bed. Just as his eyes were closing heavily, a text came through from Fee saying she needed to talk. Groaning, he dialled her number.

'Hey, what's up?' he asked, rubbing his brow.

'Are you okay?' she said. 'You sound beat.'

'I kind of am. What's going on?'

'I just lost a patient,' she said, and burst into tears.

He sat up in the bed, a shiver running down his spine. 'Oh Fee, honey. Don't cry. I'm sorry I'm not there with you. What happened?'

She explained about the surgery, and how the elderly patient had gone into cardiac arrest.

'Take me through the procedure step by step,' he said.

Haltingly at first, she began to talk. Jake struggled to stay awake and take in what she was saying. When she finished and trailed off, he shook himself and responded in the most soothing way possible.

'You did everything you could,' he said. 'From what you've said, it was just her time to go. You didn't miss anything and you did your best.'

'That's all very well unless you're the one who was responsible at the time,' she said sadly.

'I know,' he conceded. 'It's easy for me to say it, but from the outside looking in, I can't believe anyone would blame you.'

They chatted for a while longer until Fee said she had to go. His heart went out to her. She would have to attend a disciplinary meeting with the hospital board and explain in her own words what had happened. It wasn't necessarily because anyone thought she was at fault, but everything needed to be documented for legal reasons and for the deceased woman's family.

As he lay down again and tried to recapture that lovely heavy-lidded sleepiness, Jake wondered if he and Fee were really living the dream after all. They had worked so hard to get where they were, but for the first time he found himself wondering if it was worth it. Why were they driving themselves so hard? Would their careers bring them happiness? Wouldn't it be easier, really, to work someplace where people's lives weren't at stake each and every day?

What felt like half an hour later, his phone sprang to life with the irritating jingle he'd chosen in a moment of madness as his alarm. Taking a deep breath, he turned it off and lay on his back with his arms above his head.

He didn't want to go to work.

He felt a shot of guilt course through him as the words rose unbidden: I don't want to go to work.

He sighed. Now that he'd admitted it, he felt marginally better. He thought of Gerry, how much he'd loved flying, how he'd always said it made him feel alive. But Gerry was gone now, and things were different. Horribly, perhaps irrevocably different.

Jake's inbred sense of duty and responsibility forced him out of bed. When he got home later today, he would request a meeting with Jim. He needed to cancel the contract he'd signed yesterday and take a step back. Perhaps he could ask for a few weeks' leave of absence.

Once the idea had come to him, he felt a weight lifting from his shoulders. Maybe if he had a few weeks to think things over, he'd come to his senses. It might just be grief that was making him feel so unmotivated. Of all the people he could talk to, Uncle Jim would understand.

Feeling a whole lot brighter, he showered and put on a fresh shirt. His uniform was a lot looser than it had been. He knew he'd lost weight and it didn't suit him especially. He'd never been anything but lean, but now he was beginning to look gaunt. Fee had commented on it last week: 'There's nothing to hold on to. You're disappearing. I hope you're eating, Jake. I know you're time-zone-hopping but you need to be mindful of your health.'

He hesitated in the hotel lobby for a few moments, then decided against breakfast. There was a snaking queue of businessmen in suits standing with newspapers aloft, waiting for tables. He wasn't in the mood for shuffling around a buffet looking at the same boring stuff. He'd grab something at the airport lounge. Coffee and a sugary pastry sounded nice for a treat.

He checked out and the receptionist called a taxi to take him to the airport. He accepted the offer of a newspaper and loitered at the door until his cab arrived. The traffic was heavy but moving. The Indian driver chatted for a while, but gave up when he only got monosyllabic answers.

At the airport, Jake thanked the driver and tipped him generously.

'I'm sorry I wasn't more talkative. I'm having one of those days. You were very pleasant,' he said.

He needed to snap out of this mood. Quite apart from anything else, he was in uniform and it wasn't good to be so grouchy.

'That's no problem,' the driver said sunnily as he thanked him for the tip.

The attendants' lounge was ridiculously busy when Jake arrived. It seemed most of the other pilots from the airline had made the same decision he had and gone there instead of their respective hotels for breakfast.

He greeted the people he knew and nodded and smiled at those he didn't. There were no tables free, so he filled a takeaway cup with coffee and, using metal tongs, slid a Danish pastry into a paper bag, then made his way towards the plane. Normally he'd leave it a while, choosing to stretch his legs instead, but he just wanted this flight over with now.

As he was walking towards the steps, his phone rang with a number he didn't recognise. His heart thudded as he listened to the voice at the other end. He was to report immediately to a room adjacent to the Gold Circle departures lounge.

'You have been randomly chosen for a spot-check screening. As you know, it's company policy to . . .' The rest of the spiel went over his head as he turned on his heel and walked numbly back to the terminal building.

Sweat began to bead on his brow. He cursed his lack of breakfast. Knowing it was futile, he gulped the hot coffee, burning his throat in the process, and stuffed the pastry down his neck. Then, brushing crumbs from his clothes, he knocked on the door of the screening room.

Everything after that was a total blur. Calls were made and people appeared from the woodwork.

'But am I over the limit?' he asked, hearing the quiver in his own voice.

'You will hear the results at your disciplinary hearing,' the official said, looking like he was enjoying his new-found power. 'But your alcohol levels are too high for us to allow you to fly today.'

Jake would travel back to Ireland as a passenger on the plane he was due to captain, and there would be a meeting to discuss sanctions and indeed his future with the airline. He couldn't even begin to know how he felt about any of this. His head was aching. Why in God's name had he drunk so much wine? That question taunted him all the way back to Dublin.

Chapter 19

SHELLY COULDN'T BELIEVE HOW MUCH SHE WAS enjoying wandering around Rondilla.

As she stopped at a little café that was beautifully shoe-horned into a narrow stone building halfway up a winding cobbled side street, a gaggle of schoolchildren alighted from a bus and hurtled towards her, babbling excitedly in Spanish. Their honeyed skin and dark hair and eyes made her smile in delight. The checked short pinafores with white collars on the girls and shorts in matching material on the boys looked so wonderfully Spanish.

Stepping inside the café, she realised that it was quite packed. She ordered a coffee and magdalenas, then pointed towards one of the three round metal tables outside. The waitress nodded and shooed with her hand to show that she should go and sit down.

As she settled at her table, Shelly gazed up at the windows along the narrow street. Each house had a tiny balcony piled high with containers of vibrant flowers. Although it was winter, there was clearly enough sun to keep the violet and crimson blooms alive.

Her coffee and sponge cakes were served in a whir of skirts as the waitress presented them hurriedly.

'All okay? Good, yes?' she asked. As soon as Shelly nodded, she was gone.

Shelly smiled. It was so different from home. Mary at the local café would want to know what you'd been up to in chronological order since she'd seen you last. She could probably write every customer's memoir if the mood took her.

The dark coffee smelled almost like the tobacco her grandfather used to smoke when she was a child. Balking slightly, she added some milk from the jug that had been provided. She hadn't expected it to be warm and frothy and was delighted with the surprise.

As she bit into the sweet light sponge of a magdalena and sipped a careful mouthful of coffee, she felt her shoulders drop from her ears. A stout elderly lady wrapped in a floral apron was sweeping her front step at the top of the street. The sun was slowly making its way towards her, illuminating the blooms on the balcony as it came. She imagined Gerry sitting opposite her. That would have made the moment completely perfect.

As she finished her coffee, Shelly felt more relaxed than she had in months. She'd come here to try and rebuild her life. She wanted to see if she could occupy her mind enough to lift the veil of sadness that had shrouded her since Gerry's passing. So she checked her sad thoughts about his absence and forced herself to recognise fully that this was a lovely moment in time. A new type of moment. She had to learn to appreciate the good times without lamenting what she no longer had. It would be difficult, but today, for the first time, it felt a little bit possible. That was a huge step forward.

Once she'd paid the waitress, she strode to the top of the street and over towards Casa Maria. As soon as she saw the hacienda again, something clicked for her. It was going to need a fair bit of work. In fact it needed gutting and redecorating throughout. But that wasn't necessarily a bad thing. It would keep her very busy for the foreseeable future. This beautiful and majestic place deserved to be returned to its former glory.

'How about we try and rebuild one another?' she said out loud. 'What do you say, Maria?'

Giggling at her own madness, she walked to the front door and unlocked it.

She was standing with her hands on her hips, looking around critically, when there was a loud knock on the door.

'*Hola, señora,*' the man said. '*Me llamo Alejandro.*'

'*Hola,*' she replied. 'I am Shelly.'

'*Mucho gusto,*' he said.

'Pleased to meet you, too.' Shelly shook his hand. 'Valentina told me that you would come today. *Mucho gusto tambien!*' She was pleased to have picked up the basic greetings from listening to Valentina at Café del Sol.

Alejandro was small in stature compared to Gerry or Jake, but he looked fit and strong, with a full head of wiry salt-and-pepper hair and a curling moustache with matching goatee beard.

'Alejandro, do you speak English?' Shelly asked.

He rocked his hand left and right to show that he knew a little.

'You have come highly recommended by Valentina,' she explained.

'Yes, Valentina is my friend. Me,' he slapped his hand on his chest, 'I builder. But I have many other people. One cousin, he is plumber, and another is electrician. We are, how you say?' He stroked his chin for a moment. 'We are team, yes?'

'That's great,' Shelly said, nodding. The suspicious part of her mind realised that if this man were a total crook, she'd be bunched. Knowing she needed to learn to trust people, she put her fears to one side and asked him if he could take a look around and give his opinion on how Casa Maria might be fixed up.

Leila rang her as Alejandro strode into the kitchen, making notes on a pad. Shelly explained that she was at the house with a strange man.

'Seriously, Mum, that sounds a bit ominous,' Leila teased. 'I hope he's not an axe murderer. I'll stay on the line in case he tries anything.'

'He seems decent,' Shelly said in a hushed tone as Alejandro walked upstairs.

'How can you tell?' Leila asked suspiciously. 'For all you know, your woman in the village has told him you're recently widowed with a bag of cash and a broken heart and that you're ripe for fleecing.'

'Valentina wouldn't do that. Granted, I don't know her that well yet, but my instincts tell me that she's decent and honest. I can't do anything with this place on my own, so I have to put my trust in *somebody*.'

Alejandro came back down the stairs a short while later, chatting on his phone. From what Shelly could gather, he appeared to be asking someone else to come to Casa Maria.

'*Es muy simpática*,' he said as he nodded at her and smiled.

Shelly knew enough to translate that he was being complimentary about her. She'd reserve judgement until he gave her a price for the work.

'*Bella*,' he said, pointing at the floor tiles in the hallway.

'I love them,' Shelly said wistfully. 'That wonderful mosaic pattern is timeless.'

She tried to imagine what it must've been like when the house was in its prime. She wondered if there were any photographs in local record books. There must be the equivalent of a council office where she could ask for information.

She was about to ask Alejandro about it when there was a shout from the front door.

'Hello?'

'Hello!' Shelly said, going out to see who was there.

'I am Eric,' said the man on the doorstep, offering his hand. 'I am the cousin of Alejandro. He call me for say you will like me for do plumbings works.'

'Nice to meet you. I'm Shelly, the owner of Casa Maria.' She felt a little thrill pulse through her as she claimed ownership of this place.

'So tell me, lady. What you need for me to do, please?'

Shelly showed him around and he tutted as he opened and closed doors. Then she waited downstairs as Alejandro appeared and led him up to the bathrooms. Leila was still on the line, thoroughly enjoying listening to the goings-on.

'I'll have to show you how to do FaceTime, Mum. This is pretty great entertainment. I'm really intrigued now, though. If you decide to go ahead with this project, I'm definitely coming to Spain.'

'Would you?' Shelly said, brightening hugely. 'I'd love to get your opinion. There are so many decisions to be made. It's a massive undertaking, but there's something drawing me in. I think I really want to do it.'

'Hold your horses until you know what it's going to cost,' Leila advised.

'Do you reckon he'll come back with some outlandish price?' Shelly asked. 'I mean, if we were in Ireland, we'd be looking at upwards of twenty grand to get the plumbing alone sorted, I'd say.'

'We'll just have to wait and see,' Leila said. 'I'd better go, Mum. Ollie needs feeding.'

By the time the men were finished bashing about and talking at the tops of their voices, the light was fading. Shelly led them to the door and said she'd wait to hear what they thought they could do, and what it would cost.

Almost hearing Gerry's voice in her head, she knew she ought to get some other quotes for comparison purposes. The only problem was, she didn't know anybody else to even attempt to ask. Perhaps, she thought, Jake could get her some ballpark figures from Ireland. After all, he'd just moved into his house, so he could ask the builder what he'd charge to rewire a large house and fix ancient plumbing. She had all the bathroom dimensions should they need them.

She stood outside, gazing back at Casa Maria. The fading light was casting a honeyed glow on the building.

'You're a little like me,' she said. 'There's a certain sense of wise experience emanating from you, but you could do with a facelift.'

She walked around the side of the house for a last look at the garden before she returned to the square. It had clearly been beautiful once. Under the jumble of weeds and brambles, she could envisage a whole lot of magic waiting to be uncovered. She would enjoy taming it.

In her imagination, the entire property felt as if it were holding its breath as it waited patiently for someone to come and rescue it from its neglect. As the light finally faded, she felt at one with Casa Maria. Almost as if the spirits within the house were beckoning to her.

Shelly had always believed that things happened for a reason. Now she felt certain that Casa Maria had come into her life to serve a very important purpose.

First things first, though, she would have to work out how she would pay for the renovations. Gerry had done all the financial stuff during the course of their marriage, although she'd had to step up and take on some of that work when she'd owned the café. But that had been a small enterprise. The thought of tackling such a massive project gave her butterflies in her tummy. Would she be able to manage this in a business sense? What would she do with the hacienda when it was finished? It was too big for one person and she hadn't the first idea of how much it would cost to run . . . So much needed to be worked out. While she knew it would be a wonderful project, she was terrified of biting off more than she could chew.

She locked up and made her way down the hill and through the winding streets to the main square. To her delight, a joyous wedding party was emerging from the church amidst much celebration.

'Beautiful, eh?' Valentina said as she beckoned Shelly to join her. 'This is a good day. A busy day.' She shook her head. 'What do you say – run off the feet?'

Shelly laughed. 'That's right. Do you have enough help? I'll pitch in if I'm needed.'

Valentina's eyes were wide. 'You mean this? Work? But you are on holiday.'

'Not really,' Shelly said with a shrug. 'I sort of feel like I'm living here now. And we are friends, Valentina. I'm always happy to help a friend.'

Valentina regarded her for a moment. 'If you really mean this, yes, I would like help. You are sure?'

Shelly nodded, delighted now that she'd offered. It would be lovely to feel part of the wedding celebration. 'I don't know how much help I'll be, but I used to run a small café at home, so I don't think I'll break any plates.'

Valentina's face broke into a wide smile. 'Come,' she said. 'I get you an apron and we make the people happy.'

For the next four hours, Shelly worked alongside Valentina, serving the revellers, popping corks, pouring drinks and enjoying herself hugely. It was a baptism of fire, but it felt good to be back working with customers again.

When the guests had all left, Valentina poured two glasses of sangria and set them down on a table with a bowl of olives. The two women sank gratefully into chairs and smiled at each other.

'That was wonderful,' Shelly said. 'I really enjoyed it.'

'I think you are crazy woman,' Valentina said, shaking her head and smiling. 'Was hard. My feet ache. You stay here for free, Shelly, this is how I pay you for such good work.'

'Not at all,' Shelly protested. 'I'm delighted you let me do it. I felt properly useful. And they were such a beautiful couple. So happy. I'm honoured to have been part of their big day.'

Valentina sighed. 'We used to have many, many weddings. But Rosa, the wedding organiser, she go away. So nobody organise the wedding here now.'

'Oh I'd love to do that,' Shelly said. 'Can you imagine how rewarding it would be to spend your time bringing people here to celebrate their special day?'

'You could use Casa Maria as a guest house and arrange the weddings at the church, and my chef at Café del Sol could do the food,' Valentina said hopefully.

Shelly stared at her, the wheels in her brain clicking fast, all the different aspects of the past few weeks coming together in a glorious vision of what could be. She felt a rush of joy at Valentina's suggestion, followed by a certainty that this was the answer she had been looking for.

'You're a genius!' she said, leaning over to grab Valentina's face with both hands and kissing her cheeks. 'I love that idea. It just . . . I don't know . . . resonates with me, deep down.'

'Really?' Valentina said, her eyes wide at Shelly's reaction. 'Would you think about this, Shelly?'

'Absolutely. I'm going to do some proper research and see if it could be an option for me. I want to renovate Casa Maria, but I don't know what I would do with it. There are so many rooms, and why would I go to the trouble of having them all done up with nobody to stay in them?'

Valentina wrapped Shelly in a bear hug, her eyes shining with delight.

'I will help in any way possible. Since Rosa went away, I have been worried. She brought many people to my business. I have not been able to sleep at night since I realised how much I needed that extra money. It is in both our interests that you make Casa Maria beautiful and get the weddings going once more.'

'I can see it now,' Shelly said thoughtfully. '*Weddings at Casa Maria*. It's perfect!'

'It was a very good business for Rosa,' Valentina said. 'She go away and live in Gibraltar with her man. He no love it here. But she love him.'

'How long was she doing the wedding planning for?' Leila asked.

'Five years,' Valentina said.

'So how come nobody has taken the business from her?' Shelly wondered.

'Who will do this?' Valentina asked. 'Nobody have the time or the money, and nobody have a hacienda like Casa Maria.' She shrugged her shoulders. 'One of the wedding planners from Marbella was interested for a while. But she soon said it was too much trouble. She no like to come up and down all the time. So she say she is not interested any longer. It must be someone who live here at Rondilla. I can ask Rosa for her information, if you like?'

'Would you?' Shelly asked in astonishment.

'*Claro,*' she said, nodding. 'Of course. She is my cousin. She will tell me, I am sure of it.'

'Thank you,' Shelly said. 'That would be incredible.'

'Tomorrow, we talk to Rosa,' Valentina said wearily. 'Now, we go to bed.'

'You said it,' Shelly said, stifling a yawn.

She climbed the stairs to her room feeling tired but alive with excitement. She couldn't help feeling that destiny had taken a hand. It felt like this whole situation was meant to be.

Chapter 20

SHELLY HAD LEFT ONLY FORTY-EIGHT HOURS AGO, but it was like she'd taken Leila's sanity with her. Everything had been going so smoothly and easily, but now it felt like the wheels had come off. Leila had gone from being confident and managing well to feeling utterly wretched. The pain she was experiencing was unlike anything she'd ever known before. It was grinding her down, making it impossible to think straight. And Ollie just kept crying, on and on, demanding food. Leila wanted to walk out the front door and keep going, never look back, anything to get away from the incessant noise that told her she was failing.

She tried, yet again, to latch him on for a feed, but the dull aching in her breast became unbearable. Her temperature kept soaring and she was aching all over, like a flu, but worse.

'How are things?' Matthew asked as he walked into the living room. 'Hey, little man,' he said, scooping a bawling Ollie off the sofa. 'What's happening here?'

Leila began to cry. Great big heaving sobs that silenced her and left her totally unable to express any feeling.

'How did he sleep last night?' Matthew asked over the din.

'He didn't,' Leila managed to say. 'I can't feed him. I can't get him to sleep. I don't have the energy to change him. I had to do a really nasty nappy in the middle of the night and he'd pooed all over his vest. I cut the dirty part off with scissors. It's over there,' she said, pointing to the offending piece of fabric. 'I couldn't bear the thought of taking all his clothes off and making him howl even more.'

'Why didn't you wake me?' Matthew asked, looking around the room in horror.

In all honesty, Leila hadn't even gone so far as thinking of waking Matthew. All she could think of was what a dreadful mother she was. Besides, Matthew was so besotted with Ollie and kept telling her how proud he was, and she couldn't shatter that illusion.

Mind you, the state of the room right now would leave him in no doubt that she wasn't coping. There seemed to be baby things covering every inch of the place. It was like this tiny being had completely taken over. It was a good thing Shelly wasn't here. She'd hate to see her house looking like a refugee camp.

'The public health nurse is coming this morning,' Leila said. 'I'll ask her to show me how to feed again. Maybe she'll see what I'm doing wrong and be able to fix it.'

Matthew said he'd do a quick tidy-up before heading out the door to work. Mercifully, the sound of the vacuum cleaner sent Ollie off to sleep. When Matthew came in to kiss them goodbye, he was lying on the sofa with his hands above his head, looking like a little angel.

'Call after the nurse comes and let me know how you got on, okay?'

'Okay,' she said, attempting to look happy. Inside she was miserable. She needed her mum. She wished there was someone to take Ollie for an hour or twelve. If she could have twelve hours of solid sleep, she'd be up for anything again. She was certain of it.

'I know you're wrecked,' Matthew said. 'But if you can manage it, would you give the estate agent a call again? See what stage we're at with the new development in Blackrock. I'd love to look at the four-bed house near Jake and Fee's place, too. Your mother is so good to let us stay here, but we should get going on our own place. Your father didn't leave you the money so it would sit there doing nothing. If we add the money from the sale of my flat to what you've inherited, we could easily afford that house. It's a really good buy and I think it would be great to get a place we can call *our* home.'

'I know, love,' she said. 'I'll get to it once the nurse is gone.'

She smiled and waved him off. That was the right thing to do. She already looked horrendous, so the least she could do was pretend to be normal. Every part of her seemed to be leaking. Her body had been invaded and she didn't feel as if she was in control of anything. She'd thought pregnancy was hard, giving up her tiny waist and bowing to the unsavoury side effects, such as haemorrhoids and stretch marks. But she'd naively assumed that once the baby was born, she'd get back to some sort of reality. How wrong she had been! Pregnancy was only the beginning. This breast pain, crippling exhaustion and horrible leaking from every orifice at once was totally incomprehensible. She honestly felt like she was slowly going mad. The thought of doing anything, even washing her hair, seemed like a mountain that was far too high to climb.

She must've dozed off, sitting upright on the sofa, because the sound of the doorbell made her jump two feet in the air while at the same time waking Ollie. He flinched and started to cry and she honestly wanted to join him.

Scooping him up, she shuffled to the door, not caring that she looked like a rather dishevelled and greasy bag lady.

'Leila Dillon?' the lady said. Dressed in a rain mac, with curly hair and perfect make-up, this person not only smelled fresh and zesty but was full of friendly smiles and obvious energy.

'Hello,' Leila said, sounding like she'd been out on the rip for a week. Coughing to clear her throat, she stood to the side and invited the woman in.

'I'm Emilia, and I'll be looking after you and baby for the next little while. Did the hospital tell you I'd be here to do the postpartum check-up?'

'Yes, I have some recollection of that,' Leila said. 'Please excuse the state of the house. My mother is away and she's letting us camp here for a while. We sold our flat and we need to get our own place.'

'It's a very nice house,' said Emilia. 'I never notice mess, and besides, most people make apologies for nothing at all. All I'm here for is to tend to you and baby.'

Emilia was professional and efficient and did all sorts of measuring and weighing. She was firm yet gentle, but Ollie really didn't like being stripped and checked over. He showed his distress by opening his mouth and screaming so loudly that it sounded as if he were being tortured.

'Oh baba,' Leila said, cuddling him and kissing his downy head. 'I'm so sorry. It's okay now.' Her breasts began to leak, which made her eyes do the same.

Emilia helped calm her down and they went through

Ollie's routine. Leila had a sudden compulsion to lie. She felt like such a failure as she told Emilia how awful the night before had been.

'When I try to latch him on, the pain is so bad that I don't know if I can carry on feeding. I actually feel as if my eyes are going to roll out my head and I'm going to pass out. Is that normal?'

'May I have a little look?' Emilia asked.

Normally, Leila would be mortified to show a perfect stranger her breasts, but at this exact moment, she'd get them out at a rugby match if she felt someone could help her get rid of the pain.

'Oh, you poor pet. I can see why you're feeling so awful and in so much pain. I strongly suspect you've got mastitis.' Emilia gently touched the nipple on one side, and Leila yelped. 'Yes, no doubt about it. That's why you have a temperature, too.'

Emilia got in touch with the doctor on call and he promised to drop in a prescription within the hour.

'The best thing you can do is feed. Once the breast gets emptied, it helps with the infection. The antibiotics should kick in really quickly, too.'

She promised to return the following day. Leila vowed to herself that she would look and feel better by then.

Once the doctor dropped the prescription in, she managed to pull on a tracksuit and put Ollie into his pram. Taking it slowly, she walked to the local chemist and got the tablets. She also bought a packet of soothers, hoping that they might help Ollie to settle that night.

The fresh air worked wonders, and by the time they got back, at least she felt they'd achieved something. The pain from wearing her bra and top was too much, though. So, seeing as she was in the house on her own, she took her top off and sat down on the messy sofa.

Matthew rang to see how she was, and he too sounded happier that she was out and about.

'Well done, darling. You're doing so well. It's all such an eye-opener really. I thought our lives would continue to tick along once the baby came. It's tough, isn't it?'

Just knowing that he understood how hard she was trying made Leila feel better. She was also incredibly grateful that he couldn't physically see her at that moment.

Feeding was still torturous, but she persisted. The soother was a godsend and Ollie seemed to love it. She hoped that by this time next week she would be feeling a lot better. After all, if she got any worse, she'd happily take herself to the local vet and ask to be put down.

By mid-afternoon, she felt able to have a shower. The warm water helped with the breast pain, and clean pyjamas made her feel like a new woman. She relaxed with a cup of tea in her hand as Ollie lay swaddled beside her. She took a photo of him and uploaded it to Facebook with a mushy comment about how much she loved him. It was stupid, but it instantly made her feel like a better mother. She smiled as the comments flooded in telling her how gorgeous he was.

As she was doing so well, she decided to phone Sean, the estate agent, while she was at it.

'We have one five-bed home in the same estate as your brother,' he told her. 'The deal fell through yesterday, but I can assure you the house won't sit for long.'

'Could we view it?' Leila asked.

'I can meet you there this evening at seven?' he suggested.

Leila agreed, but as she ended the call she suddenly

wondered how the hell she was going to haul herself and the baby to a viewing. She'd have to wear a top as well.

Matthew sounded really excited when she phoned him. 'I'll swing by and collect you. We won't need to stay long: if you don't love it, we'll leave.'

She knew he was right, but the thought of going out in public again filled her with anxiety. All her energy was gone. Her tank was running on empty, and she simply wanted to crawl into bed and sleep. She could feel tears starting to well up at the idea of what lay ahead.

Just then her phone rang and distracted her. It was Fee. Leila closed her eyes as Fee rattled on about wedding venues and houses.

'Leila?' She knew her name was being called, but she hadn't the energy to reply. 'Leila, answer me. Is everything okay?'

She managed to grunt that she was tired and she'd call Fee later on.

When Matthew came in the door to take them to view the house, Leila was dozing on the sofa with Ollie beside her.

'Hi, you two,' he said. 'Are you nearly ready to go?' He looked at her pyjamas and raised an eyebrow. 'I think it might be good if you put some clothes on, love. I know we're the customers and all that, but you might regret going in your pyjamas. Especially without the top on.'

'Maybe you and Ollie could go and look. If you both like it, I'm sure it'll be fine for us to live in.'

Matthew laughed and picked Ollie up. The baby's head rolled slightly.

'Sorry, baba,' he said. 'Jeepers, I'm not very good at this.

I might break him before his first birthday.' Ollie didn't seem remotely put out as he snuggled into Matthew.

'I'm sorry I look so dreadful,' Leila said. 'You weren't meant to see me looking like this. I fell asleep . . .'

'It's okay, love,' Matthew said.

'Thank you for not laughing at my poor diseased breasts.'

Leila hauled herself up the stairs and pulled on a pair of maternity jeans and a top. She detested all her maternity clothes. She'd stupidly thought she'd be back in her normal jeans in a heartbeat. Instead, her tummy was like a space-hopper and her pre-pregnancy clothes all looked like they'd been made for an elf.

Ollie was wearing a divine little onesie with a hood complete with bear's ears. Matthew had even managed to get him into the car seat.

'Ready, love?' he asked, looking very proud.

She couldn't face wearing a coat, fearing it would chafe her sore breasts, so she threw on a soft shawl instead.

As they drove into the newly built estate minutes later, both of them agreed that it had a lovely feel to it.

'There are plenty of green areas and very few of the houses are overlooked,' Matthew said.

'That's where Jake and Fee are,' Leila said, pointing to the first turn to the left. 'According to the directions, we're the next block down.'

The house they were viewing was at the very corner of the estate. It had a sizeable garden, and as it was the last house, it was very private. Leila had already made up her mind that she'd happily live here. She loved the thought of having Fee and Jake nearby, and it was only minutes from Shelly. Plus, seeing as it was a new build, by rights there shouldn't be any problems lurking within the walls.

Matthew was more scrupulous, and she could tell from the minute they walked in that he was planning on giving Sean a run for his money.

Matthew carried Ollie in his car seat, leaving Leila to walk around freely.

'It's all done up,' she said, in surprise.

'It was the show house,' Sean said. 'So all the furniture and carpets and curtains are included.'

Leila walked from the hall into the kitchen and gasped. It was all about light and airiness, and the high-shine cupboards and floors made her want to squeal with delight. There was a nice-sized eating area and family room where they could relax and watch television. The second living room was large too.

The utility room made Leila more excited than Matthew could fathom.

'Don't you see? We'll have all our machines out here and there won't be washing everywhere,' she said.

Matthew was busy delving into cupboards and looking at sockets and fixtures, so Leila went up the stairs. The carpet was soft and deep, and looked as if it had been knitted by fairies. It was slightly pink-tinged and she adored it.

The bedrooms, three of which were en suite, were like stepping into a plush hotel. She wished she could fling herself onto the master bed and sleep for a week.

Matthew eventually joined her.

'I love it,' she breathed. 'I wouldn't even change the toilet paper. It's gorgeous.'

'Keep your voice down and hide that smile,' Matthew said. 'Don't let our new friend know that you're interested.'

'Interested? I would pack a suitcase and move in this

second if we could. Did you see the bath? Do you think he'd mind if I got in? I'd love nothing more right now.'

Matthew handed her the car seat and looked at all the upstairs rooms in detail.

'Well?' she hissed. 'What do you think?'

'I think it's great,' he said, hugging her. 'But I'm a little concerned that it's the first house we've looked at properly. Shouldn't we wait and see what else is available in the area?'

'But I've been downloading information on properties for months, from well before Dad left me the money, and I know this ticks all the boxes. I never thought we'd be able to afford anything as gorgeous as this. It's a forever home, Matthew. I think we'd be crazy to let it go.'

'I do love the idea that it's all done for us,' he said. 'You've got so much on at the moment with this little man.' He looked down at Ollie, who was fast asleep. 'My only concern is that this will clear out your nest egg.'

'So?' she said, looking puzzled. 'It'll use up all the money you've got for your flat as well. But we won't have a mortgage.'

'Well, you're the banker. I don't know that I'm comfortable with you spending every last cent you own.'

'But you're doing the same, love. It's not as if I'm lashing out on shoes and bottles of wine and you're buying a motorbike. It'll be our home. We won't have a massive debt like everyone else our age and we can be confident that Oliver will grow up in a lovely neighbourhood.'

'I know,' he said as he buried his nose in her hair. 'It's pretty darn fantastic, isn't it?'

They made their way back down the stairs, where Sean was waiting patiently.

'So what are you thinking?' he asked. 'Not to put too much pressure on you, but there are several other couples interested in viewing this and—'

'Right,' said Leila. 'I've had no sleep since our baby was born. I have a crippling dose of mastitis and I'm hanging on by my fingernails here. So I'm not in the mood for playing games. Please don't annoy me by saying that there's a queue of people just around the corner with bags of money wanting to give it to you. This property isn't cheap and we've already told you we're cash buyers.'

'Of course,' said Sean, raising his hands defensively. 'I didn't mean to annoy you.'

'Give us until the morning and we'll let you know. We're very interested. We won't mess you about and we will give you a definite answer before ten o'clock.'

'We can't say any fairer than that,' Matthew added.

Sean barely had time to answer before Leila was gone out the door. Matthew gave him a lopsided smile and told him they'd talk to him in the morning.

It took a few minutes to get the baby seat back into the car. Leila hadn't the energy to even guide Matthew, so she sat in the passenger seat as he fiddled and cursed.

'Does all this get easier with time?' he asked.

'It must do or the population would've ceased,' Leila said.

They chatted about how it would feel to drive in and out of Furzedale Close each day. Both of them loved the thought.

'Should we call Jake and Fee and ask them if they'd mind us living on their doorstep?' Matthew wondered.

'No!' Leila said with a laugh. 'They don't own the entire

place. Besides, we're not in their cul-de-sac, so it's not relevant.'

Leila was utterly wrecked when they got home. She took her antibiotics and accepted Matthew's offer of making dinner. He wasn't exactly Jamie Oliver in the kitchen, but she knew he'd manage something tasty.

Ollie needed feeding again, and she sat on the sofa ready to do the honours. The second she thought of having to even undo her bra, tears began to well in her eyes.

'What is it?' Matthew asked in concern.

'I can't do it, Matthew. The pain is so awful and I feel so sick . . . I wish there was some other way. It's getting to the point where I'm dreading Ollie getting hungry. It's putting me off him. My boobs are sore with just my clothes resting on them, let alone having him suckling on me.'

'But didn't the doctor say that you've to feed through the pain?'

'Yes,' she said as she tried to latch him on.

The next hour was excruciating. Ollie kept pulling away and screaming as Leila sobbed silently. She felt like the most useless lump in the universe. Her Facebook feed showed her friends with babies coping beautifully, and here she was, weeping and hopeless. When she saw a selfie of Fee and her friend Norah out at a bar she loved in town, it nearly sent her over the edge. She was about to ask Matthew to walk up and down with Ollie in an attempt to calm him when he suddenly strode out of the house and slammed the front door behind him.

Now that she was by herself, Leila stopped all attempts to hide her anguish and allowed the tears to flow freely. Laying Ollie in his basket, she sat back on the sofa, dropped her head into her hands and had a really good cry.

She didn't even hear Matthew coming back. She jumped in fright as he plucked Ollie out of the basket, his tears stopping instantly, and watched astonished as her son horsed into a pre-made bottle of formula.

'Oh my goodness,' she said in awe. 'A bottle . . . Matthew . . . I . . .'

'Sorry, Leila,' he said. 'I'm sure you'll get the hang of feeding soon. But just for tonight you need to go to bed, sleep through the night and see how you are tomorrow.'

'Really?' she asked, the very words sounding blissful.

'The lady at the chemist said to put these gel-pad things on your nipples. Apparently they're cooling and will help. She buys them in from the States and she said they were a life-saver when her own baby was born.'

Matthew had Ollie tucked into the crook of his arm and was giving him his bottle as if it were the most natural thing in the world. For a second, Leila felt a shot of resentment at her baby for not missing her milk, but she pushed the thought aside. Not waiting to be asked a second time, she stooped to kiss Matthew and then Ollie, and went straight up to bed.

Within minutes, she was tucked up in her pyjamas, closing her tired, burning eyes. The cool gel pads on her nipples were the most astonishingly wondrous thing she'd ever encountered. But even as her mind tried to sink into sleep, the awful racing started up again. Guilt flooded her. She had failed her baby. She had failed at being a mother before she'd even really begun.

Tears slid down her face as she tried to rationalise things. She'd tried to breastfeed and it hadn't worked. That didn't mean she was a bad mum, right? So why did she feel as if she'd fallen at the first hurdle? What kind of child was

Ollie going to turn into if she couldn't even feed him properly? It had taken Matthew's initiative to get things on an even keel. Plus there was so many articles suggesting that breastfed babies got a better start in life. Now Ollie was having a crappy start, where she'd practically starved him and got an infection in the process.

Too tired to even cry any more, Leila pulled the covers right up to her chin and passed out.

Chapter 21

FEE WAITED AT ARRIVALS IN THE AIRPORT WITH A knot in her stomach. Jake had called to say that he needed a lift home and he'd explain everything when he saw her.

She was buzzed up after a brilliantly successful knee replacement surgery that she'd ended up helping with that evening. Joints weren't her speciality, so she'd never gone there, but the process had fascinated her. To celebrate nailing it, Norah had suggested a drink in town, and Fee had readily agreed. She had taken just one sip of her cocktail when Jake had called, and she'd had to bail on Norah, promising to make it up to her in the future.

Normally she might have told him to take a taxi, that she'd had a drink. But Jake had sounded a little on the quiet side when he'd phoned; nothing too out of the ordinary, but it had made her wonder. She assumed there was either an issue with his car that he'd forgotten to tell her about or he was ill. Either way, he needed her to be there, so there she was.

When he walked through arrivals, she did a double-take. He was pale and drawn-looking, and instead of strutting with his head held high, looking like a movie star as he normally did, he was slouched over like a beaten puppy.

Rushing over, she tried to hug him.

'Let's get out of here,' he said in uncharacteristically harsh tones.

She followed, having to trot to keep up. She paid for the parking ticket and was sitting in the car before she spoke again.

'What happened?'

'I've been suspended until my case comes before the board. It could take weeks or months. Nobody knows how long.'

'Pardon?' she asked, staring at him in horror.

'I drank too much wine last night. I took a chance and I got caught in New York this morning. They breathalysed me and I failed the test.'

'Oh Jake!' Her heart was thumping as she tried not to panic. 'I'm so sorry. Are you okay? Was it awful?'

'It was up there with my father's funeral in the fun stakes. But nobody has died. I didn't kill a planeload of passengers and I get to take some time off. Whoop-de-do,' he deadpanned.

'But were you actually over the limit?'

'They wouldn't tell me. Apparently my levels were too high for their liking, so that's that.'

She started the car and drove out of the airport. Not sure of what she should say or do, she decided to let him talk it out. That was what Jake usually did. But they reached home and walked into the house in stony silence. In the hallway, she tried to hug him. He shrugged her off and went up the stairs and into the bathroom. Minutes later, she heard the shower being turned on.

Flicking on the kettle, she figured he'd come down

shortly, looking sheepish and wanting to talk. She made a pot of tea and put some bread in the toaster.

After what felt like an age, there was still no sign of him, so she went up to the bedroom. He was in bed with the lights off and the covers pulled up to his chin.

'Hey,' she said, sitting on the edge of the bed. 'We should talk.'

When he didn't answer, Fee felt totally dejected. She walked out of the room and went down to clear away the tea and toast. She couldn't believe Jake was shutting her out. He'd never acted like this before.

All she could do was put herself in his shoes. If she were caught drinking and had been sent home from the hospital with the prospect of an inquiry and all that it entailed, she'd be struck dumb too.

She'd give him until tomorrow to get his thoughts together. She was slightly worried, as she needed to leave the house at six for the early shift. She didn't want to leave him alone while he was so upset. But knowing Jake, he'd be awake by the time she'd finished her shower in the morning.

Not wanting to disturb him, she used the flashlight on her phone to find clean clothes for the morning and get into bed. He had his back to her and seemed to be breathing evenly, so she didn't attempt to talk.

Even after Fee's alarm clock went off the next morning, followed by the noise of the shower pump filling the room, Jake didn't open his eyes. Knowing she couldn't be late for work, Fee crouched to kiss him goodbye. He didn't so much as flinch.

All the way into the hospital and during her first few hours of work, she kept expecting him to call. Her pager didn't go off once. One thing led to another and she didn't manage to take a proper break until her shift ended. Checking her mobile phone in her locker, she hoped there'd be at least one missed call. There was nothing.

As soon as she drove out of the hospital car park, she dialled Jake's number. It went to voicemail. She put her foot down and concentrated on getting home as quickly as possible.

Fully expecting him to be stuck in bed in the depths of depression, she ran into the house and straight up the stairs, taking two steps at a time.

'Jake?'

She was gobsmacked to find the bed made, the curtains open and everything spotless.

'Jake?' she called again, running back down to the kitchen.

She went from room to room, and it was only when she returned to the kitchen that she saw it: an envelope propped up against the newly acquired salt and pepper mills. She tore it open and pulled out the single sheet of paper.

Fee,

Sorry for the drama, but I've gone down to Mum in Spain. I need time and space to figure things out.

Jake x

Fee's heart thudded in her chest. What did he need time and space from? Her? His job? Both? As she gazed around their new home, it felt far too big and shiny and modern.

She wished she could make a pot of tea and sit down and talk about things. But the one person she usually went to was Jake, and he was gone.

She phoned Leila, hoping he might have told her something.

'No,' Leila said, sounding shocked. 'I haven't heard from him at all.'

'Oh God, Leila, what will I do?'

'Jake has always been a weirdo, Fee. You of all people should know that. It's either flying or you that fills his head. So I'm guessing that he's freaking out now that one of his passions has been taken away. Let him lick his wounds and hopefully he'll get away with a suspension.'

'What if he loses his job?' Fee said, breathless with worry. 'I mean, he's worked so hard and things were going in the right direction. We both have such amazing plans for the future, but none of them involves him being unemployed.'

'Try not to freak out,' Leila said. 'It'll work out, Fee. Everything always does for you two.'

'O-kay,' Fee said, detecting a bit of a snipe. 'Is everything all right with you?'

'Yup, just dandy.'

'Right. Listen, I'm sure you have a lot on your plate with the baby and all that. I shouldn't have bothered you. As you say, it'll all be fine.'

'So we got the house, by the way. The one we were looking at around the corner from you. We're going to be neighbours. Yay.'

Leila sounded as if she'd just told Fee she had a couple of weeks to live, not that she'd bought her dream home.

'Wow,' said Fee. 'That's a big decision. But shouldn't you buy something a little smaller, like we did? Start off small and work your way up? If you use every cent of the money your father left and something goes wrong—'

'We love the house, Fee,' Leila interrupted brusquely. 'We already have Ollie, so it's the right choice for us. Matthew has put money into it as well. It's not just the money Dad left me. We're buying it half and half. I wouldn't want you to think that Matthew isn't paying his way.'

'What, like me, you mean?'

'Ah, Fee, I wasn't suggesting that at all . . .'

'Weren't you?' Fee said angrily. One part of her brain was shouting at her to back down, but the other part had reared up and was ready to fight its corner. It was like having her deepest fear laid bare: that people were talking behind her back and saying she was a sponger, a freeloader, a kept woman.

'Fee, look, I'm having a really hard time of it right now. Things aren't working out the way I'd hoped, and I'm feeling dreadful.'

'I see. Well I'm really sorry that I bothered you with Jake's issues. I'll leave you to it.'

Fee hung up and burst into tears. How could Leila be so flippant about Jake? His entire career was at stake here. All she could think about was her damn five-bedroom house.

Besides, she thought Leila was wrong. Not that her opinion counted, clearly. She would never have allowed Jake to spend so much on a house right now. It didn't make sense. He had tried to persuade her to go for something bigger, seeing as he had the money for it, but she had insisted they stick with the starter house, just as they'd planned before the money came along. It was by far the most sensible way to approach a first buy. And anyway, Leila and Matthew had one tiny baby, not five hulking teenagers. There was lots of time to work their way up. She wasn't going to say it to Leila either, but on top of all that, for the money they were paying, she would want somewhere a bit more private, with nobody else near her.

Feeling too upset to sit for the entire evening on her own, Fee decided to use the time to visit her parents. It was never easy taking Jake over there. They were so uppity and defensive that he ended up feeling uncomfortable. This way she could give them her undivided attention and there'd be no unnecessary awkwardness.

The minute she sat down at their kitchen table, she regretted her decision.

Her mother wanted to know why she wasn't at work. Her father wanted to know if Jake had kicked her out. Once they were satisfied that everything was all right, they wanted to discuss the wedding. The very last thing Fee wanted to talk about right now.

They had no interest in the party or the meal or the dress or the make-up of the wedding party. All they wanted was for her to get in touch with Father Tracey from the local parish and choose the prayers and hymns.

'I don't know if we'll get married in a church at all,' she admitted. 'We haven't discussed it yet.'

'What do you mean?' her father said.

'Well, we might do something abroad. Have a ceremony on a beach, perhaps.'

'How?' her mother asked, with wild-eyed confusion. 'How would Father Tracey get onto a plane with his bad knee, let alone trudge through searingly hot sand to conduct the ceremony?'

'It doesn't work that way, Mum. All the resorts have their own celebrants. I wouldn't expect Father Tracey to be there at all.'

'How can you get married without Father Tracey?' her father asked, shaking his head as if she'd just suggested Jack the Ripper should be the celebrant.

'I'm marrying Jake, Dad, not Father Tracey, so we won't worry about it.'

Fee could feel a headache coming on. She couldn't sit listening to her parents squabbling, and there was no way she could confide in them, so she made her excuses and left.

Much to her relief, Shelly rang just as she got home.

'Shelly! Please, can you tell me what's going on with Jake? I'm so worried about him.'

'Well I can tell you that he's on his way here,' Shelly said, sounding a lot happier than Fee felt. 'He told me he'd asked for a leave of absence and that he's coming down to me for a week or so. I presumed he'd cleared the idea with you first. I'm clearly delighted, but I don't want to step on anyone's toes.'

Shelly sounded so utterly thrilled at the prospect of having Jake's company that Fee couldn't possibly tell her that none of this had been discussed and that Jake had totally pulled the wool over her eyes.

'Ask Jake to call me when he's settled,' Fee said. 'Enjoy your time together. How are you managing, Shelly?'

'I'm taking each day as it comes,' she said. 'But it's really beautiful here. I have lots of ideas zooming around my head and I am more grateful than you'll ever know that Jake is on his way. Thank you for lending him to me.'

'Oh, please!' Fee said, wanting to sound nonchalant. 'He's not mine to lend. He's your son and I know he's desperately worried about you. It'll be great for you to spend a week together.'

Fee put the phone down feeling stunned. None of the things she'd said to Shelly were a lie. She genuinely was happy that he was going to be with his widowed mother. But she couldn't get her head around the fact that he'd sneaked off without so much as a phone call, and that he was blatantly lying to his mother.

What was he playing at?

Anger boiled through her as she tried to get things in perspective. She thought of the patient who had died on her operating table. She thought of poor Gerry, lying in his grave, of the finality of both situations. Jake had made a mistake and they would have to figure out a way of putting it right. That was as far as it went.

Feeling hungry and tired, she decided to fix herself a cold supper of salmon and brown bread, with a glass of wine to take the edge off her seething emotions.

She was just about finished eating when her phone buzzed, and Jake's name came up on the screen.

'Hi,' he said, with the din of what sounded like live music in the background. 'How was your day?'

'Fine,' she said. 'But I would've appreciated it if you'd discussed your jetting off with me before you left.'

'Yeah, sorry about that, Fee. It was a spur-of-the-moment thing. I need to sort my head and I know Mum is finding her feet down here. So it felt right that we should do that together.'

'Uh-huh, but yet again, I would've appreciated it if you'd told me first.'

'Don't be all pissed off, Fee,' he said. 'I'm feeling relaxed now. Mum is made up that I'm here. Let's make the most of this situation, yeah?'

'What? Let's all be delighted that you've been suspended for almost being over the limit while attempting to fly a plane? Oh super! Silly me for thinking this is anything but wonderful.'

The line went dead.

'Hello? Jake?'

Fee looked at her phone and it confirmed what she thought. He'd hung up on her.

Looking at her watch, she knew she needed to go to bed. She was on the early shift again tomorrow. Much as she would love to sink the entire bottle of wine, she knew it wouldn't exactly help matters if both of them were fired for being drunk in charge.

She cleared everything away and set out her clothes for the morning. By the time she'd cleansed her skin and brushed her teeth, she was wide awake again. She tried reading, but was too cross to even take in the words. There was nothing she wanted to watch on television, so she lay there, by herself, boiling with rage.

Chapter 22

SHELLY WAS DELIGHTED TO SEE JAKE.

He'd sat with her and Valentina last night, discussing the idea of her taking over from where Rosa had left off with the wedding planning business. Their chat seemed to have lit a fire under Valentina, who sprang into action first thing the next morning. When Shelly came down for breakfast, Valentina steered her into the back room where the computer was. Rosa was waiting to talk to her via Skype.

'I loved my business, but inside my heart was so heavy,' she explained. 'I was always surrounded by people who were so in love . . . people who were doing what I dreamed of doing myself.'

'I'm not in a great position with my own heart right now,' Shelly admitted. 'My husband died a few months ago. Do you think I'm crazy to even consider delving into the world of love and romance? Will I torture myself unnecessarily?'

'Ah,' Rosa said as she tutted. 'Life can be very cruel. Are you in Rondilla alone?'

'No, my son is here with me at the moment,' Shelly said, feeling a little defensive. The last thing she wanted was for this stranger to pity her. Besides, she desperately wanted to keep going with her project.

'So you will have help from your son?'

'I haven't had a chance to discuss it with him properly. But he's a pilot, so he won't be here for long. I did tell him about my idea last night, and he thinks it would work very well. I would listen to him. He's a good businessman.'

'I think you need something to occupy your mind, Shelly. Heartache and grief can become a dark and heavy burden. If you can channel the happiness from the couples, this will be a good thing for you.' Rosa paused. 'The reason I think it didn't work for me is because I had *never* met a sweetheart. I thought I would go to my grave without ever finding love. So it began to eat me up.'

They chatted for a while longer. Shelly was genuinely surprised and touched by how giving and open Rosa was with her business advice. After they ended the call, she sat back in the chair, mulling it all over.

She was at a crossroads in her life, there was no doubting that, but the pull towards Rondilla and Casa Maria was incredibly strong. Having listened to Rosa, she knew this plan would work. It just made sense. Even though she had plenty of fears and doubts, she decided that she was going to give it a try. She was going to throw everything into getting Casa Maria ready while simultaneously attempting to line up some weddings, to get a feel for the potential of her venture. The thought was a balm to her aching heart. If she were flat-out busy, she'd have less time for being swallowed by grief. The project would give her a whole new purpose in life. And that was why she was here, after all, wasn't it?

As she emerged from the back office and into the restaurant, Valentina was waiting, eager to talk to her.

'You find lots of answers, *sí*?' she asked. 'Rosa is . . .'

She kissed her clasped fingers and tossed her hand into the air. 'She had a good business and I think you would be perfect for this too. You will make a good job of it, I think!'

'Thank you,' Shelly said, grinning. Valentina was like an angel who'd walked into her life at a time when she needed her most.

'Jake!' she said, as he came down the stairs looking a little sleepy. 'Come and have breakfast with me. I have more news, and then I want to show you Casa Maria.'

'Whoa, Mum! I thought I was coming to Spain to relax. It's like Grand Central Station here this morning.'

They sat in the café and ate tortilla followed by a pot of dark aromatic coffee. Afterwards, they made their way up the hill towards the hacienda.

'I'm a bit nervous now,' Shelly said with a giggle as they pushed through the gates.

'*Hola, señora!*'

They looked up to see Alejandro leaning on a shovel. The entire entrance had been levelled and already the place looked neater. She had asked him to clean up the outside, not sure whether or not she'd even go ahead with the inside. But she'd figured that either way, the front needed to look presentable.

'*Hola,* Alejandro,' she said. 'My God, did you dig all that by yourself?'

'*Sí,*' he said matter-of-factly.

'This is my son, Jake.'

The two men shook hands and exchanged pleasantries, then Jake stood and stared at the house.

'Gosh, it's a lot bigger than I'd thought. It really would be a guest house rather than a private holiday home, wouldn't it?'

Shelly nodded and bit her lip.

'Dad must've wanted you both to retire to here while still having something to keep you occupied. There's no way he bought it as a weekend retreat.'

'First impressions . . .' Shelly asked. 'Do you like it or loathe it?'

'I certainly don't loathe it. It's a stunning place. But I'm a bit worried that it's too much for you to take on alone.'

'Please, you come. I have drawings. Come, come,' Alejandro said. Jake looked at Shelly with puzzlement.

'I asked him to give me a price for renovating it,' she whispered.

'What, the whole house?' Jake asked in confusion.

Shelly nodded.

'Does he live in a cottage with Snow White and six other small men, each of whom is trained to do a different type of building work?'

'Sort of.' Shelly giggled. 'He has cousins and other people who can come and be his team.'

While Shelly went into the kitchen with Alejandro to look at the initial plans, Jake took a tour of the house. By the time he rejoined them, they were crouched over huge architect's diagrams spread on the floor. Clipped to the top left-hand corner of the page were several black-and-white photographs.

'Is this Casa Maria?' Jake asked in awe.

'*Sí*, from many, many years ago,' Alejandro said proudly. '*Bellísimo*, eh?'

'Incredible,' Shelly breathed. As she stared at the photograph of the main front room with its decorative cornices painted in a dark colour, and the richly patterned rugs that brought warmth to the polished wooden floors, she longed to lounge on the oversized plush couches. The sweeping brocade drapes pulled back by thick tasselled cords made her want to weep with joy.

'Where did you find these photos?' Jake asked Alejandro as he pulled them free of the paper clip and examined each one.

'My mama,' he said. 'She work here for many years.'

'Really?' Shelly said. 'Would she come and speak to us? Could we meet her? I would love to get some ideas, if she would share them.'

'Eh, no,' he said evenly. 'She no come to Casa Maria no more. Never, never. She say Casa Maria have bad memories for her.'

'Why?' asked Shelly, a shiver running down her spine. 'Did something happen here?' She gazed up at the high ceiling, wondering why this magnificent house had been boarded up and left to rack and ruin. It made no sense.

'Casa Maria was once very beautiful, as you can see.' Alejandro pointed at the photos. 'But for many years, she stay with nobody. She sad now. But you can change it.' He nodded earnestly. 'You can make this *casa* come alive once more.'

'Yes, especially if we have some magic beans and a beanstalk with pots of gold at the top to spend on it,' Jake said, laughing. 'Alejandro, do you mind me asking how you came up with full architect drawings overnight?'

Alejandro looked from Shelly to Jake and hesitated before speaking. 'Señor Gerry, he . . . he speak with me many times. He talked to an architect in the city, in Marbella. He show me these, say he will make agreement with me. But he no come back. I no understand why, and then Señora Shelly, she come.' He looked sad.

'You met my father?' Jake said, and Shelly could hear the catch in his voice.

'*Sí.*' Alejandro nodded. 'A good man. Very good. He want to make the house live again, this is what he say. He had fire in his eyes when I talk to him. He was . . . under a spell.' He shrugged, unable to express himself fully, but Shelly knew exactly what he meant.

'Thank you for telling us that,' Jake said, and smiled warmly at the older man. 'I like to think of Dad here, walking around, picturing how it could be.'

Alejandro nodded kindly. 'I understand this,' he said simply.

Jake began studying the drawings more closely. 'It looks like a solid plan,' he said to Shelly. 'What do you think?'

Shelly thought for a moment. 'The way I see it is that Gerry bought this place for us to renovate together. He never knew I'd be doing it without him. But the plan is a good one. I'd like to honour his wishes.' She paused. 'In fact, it's not just that. I want to do this for me too, for my future. I know it seems crazy, and like you said, it's a big undertaking, but this place has got under my skin. I can't walk away.' She smiled at the two men, who were listening to her in silence, then thrust out her hand towards Alejandro. 'If we can agree on a price,' she said, 'you've got yourself a deal.'

The look of delight on Alejandro's face lifted her spirits.

Jake was smiling. 'If you're absolutely sure, Mum, I think you should go for it. Why not?'

'Why not indeed?' Shelly said with a laugh.

'I am so pleased,' Alejandro said.

'Okay, well can you sit down with me and we'll go through the incidentals?' Jake said. 'I need to see the figures broken down so we can try to figure out how much each element is going to cost.'

Alejandro was more than willing to get started immediately. He and Jake walked around the house together, identifying and discussing the many problems. There was much to be done, but thankfully there seemed to be an astonishingly small amount of damp. Although it had been left idle for many years, the house had clearly been well sealed.

'This is a shame,' Jake said, pointing to the staircase. 'It's beautiful wood.'

'You know about this?' Alejandro asked.

Jake shrugged. 'I love to make things from wood in my spare time. Just a hobby. But I don't get to do it half enough. I'm a pilot, so I'm away a lot. Not much time off.'

'Okay,' Alejandro said, nodding. 'But maybe you like to try to work on this?'

Jake looked at him in surprise. 'You'd trust me to do that?'

Alejandro nodded. '*Sí*, of course. Is nice when an owner get to work on a house. More personal, you know?'

Jake studied the staircase. 'You know what, Alejandro, I think I would like to try. Just promise me you'll throw me out if I'm messing up.'

Alejandro laughed. 'Okay. I promise this.'

They went outside to continue their survey. Jake was delighted by the outbuildings, which sat in the middle of a wild and overgrown garden. One long mews-type building had a smaller one attached, and Alejandro ushered him towards this, saying, 'Come, come, you must see.'

Jake was intrigued. Alejandro pulled open the door to the building and stood back. Jake stepped inside and looked around in silence. It was dank and musty, but it was a workshop. An Aladdin's cave of tools and benches.

'It's like a woodworking studio,' he said, looking over at Alejandro.

The other man smiled. '*Sí*, it belong to the gardener, my mama tell me this. He did garden and any jobs in house, you know, like . . .'

'Handyman?' Jake said.

'Exactly,' Alejandro said, looking around appreciatively. 'Fine workshop. I show your father, too.'

'You did?' Jake said. 'He must have loved it.'

'*Sí*.' Alejandro smiled. 'This is what I show you.'

Jake looked to where he was pointing, and his heart lurched in his chest. There, on the back of a high stool, hung Gerry's jacket. He'd recognise it anywhere. It was a light blazer, the kind he tucked into his flight bag for days off. His hand went to his mouth and he had to swallow down the lump in his throat. 'Wow,' he said.

At that moment, Shelly appeared in the doorway.

'I haven't been in here yet,' she said, stepping inside. 'What's in . . .' She stopped at the sight of Jake's face. 'What is it?' she said quickly. 'What's wrong?'

'Nothing,' Jake said, smiling. 'Alejandro just showed me something wonderful.' He pointed over to the stool.

Shelly looked over, and a gasp escaped her when she saw the jacket.

'Oh Lord,' she said faintly. 'Gerry.'

Jake moved quickly to her side and took her hand. Alejandro looked concerned.

'I'm fine, sorry,' Shelly said. 'I just didn't . . .'

'I know,' Jake said. 'Isn't it brilliant? Thank you so much, Alejandro.'

The older man nodded and stepped back outside, leaving them alone. Jake went over and picked up the jacket and brought it to Shelly. As if in a trance, she stared at it, then held it to her face and breathed in deeply. It still held the faint scent of Gerry's aftershave.

'It's okay, Mum,' Jake whispered.

'Yes, it is,' she said, taking the jacket away from her face and smiling at him. 'I think he's here, Jake, can you feel it?'

Jake looked around. This place did have a very unique feel to it. It was almost as if Gerry had deliberately left a piece of himself here for them to find.

'Yeah,' he said, nodding. 'I think I can.'

'I think we'll leave this where you found it,' she said, holding out the jacket.

As Jake took it from her, he heard a slight rustling from the inside pocket. He flapped open the lapel and put his hand into the pocket, drawing out a crumpled piece of paper with pencilled notes scribbled all over it in Gerry's handwriting. He and Shelly examined it in silence. It was a higgledy-piggledy listing of things to do, ideas, notes to himself. And in a roughly drawn box, with the words inside underlined, Gerry had written: *Ask Jake about doing some of the woodwork?*

Jake couldn't form words. Shelly put her arm around him and squeezed him.

'I keep thinking the word "destiny",' she said quietly. 'I thought it was just mine, but maybe not.' She smiled up at him.

Jake couldn't stop staring at those words, written in his father's hand. At that moment, a certainty took hold of him: Shelly was meant to do this, and he was meant to help her. He made a silent promise to himself that he would do all he possibly could to make his father's dream a reality.

He hugged Shelly. 'Come on,' he said. 'Let's go talk money with Alejandro, and get this thing up and running.'

While Jake and Alejandro sat on the old rickety window bench in the kitchen to go over things in detail, Shelly went through the photos again, fascinated by the house's former self. She looked at them all closely, but even so, it was only after going through each one about four times that she spotted her. There was a photo of a book-filled room – Shelly wasn't sure exactly which room it was – backlit by the light falling through the long sash windows. As her gaze kept returning to the curtains and the carving on the bookshelves, she suddenly realised there was a person in the picture. A woman. She held the photo close, squinting, trying to see right into the past.

The two men were still deep in conversation, so she went to her handbag and took out the small magnifying glass she always carried with her – a sign of encroaching age that she tried not to let anyone see – and held it up to the photo. She was right, there was a woman there. She was curled up tight in an armchair, reading a book. She was almost indistinct, pushed out to the edge of the picture, but she was there.

'I think things are okay here, Mum,' Jake said, nodding at her. 'Alejandro has given us the price he offered to Dad, and it seems fair to me.'

Shelly put down the photo and walked over to them. 'That's fantastic,' she said, feeling relieved. 'I really don't want to take out a bank loan at my age.'

Jake shook his head. 'I don't think you'll have to. Alejandro has been very fair. As long as there are no nasty surprises, it should work out okay.'

'Fantastic,' Shelly said, smiling warmly at Alejandro. 'And now that that's sorted, Alejandro, could I speak with your mother at some point? I know she doesn't want to come here, but do you think I could go visit her? I would like to ask her about these photos, about colour schemes and things. The photographs are amazing, but they're all in black and white. It would be lovely to remain true to the original design.'

Aware that there would probably be a language barrier, Shelly promised herself for the hundredth time that she would sign up for a language class. At least now she had a real impetus to do it – she was fascinated to learn what had gone on here so many years ago.

'I try,' Alejandro said, not sounding too hopeful.

Shelly picked up the photo she had been examining. 'Which room is this?' she asked him. She was curious to see if he mentioned the figure in the picture.

He glanced at it and said, 'The library. The room to right of front door, yes?'

Shelly nodded and watched as he put the photo down. She felt pretty certain he had no idea there was a woman captured in it. She was about to ask him about it when Jake cut in.

'I'm not here for long,' he told Alejandro, 'so I'd like to get cracking on the stairs.'

Alejandro smiled at his enthusiasm. 'Okay, we look at the wood, see what we deal with.'

'Great,' Jake said, standing up. 'And is there a lumber yard or something nearby that I could go to?'

Alejandro nodded. 'I show you. You can borrow my van.'

'Really?' Jake said. 'That would be amazing, thank you.'

While Shelly went out to look at Alejandro's handiwork in the garden, Jake took a loose baluster from the handrail of the staircase and brought it out to the workshop. Once he'd sanded it gently, removing the old lacquer layers, he could see that it was cherry. Feeling excited about everything that was happening, he decided to give Fee a call. She didn't pick up, so he left a message telling her she would love Casa Maria.

Realising Leila was also home alone, he gave her a call too.

'You'll have to come out and see this place, Leila,' he said excitedly, tripping over his words as he rushed to describe it all. He told her about finding Gerry's jacket, and how excited he was by Shelly's plans for the place. 'Why don't you try and come down?'

'I'm not sure,' Leila replied. 'Christmas is so close. It's a bit messy with baby Ollie, too.'

'How is the little fella?' Jake asked.

'Great,' Leila said sharply. 'Why?'

'Pardon?' Jake said.

'Why do you ask? Has Matthew told you I can't look after him properly or something?'

'Leila, what the hell are you on about?' he said, perplexed.

'Nothing. Forget it. I think I misunderstood, that's all.'

'Fair enough. Listen, I'd better go. Chat to you soon.'

He purposely avoided the subject of his suspension from work. He didn't want to highlight it too much to Leila, mostly because he didn't need his mother finding out. Things were lovely and chilled here in Spain and he was enjoying the little bubble he'd created. Knowing the serenity couldn't and wouldn't last, he tried to block all thoughts of his messy work life from his mind.

He put his phone back in his pocket and looked happily around the workshop. It was the weirdest thing, but this place, even though it was half ruined, had such a homely feeling. He put his hand on Gerry's jacket and rubbed it.

'Thanks, Dad,' he said. 'This is amazing.'

Chapter 23

LEILA WAS FURIOUS WITH JAKE AND FEE. THEY were so bloody cocky, acting as if they knew it all. Who did Fee think she was, telling her not to buy the house? Just because she and Matthew didn't work as surgeons or pilots didn't mean they couldn't afford a nice house.

She loved Fee, but she did have all these airs and graces about herself. Being a surgeon was an amazing achievement, but Leila got the feeling that she was now looking down her nose at her because she was at home with Ollie.

Well, little did Fee know that being a new mother was the hardest bloody job *ever*. There was no exam available for learning how to look after a baby. Nor was there any guarantee that you'd even be able to feed that baby. This morning as she'd given Ollie his bottle, he'd nearly taken her hand off. As soon as he began to suck, his eyes had actually rolled in delight. He clearly preferred the formula to her milk. Knowing she was being utterly silly and that it shouldn't matter one jot, she'd sat and sobbed as he'd fed hungrily.

She flicked the kettle on. The house was quiet and she felt lonely. She missed Shelly. Sharing baby-minding was lovely; doing it on your own was a bit of a drudge. She checked her phone, and then put up a post about how there was nowhere she'd rather be than with Ollie. The lie tasted bitter in her mouth, but it was far better than telling the grim truth.

Matthew had told her again this morning that she was doing a great job – as he skipped out the door to work and freedom and adult conversations and lunch breaks. What she wouldn't give to eat one meal with both hands. Every time she sat down to a snack, Ollie seemed to sense that she was trying to have 'me time' and kicked off. She was forever eating with one hand and holding on to him with the other. The whole thing was just too exhausting for words.

Maybe she should go back to work now? Put Ollie in a crèche where the people had more experience than her? That way he mightn't be ruined by the time his first birthday came around. She could use the excuse of the new house and tell Matthew that they'd be better off if she got going with work and earning again.

Feeling utterly heartbroken, she made up her mind that it would be in Ollie's best interests. She loved him more than she had ever imagined it possible to love anyone. She couldn't risk destroying him.

She'd hold out until after Christmas and then slip it in that she felt it might be best if she went back to the bank a little early. She experienced a moment of certainty, then her mind wavered. From what Shelly had told her, things were going really well in Spain. She was so looking forward to seeing this Casa Maria place, but if she returned to work, that wouldn't happen for a while. She was so confused, she didn't know what she wanted to do. It seemed like she could no longer make a decision. Her brain kept doing this – throwing up questions and obstacles – until even the act of thinking felt exhausting.

Her phone pinged. A comment on Facebook from Fee: *Lucky you! Enjoy!* Leila stuck out her tongue at the phone and her shoulders drooped. She was so irritable these days. Everything annoyed her, particularly her child-free brother and his girlfriend. The way he'd shot off to Spain without a thought seemed almost designed to illustrate to her how trapped she was in her life.

Sighing, Leila forced her mind to try to focus on what she wanted to do. If they pushed it, she and Matthew could be in the new house straight after Christmas. Yes, that was a good plan, she decided. The next second, she was overcome with terror at the thought of being there on her own for any longer than necessary. Fresh tears welled up in her eyes.

The deal had been closed on Furzedale Close and she knew she was one of the luckiest girls in the world. It was a beautiful home for them to enjoy as a family. Plus the antibiotics had kicked in and the mastitis was gone, but so too was her milk. Ollie was totally divine, not the best sleeper, but then she was guessing that was normal. She tried to stack up the positives and feel good about them, but she felt like such a mess and a failure that she was beginning to believe she didn't deserve any of it.

As she reached to pour the boiling water into her cup, Leila noticed the flyer propped up against the toaster. It was one the public health nurse had given her, but she'd put it away in a drawer. A mother-and-baby group didn't sound like a good time to her. Probably just a load of women moaning about their husbands or whatever. She picked it up and looked at it. Matthew must have found it and left it there, she thought. The group met in the church hall not far away, and today was one of their twice-weekly meeting days. She glanced at the clock. It was due to start in an hour.

She wasn't really much of a joiner, but she was feeling so desolate and lonely this morning, she decided it might be worth a try. The nurse had said she'd meet women in the same boat as her. Might be nice to talk to another drowning victim, Leila thought ruefully.

'Right, come on, Ollie,' she said, suddenly feeling desperate to get away from these four walls. 'We're going out, little man, and you're going to meet some of your own kind.'

An hour and ten minutes later, Leila was standing outside the church hall as the rain teemed down, pinging off her waterproof jacket. She was dithering, as usual, her tired brain unable to decide whether to stay or go. Frustrated with herself, she was just turning around to go home when a woman dashed up the path behind her with a baby in a Rock-a-Tot.

'Bloody hell, the weather in this country would drive you to drink, wouldn't it? Go on in. Push the door.'

Leila didn't have the confidence to admit she was chickening out and running away, so she did as she was told. Inside there were at least twenty other mums with babies and toddlers of varying ages. They were sitting in a circle, with their little ones on their laps.

'Sorry I'm late. How's everyone?' the lady behind Leila said.

Leila hovered awkwardly near the door, wishing she hadn't come, longing to get out of there.

'Do come in!' said the woman, smiling at her. 'I'm Nina, and you'll meet all the others in due course. We all wanted to charge out the first time we came, too. Don't worry, we don't bite!'

Leila felt her cheeks flushing as she attempted to pretend she'd had no intention of leaving.

'Come and sit with us,' said another mum. 'What's your name?'

'Leila.' She lifted Ollie out of the buggy. 'And this is Ollie.' She knew she was being horrible, but she shunted him about quite roughly to ensure he woke up. Thankfully, he didn't scream the place down.

Leila sat down beside the lady who'd beckoned her over and turned to smile gratefully at her. The woman's baby was cuddled to her chest, and Leila flinched when she saw her. She was absolutely tiny, like a toy doll. There was a thin plastic tube going into her nose, and it was taped to her poor little cheek with plaster.

'Hi there, I'm Sarah, and this wee mite is Lola.'

'What happened to her?' Leila asked. 'The poor little thing.'

'Oh, she's a premmie baby. She came at thirty weeks and tried to frighten the living daylights out of us all, didn't you?' Sarah said, kissing her. 'She's doing really well and she'll have her feeding tube removed soon. So we'll all be celebrating then!'

Two of the mothers were breastfeeding while chatting, and one was even eating a biscuit at the same time.

'How old is Ollie?' one of the women asked.

'Two weeks,' said Leila.

'Oh.' A few of them groaned.

'Fair play to you being outside and dressed. Is he your second or third?'

'No, he's my first,' Leila said hesitantly.

'Well you're doing really well,' said one of the breastfeeders. 'I think I was in my pyjamas for about two months with my first. You look great, and so does Ollie.'

'I can't do the breastfeeding. I got mastitis and now he's on bottles and I feel like a failure.' It came out all in a rush, taking Leila by surprise as much as her audience. She had no idea why she was telling a room full of strangers her most shameful and darkest secrets.

'Oh God love you,' said breastfeeder number two. 'I had mastitis with my second. It was pure hell. I wanted to die.'

'Me too,' said Leila, wanting to hug her for understanding.

'I cried for a week and thought my daughter was going to be damaged somehow because she wasn't breastfed. All I can tell you is that she's as sharp as a tack now, and once I got my head around her being on a bottle, I never looked back.'

'But you're managing so well this time,' Leila said.

'Yes, because I had a lot of help. I stayed in the hospital for a bit longer, and I had a private room. But she's my last, number four! You learn as you go along.'

The women were full of chat, and Leila couldn't believe how honest they all were. They talked about everything from hating their husbands during labour to never wanting sex ever again. It wasn't miserable moaning as she'd feared; they made her laugh with their spot-on humour, and she joined in the chat freely and felt as if she'd known them for years.

By the time the session was over, she felt a thousand times better. She was so glad she'd made the effort to come along.

'Hope you didn't think we're all a bunch of nutters,'

said Nina with a giggle. 'We don't exactly solve the world's issues in here, but it's good to know that everyone else is attempting to stay sane too.'

'I really enjoyed myself,' Leila said sincerely. 'It's absolutely brilliant to know that I'm not the worst mother in the world. I thought all other babies slept eight hours a night and that everyone else could breastfeed.'

'We hope you come back next time,' said a glamorous blonde called Stephanie, who looked like the least likely person to sit on a carpet-tiled floor and talk about baby puke.

'I'd love to come back,' Leila said. 'Thank you all for helping me to feel that my baby might survive his first year of life!'

The rain was heavier than ever as she left, so she put Ollie straight into the car and drove to the shopping centre. Buzzed up by her new experience and the certain knowledge that she wasn't evil or a terrible person, she decided to cook a celebratory dinner for her and Matthew tonight. It was crazy that ninety minutes could make such a difference. She'd have to get a handle on her brain and not let the miserable thoughts take over. She was being so judgemental of those around her, and that had to stop.

She took out her phone and texted Fee. *Sorry I was so ratty earlier. I love you & don't want any bad blood. Will u come 4 dins 2nite? Promise I won't scratch ur eyes out x*

Fee answered immediately. *I'm sorry 2. I can be a right bossy cow. Don't mind me. Thanks 4 the invite. C u l8r. Luv u 2 xx*

Relief washed over Leila. She hated fighting with anyone, especially darling Fee. She was the closest thing she had to a sister after all.

She bought steaks and two bottles of red wine along with vegetables and a chocolate cake. Then she put up a post on Facebook saying she was cooking for two of her favourite people. She got lots of comments telling her that she was amazing to be doing anything for anyone with a new baby on her hands. Leila smiled, enjoying feeling like Miss In-Control in the eyes of the world.

As she walked back to the car park, she drooled over the dresses in the windows she passed. It wouldn't be long, she promised herself, before she could shop for normal-sized clothes again. She'd been doing really well with her weight loss. She hadn't put on a massive amount in the first place, but she was determined to be back in her jeans early in the new year. One of the mums she'd just met at the group had been warning them all to beat the weight off sooner rather than later. Leila had found her hilarious. She had a perfect figure and her daughter was only three months old. She'd admitted to the group that after her first son was born, she'd just kept eating.

'I thought I'd be as skinny as a whippet because I was breastfeeding. What a load of crap! I ended up losing my bump all right – I filled in around it and it disappeared into a load of lard.'

'But you're tiny now,' Leila had said with a grin.

'Oh, I learned the hard way, believe me. Ten months at a slimming club, and I made myself stand in a skimpy red bikini every night at home. I'd look in the mirror and sob.'

'That sounds a bit harsh,' Leila had said, somewhat shocked by such extremes.

'It was,' she'd replied. 'It was horrendous. But I was determined to get back to my former shape. When I got pregnant again, I was damn careful. I couldn't wear the red bikini, so I hung it up in the bedroom instead.'

'Your poor husband must've been traumatised by that bikini,' Leila laughed.

While she knew she wasn't going to go so far as to buy a skimpy bikini, Leila did want to get her shape back. Matthew was being so good about her wobbly body. He hadn't said a single disparaging thing. In fact, he was nothing but loving and sweet. She knew he was one in a million and she couldn't bear the thought of him deciding he didn't fancy her any more.

A part of her was glad he hadn't seen her giving birth. It was so barbaric and undignified. She shuddered at the thought of it. Fresh appreciation of Fee washed over her. Of course, that was another reason she wanted to get into shape. The wedding. She'd have a chat with Fee about bridesmaid dresses tonight as well.

Back home, with her shopping put away and Ollie napping, she decided to grab the opportunity to call Shelly.

'Hi, Leila!' Shelly said when she picked up. 'I was going to call you later. How are you? How's Ollie?'

'Hi, Mum. We're all great.' She filled her in on all her news. 'How about you, any news on the house?'

'Yes, as a matter of fact, there is,' Shelly said, sounding excited. 'Jake and I have made the decision to definitely go ahead with the renovations.'

'Great stuff, Mum!'

'And the best bit is that I'm setting up a new business as well!' Her enthusiasm was infectious as she told Leila all about her conversation with Rosa.

'Sounds like a decent plan,' Leila said. 'Are you certain you'll manage on your own?'

'Well that's just it,' her mother said. 'I was going to see if you'd come down for a little bit after Christmas. Jake is going to do what he can. There's an old woodwork studio here, so he's right at home.' She explained about the stairs and how Jake was flinging himself into working on them.

They finished their chat and Shelly promised to book her flights home for Christmas and send on the details. Leila said she'd talk to Fee tonight about Christmas dinner, while Shelly should mention it to Jake. She suggested it would be easier for them all to be together this year.

'The first Christmas without Gerry is going to be heart-breaking,' Shelly said, as her voice caught in a sob.

'Oh Mum, we'll be with you.'

The rest of the day passed in a blur of feeding and baby bathing and cuddling. At six o'clock, Leila started getting things ready and setting the table. She gave Ollie his bottle and settled him in his bouncy seat. Matthew arrived first, looking animated.

'How was your day?' she asked. 'You look like you've won the Lotto!'

'I may as well have,' he said. 'You won't believe it! I got the agency for Lexus for the garage.'

'That's amazing, love. You've been trying for that for a long time. It'll bring a whole new element to the place.'

'It means I can dump some of the less expensive models and try to get away from second-hand cars altogether. The repairs will continue, and seeing as I was servicing most of the Lexus cars in Dublin as it was, this just makes it official.'

'Fee is on the way. I think we should have a glass of wine to celebrate and toast your success.'

Leila hadn't had a drink since finding out she was pregnant.

She had been sorely tempted at times since Ollie was born, but she'd known that if she started, she would have trouble stopping. Tonight, though, things felt good and positive, and she was more than ready to toast a good day all round. Matthew uncorked a bottle and got out two glasses.

'Big moment,' he said, grinning at her. 'I wasn't there to get you that G and T you craved. But your first drink in nine months! This should be good.'

He poured and handed her a glass. Slowly she raised it to her lips and sipped. It tasted absolutely divine. My God, she'd missed that. She could feel the wine relaxing her immediately. She savoured each drop. Matthew put a match to the fire, scooped Ollie onto his lap, and the three of them enjoyed the cosy mood.

'This is one of the positive things about not breast-feeding,' she said sadly as she enjoyed her wine.

'You're not still worried about it, are you, love?' Matthew asked.

'I was a bit,' she said, realising it wasn't something a man could properly appreciate. 'But I'm feeling better about it now.'

'Good.' He smiled, nodding at her wine glass. 'That's the best consolation prize I could give you.'

Fee arrived soon afterwards and practically melted into the armchair.

'Wow, that was a seriously busy day. Thank you so much for inviting me over, Leila. I know I would've gone to bed with nothing to eat otherwise. Plus it's nice to be able to sit and chat to people who aren't patients.'

'I'm glad you came. Will you stay the night here?'

'Yeah, if you don't mind, that'd be lovely. Then I can have a glass of wine. I'd love that.'

They chatted about anything and everything and Leila brought up the subject of Christmas.

'I know you might need to go to your folks,' she said to Fee, 'but maybe you and Jake could stay here that night and you could juggle the two?'

'I'll think about how to arrange it,' Fee said. 'And who else will be coming? Would your parents join us, Matthew, seeing as little Oliver is on the scene?'

Matthew's parents had gone to live in the North soon after he'd left school. They had little or no contact and he preferred it that way.

'Not a hope,' he said. 'It's weird, I know, but they didn't have any interest in me and it won't change for Ollie. They're funny fish, and I've long since come to the realisation that I'm better off concentrating on what matters.'

'I understand,' Fee said. 'My folks are as odd as two left feet. I get my sanity from the Dillons.'

'Cripes!' Leila laughed, filling up her wine glass. 'If you're both looking to us lot for normality, I think you're barking up the wrong tree!'

The three of them burst out laughing.

'All jokes aside, though,' Matthew said, 'what you guys have is rare and wonderful. You all get along and you look out for one another. Not every family has that.'

'I agree,' said Fee. 'My parents are stuck in a time warp. They're so set in their ways, and there are times when I feel like shaking them.'

'But they're happy, aren't they?' Leila asked.

'I suppose they are, in their own way. I find it a bit depressing, though. They don't go out, don't go on holiday and don't see anyone.'

'Will you ask them to come to Christmas dinner all the same?' Leila asked. She'd never met Fee's parents, but she figured they couldn't be *that* bad. After all, Fee was about as trendy and with-it as you could get.

'I'll certainly mention it to them, but I don't think they'll even entertain the idea,' Fee said.

The dinner was delicious. Leila made potato gratin and spinach and Matthew cooked the steaks. Luckily, all of them were happy to eat them well done.

'I think I may have been a bit overzealous with the frying pan,' he said with a grin.

'Yup, mine looks like it's been scorched by a flame-thrower. But we won't worry. Top up my wine glass there, Matthew. There's no drought as far as I'm aware!'

Fee offered to give Ollie his bottle, and Leila asked her to do it in his bedroom.

'According to the book I'm reading, he's to get his bedtime feed in a dimly lit room before being put into his cot. The idea is that he'll sleep all night.'

'What's the longest he's slept so far?' Fee asked. 'I need to know all these things for when we have a baby.'

'Are you planning one?' Leila asked, looking excited.

'Not just yet. But some day. I think we'll do the wedding first and then see.'

Matthew and Leila, fuelled by the red wine, had a little cuddle on the sofa while Fee and Ollie were gone.

'It's nice to have you all to myself for a minute,' Matthew said. 'Our lives have changed so much, haven't they? One second we're in the flat, and now look at us. We're parents and about to move into our own amazing home.'

'It's pretty great really,' Leila said. In her own head, she had let go of the breastfeeding issue. She needed to be thankful for what she had. Enough was enough and she was going to concentrate on enjoying her life.

Fee appeared a short while later, looking as if she were ready to drop.

'The dimly lit room and swishy music you have up there has worked on me, never mind baby Ollie. I'm hitting the sack. I've to be up early anyway. I'm going Christmas shopping.'

'Night, honey,' Leila said, standing to kiss her. 'Oops, I think I'm a little tipsy!'

'Good for you!' Fee laughed. 'Would you like me to take the baby monitor and give you guys a break tonight? I'm not working tomorrow, so I can sleep in the afternoon if I need to.'

Leila looked at Matthew and smiled. 'Are you sure?'

'Of course! It's my godmotherly duty.'

Leila and Matthew decided to leave the cleaning-up until the morning and cracked open another bottle of wine.

'I don't want much more,' Leila said. 'I'll be pie-eyed and I can't afford to be dying with a hangover tomorrow. Mum is coming back in a matter of days and I need to get the Christmas food ordered.'

Matthew made it very clear that he didn't give a hoot about anything other than Leila. As they moved together, he whispered, 'Is it too soon to make love?'

'No, I don't think so,' she said.

'I've missed you,' he said. 'We'll be gentle, and you tell me if you need to stop.'

As they made love, Leila felt pretty uncomfortable physically and didn't exactly enjoy it, but she certainly felt as if they were a real couple again. Pleasantly fuzzy from the wine, she went up to bed and fell into a deep sleep.

Chapter 24

FEE HAD ENJOYED MINDING BABY OLLIE LAST night. He was the sweetest little dumpling. He'd been so good and had only woken once. She still hadn't spoken to Jake properly, but her night with Leila and Matthew had calmed her down. The talk of Christmas and all the plans had made her feel sorry they'd argued. She loved Jake to bits and didn't want to carry on with the bad feeling.

It was early in the morning, and as Ollie drank his bottle, she dialled Jake's mobile. She hoped he was awake and would pick up. He was as stubborn as a mule when it came to saying sorry or putting things to one side.

'Hey,' he said amidst dreadful noise.

'Hi,' she said. 'Where are you? It sounds really noisy. I wasn't even sure you'd be awake, let alone out somewhere.'

'I'm in the workshop and there's a sander on.'

'How are you?' she asked tentatively.

'Better than I've been for ages,' he said. 'I'm loving this, Fee. I got up at five o'clock this morning and came straight out here. I've been ploughing away with the radio on and it's like I'm a teenager again.'

'Great,' she said, feeling confused. 'Have you spoken to Shelly about your flying ban?'

'Nope, and I don't intend doing so. Just forget about it until we have to deal with it, okay?'

'Jake,' she sighed. 'I'm not getting this. Why are you so relaxed about the fact that the career you fought tooth and nail for could be slipping through your fingers?'

'Life is precious, Fee. Life is short. What will be will be. Stressing constantly and ending up with ulcers, or even worse, a heart attack, just isn't worth it.'

'But Jake—'

'But nothing,' he interrupted. 'Mum has enough going on right now. As far as she's concerned, I'm here with her for a bit. We'll be home the day after tomorrow for Christmas. So let's just see what happens, okay?'

Fee knew that she wasn't going to get Jake to see things the way she did. Maybe he was right and she was wrong. But this wasn't the guy she'd fallen in love with. This wasn't the guy she knew, full stop.

She stayed with baby Ollie until Leila appeared. When she did, it was obvious she was feeling the effects of the wine.

'Will you be okay? Is Matthew working all day?' Fee asked. 'I can stay here if you need me this morning?'

'He'll be home at lunchtime because it's Saturday. I'll be fine. I don't think I'll drink the guts of a bottle of red wine on my own again, mind you. It's not so great with a baby to mind!'

Fee fed her paracetamol, then packed up her things and headed home to put on a wash. As she gazed around at the empty, silent house, she got that feeling again. She couldn't say it to Jake, but she didn't consider this house to be hers as well as his. Gerry had paid for it. But he'd left the money to Jake, not her.

The sooner they could save up and move to a bigger house, one that had *both* their money behind it, the happier she would be. They still had the deposit they'd managed to save before Gerry died. Fee had been squirrelling as much cash into it as she could, topping it up regularly and ensuring it was growing nicely. All the extra shifts were starting to pay off. She hadn't bought an item of clothing or a pair of shoes in months. Everything she did was channelled into their savings.

The fact that she wasn't paying rent at home any longer was making a massive difference too. She'd been giving her parents a generous contribution ever since starting her first job. She'd told Jake that she'd give him rent money for this house, but he'd blown her out of the water.

'Why on earth would you do that? The beauty of having this place paid for is that we don't have a noose around our necks.'

But how would her plans come to fruition if Jake was going to dump his career and become a carpenter, of all things? This wasn't what she'd planned, and quite frankly, it wasn't what she'd signed up for.

Feeling confused and dreadfully worried, she drank a coffee while texting Norah to see if she was free. No luck. She was shopping with her sisters. Fee hoped she might ask her to come and join them, but no such invite was forthcoming. This was the downside of working so hard, she thought to herself: it meant you had very few friends. She finished her coffee and decided to visit her parents.

As always on a Saturday, they'd been to the supermarket, cleaned the already clean house and were now having a rasher and egg for lunch.

'We didn't know you were coming,' her mother said, looking hassled. 'I'll make you some now.'

'Stay sitting, Mum,' she said. 'I'm only dropping in to see if you need anything. I'm going shopping for the afternoon.'

The conversation was stilted. She knew they were unhappy with her. They'd been furious about her moving out and living in sin, as they put it. But she'd chosen to ignore that. She had learned many years ago that her parents didn't approve of most of what she did. From the day she'd got highlights in her hair to the time she'd come home saying she wanted to be a doctor, she'd been met with disapproval. Her mother thought she should be a housewife and her father wasn't allowed to have an opinion.

Until now she'd just done her own thing and taken the flak, but she was getting a bit fed up with their attitude.

She decided to plunge straight in to the topic of Christmas.

'I was wondering if you'd consider coming to Jake's family home for Christmas dinner this year. On account of Gerry passing away, Leila thought it would be nice if we all got together.'

There was silence as her mother stared at her, knife and fork held aloft, mid-chew, frozen in shock.

'You don't have to answer now,' Fee said. 'Maybe you'd think it over, though.'

'Fiona,' her mother managed. 'We paid for our turkey back in October. The ham is ordered from Mr Lindsey's butcher shop, the same as it has been since before you were born. Why would we want to do something different on Christmas Day, especially at a moment's notice?'

'Because I'm asking you to, that's why. My life is changing, Mum. I'm with Jake now. His mother is a widow and I thought you might have it in you to dig deep and find some sort of Christian values.'

'Now hold on a minute, Fiona,' Dermot said, white-faced. 'Your mother and I are the most Christian people I know. We have strong values, we don't drink or smoke or take the Lord's name in vain. We're—'

'Dad.' Fee put her hand over his. 'I'm not trying to start a row. I only wanted to make a suggestion. Clearly it's not welcome. So how about we pretend I never said anything?'

'You can't unsay it, Fiona,' Deirdre said dramatically.

'Okay then,' Fee said. 'I *did* say it, but you don't want to do it, so that's the end of the story.' She stood up and pulled on her coat.

'Thanks for coming over, dear,' Dermot said. He was about to smile when Deirdre took over.

'You've ruined our lunch. You've upset the apple cart and you've suggested that your father and I are less than charitable. Christmas? Huh, this is more like Purgatory. And by our own daughter's hand.'

Fee knew she was going to say something she'd regret. Her hands were shaking and she honestly wanted to grab her mother's birdlike shoulders and shake her until her teeth rattled in her head.

Clenching her jaw shut, and without so much as a backward glance, she turned and walked out of the house.

She would have given anything to be able to call Jake and meet up with him to talk about it and laugh it off. He could always make her laugh when she was stressed, especially about her parents. But Jake was far away and there was no one else. Sighing, she started the car and turned in the direction of the shops, knowing she had to sort out the last of her Christmas presents.

At the shopping centre, she started with a large cappuccino and a sugary pastry before picking out rather extravagant gifts for all of Jake's family, even though she was well aware that throwing money at people wasn't what it was all about. Particularly with the Dillon family. They cherished togetherness. All the same, they'd be her people going forward and she wanted them to know that she appreciated them. She struggled when buying her parents' gifts, partly because there was nothing they liked, and partly because she was so cross with them.

It was early evening by the time she was snaking her way through the traffic on her way home. When she reached the house, she was taken aback to see that the lights were on. Opening the front door, she called out cautiously. Jake appeared at the top of the stairs, wearing a tracksuit and with wet hair.

'Hey,' he said, walking down the stairs. 'I tried calling you, but you didn't answer.'

'Ah shoot, sorry. I went to see my parents earlier and I put my phone on silent. I must've forgotten to turn it back on. I didn't know you were coming home. I thought you were staying in the workshop being a whittler for the rest of your life.' She couldn't hide the sour edge to her voice.

He stared at her as if he was going to argue, but changed his mind.

'I got a call from Jim. I've to attend my disciplinary the day after tomorrow,' he said with a shrug. 'All the flights were booked up, so I had to come today. Mum is following tomorrow. Listen, I've been having the most amazing time down in Spain. I can't wait to show you Casa Maria. I think you'll love it.'

'Jake!' she said, dropping the bags on the floor and walking swiftly towards him. 'How can you tell me that you've to attend a disciplinary the day after tomorrow and swiftly move on to telling me about Spain? This is major. What if you lose your job? What does Shelly think of all of this?'

'Mum was thrilled to see me working with wood.'

'She *does* know about your work situation, doesn't she?' Fee asked.

'You worry too much,' Jake said as he hugged her and kissed her on the lips. There was a spark in his eyes that she hadn't seen for a long time.

'What will be will be, Fee. I told you that this morning. I'm sick of being worried and stressed out. Maybe it's a sign. Maybe I need to stop being a pilot for a while. Maybe forever.'

Her heart stopped. She stood back from him and looked at him as if she didn't recognise him.

'But what would you do instead?'

'Let's not worry about it now,' he said firmly. 'I can't tell you what's going to happen until I speak to the men in suits. For now, I've made roast chicken and we are going to plan a trip to Spain.'

Fee didn't tell Jake about her parents and how difficult they'd been. She didn't tell him that she wanted to try and buy a bigger and better house. She didn't say that she thought the entire notion of this hacienda was insane. Instead she sat looking at photo after photo after photo on his phone, pretending she was fine.

After dinner, she went for a shower. Only then did she allow the tears to fall. She'd spent so many years in her parents' house acting. Acting as if she was happy with her life. Acting as if she felt she belonged. Acting as if it was her perfect home. What had kept her going was the notion that someday she'd be free. And then the promise that she and Jake would forge a new and better life together. Jake got her. He shared the same ambition and drive. They were on the same page.

But now it seemed she was on her own once again. Living in a house where she was out of sync with everyone else. Pretending to be something she wasn't in order to keep the peace. It was eating her up inside, and she honestly didn't know for how long she could continue to do this.

Chapter 25

SHELLY DECIDED TO DROP BY CASA MARIA ON HER way to the airport. She'd settled up with Valentina and they'd exchanged gifts. She gave Valentina perfume and a brooch she'd found in a market in Marbella. Valentina gave her a beautiful necklace and some flowers pressed from her garden. It was so thoughtful, and the two women were half crying and half laughing as they wished each other a Merry Christmas. Shelly had no firm plans as to when she'd be back, but she assured Valentina that it would be soon.

'Now that we're getting things started, I can't bear to be away from here. I'm so excited about this.'

She made her way to Casa Maria, feeling sad to say goodbye to it too. She had a small gift for Alejandro, which she intended to leave for him to find. As it happened, he was at the house. As Shelly walked down the driveway, she heard him having an animated conversation with a man she didn't recognise.

'Is everything okay?' she asked, as he approached her, looking ruddy-faced.

'No, *señora*. It's bad, bad, bad.' He shook his head and tutted. '*Es el techo,*' he said, pointing upwards.

'The ceiling?' Shelly asked, scrunching up her nose as she attempted to translate.

'No.' He shook his head again and scratched. '*El techo* . . . eh, roof.'

'The roof? What's wrong?' Shelly asked.

'She broken. Much of roof broken. Man here, he say that we need to fix all.'

'Replace the entire roof?' Shelly asked, astounded. 'Really? How come we didn't know this before?'

'I find problem when I go to fix big bedroom here,' Alejandro said, pointing up at the main bedroom at the front of the house. He took Shelly up and showed her where there was some discoloration in the ceiling. She'd noticed it before, but hadn't thought it was anything too worrying.

'Roof, she is rotten. She have bad fungus living in wood.' He handed her a quote that the man had just shown him. 'This is best price I can find,' he said.

Shelly gasped when she saw it. 'Thirty thousand euros!'

Alejandro nodded gravely. 'I sorry, Señora Shelly.'

Her head reeled. What had Jake said – *as long as there are no nasty surprises*? Well, this was about as nasty as a surprise could get.

'It's not your fault Alejandro,' she said quickly. 'Look, you'll have to leave it with me. I'm going back to Ireland for Christmas with my children. I will call you. I don't have this much money to spare. I need to think about it.'

He nodded sadly, as if he'd known this might be the case. A car horn beeped, and Shelly turned to see the taxi driver waving at her from outside the gate.

'I have to go,' she said. 'Merry Christmas, Alejandro. I'll think it over and look at the figures, and we'll talk as soon as I get back. Take care.'

* * *

The flight was crowded and boisterous. Shelly sat stiffly in her seat, mentally going through the figures, considering the options, trying to find a solution. She was preoccupied for the whole flight, and by the time she landed in Dublin, she had pretty much decided, with a heavy heart, that she needed to cut her losses and sell Casa Maria.

If she paid for the roof to be fixed and the place didn't work out as a guest house, she'd be bunched. She couldn't afford to leave herself open to massive debt at this point in her life.

She wanted to sit down and have a good cry about it, but this wasn't the time. As the taxi sped towards her house, she gave herself a good talking-to, insisting that she had to be upbeat and positive in front of the children. She had to enjoy Ollie and be fully present with him. She had to get through Christmas. After that, she could go to pieces. But not until then.

The taxi dropped her off and she rooted in her bag for her keys and unlocked the front door. It felt like she was stepping into someone else's home. She stood in the hallway and called out tentatively, 'Hello?'

The living-room door burst open and Leila came running out, pulling her into a hug.

'You're here,' Leila squealed. 'I've missed you so much.'

Shelly smiled and let herself be led into the living room, where she was delighted to find Matthew, Ollie, Fee and Jake waiting for her.

'Everyone is here,' she said, and promptly burst into tears.

'Mum,' said Jake, rushing to hug her. 'Come on now.'

'I'm just so happy to see you all,' she blubbed. 'And little

Ollie – oh, come here and give me a hug, you gorgeous thing.'

Ollie was passed to her and they all sat down. Matthew went to bring in the tea, coffee and cakes he'd prepared on trays. Shelly held Ollie close, delighting in his warmth and baby smell.

As they passed round the drinks and caught up with one another, Leila asked her about Casa Maria and how things were progressing. Shelly was tempted to gloss over it and not say anything about the roof, but then decided it was better to get it out of the way and not have to worry about letting it slip over Christmas.

'We've hit a problem,' she said.

Jake sat forward, immediately concerned. 'What is it? I'm coming back in the new year, I can help sort it.'

Fee shot him a look, but said nothing.

'I'm afraid it's bigger than any of us can fix,' Shelly said, willing herself not to break down in tears. 'We've discovered that the roof is rotten. It all has to come off and be replaced.'

'Oh God,' Jake groaned. 'How much will that cost?'

Shelly took a deep breath. 'Thirty thousand euros. More than I can afford, I'm afraid.'

Jake frowned, and a stubborn look crossed his face that Shelly knew only too well. He looked just like Gerry when he did that. It usually meant wild horses weren't going to drag him away from whatever he'd decided to do.

'There has to be a way,' he said, his voice hard. 'We can't give up. I know the others haven't seen it yet, but I've been trying to convince them to come to Spain to ring in the New Year. Matthew can swing the time off. Leila and Ollie are up for it, aren't you?'

Leila nodded.

Shelly looked at Fee. She had an odd look on her face, but she forced a smile and said, 'Sounds good. I'll see what I can do. But don't let me hamper your plans.'

Jake looked preoccupied as the others talked about novel ideas for raising money, and how to organise the New Year celebrations. Shelly held on to Ollie as if her life depended upon it.

'Oh, I've missed this little man. I don't know if I'm right to be down in Spain while my only grandchild is here. Maybe this problem has cropped up to tell me to stay here with all of you.'

'Nonsense,' Jake said emphatically. 'It's just a temporary setback. We should have expected it really, the house is so old.'

'And once we get settled in our new place, I'll be freer to come and see you in Spain,' said Leila. 'Ollie is doing really well now too. He's a little bruiser, as you can see.'

'But you're going back to work soon,' Shelly said. 'You'll need my help and I won't be here.'

'We'll work it out, Shelly,' Matthew said. 'None of us wants you to regret things. You've been certain you really want to do this. There were always going to be problems to overcome along the way.'

'Sure, if the worst comes to the worst,' Leila said, 'you could sell it once it's renovated and get your money back.'

'And if Dad was alive today,' Jake added, 'you'd most certainly be moving over there to do the renovations, as he'd planned. So you're not abandoning anyone. We can come to you whenever you like.'

'And you can come home any time, too,' Leila said.

'You're very quiet, Fee,' Shelly said. 'What do you think?'

Fee looked up, surprised to be asked. 'Oh, er, well I'm not . . . I mean, it's your decision, Shelly.'

'I know, but all of your opinions matter to me.'

Fee squirmed as they all looked at her. A part of her brain was screaming at her to lie, but she was sick to the back teeth of lying.

'I'm probably a bit out of the loop,' she said carefully, 'and I haven't seen it, but I think old buildings can quickly become a money pit. You've got a long time left to live, all going well, so you have to think about providing for yourself. If you sink your savings and Gerry's pension into this one thing, there's a chance you'll lose all that money and regret it later. I'd be more inclined to play it safe and sell it on. There are plenty of projects you could take on here in Ireland, and that way you wouldn't be away from your family.'

When she finished speaking, there was total silence. She felt her face flushing red and cursed herself for speaking her mind. She glanced over at Jake. He looked so angry, she wouldn't have been surprised if he'd stood up and ordered her to get out.

Shelly spoke first, obviously sensing how the mood had changed. 'Thank you so much, Fee,' she said, nodding her head. 'It's essential to consider the opposing viewpoint, especially when it comes to big life decisions. Thank you for being brave enough to give it to me. I'll take everything on board and think it over carefully.'

Later on, they cooked dinner together and slowly the mood levelled out again. Shelly asked Fee about her job and was delighted to hear how well it was going.

'There were times in the past few years when I honestly thought I'd go mad,' Fee admitted. 'The hours didn't reflect my pay packet. But now it's a lot better.'

Shelly adored Fee. She was bright, ambitious and such a beautiful girl. In skinny jeans and a tight-fitting long-sleeved T-shirt, with a silk scarf tied at her neck, she looked like someone from a catalogue. And today she had shown a new side – the ability to be honest in the face of those who disagreed with her standpoint. Shelly could tell that Jake was annoyed with Fee for what she'd said, but she greatly admired her for it. Jake might not realise it now, but being with someone who would stand up to him at the important moments was a very good thing. Fee had risen even higher in Shelly's estimation on the back of her comments about Casa Maria.

She was also delighted to see how Leila was coping, and how besotted she and Matthew were with Ollie. They made a wonderful family.

Jake was her worry. There was something not right with him. She knew he'd tell her at some point, but she also knew her son was struggling. He'd been so close to Gerry and she was worried that he felt outnumbered in the family now.

While he and Matthew got on just fine, they had no real connection. They wouldn't go for a pint or a run together. Shelly made a mental note to go for a walk on her own with Jake at some point over the next few days, in the hope that he might open up to her.

As she climbed into bed later that night, she was still going over the Casa Maria problem from every angle. The kids were being wonderful about it. But while she understood them wanting her to fulfil Gerry's wishes, she would be the one who stood to lose her shirt if it all went wrong. She had nobody to back her up if that happened. Nobody to turn to. Fee was right: she needed to be cautious. This was too big a project to take on out of a sense of nostalgia. It couldn't be just for Gerry; it had to be for her, and it had to make sense.

Chapter 26

THE FOLLOWING MORNING, IT WASN'T ONLY THE front lawn that was frosty as Jake put on his suit and prepared for his disciplinary hearing. He was still upset about Fee's comments about Casa Maria yesterday. He couldn't for the life of him understand why she would try to talk Shelly into selling it. He'd explained how he felt about it, yet there she was, being all conservative and suggesting they just let it go. Every time he thought of it, he felt his blood boil. For her part, Fee was clearly incredibly annoyed with him and his attitude to today's hearing. They got ready in silence, until finally he couldn't bear the tension any longer.

'It'll get sorted, I promise,' he said, trying to catch her hand so he could hug her.

'Whatever you say, Jake. As you've been at pains to point out, it's *your* life, and what will be will be.'

They parted without a goodbye kiss, a strained silence separating them.

The drive to the airport was a weird one. It suddenly hit him, with unexpected force, that this could be his last time driving there as a licensed pilot. Now that he was faced with the prospect, it didn't seem like such a marvellous idea. His father would turn in his grave if he knew what was happening. For the first time in ages, Jake didn't feel he could talk to Gerry. Instead, he felt ashamed and foolhardy. He tried to find his earlier carefree attitude, but he was tense and anxious and suddenly fearful of the outcome and the repercussions it would have on his whole life.

When he walked into the room where the hearing would be held, there were six people waiting for him behind the table, five men and a woman. None of them looked exactly welcoming, until he spotted Jim at the far end. His immediate thought was to smile and raise a hand in greeting. Jim moved his head only slightly, but Jake knew he shouldn't acknowledge him.

'So, Mr Dillon,' the woman said. 'We've looked over your files and we've discussed your record over the time of your employment. Your boss, Jim Byrne has spoken out on your behalf.'

'Thank you,' Jake said. He knew that the worst thing would be to hang his head, so he sat ramrod straight and faced his destiny like a man.

The talking went on for quite a while, and slowly the colour drained from his face as it became apparent that two of the board were intent on revoking his pilot's licence. His mouth went dry and he glanced over at Jim, who was looking grave and worried. Jake honestly felt he was scuppered. They asked him to leave the room while they agreed on their final decision.

As he paced up and down in the corridor outside, he realised that he needed Gerry more than he ever had before. He begged his dad to forgive him and to allow him to continue to fly.

When he was called back into the room, he tried to remain calm. Why had he thought this didn't matter any more? All his hard work was about to be wiped away. Fee's anxious face and tortured look came rushing back. He'd been a total moron. He'd broken his promises to her and left her wondering who the hell he was.

And Shelly – she had enough to cope with right now. What if he had to go home and say, *Merry Christmas, Mum, I'm now unemployed . . .* The thought made him shudder.

Jim was the one who stood up to deliver the panel's verdict.

'The decision wasn't unanimous, Mr Dillon,' he said, 'but the majority has ruled that you will be allowed to return to work, subject to a routine exam. You would be due to sit one at this time anyway.'

The regular exams were the bane of Jake's life, but he'd got used to them. Like all the other pilots, he knew they were compulsory in order to hold on to his qualification. Jim had told him he'd need to sit an extra one if he were to take up his new post as captain. So he should've been studying instead of fluting about acting as if he were a teenager on a gap year.

'Really?' he asked, looking astonished. His legs felt like jelly. 'Thank you so very much. I appreciate your faith in me.'

'There's no thanks required,' the woman said. 'Just take this as a very severe warning and don't pull a reckless stunt like this again. For the record, you were dangerously close to being over the limit. Had that been the case, you would *never* have flown as a pilot again.'

Jake walked out of the room and up the corridor before leaning against the wall and gulping in deep breaths. Thank God for Jim. Clearly he'd saved Jake's skin. Apparently the airline would get in touch and tell him when he was to take the test. The ball was in their court for now. He was too terrified to ask whether or not his promotion was still on offer. Either way, he knew he'd be thrilled to be reinstated in any job with the airline.

Relieved beyond belief, he sent a text to Jim, thanking him and telling him he very much looked forward to seeing him at Christmas dinner the day after tomorrow. Leila had asked Jim to come along, and he'd accepted. It would be nice to relax together for a change, without Jake's mistake hanging over them.

Fee was still at work, so Jake texted her too, to let her know he was off the hook. He also apologised for his cavalier attitude, hoping that would smooth things over between them. She didn't reply.

He'd done no Christmas shopping, so next he drove to the shopping centre. It took him almost two hours to get into the car park and find a space, but he knew he needed to get sorted. It was late by the time he reached home. Not sure of when Fee had said she'd finish her shift, he showered and went to bed to watch television. Terrified to even have a glass of wine to celebrate, he opted for a cup of tea. He was utterly exhausted, and fell asleep next to the empty space in the bed.

Jake woke up alone on Christmas Eve. He reckoned Fee had a long surgery and had opted to stay in the hospital. He had slept well and now felt reinvigorated, so glad to have the cloud gone from over his head. He resolved to make Christmas as good as it could be without Gerry, and to make things up to Fee. He dressed quickly and headed straight over to Shelly's to help with preparations there.

When he got to the house, it was empty. Someone had made an effort to put the decorations up, but had obviously abandoned it quickly. Jake knew how they felt – putting up decorations when Gerry wasn't here to share Christmas with them seemed like sacrilege. But it was baby Ollie's first Christmas, and Jake was damned if he was going to let him be photographed in a sad-looking, dark house with no life in it.

He set to work untangling the Christmas tree lights – the job from hell. He worked solidly for about two hours before he heard a key in the lock and bright voices coming towards him. The door to the sitting room opened, and Leila stopped in surprise. Her hand flew to her mouth.

'Oh,' she gasped. 'You've done it. Oh Jake, it looks fantastic. I tried, but . . .' She trailed off, and Jake went over and hugged her.

'I know. It was too hard. I thought I'd surprise you by getting it done.'

She leaned against his chest. 'Thank you,' she whispered.

Shelly came in, and oohed and aahed over the transformation.

'We have to make sure Ollie has a good first Christmas,' Jake said, tickling his nephew. 'And where did they cart you off to, little man?'

Leila smiled. 'We went to look at my new house!'

'It's just gorgeous,' Shelly said. 'And you're near enough to babysit loads, Jake.'

'That thought never crossed our minds,' Leila joked.

Jake grinned and swatted her arm. 'Yeah, right. I've no doubt my every day off between now and his twenty-first is already pencilled in.'

'You better believe it,' Leila said. 'Right, this darling boy is tired out now. I'll go put him down for a nap and we'll have a coffee.'

When Leila and Ollie left the room, Shelly seized the opportunity to talk to him.

'Jake, I don't want to pry, but I've a feeling all is not well with you.'

He sighed deeply. 'I'm okay now,' he said. 'I didn't want to worry you before, but I had a bit of trouble at work. I was spot-checked and was almost over the limit to fly.'

Shelly looked shocked; she couldn't help it. Jake and Gerry had both been so disciplined and careful about alcohol. They took their responsibilities very seriously. She couldn't believe Jake had slipped up like this.

'It's okay,' he said quickly. 'The hearing was yesterday morning and I got away with an official caution. Jim spoke up for me and said that my track record was impeccable. He even mentioned Dad.' Jake looked ashen-faced. 'I felt so ashamed, Mum. I wasn't over the limit, thanks be to God. But it was too close for comfort.'

Shelly took a deep breath. 'Your father would have gone into a total meltdown if he heard this, I won't lie. But you're a good man, Jake. What happened?' She looked him in the eye, and it was as if a mist had lifted. 'Don't bother telling me it was a mistake. I'm your mother and I know you far better than that. If you drank too much, you did it knowing that was what you were doing. Why did you take a risk like that?'

Jake looked shocked for a second, then his shoulders sagged and he rubbed a hand over his face. 'You're right,' he said, so quietly she had to strain to hear him. 'I can't bear to admit it, but . . . yeah, I did know what I was doing. I think I did it on purpose, Mum,' he said, looking stricken. 'I didn't know if I wanted to be a pilot any more.'

The words hung in the air, and Shelly's heart broke for her son.

'How do you feel now?' she asked, keeping her voice steady. He didn't need a dramatic scene right now; he needed understanding.

'I'm so relieved that they didn't ban me for life. I'm delighted that I have a choice now. After all, I've put so much work into getting where I am.'

'But you're still not one hundred per cent sure that you want to keep flying?' Shelly asked.

He nodded sadly.

'Have you told Fee?'

He stared directly at her. 'What do you think, Mum? How can I tell her that I think there's a strong possibility I'd rather sit in the workshop at the back of Casa Maria and make pieces for the staircase than fly a plane and earn decent money?'

'Fee loves you, Jake. You need to talk to her. And in the meantime, what have you decided about work? When will you go back, if you decide to do that?'

'Jim just called. I have two weeks' leave of absence. I've to report to my superior prior to each flight, and I've been fined and slapped on the hand.'

'Did you tell Jim that you're considering not going back?' Shelly asked.

'God, no! How could I when he stuck his neck out for me like that?'

'No, I don't suppose you could.' Shelly sighed. 'Don't make any rash decisions just yet. Let's get through tomorrow and enjoy the time together first.'

'Thanks, Mum.'

'That's okay, love,' she said, hugging him. 'I just want you to be happy.'

Shelly bit her lip. She'd come home to Ireland feeling that she ought to sell Casa Maria because it would be in her family's best interests. Now she was confused. Selling the hacienda was going to break her heart, and by the sounds of it, Jake was firmly against that idea too. She was beginning to suspect that Casa Maria was some kind of a lifeline for him, a comfort zone in a world that felt colder and more uncertain without his father in it. She was really torn in two about her decision.

Jake's mobile phone started ringing.

'Hi, Fee,' he said, pulling his fingers through his hair.

Shelly went over to the box of decorations, to give him space to take the call. She began to take out the old bunting, smoothing the strings out, ready for hanging.

'What do you mean?' Jake said loudly. He looked more and more agitated as he listened to Fee. 'Okay. Do whatever you have to do . . . Right . . . Yeah, well I'm staying here tonight as planned. See you later.'

He put his phone back in his pocket and looked exasperated. 'She's working tomorrow,' he said in a flat voice.

'On Christmas Day!' Shelly said. 'How come that wasn't arranged before now?'

'It was, apparently, but someone is sick and Fee felt she should offer to stand in, seeing as she's new. Apparently the other surgeon who was in line to do it has kids.'

'Well . . . that's fair enough, I suppose,' Shelly said.

'The good news is that she will get New Year off. So maybe we can all go down to Spain,' Jake said hopefully. 'It would be lovely to spend a week with you.'

'Let's see what pans out,' Shelly said.

She'd love nothing more than to go to Rondilla, but she felt she needed to make a decision first. She didn't want to become any more attached to the place if she was going to have to sell it.

Chapter 27

CHRISTMAS DAY ENDED UP BEING BETTER THAN any of the Dillons had hoped. While there were plenty of tears, the addition of baby Ollie lifted their spirits no end. The fact that Jim was joining them too only added to the sense that they could get through this together.

Jake was disappointed that Fee had to go to work, but he figured there was no point in sulking as she couldn't do anything about it. Besides, it got him off the hook in terms of having to spend a long period of time with her miserable parents. He and Fee exchanged gifts early in the morning and she begged him to accompany her to Deirdre and Dermot's house for a quick visit before she went to the hospital.

They dropped in at a quarter to ten, catching her parents on the way out the door to mass.

'Happy Christmas,' Jake said, handing them a bunch of flowers and a bottle of whiskey. 'Sorry we can't stay longer. Fee has to work, as you know, and I need to get back to my mother.'

'God bless her, being a widow at this time of year,' Deirdre said. 'I'll light a candle for her at church this morning.'

'That's kind of you,' Jake said. 'I'll tell Mum. I know she'll appreciate it.'

'The good Lord would appreciate it if all your family took the time to go to mass,' Deirdre said.

'Mum!' Fee said.

'I meant no harm, Fiona. I was merely stating a fact.'

'I'm sure the good Lord has me down to a T by now,' Jake said easily. 'Enjoy mass and I hope to see you both soon.'

'Mass isn't a rock concert,' Deirdre said, straightening her hat. 'We don't go there to be entertained. We go to give thanks and to be part of a community.'

'Good for you,' Jake said, refusing to drop his cheery demeanour. 'Merry Christmas to you, Dermot,' he said. He dropped his voice. 'I hope you get a chance to have a couple of drams later on.'

'I do too,' said Dermot, a fleeting smile appearing on his lips.

'Can we drop you off at church on the way?' Fee asked.

'No thank you,' Deirdre said. 'We're all organised as usual. Goodbye, Fiona. Mind how you go, and put in a good day's work. Don't feel guilty about working on such an important day. I know you and Jake have no regard for such things.' She sniffed and walked towards the front door.

'Let's go,' Fee said to Jake, looking as if she might throttle her mother. 'See you, Dad. Take care. I've left gifts under the tree for both of you.'

'We bought you a goat to share,' Deirdre said.

'I hope you didn't cut him in half,' Jake said in feigned shock.

Deirdre looked him up and down with disdain. 'He's gone directly to a needy family in Africa.'

'Excellent,' Fee said, sighing.

'I hope he survives in the Jiffy bag,' Jake said.

Fee dug him in the ribs. 'Shut up,' she whispered.

As they drove off, Jake's shoulders were shaking.

'What's so funny?' Fee demanded, flaming with anger and irritation.

'Half a goat,' he said, and burst out laughing.

Fee grinned and looked out the window. He elbowed her and roared with laughter. In spite of her annoyance, Fee had to laugh too.

'There's nothing else for it, darling,' Jake said. 'If you take them seriously, you'll go insane.'

'Now can you see why I had to get out of there? Why it was worth studying my ass off to climb out of the fug of beige blandness and into a world where people have a life?'

'I get it,' he said. 'I always have. But you need to relax a little now, Fee. You've done it. You're amazing and I love you. The future is bright.'

'Can I paint our entire house neon pink?' Fee asked as she began to smile.

'If you want. With green spots perhaps?' They both laughed. 'Did you agree to work today so you wouldn't have to see them?' he asked.

She looked sheepish. 'It was a genuine last-minute panic, but yeah, I did volunteer very readily. I'll be back by ten this evening and we'll have a drink, okay? They'd never have agreed to come to your mum's, and I would've had to sit in their kitchen in silence with the highlight of the day being the *Coronation Street* Christmas special.'

Jake kissed her as she got out of the car. One of the other surgeons was giving her a lift home at the end of her shift.

'It'll all be better next year,' he said. 'Let's make a pact that we'll be married by then. If you're married to me, you have to make my dinner and sit with me, or else!'

'That sounds great,' she said, but she looked jaded.

Jake drove home hoping that lots of things would be different next year. He wanted Fee to be happier, but he wanted to be happier too.

By the time he got back to the house, the dinner preparations were well under way. The huge turkey was in the oven, and Leila was peeling a small mountain of potatoes. Leila and Matthew had insisted that Shelly relax and do nothing, which meant Shelly was on edge and things in the kitchen were a bit tense.

At four o'clock, Jim arrived, laden down with gifts for everyone. He was introduced to Ollie, and they lit the fire and opened the wine and enjoyed catching up with each other. By dinner time, Leila was a few glasses on and possibly not as meticulous as she needed to be for her first Christmas as chef. They ended up having to cook the turkey legs on the frying pan as they were still pink.

They all cried as they toasted Gerry, and Leila insisted they hold hands and make a vow that they would continue to look after one another. Jim did a second toast for Martha and they all cried again.

By half nine, Leila was done in. She apologised to everyone and went off to bed, taking Ollie with her. Jake and Matthew got stuck into the washing-up. Jim and Shelly sat by the fire, enjoying a final glass of wine.

'Well, you did it,' Jim said, raising his glass to her.

'Did what?'

'You survived your first Christmas as a widow.'

'Yes, I did,' Shelly said with a sad smile. 'And it's thanks to you all. I couldn't have done it without family and a good friend.'

'Next year won't be as hard,' he said. 'Time helps.'

Shelly nodded tiredly. 'I hope so,' she said.

'Jake tells me you're serious about the place in Spain? Gerry mentioned it to me, that he wanted to retire there with you. I thought it was a wonderful plan.'

'It was,' Shelly said, sighing, 'but I don't think it's going to work out after all.'

'Why not?' Jim asked. 'Have you lost your heart for it?'

'Oh no, quite the contrary. I've fallen in love with the place and I now feel happier there than I do here.'

'Fewer memories?' Jim said.

Shelly nodded. 'Exactly. And I've made friends there and it's a lovely community, but the thing is, just before I left, we found out that the roof is rotten. It would cost thirty thousand to repair it, and on top of the rest of the renovations, it's just too much.'

'You can't afford it?' Jim asked.

'No – and before you say it, Jim,' Shelly said quickly as Jim opened his mouth to speak, 'I won't accept any help. My one condition is that if I do this, I do it without loans. I don't want debt at this stage in my life.'

'Very wise,' Jim agreed. 'But that wasn't what I was going to say.' He leaned forward. 'Don't you realise that you have an extremely valuable asset right here?'

She looked at him, not taking his meaning for a moment.

'This place,' he said, gesturing around the room. 'The market is up at the moment, so you'd get a very good price for the house. If you sold it, that would free you up to finish the house in Spain and still have a nest egg to give you a sense of security as you get older.'

Shelly sat back suddenly, stunned by the obvious. Selling the house had never occurred to her before, but now that Jim had said it, she could see that it was a really good decision. The children were in their own homes now, she was here less and less, and it didn't feel like her home any more. Why hang on to a house that was far too big for one person? It was so clear all of a sudden that she started laughing.

Jim looked at her questioningly. 'Is that good laughter, or I've-just-lost-my-marbles laughter?'

Shelly laughed even harder. 'I lost my marbles long ago,' she said, making him smile. 'It's just . . . it's so obvious and it never, ever occurred to me. That's an absolutely brilliant solution, Jim.'

He nodded. 'Sometimes you need to bounce an idea off someone to get perspective. I'd say Gerry was planning to sell this place when the time was right. You've provided for the children, so what's left is rightfully yours. Use it to live the life that will make you happy.'

Shelly took his hand. 'Thank you. You're like another gift Gerry left to me, Jim. Your friendship is so important. And you've just lifted a weight from my shoulders tonight.'

Jim grinned at her. 'Glad to be of service. Now, do you think you could call a tipsy old man a taxi?'

Shelly laughed. 'Absolutely.'

Once Jim had been seen off safely, Shelly went into the kitchen, where Matthew and Jake were enjoying a post-clean-up beer.

'Do you two mind if I ask you something serious?' Shelly said. Her mind was buzzing with the house idea and she wanted to see if it would be met with resistance. This was, after all, her children's family home. They might have an opinion on what should happen to it.

'Sure,' Jake said.

'I'm asking you as Leila's representative,' Shelly said to Matthew.

'Right, this is definitely serious stuff,' he said, putting down his beer.

'I was telling Jim about Casa Maria, the roof, the cost, and he reminded me that I have a valuable asset at my disposal. This place.' She watched them carefully for their reaction, and to her relief they both smiled.

'Of course,' Matthew said. 'That makes total sense.'

'Are you absolutely sure?' Shelly said. 'If I keep it, you lot get it in the will. But if I sell it . . .'

'Don't even think about that for a second,' Jake admonished her. 'You and Dad have set me and Leila up for life. This house is yours. If you want to sell it to resurrect Casa Maria, I'm one hundred per cent behind you.'

'Me too,' Matthew said, nodding. 'And I think I can safely speak for Leila when I say that.'

'Oh good,' Shelly said, delighted. 'It had never occurred to me, but once Jim said it, like you say, Matthew, it makes sense.'

'Here's to saving Casa Maria,' Jake said.

'To Casa Maria,' Shelly and Matthew repeated.

'Right, well I'm exhausted after all that,' Shelly said. 'Thank you both so much for all your hard work today. It was lovely. I'll see you in the morning.'

'I'll head up too,' Matthew said. 'Any more of those beers and I'll be snoring loud enough to keep you all awake.'

'Fair enough,' Jake said. 'I'll wait for Fee.'

* * *

Jake stayed by the fire, eyes heavy, until after midnight. Finally he gave up and went to bed, leaving the lights on downstairs for Fee.

He woke again at two and felt the other side of the bed. Empty. He sat up and dialled her mobile number. It went to voicemail, so he left her a message asking her to call him.

He slept on and off until he heard the front door closing at three thirty. He listened as Fee crept quietly up the stairs, across the landing and into the bedroom.

'Where were you?' he whispered into the darkness.

'Oh, I thought you'd be asleep,' she said, sounding shocked.

'How could I be when I was waiting for you?'

'Sorry. Go to sleep.'

He turned over and did just that. He'd talk to her in the morning.

When Jake woke the next morning, it was already half nine. Yet again, the bed was empty. He smiled to himself. Fee was probably tucking into a turkey and ham breakfast. He pulled on a sweatshirt and trackie bottoms and followed the noise of chatter down the stairs.

'Morning!' he said, yawning. 'Are you all eating turkey and ham for breakfast?'

'Not quite,' Shelly said. 'But we will be having that for dinner!'

'I won't complain,' he said. 'Where's Fee?'

'We thought she was with you,' Leila said, looking up in alarm. 'Didn't she come back last night?'

'Yes, she did eventually,' Jake said. 'But I didn't know she was heading off again so quickly.'

He racked his brains to try and remember if she'd told him she was leaving early. She was always saying he didn't listen, so she must've said it at some point. He dialled her mobile; again it went straight to voicemail. With an angry sigh, he assumed she was back at work.

'We're going over to the new house today,' Leila said. 'We think we'll try and sleep there for a couple of nights and then go to Rondilla for New Year. Break the place in before we go see Casa Maria.'

'I've been on to Valentina. She can give us two rooms, and there's another room available at a guest house nearby if you and Fee think you could make it.' Shelly looked so hopeful that Jake knew he'd move mountains to make it happen.

'Sounds brilliant,' he said. 'I'd love everyone to see Casa Maria. It would be kind of like Dad being there to ring in the New Year as well, seeing as it was his idea.'

'I agree,' said Shelly.

Jake said he'd take on the responsibility of booking the flights, while the others got things ready to move to Leila and Matthew's new house. Once a good amount of stuff was packed and lined up in the hall, he and Matthew did a few trips, transferring all the essentials to the new place. When they were satisfied they had enough to keep them going, Jake drove over to his own house.

There was no sign of Fee, or that she'd even been there. They hadn't bothered putting up a Christmas tree or doing anything to make the place festive. Now he felt a bit bad. They'd have to make an effort to make the place more homely in future.

He smiled as he spied a pile of bridal magazines. Fee was so black-and-white, all business and no sign of frills, yet deep down she clearly had a bigger feminine streak than he'd guessed. He picked up one of the magazines and flicked through it. None of the stuffy-looking hotel venues appealed to him. The thought of having to wear a tuxedo and spend his day talking crap to people he barely knew filled him with dread.

An idea came to him. What if they handed the wedding planning over to Shelly? It would give her a reason to get Casa Maria renovated and would be a fantastic family occasion. Plus it would give Fee the perfect reason to go to Spain for New Year, so she could suss it out and start planning around the venue.

Buoyed up by the idea, he figured he'd better keep shtum until Shelly made a final decision on Casa Maria and until Fee had laid eyes on the place. That would be enough to convince her, he was sure.

He watched a bit of telly, but after a while decided to head back over to his mum's. They were due to meet there again for dinner, to finish off the leftovers. Leila and Matthew had no food organised and they didn't want to go to the supermarket until tomorrow. He smiled as he read Leila's Facebook post, complete with a photo of her boxes stacked up in the reception area of the new house. The place looked fabulous, there was no doubt about that.

Over at Shelly's house, they sat in the living room and had a glass of wine, waiting to see if Fee would turn up. By eight o'clock, they figured they ought to go ahead without her.

'I've left a message on her phone,' Jake said. 'She'll be here at some point, I'm sure. All I can say is that she's coming to Rondilla for New Year, come hell or high water. The hospital is taking the Mick at this stage.'

Jake stayed at the house, not wanting to drive after drinking so much wine. He texted Fee to let her know. By ten o'clock he'd gone to bed, feeling pretty disgruntled with her and her ongoing silence.

Chapter 28

IT WAS THE THIRTIETH OF DECEMBER, AND everyone was waiting at departures for Fee to arrive.

'I purposely booked the afternoon flight so she'd have plenty of time to get here,' Jake said, looking apprehensively at his watch.

'I really hope the hospital doesn't hold her back,' Shelly said. 'We've barely seen her for the past few days.'

'It can't be legal for her to work all the shifts she's been doing,' Leila said as Matthew jigged Ollie to keep him quiet.

Just as they were about to go through Customs, Fee arrived, looking purple in the face and hassled.

'So, so, so, so sorry,' she said, rushing over to join them.

They got through Customs and onto the flight just in time. Jake decided not to say a word. He was sick of asking her where she'd been and why she hadn't come home. Clearly her job was more important than anything else. Guiltily, he knew deep down that he'd been like that himself at one stage. He'd have walked over hot coals to better himself once upon a time. He softened and looked at her. She was so beautiful. She was clever and amazing and he shouldn't be annoyed with her for doing her job. He reached over and took her hand. She smiled and leaned in and kissed him on the cheek.

* * *

By the time they landed, Fee felt as if she could sleep for a week. She'd been double-shifting for the past few days, and although it was damned exhausting, she'd clocked up a serious amount of cash. She hadn't mentioned it to Jake, but she'd seen a castle in one of the bridal magazines that she thought might suit them as a venue. It was plush and luxurious and would make for a memorable day. She didn't want to spring the idea just yet, but she thought she might as well start saving for it, just in case.

She'd realised that *nobody* wanted to work over Christmas, so she was finding it easy to get her name on the rota for as many shifts as she liked. Jake was occupied with Shelly. Her parents were doing the same thing they'd done since Noah floated off on the Ark, so nobody would really miss her. She hadn't told Jake yet, but she was only staying in Spain for two nights. She'd booked her return flight and was getting off the plane and dashing straight into a night shift. Her hospital had an accident and emergency department, which meant that surgeons were always needed on duty. She knew Jake would give her the puppy-dog eyes for a minute, but he'd be fine when push came to shove.

Besides, if this Casa Maria place was going to be renovated, they'd be consumed with planning that. They wouldn't miss her that much. Fee knew she had to keep her focus on earning her half of the bigger house they would buy. She had to keep her priorities in order.

The taxi ride to Rondilla astonished her. As they climbed higher and higher, she wondered how on earth Gerry had found this place. Jake gave directions to the driver, and before long they pulled up outside a set of huge iron gates.

'Here we are,' he said, sounding as excited as a small child at a sweet shop.

Shelly got all teary and put her arm around Fee. 'What do you think?'

Fee stared through the gates and caught a glimpse of the house at the end of the driveway.

'Let's go inside,' she said, pulling her small suitcase behind her. The other taxi containing Leila, Matthew and Ollie arrived, and they walked up the driveway together.

There was no doubting that Casa Maria was gorgeous. Fee could imagine spending time here. But not right now. Later in life, when she had things sorted. When she was driving the car of her dreams and living in the house of her dreams. Right now it seemed like an added stress that wasn't part of her five-year plan.

'Do you get the vibe?' Jake asked. 'Isn't it magical in some way? Mum and I both felt it, and we know Dad did too.' He looked so earnest that Fee felt she should play along.

'It's great, Jake. I think it's the perfect thing to occupy your mother's mind. It'll keep her busy and we can get on with our lives.'

Jake's smile dropped. 'What do you mean, we can get on with our lives? I want to help Mum. I want to be part of this renovation process. Wait until you see the most exciting part.' He took her hand and led her through the kitchen and out the back, to the end of the sandstone mews building.

'Ta-da!' he said, pushing open the large wooden door, looking flushed and emotional.

'This is the workshop you said you found your dad's jacket in, right?'

'Yes,' he said. 'It's incredible. Look at all the tools, and the workbench. Isn't it just fantastic?'

She nodded silently.

'Look.' He grabbed a piece of broken staircase. 'This is one of the original balusters. I'm going to use it to copy. By the time I'm finished, the stairs will look the way they once did. I got special stuff to treat the wood, and sandpaper and—'

'Jake!' Fee said, feeling as if she might scream. 'I'm glad you're intending to help Shelly. That's nice of you. She needs her family right now. But going forward, you're going to be working crazy hours. We both are. So realistically there won't be that much time for fluting about here.'

'I intend *making* the time to *flute* about here,' he said, looking angrily at her.

'But what about your job? You need to try and claw your way back into favour, Jake. You were hurtling towards being the golden boy and you've blotted your copybook. That's not the end of the world, but make no mistake, you need to show Jim and all the other people who believe in you that you're as good as, if not better than, your father.'

Jake stood and stared at her with such confusion in his eyes that she felt compelled to hug him.

'Hey,' she said. 'It's okay. We'll get there together. I'm right here beside you.'

'Yeah,' he said bitterly. 'You're here beside me so long as I want to attempt to take over the airline. As long as I toe the line you've drawn for me. But what if I tell you that I don't want to fly any more? What if I say that I want to become a carpenter and screw the rat race and screw the whole notion of earning more money than I can spend?'

'You're suffering immense grief right now,' she said, struggling to stay calm. 'Christmas is a really emotional time of year for everyone. You need a bit of time away.

That's why we're here. Don't stress yourself trying to work things out.'

Fee felt as if she was drowning. What had happened to the Jake she'd fallen in love with? What about their dreams of having it all and climbing the ladder of success rung by rung, hand in hand?

She'd read up about grief. It affected people in a whole host of ways. This was probably totally normal. But she sincerely hoped the *real* Jake returned soon.

That evening, they sat in Café del Sol and Valentina brought them a huge selection of tapas. Fee could see why Shelly had fallen in love with Rondilla. The beautiful square and picturesque narrow cobbled streets and higgledy-piggledy houses were like something from a postcard. Valentina was cheery and friendly and it was clear that she and Shelly had made a special connection.

She was pleased, relieved even, that Shelly had a friend here. It would make things easier when she was here alone. Leila and Matthew weren't going to stay too long. Both of them had to return to work, and she and Jake were the same.

As they were finishing their food, Alejandro appeared. They were introduced to him in turn and shook his hand, then Jake took him aside. Fee watched as they pored over some pages. She felt sorry for the man – he'd just stepped in for a quiet drink, and here he was being roped into Jake's vision. She sipped her drink and felt as if all the colour had drained out of the world.

She was literally falling asleep as they eventually went to the guest house up the road. When they climbed into bed, Jake wanted to make love, and she had to tell him she couldn't. Within minutes she was asleep.

The following morning, in case he thought she wasn't interested, Fee woke him with kisses. They stayed in bed for a couple of hours, savouring the quiet and relaxed time together.

He stroked her face. 'Isn't this place such a dream?'

'It's certainly relaxing,' she said, stretching and contemplating a shower. 'Will we go up and see what's happening at Casa Maria?'

'Oh yeah,' he said. 'I'm meeting Alejandro and two of his cousins there this afternoon. They need to get going on the roof as soon as possible. And Mum spoke to Sean Carlisle yesterday. You know, the guy who runs the estate agency where we bought our house?'

'Leila and Matthew used him too, didn't they?'

'Yeah, so he's going to assess Mum and Dad's place, but he said straight up that he thinks it'll sell really quickly.'

'That's good news for Shelly. At least she won't have to worry about bridging loans or any of that nonsense.'

By the time they pitched up at Casa Maria, the place was a hive of activity. Fee was impressed that the locals were here and willing to work on New Year's Eve.

'Alejandro has no children,' Shelly said when she mentioned it to her. 'I asked him just now if his wife was annoyed that he was here all the time. Turns out he still lives with his elderly mother and he's unattached.'

'Could be a little boyfriend for you,' Fee said in jest.

Shelly's face fell, and for a moment Fee thought she might cry.

'Oh my goodness, that was meant to be a joke. It was a bad one. I'm so sorry, Shelly. Don't mind me, I think all this time off is going to my head.'

'I know you mean no harm, love,' Shelly said, hugging

her. 'But I reckon it'll be a very long time before I'd even look at another man. Alejandro is a kind person and an enthusiastic worker. That's all.'

Fee wanted to kick herself. She should never have been so unthinking.

The rest of the day was spent making plans. Alejandro gave them the name of a fabric shop where he could get a good trade discount. The plan was that the girls would go there the day after tomorrow. Fee didn't want to say that she'd be in work, starting a day shift, having had three hours' sleep after the extra night shift she'd signed up for. Instead she smiled and nodded and acted as if she was interested in the notion of a day spent choosing curtains.

Some day, she mused, she would thoroughly enjoy choosing curtains, but it would be with a swish interior designer for her and Jake's mansion. For now, all her concentration was on their five-year plan and her goals. By the time she turned thirty, she wanted to be in a very different place from where she was now.

That evening, Shelly had booked a table at Café del Sol. Thinking they'd be the only ones there, Fee chose a pair of dark denim jeans and a sparkly top. She was afraid of turning her ankle in high heels – those cobblestones looked pretty, but they were a liability in reality – so she opted for trainers.

Pulling her hair back off her face, she put on minimal make-up and a spot of lip gloss. She'd need to curb her drinking tonight, seeing as her flight was at lunchtime tomorrow. This place was so far from the airport that she'd have to leave at nine in the morning at the latest.

Everything was planned in her head. She'd tell Jake later on that she'd had a call and needed to return to Ireland. She'd apologise and look desperately sorry. He'd be disappointed for a bit, but he'd get over it. He had Alejandro to play with, and they were all due to come home to Ireland in three days anyway.

Life would return to normal then. He'd be back at work and soon she'd be able to show him how much money she was earning. The thought of it give her a little shiver of excitement. They were on the up, and it felt great.

'You look so gorgeous when you smile,' Jake said, hugging her.

'You're very smartly dressed for a quiet dinner with family,' she remarked.

'It's New Year's Eve and I reckon it'll be buzzing tonight.'

She laughed and kissed him. 'If you say so.' But as they walked hand in hand down the street towards the square, Fee was stunned by the sight that greeted them. There was bunting strung around, and lots of twinkling lights. Every house and restaurant had made a massive effort to jazz the place up.

She glanced at Leila, who was in a gorgeous dark pink top with a tulle skirt and high shoes. Shelly was wearing a shift dress with matching coat.

'Wow, I didn't realise it was such a big occasion,' Fee said. 'I figured because we were in a one-horse town that it would be just us.'

'Oh no!' Shelly said. 'Rondilla is one of those places that appears to be sleepy until it's party time. The sense of community is wonderful.'

'Should I change?' Fee asked, feeling out of place. She bit her lip. She didn't really have anything to change into.

She hadn't given much thought to her wardrobe for this trip.

'Not at all,' Leila said, handing her a glass of bubbly. 'You'd be like a supermodel even if you appeared in a grass skirt.'

'But look at your lovely outfit . . .'

'I need some drama to hide my flabby bits. You don't, Miss Skinny who hasn't had a baby! Cheers!' Leila said, clinking her glass.

Music started, and people seemed to pour from every corner of the village to congregate in the square. A while later, as the family sat at their table, a huge paella was placed before them, with crusty bread and olive oil for dipping.

'Fee, you don't have a drink!' Shelly pointed out. 'Get your finger out, Jake, please.'

'Oh no, I'm fine,' she said, feeling this might be a good time to let them all know she was leaving in the morning. 'I got a call earlier asking me to return to work tomorrow.'

'Oh no!' Shelly said, looking crestfallen. 'I hope you said no.'

'Absolutely,' Leila said. 'Tell them to shag off. You've barely slept for the past few weeks.'

The conversation turned to the wine and Fee had to wait before she interjected again.

'Actually, I've had to agree to go in,' she said.

'What are you talking about?' Jake said with a laugh.

'I'm leaving at nine in the morning.'

Silence descended as Jake's smile disappeared. 'I see.'

After a couple of seconds that felt like an hour, Shelly changed the subject and commented on how European baby Ollie was being.

'Look at him, taking it all in!' He was sitting happily in his bouncy seat, staring wide-eyed at all the goings-on.

'He's usually awake at this hour while we're trying to get him to sleep,' Matthew agreed. 'He should probably stay here until he's ready to go to school.'

Fee tried to make conversation with Jake a couple of times, but he barely looked at her. He seemed to be intent on talking to Matthew, with whom he hadn't anything in common prior to tonight.

'Leila teases me rotten about my models,' Matthew was saying.

'I get that,' Jake said. 'I don't get model cars per se, but I totally understand having a passion. For me, it's woodwork. You're into cars, so making model cars is a nice diversion for you.'

'Yeah, except he wants to put his toys in a glass case in our new house,' said Leila.

'There are only a few, and they're actually quite sought after,' Matthew protested. 'Anyway, you want to put those creepy ballerinas on the mantelpiece.'

'They're my two bronze sculptures and they're magnificent,' Leila argued.

'Why don't you agree to disagree?' Shelly said. 'That's what relationships are all about. Your father and I were constantly fighting at the beginning of our marriage. He was a workaholic and I resented being put second.'

'Dad never put you second,' Jake said. 'He idolised you, Mum.'

'Yes, he did,' she agreed. 'But he also needed to learn what really mattered.'

'How did he learn that?' Matthew asked.

'I made it easy,' Shelly said. 'I knew he was climbing

the ladder of success, but I had to warn him that he might end up sitting on the top rung alone. Then I told him I would leave if he didn't cop on.'

They all laughed, but Jake looked directly at Fee.

Boiling with anger, she waited until after the countdown to midnight before excusing herself.

'I'll walk you back,' Jake said calmly.

She thanked him and hoped that this would be the end of his prickly mood. To her astonishment, as soon as they reached the guest house, he handed her the key and turned on his heel.

'Where are you going?' she asked.

'Back to my family. It's New Year's Eve. Our first without Dad. I need to be with people who are as emotional and connected as I am.'

'That's not fair, Jake. I miss Gerry too.'

'I never said you didn't. But you are clearly on a whole other agenda to me at the moment. So I figured it would be better to allow you to get on with that.'

'You've changed,' Fee sighed.

'No,' said Jake, as he kissed her cheek. 'You haven't adapted to the mitigating circumstances that have rocked my world. You had a plan, and it's obvious to me now that no matter what happens, you'll forge ahead. I don't know if we're on the same journey any more.'

As he walked away, Fee felt as if her world was crumbling.

Chapter 29

LEILA WAS WORRIED ABOUT FEE. THEY USED TO spend so much time together before Ollie was born. She knew it was probably down to the fact that they'd both been juggling so much coming up to Christmas. But she'd never felt disconnected like this before. At the moment, she couldn't tell what Fee was thinking.

Jake appeared back at the table.

'What's going on?' Leila asked as he sat down with a tight smile.

'Nothing,' he said, pulling his fingers agitatedly through his hair.

'Where's Fee gone?'

'Back to the room.'

'Wasn't she having fun?' Leila asked with concern. 'I didn't get a chance to chat to her much because Ollie was bawling earlier on. He went from little contented baby to Mr Crazy Boots. I was going to hit the sack myself, but he's out cold now, so Matthew and I figured we may as well make the most of it.'

'Good for you,' Jake said kindly. 'You're doing a great job, Leila. I'm so proud of you. Most new mums and dads would be tucked up inside instead of travelling and out having fun.'

'Thanks,' she said, looking him directly in the eye. 'So what's happening with Fee?'

He shook his head and patted her hand. 'Something and nothing. She's going back to Dublin first thing in the morning. It seems they can't do without her. Either that or she can't do without them.'

'The only thing I can say in her defence is that it can't be easy for her. She's obviously under a lot of pressure right now. Qualifying as a surgeon is only the beginning. She still has to prove herself.'

'I know all of that,' he said calmly. 'Honestly I do. But that's not really the nub of the issue.'

'So what is?' Leila poured him a glass of wine and one for herself. She lifted her glass and he clinked his against it. 'Cheers, bro. It's been a weird year. Let's hope this one is a little less rocky.'

'Cheers, big ears,' he said.

'So back to Fee . . .'

'Yeah.' He sighed heavily. 'I'm afraid we're drifting apart, Leila.'

'No!' she said. 'Please don't say that. We all love her so much. She's a part of our family.'

'Don't you think I know all of that?' he said desperately. 'But if it's not working for us and we're no longer on the same page, how can we have a future together?'

'What's going on here?' Shelly said, pulling up a chair. 'You two look very serious. Is everything all right?'

'Fine, Mum,' said Leila with a smile. 'Come and sit with us. How are *you* doing?'

'Better than I'd imagined,' Shelly said with a brave smile. 'Obviously I'm missing your dad, but I couldn't have dreamed we'd all be here in Rondilla tonight. Amazing how the world turns, eh?'

Leila put her arm around her mother and squeezed her. 'You're a trouper, Mum, and none of us can get over how fantastic you're being.'

'Hear, hear,' said Jake. 'So what do you think of Casa Maria, Leila?'

She looked at them and grinned. 'It's beautiful. I can understand why both of you are so taken with it. I love the fact that Dad bought it and we have a chance to fulfil his wishes.'

Shelly began to talk about her plans to sell the house in Ireland to pay for the roof. Matthew had filled Leila in on all this, but Shelly hadn't had a chance to talk to her two children alone about it.

'I could always set myself up with a little apartment somewhere in Dublin as well, if I decide I want to,' she said. 'I don't see the point in having a big family home sitting there gathering dust, especially when I need the money out here.'

'We're totally behind you,' Leila said, and Jake nodded in agreement.

Alejandro and Valentina and a couple of the builders came over with glasses of sangria in their hands, asking if they might join the table.

Leila excused herself and whispered to Matthew to keep an eye on sleeping baby Ollie. 'Fee's gone back to her room. I'm going to pop over and check on her, if that's okay.'

'Sure, take your time. I think our little prince has bawled himself to sleep!'

Grabbing two glasses of bubbly, Leila tiptoed across the square and up the little cobbled street to the guest house.

Not sure how to get inside without waking the entire street, she texted Fee.

Seconds later, the door opened.

'Hey, may I come in for a couple of minutes?' she asked.

Fee nodded, looking miserable.

Leila produced the two glasses of Prosecco and handed one to her.

'Thanks, Leila, but I think I've had enough. I've to fly in the morning.'

'Bring it up to your room and I'll drink it,' Leila said.

In the privacy of the bedroom, the two girls sat side by side on the bed.

'Are you okay?' Leila asked. 'I'm sorry I haven't been much of a friend lately.'

'Hey, you've been so busy having babies and moving house. Gosh, it's all going on with you, isn't it? You look wonderful, by the way. You're an ad for motherhood.'

'Thanks,' Leila said, squeezing her hand appreciatively. 'So, formalities out of the way, what's going on with you?'

'I'm fine,' Fee said, looking at the floor. 'I'm under so much pressure, that's all. I think Jake is having a bit of a hard time getting used to life without Gerry. My heart goes out to him . . .'

'But?' Leila said.

Fee looked up at her and smiled wearily. 'You know me too well, Leila. I don't want to sound like a cow. Honestly, I understand that Jake has literally had the rug pulled from under him, but I'm worried that he's throwing in the towel and sitting back.'

When she looked up and realised that Fee was crying, Leila reached to hug her. 'Hey, don't get so upset. I'd say it's exactly what you figured. Jake is freaking out since

Dad died. He's had a slap on the wrist and I bet he'll be back like a force of nature now.'

Fee shook her head. 'Something has changed with him. He's sort of given up. He's talking about staying over here with your mother for a while.'

Leila picked up the other glass of Prosecco and made sure Fee didn't want it before taking a big swig.

'All I can say, Fee, is that Jake has never put a foot wrong. He's always excelled, always done what he was meant to do. So maybe he's having a bit of a kick-back. He's not stupid. He'll keep his head above water. I know it goes against the grain with you, but why don't you try and bite your tongue and bide your time? It might help you both in the long run. Let Jake get this out of his system and then you can go forth as the power couple we all adore.'

Fee seemed a lot happier as they hugged goodbye. Leila was feeling stupidly trolleyed as she swayed back to the restaurant. She loved Fee to bits and there was no doubt in her mind that she and Jake would work it out. For now, her greatest concern was navigating the cobblestones in high heels after far too much booze. Giggling, she nearly came a cropper several times.

'There you are,' Matthew said as she arrived back at the table. 'The locals are starting a dance-off. It's brilliant!'

As they sat and watched the fabulous flamenco-style dancing, Leila felt confident that Fee and Jake would be totally fine. Jake looked happier than she'd seen him in years. The fact that he and Fee weren't getting on had clearly been forgotten, and he was currently clickety-clacking across the dance floor as though he was on *Strictly Come Dancing*.

'Someone's going to have a sore head in the morning,' Leila slurred to Shelly, nodding towards Jake.

'He hasn't actually drunk that much,' Shelly said. 'That's the alarming thing. He's doing this of his own free will!'

Several moments later, Leila felt as if the world were spinning. Her vision was blurring, and she needed to lie down.

'I don't know why I'm so hammered all of a sudden,' she said, as Matthew led her to their room while holding Ollie with the other hand.

'Make sure you don't wake Oliver,' she said, whispering *very* loudly.

'You're making such a racket, it's a miracle he's not bawling again,' Matthew said with a grin. 'You go to bed and I'll settle him in his travel cot.'

As soon as she lay down, Leila knew she was going to be sick. She'd never had spins like it. Attempting to call out, she made a weird groaning noise and lurched out of bed with her hands clasped over her mouth. Staggering and retching at the same time, mercifully she made it to the bathroom.

'Are you okay in there?' Matthew asked.

'I'm fine, leave me alone,' she said miserably.

Once she started crying, she couldn't stop. The vomiting went on for another hour. By the time she crawled out and into bed, she felt as if she might die. To be precise, she *wanted* to die.

'I think the mixture of Prosecco and sangria got to you,' Matthew said as she curled into a ball and fell into a fitful sleep.

* * *

New Year's Day, and all was quiet as the village slept off the revelries of the night before. Leila's head emerged from beneath the sheets and she opened one eye, hoping to feel less like death. All she could think of was food.

'I'm starving. I need to eat lots of stodge,' she said.

Matthew had clearly woken a while earlier, as he'd already made Ollie's bottle and got him dressed.

'I'll take little monster man downstairs,' he said. 'Follow us when you're ready. No rush. We're happy, aren't we, Ollie?' He kissed Ollie's fuzzy head and lifted his hand to make him wave at her.

After they'd gone, she lay on the bed with her arms above her head. Knowing she needed food, she dragged herself into the shower and pulled on a pair of leggings and a tracksuit top. She couldn't bear the thought of water on her head, so she didn't wash her hair. Instead, she pulled it back into a bun and hoped for the best.

The restaurant was surprisingly busy. Matthew and Jake were in deep conversation, and there was no sign of Ollie or her mum.

'Hi, boys,' she said, sitting down beside Matthew.

'Holy jamoley, sis,' said Jake, doing a double take. 'You look rough.'

'Thanks,' she said drily.

'Sorry, I don't mean to be rude, but you look like you've been run over. Are you okay?'

'I was sick as a dog last night,' she said. 'I'm blaming your fiancée. I went to chat to her and brought her a drink. She wouldn't have it, so I drank both.'

'Ah, I see,' said Jake. 'Well you'll be pleased to know she's probably already back in Dublin in her scrubs, slicing people open. So all is cool in her world.'

'Don't be too hard on her, Jake,' Leila said. 'She's doing her best. She needs to get ahead.'

'Yup,' he said, making it clear he didn't want to discuss the matter. 'I know that Fee is forging on up the ladder. She'll be halfway to the moon by spring. Good for her.'

Matthew pinched Leila under the table to let her know she needed to let the subject drop.

'We're going up to the hacienda after breakfast,' he said. 'Jake wants to show me all the woodwork he's planning on fixing. It sounds as if he's got great stuff happening.'

'Mum wants me to accompany her to some fabric place tomorrow,' Leila said with a yawn. 'It sounds great. Fingers crossed I'll be able to actually see by then. Am I cross-eyed?' she asked Matthew.

'A bit,' he admitted. 'I think I'll mind Ollie today in case you walk into a tree or drop him.'

Leila grinned because she knew that this was the reaction Matthew expected. But really she just wanted to lie down and make everything go away.

She felt marginally better after a big breakfast and two mugs of coffee. They were walking towards Casa Maria when her mouth filled with saliva once more. She began to sweat and had to clamp her hand over her mouth. There was nowhere to run. They were in a tiny street with houses on either side.

In utter panic, she rifled through Ollie's changing bag and managed to find a nappy sack just in time to be sick.

'Sorry,' she said miserably. 'I can't believe I'm so ill.'

'Maybe you've picked up a bug,' Matthew said. 'You were tipsy last night, but I didn't think you were *that* bad. Why don't you go back and lie down? I'll take Ollie on up to Casa Maria and see everyone.'

Knowing she couldn't risk being sick again, Leila did as he suggested. The second her head hit the pillow, she fell asleep. She didn't stir until Matthew appeared, looking a bit put out.

'What time is it?' she asked in confusion.

'Two o'clock,' he said.

'Oh no, I'm really sorry. I hadn't intended sleeping that long.'

'How are you feeling now?' he asked.

'Better, but I'm starving.'

'You'd better not eat too much or you'll be sick again. Do you think you can mind Ollie for a while?' he asked. 'Jake and I are going with Alejandro to meet the roofer.'

'Sure,' she said, holding her arms out to take the baby.

Once Matthew had left, she put Ollie in his bouncy seat, then made her way shakily to the small en suite bathroom and turned on the shower. The cascading warm water was a joy, and she might've stayed there all afternoon if Ollie hadn't grizzled so much.

She made her way down to the restaurant. Valentina hugged her and was so kind it made her want to wail. Instead she ate soup and sourdough bread, then took Ollie to find Shelly.

They spent the afternoon making notes of what they needed to find at the soft furnishing warehouse the following day. Leila was grateful to be feeling more or less normal again, and vowed to leave the Prosecco to others in future. No more bubbly for her!

By the time they congregated later that evening, Matthew and Jake seemed to have bonded with Alejandro. They were sitting having beers at Café del Sol.

'You're like locals, you two boys,' Shelly said. 'Have you had a productive day?'

'Yeah,' said Jake, looking animated. 'The roofers were oblivious to the fact that it's New Year's Day. They can start immediately. Alejandro was amazing on our behalf. The least he deserves is to have a few beers and let us buy him dinner.'

'Beer is very good,' he said. 'But I must return home in ten minute.'

Shelly had never wanted to pry into his life, but she was curious about him the more they got to know him.

'You have to go see your mother?' she asked lightly.

'*Sí*,' he said, nodding. 'I don't like to leave her alone in the evening.'

'You're a good son,' Shelly said, smiling at him.

'You have two very good sons,' Alejandro said, pointing at Matthew and Jake. 'Wonderful help. Matthew fix my truck.'

'Really?' Shelly said, looking in delight at Matthew. 'I'm glad he was able to lend a hand.'

'*Sí*.' Alejandro smiled warmly at Matthew. 'It make noise for two month now. I no understand. But he, he take one look and says, "Oh yes, is easy." Now, no noise.' He looked thoroughly happy with this unexpected turn of events.

'My pleasure,' Matthew said, raising his glass towards Alejandro. 'It was a simple problem to fix, and you are fixing so many problems for us.'

Alejandro ducked his shoulders shyly. 'I hope so,' he said.

'Here's to a new year,' Shelly said, raising her own glass, 'and a new Casa Maria.'

Chapter 30

THE HOUSE WAS LIKE A TIP. GRANTED, FEE HADN'T spent much time there, what with the trip to Rondilla and her subsequent workload. She'd barely slept in the past week at all. There were clothes everywhere, and plates piled haphazardly in the sink. Between the total lack of Christmas stuff and now her dreadful housekeeping, they weren't exactly winning in the creating-a-beautiful-home stakes.

Jake was due home from Spain tonight, and she'd admitted defeat and taken the weekend off, knowing he'd only get annoyed if she was working again. She'd decided to use the day to sleep in and then do grocery shopping and try to make an effort to clean the place up. She hoped her efforts would ease things between them.

They'd spoken on the phone this week, but their conversation had been strained.

'Any more news on the roof?' she'd asked. 'Has the rain stayed away and let the men make a start?'

'It's been dry and really pleasant. Like a summer's day back in Ireland,' he'd said. 'There must've been twenty men here today. I think it will be finished soon. Meanwhile, there's been all sorts of work going on inside too.'

He only seemed to become animated when she asked him what he'd been doing specifically.

'I've started making the balusters,' he said, his voice become light and excited. 'It's coming on nicely. Alejandro is actually trained in carpentry, so he's been great. He's a really lovely man.'

Fee was glad that Jake was working with Alejandro. It was good for him to have a male influence in his life again. He must be missing Jim, seeing as he wasn't at work.

As she blow-dried her hair and put on a bit of make-up, she couldn't help grinning. She felt like a 1950s housewife making things lovely for her husband when he came home. All she was missing was the pinny and housecoat.

She heard the front door open and ran down, surprised.

'You're here!' she said, stating the obvious. 'I wasn't expecting you until this evening.

'I got an earlier flight,' he said. 'We need to talk.'

There was such loaded emotion in his voice that Fee's heart plummeted.

'Is everything all right?' she asked.

'It will be,' he said. 'I've spoken to my superior just now.'

'Who, Jim?' she asked, confused.

He nodded. 'Yes, and Alistair too. I've asked for some extra unpaid leave from the airline.'

'What?' she whispered. 'But why? I thought you were pleased about your promotion. I thought you were relieved that you hadn't been caught over the limit . . . You're on the way up, Jake. Why would you jeopardise it all now? You've worked so hard. It's what you've always dreamed of.'

He squeezed his eyes shut and shook his head.

'It's not what I want, Fee. It hasn't been for a long time.' When he opened his eyes and looked at her, there was such pain there. 'From when I was a boy, my dad instilled in me that I should be a pilot. I idolised him and wanted to be like him.'

'Of course,' Fee said with a tight smile.

'I thought it was what I wanted, but since he's gone, something massive has shifted inside me. Now that I'm doing the woodwork, I feel like a different man. The racing inside my head and the heavy sensation in my chest is easing.'

'You're probably just dealing with your grief now, that's all. Maybe you're getting used to life without Gerry.'

He looked at her with an odd expression. 'I'll *never* get used to life without my dad. He was one of the closest people to me. I'm trying to adapt, but that's nothing to do with what's clicked in my head.'

'I don't understand . . .'

'I know you don't,' he said kindly. 'I know you will struggle massively to attempt to appreciate where I'm coming from. But I need to press pause on my life.'

'For how long?' she asked, her voice breathy and strained.

'I don't know. My job at the airline will be kept open for a few months, so that gives me a little bit of wriggle room.'

'But what will you do? Be a house husband and spend your time ironing?'

He took a deep breath. 'I want to go to Spain while Casa Maria is being refurbished.'

Fee felt her throat contracting. 'So what are you saying?' she managed. 'Are we finished? Do I not fit into your new life where you're covered in wood chips and keeping odd hours?'

'I'm asking you to stand by me, Fee,' he said. 'I love

you, but I don't love my life. If I were to continue as is, I know I'd be miserable.'

'But . . . excuse my stupidity here . . .' She thought she might explode with anger and disappointment. 'How are we meant to conduct a relationship and be engaged if you're in Spain and I'm here?'

'It'll only be for a while,' he said.

'I see.'

Fee could feel her pulse quickening. Sweat beaded her spine and she honestly wanted to slap him. Unable to think of anything constructive to say, she grabbed her coat and walked out the door.

The cool air and dancing rain made her pull her Puffa tightly around her. Why couldn't things just run according to plan? She'd worked her ass off to get to where she was. She'd thought they were on the same page, and now it appeared she'd misjudged Jake completely. The arrogance of him, swanning in the door and asking her to hold the fort while he played at whittling with his mother! She'd put up with a hell of a lot lately; she'd been a staunch support to him after Gerry's death, but when did her turn come? When did he show that she was his number one? She felt sick and cheated. She'd poured herself into this, been everything to him, and now it felt like he was turning his back on her. Her pride was stung. Here she was, a surgeon; she kept herself slim and fit, she ate right, exercised, worked hard, and her fiancé found it easy to walk out on her, to leave her behind. What kind of man was he now? And what kind of a woman did loving him make her?

Her brain spinning with anger and indignation, she turned on her heel and marched back to the house. Jake was leaning against the counter in the kitchen, and he straightened up when she walked in. He opened his mouth to say something, but she got in before him.

'I can't do this,' she said. 'I'm not the type of person who can forge on ahead while you sit and do nothing. If we're not thinking the same way and wanting the same things, it's no good. We'd be better to quit while we're ahead.' She slid her engagement ring from her finger and handed it to him. 'I'll move my things out now to save any embarrassment or awkwardness.'

'Fee, no! Please,' he said sounding desperate. 'Don't do anything rash. Listen, I've to go to Mum's and organise for the house sale. I can stay there. Besides, I won't be here for the next while. Don't go back to your parents. I know you were miserable there.'

'But this is your house, Jake.'

'It's *our* house,' he corrected her. 'Your name is on the deeds as well.'

'But your father's money bought every last brick of it. So in actual fact, it's not mine at all.'

'Fee, why are you being like this?' he asked.

'I'm not being like anything; I'm stating a fact, that's all. And before you even think it of me, I won't fight you for half of this place. We can be grown-ups and get it all put into your name.'

'Can't we wait a while and see how we go?' Jake asked. 'Let's not make any rash decisions.'

Fee walked out of the kitchen and marched upstairs. She couldn't even be in the same room as him. What was he playing at? Would he be going around in Jesus sandals with long hair and a beard soon? She had zero interest in supporting a layabout for the rest of her life.

* * *

Jake bit his lip, unsure what to do. He'd never seen Fee so angry. He figured he should leave her alone for a while. He knew she could be incredibly stubborn, so it was important he didn't aggravate the situation.

He went upstairs and found the bedroom door closed tight.

'Fee?' he said.

There was no answer.

'Look, I'm so sorry. I didn't foresee any of this. I'm sorry I've upset you. I'm going to go now, give you some space. Please don't leave the house. You'd be miserable back at your parents' and you'd have to deal with the questions. You stay here. I'll go. I'll stay at Mum's until you feel ready to talk to me.'

No answer. He leaned his forehead against the door for a moment, willing it open and for Fee to be standing there, smiling, ready to make up and let it go. After a few minutes, he knew that wasn't going to happen.

'Okay. I'm going now. I'm sorry.'

He went back downstairs, grabbed his bag and took a last look around the house, hoping it wouldn't be too long before he was back here, on better terms with Fee. Then he went out to his car.

He knew what he would do now. He was going to get things moving on the house sale. He called the estate agent and arranged for someone to come round to value it. They promised to send a photographer as well. He knew there were some items Shelly would like shipped to Spain, so he would get started on the process of dividing everything into a 'sell' pile and a 'keep' pile. There was lots to be done.

As he started the car and pointed it in the direction of his old home, he was surprised by how light he felt. After all these weeks worrying about Fee, if he was being honest, it actually felt like a relief to have things out in the open. He didn't want to hurt her, but their different life interests just couldn't be denied. He felt himself buzzing on the sense of freedom. He would get stuck into the work, order a takeaway, keep himself busy. He didn't have to explain himself to anyone, and even though that thought made him feel guilty, it also made him feel pretty good.

He looked up at the bedroom windows of their house. Then he put the car in gear and took off quickly.

Fee was sitting in the living room, lights on, curtains open, a glass of wine on the table in front of her, when there was a knock at the door. Tears of gratitude prickled her eyes as she flew to open it.

'Norah,' she said, hugging her friend and promptly bursting into tears. 'Oh you liar, you said you were off when I texted. You've come straight from a shift, haven't you?'

'Never mind that now. First things first, I need wine, and lots of it.'

As she filled her in on what had happened, Fee waited for Norah to explode and tell her that Jake was a bastard and their relationship had been doomed from the start. Instead she sat and mulled things over.

'Well?' Fee said after a couple of minutes. 'What do you think?'

'I'm trying to get my head around it. I'm trying to fathom what's happened to break Jake, because it's not that he doesn't love you, Fee.'

'But he's acting like a total nutjob. He's broken all his promises to me, and more to the point, he's gone back on his promises to himself. That's not the man I know and love.'

'And he's thinking he wants to be a carpenter,' Norah said, shaking her head. 'What's the connection there? Did he and his dad do a course together or something?'

'No,' Fee said in exasperation. 'His dad was a pilot, a captain. A highly regarded one at that. This notion of playing with bits of wood was something Gerry encouraged as a hobby. But the poor man must be turning in his grave right now. All he ever wanted was for Jake to follow in his footsteps.'

'Well that's it, isn't it?' said Norah. 'He's freaking out and going in the complete opposite direction because he feels his entire life has spiralled out of control. He's reacting to grief.' She took a deep slug of wine and shook her head. 'But he's doing me out of a possible shag while he's at it. I was supposed to be inundated with offers from the opposite sex at your wedding.'

In spite of her anger and sadness, Fee couldn't help bursting out laughing.

Norah looked over at her and smiled, taking her hand and stroking it.

'I'm sorry things have come to this. But I honestly think you two are meant to be together.'

'I thought so too, Norah. But Jake has changed. He's not the man I fell in love with. Much as I'd love to be able to say that it doesn't matter and I'm okay with him being an untrained carpenter living in an outhouse in Spain knee deep in sawdust, I'm not. *I* haven't changed. The goalposts haven't moved in my world.'

'No, they haven't, and as surgeons it's in our nature to fight for what we believe. To slog our guts out to achieve what we need. So unfortunately I understand that you can't be who you're not either. I'm exactly the same: I can't compromise. Why else do you think a fine specimen like me is still on the market, hurtling swiftly towards the eternal shelf?' Norah smiled sadly.

They chatted for another hour before Norah announced reluctantly that she had to go home and sleep.

'You can stay here if you like,' Fee offered.

'Thank you, doll, but I've nothing sorted for tomorrow. You know how it is.'

'I sure do,' she said, stretching and yawning. Her eyes were burning from crying, her heart felt heavy in her chest and she would quite happily crawl into the nearest kitchen cupboard and stay there for a week. But she knew that her life needed to continue. Now more than ever she needed to channel that drive and vigour that had brought her this far.

'Thank you for rushing to my side tonight. You're one in a million, and I promise the next time I get engaged you'll be first on my list as bridesmaid again. And if you get there before me, will you return the favour?'

'Deal,' said Norah, as they hugged goodbye.

Fee locked up and set the alarm, then trudged up the stairs to her empty bed. Her parents were going to be apoplectic with rage when she told them she wasn't getting married after all. She could hear them now, ranting and blessing themselves and lamenting the fact that she was now damaged goods, just as they'd gloomily predicted.

Chapter 31

IT WAS THURSDAY MORNING AND SHELLY WAS preparing to say goodbye to Leila, Matthew and baby Ollie. She was dreading it, but she knew that Rondilla was where she needed to be right now.

Besides, Jake was due to return either tomorrow or on Saturday. Things had moved at an extraordinary pace with the house in Ireland. There was a bidding war going on and three parties were interested. He'd said he'd stay until it was settled. She appreciated his help so much. He'd done sterling work, sending things in a container to Rondilla while having the rest put into long-term storage.

Shelly was up at Casa Maria, gathering her notes while getting ready to leave for the interiors warehouse. Originally she'd planned to go with Leila but time had run away with them, so she'd have to do it alone. She was trying not to feel sorry for herself when Leila, Matthew and the baby appeared.

'We've made a decision,' Leila said.

'What's that, love?' Shelly said with a smile.

'Ollie and I would like to stay for another few days. Matthew is going back to work and I'll only be at home by myself.'

'But your new house must be calling to you,' Shelly said in shock. 'Please don't stay because you feel you have to. I'm fine here.'

'I'd like to,' Leila said. 'I'll give it another week and then we'll go home.'

'I can spare them until then,' Matthew said with a reassuring smile.

They all got into the taxi that had been ordered for the airport. After they dropped Matthew off, the women and Ollie went on to look for soft furnishings.

'Alejandro says he can bring all the wooden floors back to their former glory,' Shelly explained. 'The tiles in the hall and kitchen are wonderful features, and he's going to clean them and reseal them too.'

'What about the bedrooms? We'll need to carpet them for it all to be plush and cosy,' Leila said.

'Yes, and I think the simplest and most coordinated way of doing that is by using the same colour palette throughout.'

'I agree. Let's keep it simple. We can add character to each bedroom with drapes and accessories. But having a continuous theme will make it all more homely.'

The first trade centre Alejandro had suggested was magnificent, but out of their league.

'I reckon you'd need to have the budget of the Spanish royal family to shop here,' Shelly said as she stroked a pair of heavy velvet curtains. They took lots of inspiration from the store and moved on to the other place Alejandro had mentioned.

Initially, they were both a bit disappointed. On first inspection, this warehouse didn't have the same opulence. But as they pulled out various rolls of fabric and made notes, it all started to seem very doable.

'I love these golden tones, and the heavy brocade would be so rich and welcoming,' Shelly said, as a lady came to assist.

They took it in turns juggling baby Ollie as they went through all the curtains they required. The lady, who was frosty at first, clearly saw all her birthdays and Christmases coming at once with the commission she was about to make.

'Money talks,' Shelly said with a wistful smile as they enjoyed a bite to eat and a cold glass of wine after their marathon shopping session. Leila was well prepared and had brought lots of nappies and formula along, so little Ollie was happy.

'He's a good lad,' Shelly said. 'Not many babies would have put up with such a long stint in an interiors shop.'

'I don't think he gets his patience from me,' Leila said drily.

'You were a good little baby,' Shelly said. 'You only got spirited as you grew older.'

'Does this wine taste corked to you?' Leila asked, wincing. 'Ugh, it's like vinegar.'

'I was just about to say it's lovely,' Shelly laughed. 'Clearly my palate is nowhere near as refined as yours!'

By the time the taxi dropped them back in Rondilla, Ollie was fast asleep. Shelly took the box of fabric samples and wallpaper cuttings as Leila cradled the baby. Valentina appeared as if by magic and scooped up the pram and remaining bags.

'You need a car,' she scolded. 'No more taxi. Too expensive,' she huffed.

'We'll get around to it,' Shelly said. 'I'm not quite ready for the kamikaze driving on these winding narrow roads.'

'Me neither,' Leila admitted. 'Besides, how often will you be going to Marbella, especially once you're up and running?'

'You will need a bus,' Valentina said. 'That way you can collect people from the airport and they give you good money for this.'

'That's a point,' Shelly said, scratching her chin. 'But I was balking at the idea of a small runaround, never mind a great big hulk of a bus.'

'Count me out,' Leila said. 'Money or no money, there's no way in hell I'm being responsible for other lives or the houses I could potentially crash into on these teeny streets.'

Valentina parked the pram in the café storeroom and followed Leila upstairs with the bags. As Leila placed Ollie in his cot and waited for him to settle, Valentina blew a kiss and whispered that there were plenty of tapas downstairs.

'Thank you, but we've eaten,' Leila said. 'We'll see you tomorrow. I'm beyond exhausted. I think I still have a bit of a bug.'

Closing the door, Valentina padded in her stockinged feet over to Shelly's room. They sat and went through the fabrics the women had chosen that day.

'I know it will all become clear tomorrow when I place the swatches in each of the bedrooms,' Shelly said.

'You will make Casa Maria even more beautiful than before,' Valentina agreed.

'I'm exhausted,' Shelly said. 'But it seems a bit more achievable after today. We have a contact for the beds and furniture too. The woman who helped us with the soft furnishings called and made enquiries on our behalf, and they're going to email a price list tomorrow. Could it all be working out?' she asked fearfully.

'Of course, my friend,' Valentina said. 'Now I leave you. I am very tired too.'

'Is everything all right with you?' Shelly asked as she noticed great dark bags under her friend's eyes.

'I am just tired, that's all,' Valentina said, patting Shelly's hand.

'Are you sure?'

Valentina hesitated and looked up at Shelly. 'There is something, but I cannot talk about it now. Please, do not ask. I will tell you when I can.'

'Of course,' Shelly said. She stood and hugged the other woman. 'I'm here if you need to talk.'

'Thank you, Shelly.'

Next morning, Shelly went up to Casa Maria at first light, bursting with enthusiasm and dying to see what the fabric swatches looked like *in situ*.

Almost everything she'd chosen looked as striking as she'd hoped. The wallpaper she'd picked out for the main reception room was far too dark, but she already knew which one to change it for. The light would be far brighter in the summer months, but all the same, she wanted to create a freshness that would shine with warmth all year round.

She called the shop and explained the change to Lara, the lady who'd helped them the day before.

'*No hay problema,*' Lara said. 'Be careful that you have the correct measurements. Ask the men to do this. Otherwise you will spend euros for nothing.'

'I understand. Thanks so much,' Shelly said.

Alejandro was incredibly enthusiastic about the building works and the garden clearance, but Shelly realised swiftly that he was just like most men when it came to soft furnishings and wallpapers.

'Eh . . . *sí*,' he said, looking hopeful, when she showed him two variations of one print.

'Which one is better?' she asked.

He shrugged his shoulders and his eyes glazed over.

'Would your mother come and talk to me? I would appreciate her help so much. She knows what Casa Maria looked like in its glory days.'

'I don't know . . .' he said, looking like he wanted to run.

'Can I call to speak with her? I'll take a nice cake and make her some tea or coffee.'

'*Espera*,' he said. 'You wait. I will call.'

The conversation, which began in hushed tones, became louder and louder, with much gesticulation and the odd foot stamp. Shelly grinned and turned her back so he wouldn't see. The hot Spanish flares of temper were short-lived, yet so passionate while they happened. From the tone of the exchange, she fully expected him to say his mother wasn't up for a meeting. But much to her delight, he nodded.

'*Sí*, Mama will see you. Four o'clock,' he said, holding up four fingers. 'You bring cake. This was the agreement, no?'

She nodded vehemently and thanked him. Dialling Villa del Sol, she begged Valentina to sell her one of her delicious almond tarts.

'Of course. I will send it with Leila and Ollie. They are here and I think they will go to Casa Maria now.'

'Perfect. I will pay you later, Valentina. You're a star.'

'A star?' she said, sounding confused.

'Yes,' giggled Shelly. 'Like a star in the sky. You are an angel.'

'Ah, yes!' Valentina sounded pleased. 'I am a star!'

* * *

By the time Leila and Ollie arrived with the almond tart in a pretty box, Shelly needed to leave.

'Will I come?' Leila asked. 'I'm kind of intrigued to meet this woman. She must have lots of stories about the house.'

'Maybe not this time, if you don't mind,' Shelly said, as Ollie grizzled and wriggled crossly in the pram. 'If you would email the fabric orders through to Lara at the shop, though, that'd be wonderful. Eric, Alejandro's cousin, is finishing with the last measurements upstairs and he's got it all written down.'

'Oh, sure,' Leila said.

Shelly set out to walk to Alejandro's house, following his clear instructions. He explained that his mother always sat in the back garden in the afternoon, so she was to use the side passage and call out to announce herself.

Feeling mildly nervous, she did as she was bid. '*Hola,* Señora Garza,' she said, dropping into an awkward cross between a curtsy and a bow. 'I am Shelly. I have cake.' She held the box out like a talisman.

'Why are you here?' the woman answered in perfect English.

'You speak English?' Shelly said in surprise.

'Yes.' She accepted the cake. 'I'm having tea; it's too late in the afternoon for coffee. Will you join me?'

'Please. Would you like me to make it?'

'You're a guest. I'm hardly going to send you into a strange kitchen and expect you to fumble in my cupboards.'

As she rose gracefully from her low deckchair, Shelly was taken aback by how tall she was. She was nothing like the feeble little old woman she'd envisaged in her mind's eye. Her hair was pulled back in a sage-green Alice band, and as she walked towards the house, Shelly could see that it hung down her back in soft white waves. Her slender figure suggested a model's proportions, and her spine was wonderfully strong and straight, in spite of her advancing years. She wore a cheesecloth maxi dress in the same shade as the hairband, with a grey pashmina to keep her warm in the January sun.

Not sure whether or not she should follow, Shelly stood awkwardly in the compact garden. Gazing around, she noticed how neat and exact everything was. The flowers were in perfect rows and the postage-stamp-sized lawn was faultlessly manicured.

Señora Garza returned with a beautifully set tray and placed it on the round mosaic-covered table. 'Sit, if you please,' she said. Shelly perched and stared at the immaculately folded napkins and matching crockery.

'Your tea set is so pretty,' she said, as the older woman handed her a cup.

'It's older than me and that's saying something. Still, some things last a lifetime.'

Shelly accepted a slice of cake and waited until they were both settled and sipping tea.

'So what brings you here?' Señora Garza said, sitting forward and looking intently at her. 'Alejandro tells me you are employing him to do a full revamp on Casa Maria.'

'Yes,' said Shelly, dabbing her mouth. 'He has lots of wonderful advice and ideas.'

'They're hardly ideas. He's working from memory and rehashing, that's all.'

'Well, I'm very grateful to him. I saw the photographs you sent. I'm so excited that you knew the house all those years ago.'

'I didn't send the photographs,' Señora Garza said.

'Alejandro took them and I didn't stop him. There's a difference.'

'Oh, I see. I apologise if this is all very uncomfortable for you.'

'It's not uncomfortable, it's actually more of an intrusion,' she said, narrowing her eyes. 'I buried my memories of that house a long time ago. I never intended revisiting those times. They hold far too much pain and misery.'

'Would you prefer it if I left? I don't want to be the cause of any further pain,' Shelly said.

'No,' Señora Garza said quickly. 'You're here now. The memories have been awakened, so the damage is done.' She sighed heavily. 'Tell me about your life. Why are you here in Rondilla? Where is your husband?'

Shelly followed the other woman's gaze to her wedding ring.

'Ah, well my husband, Gerry, died almost seven months ago.'

'Was he ill?' Señora Garza leaned forward slightly.

'Not that we knew about. He had a heart attack, but he hadn't been sick before that. He was a wonderful man. I miss him dreadfully.'

'Alejandro didn't tell me much; our relationship can be strained,' she said pausing momentarily. 'He only said that your husband bought Casa Maria. How soon before his death, do you know?'

'Only a few months,' Shelly said.

'I see. I'm sorry for your troubles.' Señora Garza nodded. 'So what has Alejandro told you about me?'

'Only that you worked at Casa Maria many years ago and that you don't go there now.'

'Of course I don't. I have no business doing so.'

Señora Garza sat back in her deckchair and stared into space. Shelly hoped she would share her thoughts. Knowing she needed to bide her time, she waited in silence.

It felt like an age before the older woman spoke again.

'How are you thinking of decorating the place? Will you go for old-fashioned decor, or try to jazz it up with modern colours?'

'I'm hoping to restore it to its former glory. I'm looking to use similar fabrics and wallpapers. If you were willing to come and see, I could show you what my daughter and I have found.'

'No,' Señora Garza said instantly. 'I won't come near Casa Maria. I haven't set foot in the place for decades. Not since that night . . .'

'What night? What happened there?'

There was another pause.

'I worked there, as you know. I was the right-hand woman to Señora Fuentes. I did everything for her,' she said wistfully. 'She was the wife of José Fuentes. He was a famous matador here in Rondilla. Back at that time, the matadors were like royalty. He would draw massive crowds to the Plaza de Toros de Rondilla.'

'I see,' Shelly said, leaning forward in fascination. 'The bullring is an astonishing place; I've visited it several times. I can only imagine what it must have been like many years ago. I have seen José Fuentes' pictures in the museum there.'

'His wife was English. Her name was Charlotte.'

Shelly nodded, as it became clear how this woman spoke English with such fluency. Her mind flew to the photograph with the figure curled up reading. She wondered if that could possibly be Charlotte, but knew better than to ask.

'She was young and terrified when she first came to live in Rondilla.'

'How did the couple meet?'

'She was brought here by another Spanish family. Her boss at the time was a matador and one of José's biggest rivals. She worked as the nanny. Her boss was injured badly and had to stay here for almost a month. José fell madly in love with her and begged her to stay.'

'And they got married?' Shelly asked.

Señora Garza nodded. 'She was only eighteen and quite out of her depth. José's parents were furious that he hadn't married a Spanish girl, and one with more social standing for that matter.'

'Was José's family very wealthy?'

'Yes,' she sighed. 'That was the beginning of their problems. He'd come from a long line of matadors. His mother was a snob of the worst sort. She was suspicious of any family that didn't have the same wealth. She saw Charlotte as a gold-digger, and the fact that she was foreign made it even worse.'

'Did she come to love Charlotte as time went by?'

Señora Garza poured more tea. Shelly didn't actually want any more and needed the bathroom, but she couldn't risk silencing or irritating this woman.

Ignoring the question, Señora Garza continued. 'Charlotte and José were married in the Plaza Duquesa de Parcent, in the church near the Café del Sol, where Alejandro tells me you are staying. Soon after the wedding, she hired me. It was 1961, and I was twenty years old. Alejandro was only a tiny baby, but my husband was unable to work. So I had to bring some money in.'

'Why couldn't your husband work?' Shelly asked.

'He was a lot older than me. His health was failing and I knew he wasn't going to survive.'

'Did he die?' Shelly whispered.

Señora Garza nodded. 'When Alejandro was two.'

'I'm sorry.'

'I was too,' she said. 'I was warned not to marry him. He wasn't a good prospect because he was so ill. But you cannot choose who you fall in love with. We had a few wonderful years together and he gave me Alejandro.'

'I feel your pain,' Shelly said sadly.

'Charlotte was very kind to me. In turn, I nursed her through a scary pregnancy. She lost the baby and almost died in the process herself. I think she used Alejandro as a replacement for her stillborn son.'

'How awful for her,' Shelly said, as the older woman's eyes misted over.

'She never had any more children. Another reason for her mother-in-law to despise her.' Señora Garza stood up. 'Casa Maria was wonderful when it was filled with life and love. I hope you can restore that. I wish you well with it. It was interesting meeting you.' She offered her long, bony hand for shaking.

'May I come again?' Shelly asked, knowing she sounded quite desperate. 'I would love to hear more.'

'I'm sure you would,' Señora Garza said. 'I expect you think it's all like a romantic soap opera. You find the tragedy of others entertaining?'

'Oh gosh, no!' Shelly said. 'I—'

'Liar,' said Señora Garza. 'I can see the hunger for knowledge seeping from every pore you possess. Who can blame you? Casa Maria is beguiling. *Adios,*' she said, making it crystal clear that she had nothing more to say.

'*Adios*,' Shelly responded, 'and thank you for having me.'

'You arrived. What could I do?'

'Yes, of course,' Shelly said, feeling like a naughty child. Given that the other woman was dismissing her, she felt she had nothing to lose by being a little pushy.

'Do you think I might come again another day?'

An eerie silence enveloped them. Shelly held her gaze and barely breathed.

'Come in a few days. At the same time. Don't bring cake. I never wanted to be fat. I still don't. I'll send the message via Alejandro as to when you may come.'

Señora Garza sat down heavily and closed her eyes, as if shutting out the rest of the world.

Unsure of what else she could do, Shelly turned and walked away.

Chapter 32

JAKE WAS GLAD TO TOUCH DOWN IN MALAGA. THE family home was as good as sold, and he needed to get away from Dublin. He hadn't spoken to Fee since she'd given his ring back. He'd have to tell his mother and Leila about their break-up, but figured it would be better to do so in person.

The rain was coming down in sheets as he flagged a taxi at Malaga airport. He'd been hoping for some slightly less inclement weather as they sped past Marbella and headed for the hills.

When the taxi finally pulled up outside Casa Maria, Jake spotted Leila trundling up the hill with the buggy.

'Hey, sis,' he said, shoving a few notes through the window to the appreciative taxi driver.

'Jake!' she said, looking exhausted and furious. 'I've just spoken to Fee. What the hell is going on?'

'Who are you talking to?' said Shelly as she approached from the garden. 'Jake! When did you get here?'

'Just this second,' he said, hugging her.

'Yeah, and I think he has some news for us, don't you?' Leila said, her eyes flashing with anger.

'I wanted to tell you both in person,' Jake said defensively. He was furious that Fee had called his family without checking if he'd talked to them first. This wasn't panning out as he'd wanted it to. He silently cursed her for making things even more difficult. 'Fee and I have sort of broken up.'

'What?' said Shelly, looking stunned. 'What's happened?'

'We're both going in different directions right now. I want to spend time here, and Fee, well . . .' He shrugged.

'Oh Jake,' Shelly said and hugged him. 'I'm so sorry to hear that. Do you think it might be resolved with time?'

'I doubt it,' he said. 'She's pretty adamant that I'm not the man she fell in love with. And she's probably right. But I don't think I want to be that person any more.'

'But what about the house?' Leila said. 'I was just talking to Fee and she's in bits, if that helps.'

'No,' Jake said evenly. 'That doesn't help. I didn't want to hurt her.'

'Well you made a right balls of that, then,' Leila said.

'Leila!' Shelly said. 'Don't be so rude. It's actually none of our business.'

'Thank you, Mum,' Jake said.

'I'm sorry, though,' she said, sighing. 'I love Fee. We all do.'

'Leave it, Mum, yeah?' he said.

Shelly nodded and linked his arm. 'Come on, we'll show you the fabrics and wall coverings we're considering,' she said.

'Mum, how can you just change the subject and act as if nothing has happened? And as for you,' Leila turned on Jake, 'what are you playing at? Fee says you haven't so much as texted her since you split.'

'Leila,' Shelly said, placing a hand on her arm. 'It's not up to us what Jake does. I'm just as upset as you are, but it's not our place to yell and shout the odds.' She gave her daughter a warning look.

Jake stared at his feet. 'For the record, Leila, I'm hurting just as much as Fee is, but I can't talk about it right now. Can you give me a bit of space, please?'

'Sure,' she said, looking sorry. 'I'm upset, that's all. I thought you guys were forever.'

'So did I,' Jake said, shrugging. 'I just need more flexibility than she's prepared to give me.'

They wandered towards the house in silence.

'Hey,' said Leila, 'Mum went to see Alejandro's mother yesterday. She used to work here back in the day. She sounds like a right grumpy old bag, but she'll be useful if she can give us some pointers.'

'Don't be disrespectful, Leila,' Shelly said sharply. 'Señora Garza was pretty stern, but she didn't know me and she has a problem with this place, so I couldn't have expected her to welcome me with open arms.'

Jake followed them from room to room and back down to the hallway, where baby Ollie was lying in his pram.

'Wow, what have you been feeding him? Protein shakes? He's doubled in size since I saw him last.'

'He sculls his bottles, don't you, baba?' said Leila with a grin.

They all turned when there was a knock at the door. Jake went to answer it.

'*Hola*,' said the woman on the doorstep, followed by a whole string of stuff he couldn't understand.

'Right,' he said. 'Come in.'

Shelly joined him at the door. 'Er, *no entiendo*,' she said apologetically. 'Do you speak English?'

'Of course,' the woman said. 'I am Avery, from the letting

agency in Malaga. I do holiday lets and I used to work alongside Rosa, helping her to find accommodation for her wedding guests. I got your details from Rosa. I believe you were speaking with her recently about setting up a wedding planning business.'

'Oh, yes! I'm Shelly. Please come in. This is my son Jake, and daughter Leila.'

As the woman walked in, the light from the stained-glass window shining on her glossy dark hair, Jake felt his heart lurch – either that or something lower down. This woman was as hot as a furnace. He hadn't really registered other women for the past five years, and he knew it made him a snake to be thinking this way so soon after the break-up, but he was registering her all right. She was stunning.

'*Hola*, Jake,' she said, staring right into his eyes. She was almost the same height as him. She smelled of citrusy cologne, and as he shook her smooth brown hand, he couldn't help noticing how perfectly manicured her nails were.

She shook Leila's hand too, and immediately cooed over the baby.

'He's charming,' she said. 'How old is he?'

'Six weeks,' Leila said.

'Was he born in Spain?'

'No, Ireland, but I think he'll be spending a lot of time here. My partner and I live in Ireland, but we love it here too!'

Shelly showed Avery into the living room, where Alejandro and the other builders had a makeshift sort of camp. Jake trailed them, wanting to see more of this exquisite creature but at the same time trying to look nonchalant so that his sister and mother wouldn't guess what was seething beneath the surface.

'Excuse the lack of furniture,' Shelly said. 'We have everything coming soon. Once the refurbishment is done, we'll be ready to host our first weddings.'

'Yes, Rosa was building up a nice business, as she may have told you. Love made her crazy, so she walked away,' Avery said sourly. 'I hope you will be too old to do anything so stupid.'

Jake laughed out loud and promptly clamped his hand over his mouth as Avery shot him a stern look.

'What happens in the future is beyond me,' Shelly said. 'I'm mourning the recent death of my husband, so right now I'm attempting to pick up the pieces. Casa Maria and I are being rebuilt together.'

'Of course,' Avery said curtly.

'Would you like me to show you around?' Jake asked.

Leila opened her mouth with a look of astonishment on her face.

'What?' he hissed. 'I'm only trying to help Mum.'

'I know what you're doing,' she said acidly. 'Don't forget your fiancée is at home nursing a broken heart.'

'She's my ex,' he whispered. '*She* gave *me* back the ring. And I'm not planning on shagging this woman in each of the bedrooms. I'm merely showing her around.'

Leila held up both hands in surrender as Jake strode past her.

'Shall we start upstairs?' he said to Avery. 'Once the bedrooms have new curtains and carpets, they'll be hard to beat. The view is second to none, and with a new plush interior, who wouldn't want to come and celebrate their big day here?'

He watched as Avery sashayed up the stairs. The pinstriped navy dress she'd chosen was the perfect balance between classy and sexy. By the time they'd looked in all the rooms, he felt disappointed at the thought of her leaving.

'Do you want to go and grab a coffee?' he blurted.

'That would be nice,' she said.

His satisfaction was short-lived. Avery had already gone into the front garden to inform his mother and Leila that they should all go to the village for coffee.

What am I doing? he berated himself. He reminded himself that he still hadn't spoken to Fee properly. But then, he thought, things were clearly over between them, or he wouldn't be feeling like this.

They walked down to Café del Sol. Avery knew Valentina from her previous dealings with Rosa, and kissed her on both cheeks. The two women chatted in Spanish for a few moments, then Shelly ordered coffee and they got down to business. Avery was extremely helpful and forthcoming with advice. She was in the hub of things in Marbella and was more than willing to help direct potential clients towards Rondilla and Casa Maria. She made it clear that it would be a two-way thing, as having a beautiful hacienda on her books would certainly make a positive impression.

'It makes me look good also, if I have prestigious properties to show,' said Avery.

'Thank you for being so honest,' Shelly said, once they were finished talking.

'Of course,' Avery said. 'It makes sense for us to share our knowledge. This way I am hoping we will be able to do lots of business together. One final thing: how do you propose to market your business?'

There was an awkward pause. Shelly hadn't thought

that far ahead yet. She was consumed with the renovation work, and the actual weddings remained a hazy idea. She was about to say as much when Leila cut across her.

'We're in the process of preparing one-, three- and five-year business plans,' she said confidently.

Shelly and Jake stared at her open-mouthed, then recovered themselves quickly as she went on.

'Initially we will depend on the website and social media to spread the word about Casa Maria,' Leila said. 'I'm currently designing the website, which will be up and running soon to catalogue the renovation process. Our feeling is that people will enjoy the story behind their wedding location.'

Avery nodded and jotted something in her notebook. 'This is good, yes, I see.'

'We will also launch Casa Maria across several different online platforms,' Leila said, 'so that each strand of the marketing plan complements the other. We will shortly have a presence on Facebook, Instagram and Twitter, and this will be followed by online ads on the key wedding websites, particularly in Ireland. I'm researching this market currently, and what I'm finding is very encouraging and has confirmed to me that this is the optimum approach in our market segment.'

'I like the sound of this,' Avery said. 'As soon as you have everything in place, email me and I can link to you across my platforms as well. We can become online partners to increase business all round.'

Leila nodded. 'No problem at all. I'll take your email address and stay in touch with you.'

Avery excused herself to use the bathroom, and Shelly and Jake stared at Leila in wide-eyed admiration.

'Where did all that come from?' Shelly said. 'Are we actually doing that?'

Leila grinned. 'I was speaking off the top of my head, but actually we should be doing exactly what I described.'

'That was brilliant,' Jake said. 'Even I believed we had a viable business by the end of your spiel.'

'I have my uses,' Leila said. She turned to Shelly. 'I've been waiting to make a proper contribution here. Jake is doing the stairs, and I'd like to have a role too. Would it be all right if I took on the online stuff and pushed ahead with letting people know we're here?'

'Yes,' Shelly said, looking a bit overwhelmed. 'But we don't want bookings just yet. I can't get my head around that.'

'No,' Leila said, shaking her head. 'I'll do what I said to Avery. I'll chart the rebirth of Casa Maria, put up photos, then people will be interested but at the same time understand it's not ready yet.'

Avery returned to the table and gathered her things. It was dark by now, so Shelly suggested that Jake should walk Avery to her car, which was parked a few streets away.

'I do not need a chaperone. But thank you,' she said.

'No!' Jake said. 'I insist.'

They all shook hands and Jake led her back up the hill.

'So I heard you say that you live in Marbella,' Jake said.

'Yes.' She didn't smile, but the initial frostiness was gone.

'Are you married?' The question had popped out of his mouth before he could stop it.

'I don't see how this is any of your business,' she said, full frostiness restored.

'Apologies,' he said, holding up his hands. 'If it makes

you feel any better, I'm a total disaster when it comes to relationships. I'm in the process of splitting up with my fiancée, so I guess I'm an idiot of the highest order.'

She smiled. He felt his heart flip.

'I'll be helping my mother with Casa Maria, so I'll be mainly in Rondilla, but if I'm down in Marbella, may I call you?'

'Won't you be busy sorting your relationship?' she asked pointedly.

'I'm pretty much at the end of sorting it,' Jake said. 'It's over; we simply need to agree on it.'

Her flicker of a smile turned to a worried frown. 'I don't think so,' she said, ducking into her car. She rolled down the window. 'I'm sorry. I didn't mean to be rude just now. I have a lot going on at home. I'm caring for my sick father. Besides, I don't mess with a mess.'

His heart dropped. She started the engine, making it clear that she was going to drive away without giving him her number. He felt like a fool, but after a few seconds she held out a business card with two slender fingers. He reached for it, and she smiled warmly before tearing off.

As he strolled back down to the square to join Shelly and Leila, he couldn't wipe the grin from his face.

'You look like the cat that got the cream,' Leila said crossly as he sat down brandishing Avery's business card. 'You're unbelievable, Jake. I'm glad Fee isn't here to see your behaviour. I feel bad even witnessing it.'

'Don't be so snappy,' Shelly said. 'Jake wasn't flirting or asking for Avery's number so he can date her. His mind is on the business, right Jake? We all know that he and Fee are going to sort things out.'

'Who knows, Mum?' he said, tucking Avery's card into his pocket.

Chapter 33

BABY OLLIE WAS SETTLED IN RONDILLA, BUT LEILA knew she needed to get back to Matthew. It wasn't fair to keep the two of them apart.

With a heavy heart, she booked a flight home, and told Jake and Shelly that she would be leaving the next day.

She spent her final day in Rondilla wandering around Casa Maria, talking through the plans with Shelly. During Ollie's nap, she made a good start on her marketing plans, doing research and making notes and coming up with the right tone for her online posts. In the evening, they enjoyed a delicious meal at Café del Sol, and Leila said goodbye to Alejandro and Valentina, knowing she would miss them.

All too soon the taxi arrived to collect her. Shelly held her in a long hug and promised to see her soon. Jake held her tight too, whispering that he was sorry how things had worked out. She felt a lump in her throat at the thought of Fee and could only manage to smile weakly at him. She was feeling so emotional about this whole Jake and Fee thing – she was surprised at just how much it had upset her.

The second the plane took off from Malaga, Leila's stomach turned. With Ollie strapped to her, she panicked as she tried to find the sick bag in the seat pocket in front of her. Leaning towards the window, she managed to vomit without covering the baby.

'Sorry,' she said as tears ran down her cheeks.

The woman beside her pressed the call button and an air steward arrived. They were all incredibly kind and held Ollie while she cleaned herself up in the tiny toilet.

The rest of the flight was like an endurance test. Her stomach lurched continuously, and each time they had any sort of turbulence, she feared she'd be sick again.

As they landed and she gathered up her bags, it took all her resolve to hold back her tears. In arrivals, however, she dissolved in a big messy heap in front of an astonished Matthew.

'Hey,' he said in concern as he bent to kiss Ollie. 'What's going on?'

'I'm so sick, Matthew,' she said. 'I vomited and narrowly missed the baby. I was so embarrassed. I thought we'd never get home.'

'You're here now,' he said as he hugged her. 'I've missed you both more than you'll ever know!'

As they drove home, Leila yelled at Matthew to pull over, and she vomited again on the side of the motorway.

'Right, we'll get a doctor out to you,' Matthew said. 'You go to bed as soon as we get home.'

She didn't argue, and was grateful to crawl under the duvet and fall asleep. She only woke when she heard Matthew coming up the stairs, talking to a woman. Confused, Leila sat up as they entered the room.

'Hello, I'm Dr Grace,' said the woman. 'I'm the doctor on call.'

'Oh, thank you,' Leila said. 'I don't know what's wrong with me. I'm feeling terrible.'

Matthew took Ollie downstairs and left them to it.

* * *

A short while later, Leila let the doctor out. Matthew was making a cup of tea in the kitchen when she found him.

'So what's the story?' he asked.

'I'm pregnant,' Leila said, and burst into tears.

Matthew rushed to hug her, but she could hear his heart beating like a bass drum.

'I can't believe it,' she said. 'Ollie will only be ten months old. What am I going to do, Matthew? My job? My body . . .' She looked down at her tummy, which was still trying its best to shrink back to where it had been before Ollie.

'Well it wasn't what I was expecting to hear, I'll give you that,' he said. 'I didn't realise you could get pregnant again so quickly.'

'No, me neither. But the doctor was saying it's a very dangerous time. That women get pregnant again like this all the time. I never suggested we use anything, because I was breastfeeding at the start.'

Leila felt so stupid. Not only that, she felt immensely guilty as she looked at Ollie. He'd be a big brother before his first birthday.

'I have to go to work for an hour,' Matthew said, looking at his watch. 'I'm sorry to rush off and leave you, love.'

'I'll be okay,' she said. 'I'll give Fee a call.' Then it struck her. Was she entitled to speak to Fee now? Would she take her call? But as well as being Jake's fiancée, Fee was pretty much Leila's best friend, so she took the chance and dialled her number.

Fee answered immediately.

'Hi, Fee,' said Leila, and burst into tears.

As soon as she heard the news, Fee said she'd call round.

'I'll be finished at work in about an hour. I've some ends to tie up and then I'll come over.'

Knowing she needed to tell her mother, Leila dialled her number next.

Shelly couldn't hide her shock, but she tried to be positive. 'It's good news. It's great news. You'll have a wonderful family before you know it.'

Leila knew that it was down to hormones, but she couldn't stop crying.

'It'll be all right, love,' Shelly promised.

'But you're gone and I'll be stuck here on my own with two babies. Realistically, I can't go back to work now. Paying for a child-minder for two will take up all my wage.'

'You need to calm down, love,' Shelly said. 'Is Matthew there with you?'

'No,' Leila said miserably. 'But I called Fee and she's coming over.'

'Oh that's fantastic. I'm delighted you two are meeting up. She's a rock of sense and she'll tell you exactly what I'm telling you: that time will sort all this out. I was so happy to have you and Jake quickly, while I was young. It's great being a young mother, Leila. You've more energy, and then you get your life back before your old age, which is a huge plus.'

When Fee arrived, there were more tears. The two women stood hugging and sobbing for what felt like an age.

'How are you doing?' Leila asked. 'I can't believe you and Jake have split up.'

'I know,' Fee said. 'I'm trying to get my head around it too.' She bit her lip and looked sheepish. 'I haven't told anyone. Not my parents or anyone at work, bar Norah.'

'Really?' Leila said. 'How have you managed to keep it to yourself? I tell everyone everything.'

Fee smiled. 'My parents are not like yours. Gerry was so warm and easy to chat to. My father is like a shadow of my mother. He hides behind her and agrees with everything.'

'Sounds like the perfect man,' Leila quipped. 'Although Matthew is great, I have to say.'

'Yes, he is,' Fee agreed. 'But my mother is so forceful and bossy. She's never accepted anyone who doesn't think like her. I know for a fact that she's furious with me for becoming a surgeon.'

'How could she be?' Leila asked. 'You're amazing and brilliant.'

'Not in her eyes. As far as she's concerned, I've failed in my womanly duty. I should be chained to a kitchen sink, waiting with bated breath for my husband to come home.'

'But she *must* be proud of your achievements underneath it all?' Leila said.

'I don't know,' Fee sighed. 'She was marginally less annoyed with me when she thought I was marrying Jake. She figured I'd be happy to stay at home and spit out babies . . .' She stopped dead. 'Sorry, Leila, I wasn't trying to get at you.'

'Don't worry,' Leila said. 'But you can't go around living a lie. Are you hoping you and Jake will work it out?' she asked hopefully.

'I don't know,' Fee said. 'I don't know if that's what I want any more. I might be better off concentrating on one thing for the moment.'

They chatted for a while, then Fee said she needed to go. 'I'm doing a couple of hours to cover for a friend.'

'But you've only just finished a full shift,' Leila said. 'You'll burn yourself out.'

'I'm fine. Sure, what else would I be doing?' Fee said sadly.

Once Fee had gone, Leila went into the kitchen and wondered what to make for dinner. There was nothing in the fridge, so she texted Matthew and asked him to pick up a takeaway on the way home. She decided to give Ollie a bath, then let him have a kick on his mat in the living room. She loved their new home, and not for the first time, she looked around in awe, barely able to believe it was theirs.

She gave Ollie his bottle and settled him in his cot. Because they were in an unfamiliar house, he immediately proceeded to howl, getting himself into such a state that his entire bottle came back up, soaking the bed and the side of the cot.

Leila found some fresh sheets and a babygro in one of the cardboard boxes. By the time she had Ollie settled, she was exhausted. She dialled Matthew's mobile again and left a message asking him to call her. She also said not to bother with food for her, as she'd gone beyond hunger.

There was no reply from Matthew, and after an hour, Leila admitted defeat and went to bed. When she was woken by the sound of thudding about, she sat up in fright. As her eyes adjusted to the dark, she realised it was Matthew, staggering about in the dark, clearly pissed as a newt.

'Where were you?' she whispered.

'Out,' he said. His voice was slurred. Knowing there was no point in attempting to have a joined-up conversation with him while he was drunk, Leila lay down and went back to sleep.

Early the next morning, as she was feeding Ollie, Matthew shot down the stairs and straight out the front door, banging it shut behind him.

Leila felt the colour draining from her face. What the hell was going on?

Chapter 34

SHELLY MISSED DUBLIN AND GUESSED THE SNOW-drops and early daffodils might be trying to poke their brave heads out through the chilled February soil right now. But she didn't miss it enough to want to go back there. If she were there, she would be missing Gerry even more. As it was, she missed him all the time. At least ten times a day she went to call or text him, to show him what was happening, only to realise she couldn't. But she was occupied and managing as best she could, taking each day hour by hour.

She was truly shocked by Leila's announcement. She worried for her daughter and wondered how she'd cope. She might suggest that she get an au pair; that way she'd have another pair of hands. They had lots of room in the house and could easily have someone live in. It could be a very good solution.

Once Casa Maria was finished and her business was up and running, she'd look into returning to Dublin regularly. She didn't want to miss out on seeing her grandchildren growing up.

Shelly had called Fee this morning. Until now she'd been unsure as to whether she should get in touch, but once she'd heard that Fee was visiting Leila, she'd bitten the bullet and dialled her number. They'd chatted for a few minutes and Shelly had hung up wondering whether she'd done the right thing. Really, it was none of her business what Jake and Fee decided to do. But it was so difficult to sit by and do nothing.

Casa Maria was coming along nicely, and Alejandro and his team were motoring through the work. He'd sent a message that morning saying his mother would speak to Shelly once more. She was nervous of meeting the prickly Señora Garza again, but her curiosity was much stronger than her anxiety. She knew that Alejandro's mother held secrets from the past and precious information about Casa Maria.

She had been warned not to bring cake, but she couldn't arrive at Señora Garza's house with one arm as long as the other. So she'd picked up a scented candle in the village. She'd made polite conversation with the woman in the shop and said the gift was for an older lady. The woman had been most helpful and had chosen something pretty and wrapped it in cellophane with a tulle ribbon.

When Señora Garza opened her front door, Shelly held out the gift, hoping it might pave the way for a more relaxed conversation.

'Are you trying to buy my affection?' Señora Garza barked.

'Oh no,' Shelly said. 'I always bring a little gift when I visit friends. I wouldn't feel right coming without anything. You said not to bring a cake this time . . .'

'Thank you,' Señora Garza said, blinking slowly. 'You can leave it on the hall table. I like candles, as it happens. I will use it. That used to be my favourite scent. I haven't had one for a while.'

'Oh good,' Shelly said. 'If you decide you don't like it, I'm sure you can exchange it.'

'I haven't spoken to Nina for many months. I used to go to the village so much more. But since I had my knee replaced, I've been bad at going out.'

'I'm sorry to hear you had to have surgery,' Shelly said.

'They want to do the other one now. But I can't bear the thought.'

'You might feel better if you do,' Shelly said.

'How would you know? Have *you* had your knee replaced?'

'No, as it happens,' Shelly said, holding her gaze. 'I think we seem to be getting off on the wrong foot here, Señora Garza. I didn't come intending to start an argument.'

The old lady's shoulders relaxed a little. 'Some things never change. Good for Nina that she's still in business. She's a good person. A kind soul.'

'Don't you venture out into the world much at all then?' Shelly asked as she was led into a small, immaculate drawing room. Decorated in muted tones with accents of rose pink, it was far more homely than Shelly had imagined it would be. She thought Señora Garza might prefer more austere surroundings, but it was actually quite pretty and feminine.

'Not really. Alejandro takes me to Malaga once a week. That's enough for me. So where did we get to last time?' Señora Garza said, sitting down on a compact two-seat sofa.

'You were speaking about Charlotte and her baby that died.'

Señora Garza paused and stared into the middle distance. Shelly didn't interrupt the silence.

'Charlotte wasn't allowed to have her English family here in Rondilla. Her in-laws forbade it. She wasn't allowed to travel back to England either. Señora Fuentes, José's mother, hired a tutor to teach Charlotte how to speak Spanish without an accent.'

Shelly shook her head. 'It was as if they were trying to make her into the girl they'd wanted him to marry all along.'

'Correct,' Señora Garza said. 'She worked so hard to be what they wanted. She'd cry after the tutorial sessions and became so unsure of herself that she only spoke when necessary.'

'How awful,' Shelly said.

'I learned English because she couldn't bear to speak Spanish. It was easier to be in her company if we spoke her language.'

'Did things improve for her?'

Señora Garza looked sad. She carried on as if Shelly hadn't spoken.

'Every year in May, Rondilla was a hive of activity. The annual bullfighting festival drew crowds from near and far. José was the king of them all, and Spain adored him.'

'It sounds as if he was treated like a pop star.'

'Exactly,' Señora Garza said. 'He was a good-looking man, but gentle and not vain. He treated Charlotte like a porcelain doll.'

'So how come he allowed his mother to be so cruel?'

'Oh, José had no idea of what that woman was doing to his darling.'

'Why didn't she tell him?' Shelly wondered.

'She didn't dare,' Señora Garza said. 'Besides, it would take a very strong woman to argue with a Spanish mama.'

Shelly swallowed hard. She, for one, wouldn't dare to argue with Señora Garza. If *she* thought José's mother was scary, she must've been a total dragon.

'The day of the top-billing bullfight arrived. I was instructed to be at Casa Maria by seven o'clock in the morning, so I could help Charlotte prepare for the event. She needed many clothes. One outfit for the fight, then another for the celebrations, and finally a gown for the evening dinner, which was to be held at Casa Maria.'

Shelly longed to know what Charlotte had looked like. She realised this was a good opportunity to find out.

'Do you have a photograph of her?' she asked.

Señora Garza nodded and stretched out a long, lean arm, pointing to a framed photograph on the mantelpiece.

Shelly stood up and went over to examine it. Her breath caught in her throat. This was the girl who had been reading in the photograph she had seen. She kept her back to Señora Garza as she composed herself. She wasn't ready to share this with her yet.

'She was so pretty. Like a little doll,' she said, gazing at the elfin-featured girl who stared out at her. Charlotte's pale brown hair was carefully twisted into ringlets. Her boat-necked black dress was fitted at the bodice before billowing out into a full tea-length skirt. It was very formal attire, which added to the lifeless look. There was no real person in the photo, Shelly mused. It didn't capture her as she must have been in life.

'She looks like a movie star,' she said. 'Not unlike Audrey Hepburn.'

Señora Garza smiled fleetingly. 'I thought so too. She used to tell me I was blind when I compared her to Eliza Doolittle in the movie of *My Fair Lady*.'

'I see it too. Most definitely,' Shelly said.

'That day, José was the last to enter the ring. He was supposed to kill the bull, but he was a showman, and so instead of finishing the animal swiftly and precisely, he decided to make a spectacle of it.'

'Wasn't that part of his job?' Shelly asked.

'It wasn't part of his job to be killed,' Señora Garza said coldly. 'Or for his wife, parents and several thousand spectators to see his lifeless body being battered and pronged and tossed about like a rag doll.'

'Oh no.' Shelly's hand shot to her mouth. 'Poor Charlotte! She must've been traumatised.'

'We all were.'

'You were there too?'

Señora Garza nodded. 'I led Charlotte out of the auditorium. She was shaking from head to toe and had gone the colour of putty. We returned to Casa Maria. The crowds followed and stood outside with candles until darkness fell and the sun rose once more. Charlotte was terrified of being in the house alone, so I brought Alejandro and we stayed for a spell.'

'She was so lucky to have you,' Shelly said, as she wiped tears from her eyes. 'Please tell me José's family took mercy on her after that?'

Señora Garza harrumphed. 'You must be joking. They went out of their way to drive her away. They figured she was the reason their son had perished. That she was cursed and had brought bad luck to the Fuentes family.' She paused. She tried to speak a couple of times, but holding her tears inside was proving too difficult for her.

'Let it out,' Shelly whispered. 'I'm not going to judge you.'

The older woman's head shot around, and her cold stare bored into Shelly's face.

'Charlotte was pregnant again. José had known and was

thrilled. They'd spoken of the child's future, and how he or she would be José's pride and joy.'

'So she wanted to stay at Casa Maria to raise the child as José would have wanted?' Shelly suggested.

Señora Garza nodded sadly. 'She should have fled back to England. I said as much to her. She should have protected herself and that child. Not a day goes by that I don't blame myself for not making her go.'

'But surely it wasn't your decision to make?' Shelly said, stricken. 'You couldn't have forced her to go.'

When Señora Garza's head dropped forward and she began to rock back and forth, Shelly instinctively rushed to put her arms around her. Much to her surprise, the old lady didn't flinch or push her away.

'I'm sorry,' said Señora Garza after a while.

'You've no reason to apologise,' Shelly said gently. 'It's terribly upsetting for you. I feel it's my fault for making you talk.'

Señora Garza dabbed at her eyes. 'I've spent over fifty years with a broken heart and furious at the universe over what happened next.'

'I don't understand,' Shelly said, sitting next to the older woman.

'Alejandro and I lived in one of the upstairs rooms in Casa Maria. At Charlotte's insistence we had moved in full time. The Fuentes family came twice a week to check on her. Each time they left, she deteriorated more. The mental abuse they showered on her was cruel. She never told them about the baby. She was terrified they would take it from her.'

'How awful,' Shelly said, shuddering.

'I would dress her in clothes that hid the child growing

inside her. They never guessed. Finally, after one of their visits, I found Charlotte curled in a ball on her bed. She was in labour and hallucinating.

'What happened to her?' Shelly whispered.

'I called a doctor, but by the time he arrived, she was gone. Her placenta had been low-lying and had ruptured during the labour. Both Charlotte and her baby daughter died.'

Señora Garza stared into the middle distance. Shelly allowed her own tears to slide down her cheeks as she stared at the photograph of the pretty young girl.

'José's family arrived the following day. They organised the most ostentatious funeral possible. They howled and bawled and made it clear to all and sundry that Charlotte had died of a broken heart. They told stories of visiting her at Casa Maria, and how she wouldn't go outside or see her English family. They twisted everything to their advantage. The villagers swallowed it all, hook, line and sinker.'

'Oh my goodness,' Shelly said. 'So they hid what had really happened from the outside world.'

'Precisely,' the old lady said sadly. 'Charlotte was buried beside José in the family plot in Malaga.'

'You must've been devastated at the funeral,' Shelly said.

'I wasn't allowed to go. Señora Fuentes told me to take Alejandro and leave Casa Maria. She had the furniture removed and the interior stripped and the place was boarded up.'

'Until my late husband bought it?'

She nodded. 'The place was left to José's sister, Isabella, when her parents died. She never wanted to set foot in it, so when she finally passed away, her son found the deeds and put it up for sale.'

'Incredible,' Shelly breathed.

'According to Alejandro, the sale was completed by the estate agents from Barcelona. So as far as I know, nobody from the Fuentes family ever came here to Rondilla again.'

'I wonder if Gerry knew the history when he bought it,' Shelly mused.

'Hardly,' Señora Garza scoffed. 'If you were an estate agent, would you tell a man with a bag of money that the place was drenched in heartache?'

'I suppose not. All I know, from a letter my husband left, is that he fell in love with Casa Maria, just as I did.'

'Well that's all fine then, isn't it?' Señora Garza said. 'All's well that ends well.'

Shelly could see that she'd said the wrong thing. Señora Garza seemed to fold into herself once more, her back ramrod straight, her eyes veiled. 'Please go now,' she said. 'I will ask you to keep what I've told you to yourself. I cannot make you, but I would appreciate it if you didn't cause a stir. I hope you can turn Casa Maria around. That you can make it a vibrant and beautiful place once more.'

'I'll try,' Shelly said. 'And I won't talk about the past if you don't want me to.'

'Thank you.'

She let herself out of the living room. As she walked towards the front door, she stopped and turned back to Señora Garza.

'Would you like to come and see the house when it's finished?'

Much to her surprise, the other woman nodded.

'I'll let you know when it's time,' Shelly said, waving feebly before opening the front door.

* * *

Shelly walked back to Casa Maria with a heavy heart. She was confused, too. Clearly, Gerry had walked into Casa Maria and loved it instantly. She herself had felt the same way. Both Leila and Jake were comfortable in the house too. How come none of them had felt bad vibes? A sense that they shouldn't be there?

As she walked up the driveway and stared at the beautiful facade of the house, she hoped the spirits that resided there were happy for her to continue with her plans.

'If you're able to, Gerry,' she whispered, 'will you talk to Charlotte and José and tell them that we want to breathe new life into Casa Maria?'

Chapter 35

AFTER MATTHEW HAD RUN OUT OF THE HOUSE, Leila sat in shock for a few minutes. Her mind conjured up all sorts of explanations, each one more worrying than the last. Eventually she picked up her phone and tried to ring him. No answer. She sent a text, begging him not to leave her in the dark. A few minutes later, her phone pinged.

Sorry. In meeting now. Talk later.

Breathing a sigh of relief that he was at least okay, she brought Ollie upstairs in his lounge seat so that she could shower and dress. Under the revitalising stream of high-pressure water, she decided to be proactive. She would go to the supermarket to stock up, then she'd make a lovely dinner and bake an Eve's pudding with custard for afters. That was Matthew's absolute favourite.

She forced herself not to dwell on his strange behaviour and what it might mean. Instead, she got busy with housework and list-making. Then she drove to the supermarket and did a big shop.

By the time she got home again, her hands and feet were utterly numb as she felt the full force of the Irish winter. She wondered what the weather was like in Spain, and felt a pang of homesickness for Rondilla. Once she'd put away the groceries and lit the fire, she called her mum. The phone went straight to voicemail. Shelly was dreadful for leaving her phone lying around and wandering off to another place. She tried Jake instead.

'Hi, Leila,' he answered, amidst lots of noise. 'I'm in the middle of drilling something, can I call you later?'

'Sure,' she said, wanting to cry.

Feeling utterly isolated and alone, she took a couple of cute snaps of Ollie and posted them to Facebook. She included a few cheery captions and lots of love hearts, making out that her life was absolutely blissfully brilliant.

She scanned her friends' pages and looked at what people had been up to over New Year. Everyone seemed to be having the best time ever. Her work colleagues had been at all sorts of parties and were organising a fund-raising lunch this week. Normally she'd be right in the thick of it, but now she was trapped. She wished the group of mums at the mother-and-baby group were contactable. She cursed herself for not being more forward and asking for some phone numbers.

She patted her tummy gently. 'Sorry, baby,' she said. It wasn't the poor baby's fault it was coming so soon. But she really hadn't a clue how she was going to cope.

Her phone rang and Matthew's name appeared on the screen. She felt relief flood her.

'Hi,' she said. 'I was beginning to think you were avoiding me!'

'No, not at all,' he said, sounding odd. 'I'm in the car with Liam and we're on our way back to the house. I need to pick up some clothes because we've got to go to Germany for a few days.'

'Oh,' she said, on the verge of tears. Knowing she couldn't say a word in front of his colleague, she said she'd see them in a few minutes and hung up.

Liam hadn't seen the house before, so he came in and wandered about, looking wildly impressed.

'This is deadly. I'm living in a bedsit with two of my mates at the moment. It stinks and the electricity keeps getting cut off!'

'Some day you'll have a nice place like this,' Leila said kindly. 'Are you finished in college yet?'

'I've to submit my last bit of project work and then I'll be done and dusted,' he said, nodding. 'It's cool of Matthew to bring me to Germany, though. I've never been. Got my suit, as you can see.' He twirled around, looking very pleased. Liam was more like a fifteen-year-old than a twenty-five-year-old, but Matthew insisted he was brilliant at marketing and that they were getting his work for much less because he wasn't yet qualified.

'Sorry it's so rushed, love,' Matthew said, pecking her on the cheek.

'When will you be back?' she asked.

'Two nights, maybe three. It's a huge trade fair and I need to try and tie up some loose ends. There'll be a lot of people there I need to link in with, too.'

'Can I talk to you in another room for a sec?' she said quietly.

Matthew looked uncomfortable. 'I've really got to get going,' he said.

Leila looked at him imploringly. 'I'm at a loss, Matthew. Are you okay?'

'Sure, sure,' he said quickly. 'It's just work, that's all.'

'Yes, but—'

'I'm sorry, Leila, but I'm running late. Come on, Liam,' he called. 'Time to go.'

Leila watched the two of them get into the car. Ollie

woke and began to scream as soon as they pulled out of the driveway. She looked at him in despair. Suddenly the house felt too big, the rooms echoing with his cries. She glanced down at her stomach, and the full reality of her life for the next few days hit her hard. She wouldn't be able to get any help with Ollie, not for a second. She wouldn't even be able to go to the loo without involving him. She felt like crying. On top of all that, her boyfriend was acting weirdly and she had no idea why.

Perhaps it was a knee-jerk reaction, or maybe it was because she had hormones flying out of her ears, but Leila flicked open her laptop and booked a flight back to Malaga. Then she began stuffing random items into a bag. She hadn't properly unpacked Ollie's things yet, so she simply added to them. She'd booked a large suitcase into the hold on the plane, so she had plenty of weight allowance.

She changed Ollie, organised a taxi and was ready and waiting fifteen minutes before it was due to arrive. She felt like her world was falling apart. Matthew had run out on her; now she was running out on him. She picked up her phone and posted on Facebook that she was off on an adventure with her gorgeous baby. Instantly three people liked her comment, which made her feel a bit better.

She heard the taxi beep its horn outside.

Rubbing tears roughly from her eyes, she added: *Am off to Dublin airport filled with vim, living the high life and lovin' maternity leave!*

Liar, she thought bitterly.

Chapter 36

FEE WAS PULLING OFF HER SCRUBS AND HEADING for an hour of sleep in one of the empty theatres. She was down for one more surgery later tonight and then she'd have a day off. She'd been working for fourteen hours now, with just a ninety-minute break, and she felt that if she didn't lie down, she'd fall down.

She lay flat out on the bed, then picked up her phone to check it once more before turning it off. She saw a Facebook post from Leila, saying she was jumping off to Spain. As she set the alarm and put down her phone, tears soaked Fee's cheeks. Leila was the luckiest girl in the world, she mused. She had Matthew who idolised her, baby Ollie who was a little munchkin, and now baby number two on the way. Plus she had the freedom and the means to hop back and forth from Spain as the mood took her.

Fee envied her. It all sounded idyllic. She looked around the theatre she was lying in and had a sudden surreal impression that she was dead, that she was laid out here waiting for the morgue to come get her. Her breath caught in her throat and she sat up quickly, taking deep breaths. Had she fallen asleep and that was a dream? Or had her life become a waking nightmare?

She didn't know what she felt any more, what she wanted. This was meant to be it, but right now she'd sell her soul to be sitting next to Leila on that plane, laughing and flying straight into Jake's arms.

Jake.

Her heart twisted in her chest. That was all she wanted, she thought miserably. My God, she'd been a total idiot. Why was she lying here crying about the things she wished she had when she'd walked away from the very thing she wanted most in the world? She looked at her empty ring finger. That was how she felt: empty to the core. She needed Jake. She'd made a terrible mistake.

Pulling her mobile phone from her pocket, she dialled Jake's number before she could chicken out.

'Hello?' he said, as some rather loud background noise filtered through.

'Jake?' she said. 'Can you hear me? It's Fee.'

'Hi, Fee,' he said. 'Wait a minute, I'm in a bar. I'll go outside.'

She could hear him walking, and all of a sudden the sound level dropped.

'Hi,' he said. 'Is everything okay?'

'Sort of,' she said, feeling suddenly shy. 'I thought we should try to talk.'

'About what?' he shot back.

'Well, the house and that kind of thing.'

'I know,' he said more gently. 'We should probably meet next time I'm in Dublin.'

'Where are you?' she asked, changing the subject. 'That didn't sound like Café del Sol, unless Valentina is having some kind of function.'

'Nah, I'm down at the port with a friend.'

'Oh, I see.' She longed to ask who the friend was, but knew she didn't have the right to.

'Jake! You want more beer?'

She distinctly heard a woman shouting to him over the music. Fee's heart twisted again, but this time it was even worse.

'I'd better let you get back to your friend,' she said. 'Sorry for disturbing you.'

'No worries. How's work?' he asked.

'Fine. Thanks for asking.'

'Good. Well I'll let you know when I'm planning on returning, and maybe we can sort the house and all the other stuff.'

Fee hung up, feeling numb. Jake had asked how her job was, but he hadn't asked about her heart. He hadn't wondered if she was getting any sleep, knowing she'd let him go. She wished she'd had the courage to tell him that she was regretting walking away from the best thing that had ever happened to her. She'd forgotten to say that she was wildly jealous of his sister and her little family.

But Jake wouldn't expect her to say any of that, or even to think it. Because she wasn't wired that way, or so he thought. All she cared about was climbing the ladder, right?

As the alarm on her phone pinged to let her know that she needed to get to surgery, Fee felt something shift inside.

Once this operation was over, she'd have to go back to the house. The house that was meant to be *their* house. Her bank account was starting to look really healthy. But what was the point if she had nobody to share it with?

For the first time in her life, she realised that she'd duped herself. No money was worth what she'd thrown away. Why, she suddenly asked herself, had she been sacrificing life for work? When was the last time she'd enjoyed a country walk or a cycle? When was the last time she had just relaxed, with no clock ticking in her ear, no alarm about to ring and send her scurrying? The thought of Jake whittling wood had seemed so stupid she couldn't even fathom it, but right now all she wanted in the whole world was to be in Casa Maria, hanging out, working with her hands, doing something just for the joy of the doing. She sobbed as the realisation hit her full force: a house was just a house; Jake was home.

As she got ready to go back to work, she tried to piece together who Jake might be out having beers with. It could be anyone. It could be nobody in particular. But what if it was some amazing woman with more brains than her? A woman who could see exactly what Jake had to offer? A woman who didn't reject him and instead cherished him and made him fall in love with her? A woman who was beautiful and looked after herself and, more to the point, him?

Making her way towards the operating theatre, she tried to get a grip on her emotions. She rubbed her tears away impatiently and quashed her feelings. Right now, she had to be Ms Davis. Inside, though, she felt like a complete and utter fool.

Jake was sitting opposite Avery in a happening little bar at the port. Marbella was beautiful at night, as was his date. She was dressed in a little black dress that set his pulse racing the moment he set eyes on her.

The conversation wasn't exactly flowing, but Jake was happy to stare at her in a daze of lust. Her body was sculpted and honed, and coupled with her soft sallow skin, she looked like a model who had stepped out of the pages of a glossy magazine.

They were sitting very close, talking into each other's ear, and each tickle of her whispering voice nearly drove him wild.

They talked about their work mainly. He didn't mention his recent troubles, of course; he just presented the attractive image of a successful pilot, confident and capable. For her part, Avery described the property economy in Spain, which was about as interesting as the property market in Dublin. It wasn't a subject that had ever held much interest for him.

Avery flicked her hair back and looked him directly in the eye.

'This is very nice,' she said seductively, moving closer. 'I'm enjoying our evening. Are you?'

'Very much,' Jake said.

They never broke eye contact as he leaned in to kiss her. It was soft and sweet, exactly as he'd imagined it would be. She placed her hand on his thigh, oblivious to the music and the crowd.

'Would you like to go someplace quieter?' he asked her.

She nodded, but as she reached for her bag, they both heard her phone start to ring. Instantly she turned her full attention to it, answering quickly. There followed a quick-fire exchange of Spanish, then she ended the call and looked at him regretfully.

'I am so very sorry,' she said, putting her phone back into her bag and pulling the bag onto her shoulder. 'It is my father. I have to go.'

Jake's heart sank into his boots. The sure thing had just evaporated before his eyes. He couldn't believe it.

'I understand,' he said. 'I'll walk you to a taxi.'

They walked quickly to the nearest taxi rank and shared a brief kiss, then she climbed into the car and was gone.

Jake watched the lights glinting on the water and cursed his rotten luck. At least she had promised to see him again within the next few days. He would just have to be patient.

He got a taxi back to Rondilla and strolled towards the square. As he rounded the corner, he was astonished to see that Villa del Sol was packed to the gills.

'Jake!' said Shelly, rushing over to hug him. 'Come and have a drink. I'm just completing my first little wedding job!'

'What? How? There's nowhere for people to stay. You never said a thing earlier on.'

Shelly grinned delightedly at him. 'They are camping in the garden at Casa Maria. I said they could park their vans at the front, away from the scaffolding, so long as they don't interfere with the building work.'

'Isn't that illegal? What if they have an accident and sue you?' Jake was worried about this impromptu event.

'They're the most gorgeous couple. They got married in Malaga yesterday and arrived in Rondilla this evening, and they wanted to have a meal with the ten friends who travelled here with them.' Shelly smiled at the happy crowd. 'They haven't come to Rondilla to cause trouble, Jake. I'm going with my gut instinct.'

The group certainly looked like a happy bunch, not the kind to get drunk and climb the scaffolding and rip the place apart.

'Well done, Mum,' Jake said, hugging her. 'You're dead right. We need more people like you in the world. Going with your gut is a good plan.'

'Thanks,' she said. 'I know this is a bit bananas, but it's a good way of dipping my toe in the water with the whole wedding planning idea. Even if they aren't actually staying as my guests.'

A shout from the kitchen let them know that the desserts were ready to be served.

'Will I help?' Jake asked.

'If you can give out some plates, we're nearly finished.'

For the next hour, Jake worked the room, never standing still. He helped serve desserts, then cleared away afterwards. He opened bottle after bottle of wine and poured for the revellers, all the while joking with the guests and thoroughly enjoying himself. If this was what hosting was like, he could see himself getting into it.

By the time they all left to take up residence in the grounds of Casa Maria, he was dead on his feet. He left a giddy Shelly and Valentina to their late-night glass of sangria and headed off to bed. Shelly was right: they were fitting in here just fine.

Chapter 37

OLLIE WAS CRYING SO PITIFULLY AS THEY LANDED at Malaga airport, Leila knew there must be something wrong.

'It's okay, little man,' she said, trying to calm him. He normally sucked a soother if he was really tired or distressed, but nothing was working today.

She grabbed their bag from the luggage belt and made her way to arrivals to find a taxi. Biting her lip, she figured she should get Ollie seen by a doctor on the way.

The driver said he'd bring them to the medical centre and that the doctor there would be able to help.

'I no wait. You wait, maybe two hours,' he said as Leila paid him. He drove off and abandoned her with the suitcase and the screaming baby. Fighting back tears and struggling to haul everything inside the medical centre, Leila felt helpless and alone.

There were quite a few people waiting, and as it was a ticketed system, she pulled one of the paper numbers from the small dispensing machine and found a seat. She rolled the suitcase into a corner, then made Ollie more comfortable on her lap, rocking him gently and stroking his hot head. She hoped he might have a little nap, but instead he screamed and screamed so loudly that the lady behind the desk came over and ushered her into a small room.

'I will ask the doctor to see you next,' she said kindly. 'The others do not have small babies.'

'Thank you,' Leila said, wanting to cry at the stranger's kindness.

Moments later, the doctor strode briskly into the room and asked her to put Ollie on the examination table. Mercifully, like the lady at the desk, this man could speak excellent English.

'How long has he had this temperature?' he asked, looking at the electronic thermometer.

'I don't know. We flew from Ireland and he began to cry on the flight. It's been awful.'

If the doctor had any sympathy, he didn't show it. He listened to Ollie's heart and checked his pulse. Shining a light, he looked in his ears and tried to examine his throat. Then he looked in his left ear again.

'Open the clothes, please,' he said.

As soon as Leila pulled up his vest poppers, they both saw the roaring red rash on his torso. The doctor examined it, pressing and stretching the skin.

'He needs to go to the hospital. They will confirm that this is meningitis. But this is what I suspect. His left ear has bad infection, and this can lead to bacterial meningitis.'

Leila burst into tears.

'You need to act quickly and you need to be calm,' he continued. 'Otherwise your baby will sense it and will get into a frenzy.'

She felt her chest tightening and the room began to spin. She knew that if she blacked out now, there was a huge chance the doctor would have her admitted to the accident and emergency department. That in turn would mean Ollie would be alone until her mother could come from Rondilla.

There was no way on earth that she would allow a stranger to take Ollie to hospital. She steeled herself, ordering her back to be straight and her brain to be calm. She could do this.

The ambulance drove at breakneck speed. Thankfully Ollie was strapped down, because otherwise he would have bounced like a little rubber ball from one side to the other.

The hospital acted very quickly once they got there. They explained that they would first take bloods, and if the result wasn't conclusive, they would need to take Ollie for a spinal tap.

'Oh please no,' Leila said, sobbing. 'My poor baby. Please don't do that to him.' She mentioned about his left ear, saying the doctor at the clinic had noticed it.

They whisked him away before she could say another word. Dropping in a puddle of misery to the floor, she put her flat palms on the cool, shiny surface and prayed. She prayed that Ollie would survive and that they didn't have to hurt him to find out what was wrong.

She knew she should phone Matthew and her family, but she couldn't actually bring herself to say the words. Instead she crawled into a plastic seat and sat there staring into space, clutching her handbag tightly.

Eventually a nurse came to fetch her.

'Come, please, and we will let you hold your baby.'

The way she said it, Leila feared the worst.

'He's dead?' she yelled. 'Has my baby died?'

'No!' said the nurse, holding her firmly. 'Look at me. You must be calm. Your baby is very sick. But you must be strong. Yes?'

Leila nodded vigorously and followed the nurse to a room where Ollie lay on a hard hospital bed wearing nothing but his nappy, with a drip going into his tiny arm. She whimpered and rushed to his side.

'We have started him on antibiotics,' one of the doctors said. 'Blood tests have been sent to the lab. We will have basic results in an hour, though the cultures will be about twenty-four hours more. But your baby is showing all the signs of bacterial meningitis. The doctor at the clinic was very astute. He noticed the inflammation in your baby's ear. It is one possible way of meningitis starting.'

Ollie had stopped crying and was gazing up at her. Leila knew she needed to let him know everything was okay.

'Hello, darling,' she said softly. 'Mummy's here. You're a great boy. You're going to be fine.'

'That's it,' said the doctor, nodding approvingly. 'We are doing everything we can. We will have more information once the blood results come.'

'Will he need a lumbar puncture?' Leila asked, still holding Ollie's gaze.

'I will do all I can to avoid that,' the doctor said. 'With the blood tests we are looking to analyse the antibodies and proteins present. But I am pretty sure that we have the correct diagnosis.'

'Why is he having antibiotics now? Before you know for sure?' Leila asked.

'We have no time. If this is bacterial meningitis, it can spread very quickly. The sooner we try to stop it, the better his chances of recovery. So we are pre-empting in the hope that we are doing the right thing.'

Leila couldn't even begin to go to that place in her head . . . the place that suggested Ollie might not survive.

'I'm pregnant again,' she said. 'Is my unborn baby at risk of being infected too?'

'While it's not ideal for a pregnant woman to be around any kind of disease, there is minimal risk to your unborn child.'

The doctor explained that he needed to go to the lab to get the blood results. Meanwhile, the nurses were incredible. They didn't leave Leila's side and kept telling her what a wonderful mother she was.

It suddenly occurred to her that nobody even knew she was in Spain. She'd put her stupid post up on Facebook saying she was off on an adventure, but she hadn't told Matthew or her mum or Jake where she was going.

Fee sprang to mind. Maybe she should call her and ask her what the chances were of Ollie making a recovery. There was a sign above Ollie's bed saying mobile phones were prohibited. Gazing around, she realised with terror that they were in the intensive care baby unit.

There was no getting away from the fact that her son could die.

Waves of nausea mixed with skin-prickling terror shot through every fibre of her being. Putting her hand on her belly, she closed her eyes and asked her father to help them. She apologised to her unborn baby, to Gerry, to the universe for sounding off when she'd realised she was pregnant again. How could she have thought for one second that having two children was a problem? *Please God, let my two babies be okay. Dad, if you can see me, please do all you can to help Ollie.*

The doctor burst back into the room.

'Have the results come through?' she asked.

'Yes, some of them, and they confirm what I suspected.

Ollie has bacterial meningitis. The antibiotic we are giving him intravenously will kill the infection. The good news is that we believe we have caught it at an early stage.'

'Does he have a good chance of recovery?' Leila asked. The words were out before she could stop them. They hung in the air as all eyes moved to the doctor.

'We cannot say for sure. This is a very dangerous infection. But we are doing our best for your baby.'

'What about his ear? Will his hearing be affected afterwards?'

Leila fired question after question at the doctor. They established that the first signs of Ollie being out of sorts had been less than twenty-four hours ago. In fact, closer to twelve. If that were the case, his chances of survival were maximised. They wouldn't know about his hearing until much later.

In the greater scheme of things, Leila knew they would deal with hearing loss if they had to. It was minor in comparison to brain damage, or even death.

Time passed excruciatingly slowly as Leila sat by Ollie's side. He lay there listlessly, his eyes closed and his breathing laboured. Eventually, with the help of the small oxygen mask they'd given him, he seemed to become a little less agitated and more relaxed.

It was dark by the time he was sleeping peacefully and she thought of calling Matthew. The nurse promised to stay with Ollie, and Leila stepped out into the corridor and turned on her mobile phone. It instantly pinged repeatedly. It seemed her entire family and most of her friends had been trying to find her. There were even notifications from Facebook showing that Matthew had been on there looking.

Biting her lip with guilt, she called him.

'Leila! Where are you? I've been worried sick.'

'It's Ollie,' she said, and burst into huge racking sobs. It took her several attempts to even get the words out. When he understood what she was saying, Matthew broke down too.

'Oh no, Leila,' he said. 'How has this happened? What did we do wrong? Was it taking him travelling while he was so young that did it? Should we have stayed home with him?'

'No,' she said, through gritted teeth. 'We can't start blaming ourselves, Matthew. There's no good in that. We love Ollie and we never wished for any of this to happen.'

'I know,' he said. 'But I'm so shocked. I just can't get my head round it.'

Leila had had most of the day to get used to the horrible news, but it was all landing on Matthew in one go. Plus she knew he'd been worried sick about her. 'It's not our fault, sweetie,' she said. 'The doctor found a bad infection in his left ear, and apparently it can stem from that.'

'Oh God,' said Matthew, sounding relieved and terrified all at once.

'I'm sorry I didn't ring earlier. I was stuck in ICU with him,' Leila said, sniffing.

'I understand,' he said. 'I felt really mean after flying off without saying goodbye properly. I didn't want to go to Germany without telling you I love you. But I couldn't get through. I figured we'd talk when I landed, but you've been off air all evening.'

They chatted for a while and Matthew admitted he'd been totally flummoxed by the announcement of her second pregnancy.

'So that's why you got drunk and acted all weird?' Leila said.

'Yeah,' he said sheepishly.

'You silly idiot,' she said gently. She was so relieved that that was all it was. She'd had visions of affairs and all sorts. Being shocked by an unexpected pregnancy was nothing compared to the horrors she'd conjured up.

'All I can do is apologise,' Matthew said, his voice cracking, 'and let you know that I will be there for you from here on in.'

'I'm not totally innocent in all this, Matthew,' she said. 'I was freaking out too. I still don't think we deserved such a dreadful wake-up call, but here we have it.'

As soon as she put the phone down to Matthew, Leila called Shelly and explained the situation.

'I'll come right now,' Shelly said.

'There's no point, Mum. They won't let you into ICU. There is something you can do, though. Could you please let Jake and Fee know? I haven't the energy to speak to anyone else tonight. And don't worry, I'll call you as soon as I know what's going on.'

Leila ended the call, then stood staring at her phone. She flicked onto Facebook, and for the first time in a long time, she put up an honest post.

I'm having the worst day of my life. Everything isn't rosy. My baby has meningitis and I'm terrified. Sorry to be so real. But my life is far from perfect and I don't care who knows it. Please pray for my baby Ollie.

Chapter 38

THE EARLY SPRING WEATHER ASTOUNDED SHELLY. It was already as warm as most Irish summer days, with temperatures in the mid teens. She was wearing jeans with a T-shirt and flip-flops and was almost too warm. Back home now, she'd be bundled up in a Puffa coat and boots, battling diagonal rain and howling winds.

Appreciating the freedom and relaxation of the place, she inhaled the balmy air. The sleepy village knew nothing of her troubles as she walked back towards Casa Maria. She'd gone into the church to light a candle for baby Ollie.

He'd been in hospital for three days now, and poor Leila hadn't left his side for a second. Shelly had called to the hospital and spent a few minutes with them. But the medical team weren't happy about having anyone near Ollie until he was safely out of the woods.

Jake had taken the whole thing very badly. Shelly knew he was close to Leila, but she hadn't taken on board quite how much he adored Ollie. Perhaps, she mused, it was due to his break-up with Fee. She still held out hope that he might see the light and go home and try to win her back. Any fool could see that they were meant to be together. She just needed Jake and Fee to realise it too.

As she rounded the corner, Shelly couldn't help being pleased with the progress at the old house. Alejandro had been wonderful when she'd mentioned moving the finishing date to May. Leila's hard work on social media had piqued interest, and she was already fielding correspondence with a couple of different people who liked what they saw in the photos, even if it wasn't finished yet. She had broken the good news to Alejandro yesterday.

'Could we talk about when you finish, Alejandro? It's just that . . . I've had an enquiry. A couple want to book Casa Maria for a wedding, with a party the day after *and* the day before. It's a big one, and they'd like to camp as well as use the house. They're friends of the couple we allowed to stay in the grounds.'

'Karma,' Alejandro said. 'You were kind to them and now they pay you back.'

'Yes,' Shelly said with a smile. 'It's nice of them to think of us, but I'd need to know that we'll be ready to welcome them properly if they're to be expected to pay all that money.'

Alejandro had reviewed the schedule and quickly agreed to take on some more men and get the job done within six weeks.

'Then you have two weeks before the big wedding.'

Valentina was delighted, too. She had fantastic menu ideas and said she'd gladly help with the catering at Casa Maria.

It seemed that every nook and cranny was being hammered or sawed or sanded as Shelly walked in the open front door. She needed to get on the phone to the soft furnishings place and let them know that she had a tight deadline now.

'Mum!' called Jake as she walked towards the staircase. 'Up here!'

She knew Jake had been up early every day, working in the studio, but she hadn't been tracking his progress carefully, especially since she'd received the news about Ollie. Now, as she gazed upwards, she realised that he had single-handedly replaced every broken baluster and the entire handrail. He'd sanded the whole thing and was applying a coat of varnish.

'What do you think?' he said, looking pleased with himself. 'It will need several coats. I want the new parts to blend in as much as possible. But you get the idea.'

'You've done an incredible job, Jake,' she said. 'It looks like the work of a professional tradesman.'

'I have no man who would do this as well,' Alejandro said, patting him on the back. 'He is very talented. Your father would be so proud.'

'And your mother is too,' said Shelly. 'Fantastic work, Jake. Thank you. Now, I'm going to make a couple of calls to make sure we're on track with the furniture and carpets and curtains.'

Once she'd called and spoken to the interiors people, Shelly felt less panicked. The curtains, sofas and carpets would be ready in five weeks. They would come and hang the curtains, lay the carpets and put the furniture in place.

'Oh that would be wonderful,' Shelly said, sighing with relief.

'This is all part of the service. You do not worry, *señora*. We do this all the time. It will be perfect.'

'I don't want to put any more pressure on you,' Shelly said carefully, 'but I have a wedding booked for May, and as I'm clicking on my emails this minute, I can see three more requests.'

'No worry, no worry! We will make it happen.'

Alejandro was as busy as a bee. Already there were three men she didn't recognise beavering away in the kitchen.

'Everything okay?' she said, smiling.

He nodded, but unusually for him, he didn't chat. Shelly was about to ask him if he was okay, but held back. Although he was a very friendly man, Alejandro was still her employee. She should keep her nose out of his business.

A loud horn beeped outside and she went out to see who was there.

Delighted at the sight of the truck from the garden centre, she waved to the driver. He yelled in Spanish, and she was about to explain that she didn't understand when one of Alejandro's men answered and told the delivery man what to do. Plant after plant was deposited on the front drive. Clearly, Alejandro had plans to put hedges all the way around the garden.

'How are we going to work this out?' she asked him as he joined her to watch the truck being unloaded. 'Have you a proper plan drawn up?'

'Yes, but I was hoping my mother would come. She was very interested in the garden many years ago. I will ask her, if you don't mind.'

'Of course,' said Shelly. 'I spoke to her again, as you know. She said she would come when the place was finished. Do you think she'd mind coming now?'

'I will see,' said Alejandro. 'If she will come, can you walk to collect her? She is fine for walk. But I think it better if you can accompany her, yes?'

'Of course,' said Shelly, not wanting to raise her own hopes that Señora Garza might actually agree.

While Alejandro called his mother, Shelly lined the plants up in a more orderly fashion; the delivery man had executed the fling-and-fire method of unloading the van.

'She say yes,' Alejandro said, putting his phone back in his pocket. 'You will go now and find her?'

'Of course,' Shelly said, flushing with delight. She wiped the clay off her hands and shot out the gate before Señora Garza changed her mind.

By the time she reached the house, the older woman was standing on the doorstep. She looked hesitant.

'*Hola*, Señora Garza,' Shelly said. 'I didn't dare to hope that I would see you again so soon.'

'Alejandro is a very persuasive man at times. He was talking so much about the garden last night that he gave me a headache. I couldn't look at one more of his terrible maps,' she said with a sniff. 'So I said it might be easier if I come.'

'I'm so happy that you agreed. If you feel up to it, I can show you the swatches of material for the bedrooms and the downstairs rooms.'

'I'll see,' she said.

She held out her arm for Shelly to link. It seemed like an odd thing to do for several reasons. First, Señora Garza was pole straight. She was also as steady as a rock. And thirdly, she was probably the least tactile woman Shelly had ever met. It almost felt like a violation to touch her.

Shelly allowed her to dictate their pace. She walked confidently until they reached the gate of Casa Maria.

'Oh my,' she said in a whisper. 'I didn't take it on board when you and Alejandro said you were doing every part of the house.'

She gazed up at the scaffolding the men had erected to

work on the upper floors. The sound of hammering and sawing from inside was constant.

Her eyes were drawn to the plants and pots of hedging that had been delivered.

'Alejandro listened,' she said quietly. 'I told him what was here once upon a time and he got it all.'

'Oh good,' said Shelly. 'Would you feel up to helping me place them, and then the men can dig them into the ground?'

Señora Garza nodded. Silently she stepped past Shelly and towards the front door. As she stood in the hallway and trailed her hand across the wall, a tiny, choked sound came from her mouth.

'Are you okay?' Shelly asked in concern.

The older woman nodded and gestured silently towards the stairs.

'Please, look wherever you like,' Shelly said. 'I'll wait here.'

Señora Garza was halfway up the staircase when she spoke.

'Shelly.'

It was only one word, but instantly Shelly knew the other woman needed support. She placed her foot on the first step and looked up at her. Señora Garza nodded.

'Who fixed the staircase?' she asked.

'My son,' Shelly said. 'He did each piece by hand.'

Together they climbed the rest of the stairs. Señora Garza stroked the coloured panes in the window on the return before venturing to the top. Almost in a trance, she made for the largest room. As they both stood there in silence, Shelly wished she knew what to say. Terrified of ruining the moment, she waited, barely breathing.

'There is something different about the atmosphere,'

Señora Garza said. 'It's calm now. Peace has prevailed once again.'

'Really?' Shelly said. 'I'm glad.'

'Is this the colour you will use?'

'Yes,' said Shelly nervously. 'I thought it was pretty. I love rose pink and cream together.'

Señora Garza turned to look at her with glistening eyes. 'It's wonderful. You are doing a good thing, Shelly.'

'Oh, you've no idea how relieved I am to hear that,' she replied.

Just as she thought the other woman might be unbending a little, she noticed Señora Garza's mood changing. Her face glazed over and she strode back out to the landing. She inspected each room before going back downstairs. Out in the garden, she began to indicate where the plants should go.

'If you want it returned to its former glory, I can certainly give you pointers,' she said. 'But you might have ideas of your own. Do what suits you.'

'It will never be the way it was,' Shelly was quick to admit. 'But I would love to try and restore it in keeping with the way it used to be.'

Señora Garza nodded, her poker face back in place. Alejandro came out to speak to them. He looked nervous as he talked to his mother.

'You seem to be doing a good job,' she told him. 'Don't let Shelly down.'

'Would you like me to take you home?' Alejandro asked.

'No!' she said forcefully. 'I want Shelly to come.'

Pleased and slightly nervous, Shelly thanked Alejandro and linked Señora Garza's crooked arm. The old lady walked away without turning back.

As soon as they were out of sight, she stopped and leaned against the wall of the neighbouring house. She closed her eyes and exhaled loudly.

'That was surreal,' she said. Snapping her eyes open, she reached up and grasped the tops of Shelly's arms.

'Something has changed, Shelly. There's been a shift. I feel as if the spirits have been lifted.'

'Really?' Shelly said. 'That's good, right?'

'Yes,' she said. 'I know Charlotte would be very happy to see what you are doing. She loved Casa Maria . . .' A sob escaped her lips. 'She loved Casa Maria,' she repeated with such sorrowful lament, it brought tears to Shelly's eyes too.

'It was so sad that she died,' Shelly said. 'I can tell she meant a great deal to you.'

'She was such a sweet and caring person,' Señora Garza said. 'She didn't deserve what happened to her. I lost all my faith in God after she died.'

Shelly let her cry and stood waiting for her to regain her composure.

'I apologise,' said Señora Garza. 'Most sincerely.'

Shelly smiled. 'Sorry, I'm not smiling at your sorrow. I'm smiling because you have such a strong English accent at times. Just there, if I'd closed my eyes, I would've sworn you were from England.'

Señora Garza's eyes lit up. 'That's nice to hear. So perhaps there is a tiny part of Charlotte still alive after all.'

'Indeed,' said Shelly as they fell into step once more.

When they reached Señora Garza's house, Shelly waited for the old lady to open the door, then turned towards the gate.

'I'll see you soon, I hope?' she said. 'Now that you've come once, I hope you'll come again.'

'I won't make a promise. I can't bear people who don't keep promises. But I think I will. I admire what you're doing, Shelly.'

It was the first time the older woman had said anything encouraging to her. She felt ridiculously pleased.

When Shelly got back to the house, Alejandro was working like a man possessed.

'Can I make you a cup of coffee?' she asked.

'No, *señora*. Thank you, but I need to hurry now.'

He bellowed at two of the men who were laughing and joking. They stopped instantly and glanced over at their boss. Shelly was surprised by his harshness. He wasn't usually so sharp.

'Is everything okay with you, Alejandro?' she asked again. 'I don't think you're as happy as usual today.'

'I think I am feeling the pressure,' he said, forcing a smile. '*Lo siento, señora.* I'm sorry to shout. I will carry on now and I will not be a bad man.'

She wanted to say that he most certainly wasn't a bad man, that she was merely concerned. But he was gone, wielding his measuring tape with a determined look in his eye.

She didn't need poor Alejandro having a nervous breakdown over this place, although she wanted everything shipshape for the wedding guests. But more than that, she'd become very fond of Alejandro and his often scary mother.

Chapter 39

JAKE HAD ARRANGED TO SEE AVERY AGAIN. HE WAS taking her to dinner in a seaside restaurant in Marbella. He pictured good food, good wine and, quite possibly, good sex. He dressed with care, grooming himself to perfection. He wanted to make the best possible impression on her.

When he came down the stairs into Café del Sol, Shelly and Valentina whistled and cat-called.

'Get a load of Mr Handsome,' Shelly said. Then a frown crossed her face. 'Where are you headed this evening?'

Jake shrugged. 'I'm just meeting someone,' he said.

'Someone?' Shelly knew she was being nosy, but looking at him, she felt very worried about what he was up to. She had dismissed Leila's talk about Avery out of hand, but now she was wondering.

'Yeah,' Jake said, obviously not wanting to discuss it. 'Just out to dinner. It's nice in Marbella.'

Shelly nodded. His aftershave wafted on the air, and with a heavy heart, she realised he could only be going on a date. Her heart went out to Fee. It looked like he had moved on already.

'Well enjoy yourself,' she said, watching as he left and jumped into a waiting taxi.

'You look worried,' Valentina said, coming to stand

beside her as the taxi's tail lights disappeared across the square.

'I had hoped he would patch things up with his fiancée,' Shelly replied quietly.

Valentina shook her head. 'I think you may have to give up this thought,' she said, moving away to greet some locals who had just arrived through the door.

'I think I may,' Shelly said to herself.

'I don't like mess. I am very particular, *sí*. I live my way or no way. This is important to me. I have never yet met a man who could fit into my life. This is why I am single. I have a certain way I like to live, and I change it for no one. I don't like animal, for example. No way. Too dirty. But some day if I have cleaning woman, perhaps I will get one small dog. Only white, with no dirty paws.'

They had been at the restaurant for forty-five minutes, and already Jake knew that this night wasn't going anywhere. The more Avery talked, the more distant he felt from her. At the bar, they had been able to disguise it by sitting close and flirting. Here, it was all about the conversation, and there simply was no meeting of minds, no spark. Avery was too black-and-white. She was a woman who needed to be in control, that much was clear. Jake felt sorry for any guy who tried to fit into her regimented life. He could tell she wasn't as attracted to him this time either.

'So what happen with this girl you were engaged to?' Avery asked. 'You finished it why?'

The thought of Fee made him feel suddenly homesick.

'I don't think she wanted the same things I do,' he said sadly.

'Which is?' Avery stared at him, tapping her long shining talons on the table.

'I'd like what my parents had. Love, fun and a family.'

'My parents separated when I was five. Now they never speak. It doesn't bother me. Whatever.'

'I can't imagine growing up with your parents not talking. It must've been difficult for you,' he said.

'I didn't know any different. No big deal.' She shrugged. 'This life that you think you want,' she said, 'I don't know if it still exists. Nobody is like this. The world is too busy.'

'No, I think you're wrong,' Jake said. 'I think it does exist. My sister has it. I almost had it with Fee.' He looked at Avery, and the reality of his situation hit him. It was like a door had been unlocked and his true feelings came pouring through. 'I miss her. We were together for years, and it's so hard to not have her in my life any more.'

'So why did you agree for this breaking up?' Avery said, rolling her eyes. 'If you miss her that much, tell her. Don't throw her away if you're not sure. For a smart pilot, you are acting very stupid.'

Jake felt as if he'd been punched in the face. 'Wow, you like to say it as it is, don't you?'

'Huh?' She looked confused.

'You don't believe in hiding what you think.'

'No,' she said, throwing an arm in the air. 'Why would I hide what I think?'

'No reason,' he said.

While he wasn't attracted to the almost brutal honesty of this lady, he couldn't help feeling she had a point. Why was he hiding his feelings? The least he could do was to sit down and tell Fee how he felt. If she didn't want him after that, he would have to let her go.

He changed the subject, but both he and Avery knew their date was over. Once they had finished their meal, he flagged a taxi to take him back up to Rondilla. The clear air and starry night sky was wonderfully welcoming, but it made him feel even more lonely for Fee.

The village seemed quiet tonight, with only some stalwart regulars hanging out at Valentina's. Jake nodded at Alejandro and looked around for Shelly, but she wasn't there. He said goodnight to Valentina and went on upstairs.

Alone in his room, he stared in the mirror. For years he'd been so sure of who he was and what he wanted. Now he was floating in limbo. He was almost thirty, after all. Not exactly old, but not getting any younger either. What was going on? Why was he suddenly questioning everything? An image of the new house back in Dublin flashed through his mind. It would be so much better if he could go back there with Fee as his wife. He smiled at the thought of her with a baby on her hip when he walked in the door.

He shook his head, wondering if he'd lost that dream forever, killed it with his stubbornness. What he'd give to have an evening with Gerry. He could ask his advice and his dad would set him straight one way or another.

One night in particular, around this time last year, came crashing into his head.

'I've the fire lit,' Gerry had said. 'Will I make us all an Irish coffee and we can catch up on each other's lives?'

He'd gone for a shower, changed into trackie bottoms and chatted to his parents. Then Shelly had gone to bed and left them to their man talk.

'I'd give my left gonad to spend the evening with you now, Dad,' he said to the mirror. 'I've no idea how to fix my life.'

Chapter 40

NEWS THAT BABY OLLIE HAD BEEN RELEASED FROM hospital made Fee cry. As she read the text from Leila, relief flooded her. She'd been so worried about Ollie, especially as any of her colleagues in whom she'd confided had been sceptical about his chances of survival. Most had said it was touch and go for an infant that young.

Leila wouldn't know for many months whether or not Ollie's hearing had been irrevocably damaged, but the main thing was that he was on the mend.

As she stared at the rest of the text, Fee had no idea how to respond.

Matthew and I want to christen Ollie next week. As his godmother, we need you there! I know it's really hard for you to get time off, but it's on a Sunday, here in Rondilla. Please tell me you can come?

While she would move mountains to help Leila and to be there for Ollie, Fee knew there was one person she ought to consult before booking her flight to Spain. She still hadn't spoken to Jake.

She felt ill at ease every time she walked into the house. She'd strongly considered leaving and posting the keys to Casa Maria, but that would mean returning home to her parents. Going there for dinner one night a week was bad enough.

Tonight was her night to visit, and she'd been dreading it all day. She decided she'd give herself time to mull over the invitation. She would text Leila later.

Work was the one part of her life that was going to plan. She was getting loads of surgeries, and although she was still doing the odd extra shift, she was trying desperately to keep regular hours.

As she walked towards the doors of the hospital on her way to her parents' house, one of the top cardiac surgeons, Greg Murphy, stopped her.

'Well done today. You were bombproof. I was observing your surgery and I was so impressed by how you handled that bleeder.'

'Thanks,' she said. 'I appreciate that.'

Like all doctors, Greg looked totally different in his own clothes, and much as she hated to admit it, Fee found him incredibly attractive.

He turned to walk away and she carried on through the automatic doors. She was almost at the gates when she heard him running after her, calling her name.

'This is probably against all the rules and not a good idea, but I don't suppose you'd meet me for a drink later?'

'I've to go to my parents' for tea,' she said. 'They can be hard going, so I don't know that I'd be able to talk surgeries after that.'

'If I promise not to mention anything to do with the hospital, would you come? Just a drink . . .' he said, hesitating. 'Just you and me.'

'Oh,' she said, blushing. 'I thought you meant . . . Oh, silly me . . . Er, right. Sure.'

'Really?' He looked so relieved that she reached forward and touched his arm.

'Hey, I'm not *that* scary! Besides, you're my superior, so it's me who should be bricking it in theory.'

'Theory is a great thing, and it's right most of the time. But matters of the heart – and I don't mean stents or bypasses . . .' He grinned. She shook her head and rolled her eyes. 'Matters of the heart,' he repeated, 'are a whole other entity. You name your place and time and I'll be there waiting.'

'Okay, say eight thirty at the Harbour Bar?' she said.

'See you then.'

'I'll have a gin and tonic if you get there first. If it's the other way around, what would you like?'

'I'll have the same,' he said, grinning even more widely.

As she continued towards her parents' house, Fee felt as if she were having an out-of-body experience. Had Mr Murphy just asked her on a date? She was still grinning when she walked into their kitchen.

'Did you win the lottery or something, Fiona?' her mother asked. 'You have the oddest expression on your face.'

'No, Mum. I'm meeting Greg Murphy tonight, to discuss work stuff.'

'Who is Greg Murphy when he's at home?' her father asked. 'He sounds like a salesman or a con man.'

'Thanks, Dad,' she said, wondering why they always had to pour acid on things. 'He's actually a very gifted cardiac surgeon.'

'Is he now?' her mother said, zoning in with more interest. 'Is he married, though, Fiona? You need to be careful of those sorts of men. Does he know you're already living in sin with Jake? Tell him from me that you've enough problems without adding him to the equation.'

'I agree,' said Dermot. 'Those fellas think that because they can operate on hearts, they have a God given right to *every* heart.'

'That's a ridiculous sweeping generalisation,' Fee said. 'You don't even know Greg.'

'Neither do you,' her father shot back. 'Unless you've been off gallivanting with him behind Jake's back. How are you going to explain your date to Jake? Or doesn't it matter?'

'In our day, no decent girl would've shacked up with a man without a ring on her finger. And as for seeing randy surgeons . . . I don't know what the world is coming to.'

Fee ate her dinner in silence. She was glad she hadn't told her parents about splitting up with Jake, but now they thought she was going out with half the hospital as well. She wondered why they couldn't be proud of her and simply tell her they loved her rather than constantly beating her down and lecturing her.

'Thanks for tea. See you next week,' she said, before Deirdre could even put the kettle on.

'But you haven't had your spotted dick with custard.'

'I think,' she said, with one eyebrow raised, 'I have enough dicks in my life. Spotted or not.'

She did get to the pub ahead of Greg, and ordered three gin and tonics. She mixed one and drank it in two gulps. Sitting back, she contemplated breaking up with her parents. She'd heard of it happening in America. She might even have seen it on a chat show. It sounded like a great plan.

On second thoughts, she knew it would be more hassle than it was worth. Trying to explain the concept alone would be exhausting.

The lounge boy removed her empty glass as Greg walked in. He'd clearly been home, and had changed into jeans and a long-sleeved T-shirt and trainers. He looked much younger out of his work clothes: really cool and pretty damn fanciable. Norah would be beside herself when she heard about this. She had been so supportive since Jake had left, a constant shoulder to cry on. Fee smiled to herself to think of the expression on her face when she told her about this unexpected turn of events.

'You look great,' she said to Greg as he sat down beside her. 'I would say you scrub up well, but in your case, you look well out of your scrubs and in your jeans.'

'Wow,' he said. 'I wasn't expecting you to be quite so forward, Ms Davis.'

She blushed, instantly regretting being so outspoken.

'Have a drink,' she said in an attempt to pull things back a step.

They clinked glasses, and she was uber aware of how close to her he was sitting, so close their thighs were touching.

'How was dinner with your folks?' he asked.

'Fine,' she said. It was on the tip of her tongue to say that they'd been ridiculously annoying tonight and give an example, but she held back. Greg didn't know them and she wasn't in the mood to explain.

'I rarely see my folks now,' he said. 'They're utterly ancient but they spend most of their time on a cruise ship, lucky bastards.'

Before she could register what was happening, he'd put his arm around her and pulled her close, leaning down and kissing her lightly on the lips. She was taken aback, but didn't quite know what to do.

'This is cosy. Unexpected, too. But I'm glad we're here. I've noticed you before, you know.'

'Really?' she said, not sure she was overly thrilled about the instant familiarity.

They chatted for a while and he ordered another round of drinks.

'So what do you get up to when you're not at work?' Fee asked.

'I like going to the gym.'

'So I can see,' she said with a little giggle. She had no idea why she was behaving like a teenage Barbie doll, but Greg seemed to have that effect on her. Unlike Jake, he was incredibly alpha male.

The drinks arrived, and as she stirred hers and poured in the tonic, she was aware of him watching her. The second she put the bottle down, he lunged forward and snogged her full-on. It wasn't exactly romantic, nor was it overly pleasant.

'That gets that out of the way,' he said. He sat back and drank some of his own drink. 'Let's down these two bad boys and get back to your flat or wherever you live. I like the idea of having a fuck buddy at work. Lots of the other surgeons have one. I know for a fact they'll all be wildly impressed with *our* coupling, mind you.'

'I beg your pardon?' she said in horror. 'What did you call me?'

'Oh come now!' Greg chuckled. 'That's why we're here, isn't it? I know you're engaged to be married, and the entire hospital knows that though I'm not married to Meg, she's my forever gal, especially as she's the mother of my kids.'

'The mother of your kids?' Fee said in revulsion. 'I thought you were single. I would never have agreed . . .'

'Oh come on! Everyone at the hospital knows all about *me.*' He pointed at himself and puffed out his chest as if he were Elvis in his heyday.

'You are disgusting, do you know that?' Fee said.

'Hey, Ms Davis, climb down off that high horse, why don't you? You're a naughty little goer yourself. Aren't you getting married to Mr Delicious the pilot soon? Bet he wouldn't be too pleased to know his fiancée is off kissing surgeons – or shagging them in broom cupboards.' He elbowed her. 'We could do that, you know? I'm getting hard just thinking about it.'

She stood up and was about to walk away when she stopped and turned back.

'For the record, I've split up with my fiancée. I didn't know you had a partner. I thought you were single. And I wouldn't shag you or anyone else in a broom cupboard.'

As she left, she could hear him shouting at her to come back. Clearly the stupid git had assumed she had as few scruples as he did. Tears seeped down her cheeks as she realised that being a high achiever didn't mean she couldn't make really, really stupid mistakes. For the first time since they'd split, she wanted Jake so badly it physically hurt.

Knowing it was probably far too late, she nonetheless made a decision to try and make amends. If Jake told her to sling her hook, it would serve her right. But she knew now that she had to try. She felt a sense of pure determination wash over her. She pulled out her phone and texted Leila: *Count me in!*

Not only would she go to Spain for baby Ollie's christening, she was going to try and win Jake back while she was there.

Chapter 41

JAKE FELT AS IF HE MIGHT VOMIT AS HE STOOD outside the large brown door of the room where he was due to be grilled. It was the day of his final disciplinary action. Because he'd asked for extra unpaid leave, citing grief as his reason, he needed to see the board once again. He'd booked an early flight out of Malaga and now here he was, waiting to hear his fate.

While he'd been working on Casa Maria, Jake had figured he didn't care which way the proceedings went today. But now that he was standing here in his suit, he'd had a change of heart.

'Jake, come in, please,' said Jim, clapping him on the back.

Jake's mouth was dry as he entered the room. The same six people sat staring back at him. He took the chair opposite the imposing row of officials. The questioning was led by one man and the others listened intently. When asked if he had anything to add, Jake cleared his throat.

'I know there is no excuse for my behaviour before Christmas. I was reckless and stupid. But I would ask you all to please consider the fact that I was, and still am, in mourning. My father was an integral part of my life. He was the reason I wanted to be a pilot in the first place, and the driving force behind my success. I was in such a bad place at the time of the incident that I was questioning my ability to continue in my job. I deeply regret my actions. You all know that I have never done anything like this before. If you allow me to fly again, I can promise you that I will act with responsibility and integrity at all times. I am ashamed of my behaviour and I sincerely hope there is a way I can redeem myself. Having had time away from my job, I feel I have recuperated, and I am more than eager to get back to work.'

Jake caught Jim's eye as he finished. Jim's wink was barely discernible, but it spoke a thousand words. Jake was immeasurably glad to have the older man in his corner.

'Jake.' It was Jim who spoke this time. 'You are being given another chance.' Jake sighed with relief and nodded. 'You need to sit a series of tests, as we told you before, and you will be screened continuously until this board is satisfied that you are back on track. We would like you to attend some counselling sessions, too.'

'I'll do whatever it takes,' Jake said. 'I'm so grateful to all of you.'

'You can go now,' Jim said. 'Your tests are tomorrow morning, and if you pass, you can start back next week.'

Jake left the room and waited round the corner until he saw the rest of the panel leave. He had a feeling Jim would delay and wait for him. He was right. When the last panel member strode off down the corridor, he peeked into the room to see Jim still sitting at the table.

'Congratulations,' Jim said warmly. 'I'm so pleased this has been cleared up. I know you'll have to work to prove yourself, but I'm not a bit concerned about that. You're a fine pilot and a fine man; you'll be back in the good books in no time.'

'Thank you,' said Jake, sinking into a chair. 'I'm so glad

that's over. I was shaking with nerves. But I'm thrilled that it went my way in the end.'

'The key thing now is to put that incident behind you,' Jim said. 'It's always difficult when you have to deal with something unexpected, but you just have to be philosophical about it.'

Jake nodded. He knew he should mention that the wedding was off, but he was dreading Jim's reaction.

'Jim, there's something I need to tell you.'

The older man raised an eyebrow. 'No good news ever followed those words.'

'Yeah, well I'm keeping with that tradition all right,' Jake said sadly. 'It's about me and Fee. I'm afraid . . . well . . . we've split up. I won't be calling on you for best man duties just yet.'

Jim's face betrayed his shock, then he quickly regained his composure. 'I'm very, very sorry to hear that. I really like Fee, and she's a good balance for you.' He regarded Jake for a moment. 'Is it . . . fixable?' he said carefully. 'Is it a triangle, or something simpler?'

'You mean is there someone else?' Jake asked. He shook his head. 'Not for me. But I haven't talked to Fee in some time and she is drop-dead gorgeous, so she could easily have been snapped up by now.'

Saying the words out loud made that possibility horribly real. He felt a lump forming in his throat and berated himself for his stupidity. He rubbed his face roughly.

'I think she's in love with you,' Jim said simply. 'And for a woman like Fee, that means something. You should go to her, Jake. I can see that you still love her and that you miss her. If that's so, you'll have a lifetime of regret if you don't go and tell her.'

Jake looked at Jim, so kind and caring. Martha's death had aged him. Jake didn't want to live a life of regret, that was for sure.

'Maybe you're right,' he said slowly. 'The idea bloody scares me, though.'

Jim's face broke into a smile. 'And when did that ever stop you?' he said, laughing. 'If Gerry were here now, he'd say exactly what I'm saying. Go to her.'

Jake nodded, knowing that Jim was one hundred per cent correct. Gerry would have been in his ear until he went and talked it out. His father would want him to be with Fee, he'd said it enough times.

He was suddenly resolved in what he had to do. 'I'm going to go over to the hospital right now and put my cards on the table.'

'That's the spirit,' Jim said. 'I want to be reading out my best man's speech this summer, as planned.'

'I'll do my best,' Jake said, grinning at him.

'Go on,' Jim said. 'Don't waste any more time.'

Jake walked briskly to the car park and got into his car. He decided to call her first, on the off chance she was at home. He dialled her number. It went directly to voicemail. If her phone was off, she had to be in work.

At the hospital, the young receptionist was busy, so he stood to one side and waited to ask her to page Fee. The place was like a zoo, and for what must be the hundredth time, he wondered how Fee stuck the stress. Every time he came in here, he was itching to get back out immediately.

Out of the corner of his eye he saw a familiar face. He turned and spotted Norah at the nurses' station down the hall.

'Norah, hi,' he called, waving at her.

She regarded him coldly for a few seconds, then very deliberately turned on her heel and walked away. Jake stood staring after her, taken aback by the viciously nasty look she'd shot him. He felt his face burning. He hated the thought that Norah would regard him as an asshole. They'd always got on so well. But clearly she'd heard Fee's side of the story and it had turned her against him.

'Sorry, sir. Thanks for being patient. Now, how may I help you?' the receptionist said.

'I'm looking to page Fiona Davis, please,' he said.

She typed some information into the computer and looked up at him. 'I'm afraid Ms Davis isn't on duty today. According to her information, she's signed off for the next four days.'

'No problem, thank you anyway.'

He walked away from the desk feeling so disappointed he wanted to cry.

'I wouldn't worry about not seeing Ms Davis,' a cocky-looking guy in scrubs said as he passed him by.

'Pardon?' Jake said, stopping and staring at him.

'She's a cold fish, that one. No wonder her fiancé dumped her. She cost me a gin and tonic and all I got was a poor attempt at a snog. I wouldn't bother if I were you.'

If it wasn't for the fact that he was being watched like a hawk and an arrest wouldn't go down well, Jake would've punched the man in the face. Anger swelled up in him at this idiot's description of Fee, and also at himself. If this guy was telling the truth, then Fee was out on the dating scene and moving on. Gutted, he slouched out of the hospital feeling like he was the one who'd been sucker-punched.

He drove over to their house next, hoping she might have turned off her phone because she was sleeping. To his dismay, there was no sign of life when he arrived there. He unlocked the door and walked in. The smell of her perfume made him want to drop to his knees and sob like a baby.

Taking a long look around the place, he vowed to do everything in his power to get Fee back. Right now, though, he needed to get his books out and fire up his computer and do as much study as he could for tomorrow's exams.

His mobile rang, and for a second he dared to dream it might be Fee.

'Hi, Mum,' he said, answering it.

'Oh Jake, you sound terrible. How did it go? Was it awful? What happened? I've been so worried.'

'Sorry, Mum, I should've phoned you. It was pretty tough, but they've given me another chance. I've to sit some tests tomorrow and I'll be monitored closely. But I have another bash at it. Jim was there and he was fantastic.'

'Ah, that's great, love. Good for Jim. I know he won't tell you this,' Shelly said, 'but Gerry helped him out of a very sticky situation many years ago.'

'Really?'

'Yes, Jim was accused of sexually assaulting an air hostess and it was really serious. But Gerry overheard her telling a friend that she was almost home and dry with getting a large amount of cash for duping a rich pilot. Your dad stood up in court for Jim and the girl eventually admitted she'd been lying.'

'Wow,' said Jake. 'I had no idea.'

'Well, that's one reason why Jim fought so hard for you today. I'm delighted it's over. I've been badgering Jim to come and visit Casa Maria, but he didn't want to while the proceedings were under way, in case there could be any accusation of bias. So now you're free of the worry and Jim's free to visit. It's all good.'

'You know, I wasn't sure how I felt about it, Mum, but after today, I'm beginning to feel that old sense that flying is what I'm meant to be doing. I think I needed a break, and I know I lost my way for a while, but I'm actually excited about getting back in the air.'

Shelly started to reply when she was interrupted by a workman with a question. Apologising, she hung up quickly. Jake had wanted to ask if she'd had any contact with Fee, but that would just have to wait. He had work to do.

He found some pasta in the cupboard and cooked it for his dinner. After that, time seemed to go in a flash. Before he knew it, it was three in the morning. He closed his laptop, climbed the stairs wearily and went to bed. It felt sad and strange to be here alone. He and Fee hadn't spent much time here together, but he could smell her face cream, and as he picked up one of her stray hairs from her pillow, he longed to see her. It made him feel awful to think that this was how her nights had been since the split. He'd been off in Spain, free of memories, but she had been here, in this bed, sleeping next to an empty space.

He slept fitfully because he was so anxious about the test. As he sipped a coffee the next morning and did a final spot of revision, he texted Fee. He needed to know where she was. She replied within minutes.

Hi, Jake. We must have crossed in the air. I'm in Rondilla. Leila invited me to Ollie's christening. I managed to get Friday until Monday off work. Wonders will never cease.

He shook his head. They had flown past each other in opposite directions. How typical was that! He hoped it wasn't an ominous sign for their future.

He had to put Fee out of his head for the next few hours. He walked purposefully to the testing room, head held high, telling himself over and over again that it would all be okay. Being a Saturday, the airport was busy and the excited milling passengers made him want to yell with frustration. He was just short of shouting, *Get out of my way, my career is hanging in the balance.*

The examiner was waiting for him in the room. She was a friendly woman, who put him at his ease straight away. She settled him at a table equipped with everything he needed, wished him luck, then went back to her desk in the corner and sat quietly correcting other papers.

Once he got going, Jake blocked out the world. It was just him and the questions. His pen flew as he mustered up every bit of information he could and put it down eloquently on the page. He finished the last question about two minutes before the examiner told him his time was up.

He sat back and stretched. 'It felt good to use my brain again,' he said, smiling at her.

'Well, if there were marks for concentration, you'd ace it,' she said kindly. She took the pages and looked at a list on her desk. 'I've only two papers ahead of yours, so I'll call you with the results in the next two hours.'

'Thank you,' he said as he left the room.

He had booked a flight for this afternoon, to get back to Rondilla well in time for baby Ollie's christening on Sunday. He headed towards the staff departure lounge, wishing all the way that he was in uniform. He missed the admiring glances. Even small children in buggies seemed to look at him as if he were some form of superhero when he was dressed in it.

The lounge wasn't busy, but he recognised one of his colleagues.

'Jake! Good to see you, mate. When will you be back? Enjoying the holidays?'

'Yeah,' said Jake vaguely, not sure how much the guy knew. They'd never been close. 'I'm headed down to Spain for my nephew's christening, but I should be back in the cockpit soon.'

They had a meaningless conversation, then thankfully the other guy had to go. Grabbing a coffee, Jake closed his eyes and willed his exam paper to be a good one.

After a wander around duty-free, he sat and had his shoes polished at one of the stands. Looking at his watch, he realised he only had another forty minutes before he needed to board his flight. If the examiner didn't phone before then, he wouldn't know his results until tomorrow, or even Monday.

Just as he was about to work himself into a frenzy, his phone rang and Jim's number came up.

'Jim?' he said, his voice cracking with anxiety.

'Hi, Jake.' Jim sounded quiet and serious.

'Is everything okay?' Jake ventured.

'Yes, thankfully,' said Jim. 'I've just had Vera on from the testing centre. She said you got the highest score she's ever recorded. You're back with a bang, Jake. Well done!'

'Oh thank God,' said Jake, leaning his head against the wall as pure, sweet relief washed over him. 'I'm so relieved, you've no idea.'

'Actually I do know pretty much how you're feeling right now,' said Jim. 'I've been there, and your father was the one who pulled me through.' Jake didn't want to divulge that he knew. 'And I'm not too proud to say that I only got back in by the skin of my teeth. I didn't have the brain power you've got. You're a natural, and it would be the airline's loss if you were let go.'

'Thank you, Jim,' Jake said. 'That means a lot.'

For the first time, Jake realised that Jim had done this for him. Not for his dad or his mum. For him. Being a pilot was in his blood. Even though he'd been told this from the time he was knee high to a grasshopper, only now did he truly believe it.

'So have you any good news for me?' Jim asked hopefully.

Jake sighed. 'Not yet. It turns out she was flying to Spain while I was flying to Dublin. She's gone over for Ollie's christening.'

'Talk about star-crossed lovers,' Jim said, laughing.

'I'm about to board a plane, though,' Jake said. 'I'm going all out to win her back. I'll let you know if and when I do have good news.'

Feeling a lightness he hadn't felt in months, Jake strode towards the departure gate. He felt full of purpose again, full of potential. Bit by bit, he was piecing his life back together again.

Chapter 42

MATTHEW ARRIVED IN SPAIN AFTER A VERY BUSY week of travelling. When he'd first heard about Ollie's meningitis, he was all set to drop everything and rush to his side. But the hospital had been adamant that only one person could be with Ollie at a time.

'Stay and get your deals done, love,' Leila said. 'There's no point in the whole world coming to a standstill. Besides, we're going to need all the money we can get going forward.'

'Why?' he asked fearfully.

'I need to give up work, Matthew,' she said quietly. 'I can't leave Ollie or the next baby. So with your blessing, I want to tell the bank I'm not coming back for the moment.'

'Of course,' Matthew said instantly. 'You need to be there with the babies. We've no mortgage, thanks to Gerry and the sale of my flat, so I'll be able to support us.'

Leila emailed the bank and they were instantly supportive, advising her to apply for a leave of absence instead. That way she'd have the option of taking her job back. Her adviser admitted that she might not get as much time as she required, but it was better than chucking it in altogether.

So Leila had made a choice. She was content, and now that Ollie was on the mend, she was excited about the new baby too.

'I know it's very soon,' she said to Shelly over a cup of mint tea outside Café del Sol, 'but maybe it'll be fabulous in the long run. They can grow up together, and unless I have some sort of crazy hormonal figary or total change of mind, I won't be having any more. Two is enough for me!'

'Never say never,' Shelly said, patting her hand. 'See how you go with two and take it from there.'

'I miss Dad,' Leila said. 'He did the most amazing thing by setting us up in a home. I will always think of him when we walk through that door. But I wish he was here to see Ollie getting christened tomorrow.'

'Me too, love,' said Shelly as she hugged her. 'I don't think we'll ever stop missing him. But that shows how much we loved him, don't you think?'

Leila nodded, then both women looked up as they heard footsteps coming towards them on the cobblestones.

'Fee!' Leila shouted, standing and rushing to throw her arms round her. 'You're here! I'm so pleased.'

'I got here last night,' she said. 'Can you believe I've actually got four days off work? Thank you for inviting me. I needed the break and to see you guys.'

As she hugged Shelly too and bent to kiss Ollie in his pram, Fee looked about in hesitation.

'Is Jake here?'

'No,' said Leila. 'He's back in Dublin. He had the disciplinary hearing yesterday and then he had to do some exams today. He said he'd try to make it back for the christening tomorrow.'

'Okay,' Fee said, as she sat and accepted a glass of water that Shelly poured from the pitcher on the table.

'How is your room?' asked Shelly. 'Valentina makes everything very comfortable here.'

'Oh it's lovely,' said Fee. 'But I was a little confused last night: where are you staying?'

'We've moved into the mews at the back of Casa Maria,' Shelly said proudly. 'We would have asked you to stay there, but we figured it might be awkward . . . you know. It's roomy, but not so much if you're trying to avoid someone.'

Fee looked desolate as she gazed down at her fidgeting hands.

'It's all such a mess,' she said. 'I wish we could turn the clock back.'

'I do too,' Shelly said sincerely. She was praying that Jake hadn't invited anyone else to the christening. It would be crushing for Fee to see him with someone new so soon.

'Do you think we can?' The look of desperate hope on Fee's face was too much for Shelly to bear. She glanced away quickly.

'It's not for me to say,' she said, cursing herself for not hiding her reaction better.

Fee was looking intently at her, and Shelly felt as if her thoughts were laid out on the table on display. She was sure Fee had guessed from her expression and her vague response that something might be in the way of her getting back with Jake. She went very, very quiet, struggling to raise a smile as they chatted.

Leila was still feeling the effects of the hospital stay. She decided to take Ollie up to the mews and have a sleep.

'I'm taking it easy this afternoon, but you're more than welcome to come and visit us,' she said. 'I just need for Ollie to be as rested as possible. I want him to enjoy tomorrow if he can. He's a little soldier, but I know I'm wrecked, so I can't imagine how he feels.'

'I think I'm going to hang out here,' Fee said. 'It's so long since I've been in a position to just relax and read a book.'

'Sounds gorgeous,' Leila said.

As she walked away from the square, Leila hoped that Jake would realise how much he'd missed Fee. She knew Shelly loved her, too. It would make things so much better if they could scrape back what had once been a wonderful little unit. Gerry was never coming back, but it would be lovely if the rest of them could hold tight.

Matthew had arrived and was busy putting Ollie's cot together. They'd decided to go ahead and furnish the mews properly. Matthew's new business dealings meant he'd be away a lot more, so they'd discussed Leila's living arrangements.

'I'd rather you were here with your mum than back in Dublin all alone. The flight is a mere hop, skip and jump, so I think we should be fluid about it while we can.'

'But isn't it a travesty leaving such a gorgeous new house empty?' Leila asked guiltily.

'All that matters is that you and Ollie are happy. The house in Ireland isn't going anywhere. Let's just do what works for the moment, okay?'

Leila was so thankful that Matthew understood her desire to be near Shelly. He was a wonderful man and she adored him.

The following morning was blue-sky beautiful. A perfect day for a family gathering. Shelly had an appointment at the hairdresser and Leila had organised for Fee to go there too. A beautician was also turning up as a surprise. They were going to look their best for Ollie's big day.

'What's all this about?' Fee asked as the lady bustled in with her make-up trolley.

'A surprise from Señorita Leila,' she said with a grin.

'Will we have time?' Shelly worried.

'Yes, you will,' Matthew said, appearing at the door with two glasses of bubbly. 'Leila wants this to be a relaxed, fun day after all the drama, so you're ordered to chill and enjoy yourselves.'

The two women started laughing.

'That sounds like Leila all right,' Shelly said, accepting her flute of champagne.

Carla the make-up lady was an incredible character and sang opera at the top of her lungs as she worked.

'I'm not sure I want too much eyeshadow,' Shelly whispered to Fee.

'The best of luck to you telling her that. I don't think she does the subtle look, so you might be better off going along with it.'

They ended up falling out of there giggling and snorting.

'You look like one of those women from *Moulin Rouge*,' Shelly said to Fee. 'I'm not saying it's not lovely . . .'

'But I look like a hooker?' Fee hooted with laughter. 'Well if it helps at all, you look like Aunt Sally from *Worzel Gummidge*!'

They weren't sure if it was the champagne on an empty stomach or the incredibly enthusiastic make-up, but the two women were still pealing with laughter as they walked arm in arm into the church.

Valentina, Alejandro and Señora Garza were already seated, along with the builders, all of whom were very smartly dressed in suits. Much to Shelly's delight, two of Leila's old friends from back home had come along, and so had Matthew's brother.

They were all getting acquainted when the priest walked in and took to the pulpit. As it was a small church, he didn't need a microphone.

'Welcome to all of you,' he said in a strong Spanish accent. 'Now I would like to ask Matthew and Leila and Oliver to join me.'

When the little family had gathered at the front of the church, the priest commenced the sacrament of christening, his voice resonating against the cool stone walls. The local women, led, Shelly knew, by Valentina, had decorated it beautifully with white blooms.

Before the holy water was poured onto Ollie's head, the priest looked up and asked, 'Who is standing for this baby?'

Fee rose to her feet. 'I am.'

There was a beat of silence, then the sound of movement from the back of the church as someone else stood up.

'And I am.'

Fee's heart froze in her chest at the sound of Jake's voice. She turned. He was standing in the last pew, evidently having arrived late, and he was looking directly at her. She gave him a small smile as the priest called them to the altar.

They stood either side of Ollie as the priest performed the ritual. Ollie was as good as gold, not even minding when the water was poured over his head.

Shelly could see the looks that were passing between Fee and Leila, and Leila and Jake. Every now and then Fee and Jake met each other's eyes, and looked away quickly. Shelly's heart broke a little bit. If Jake were dating someone new, how could things work out for them?

When the christening was finished, the priest announced that Leila and Matthew had asked him to perform a special blessing on their family, including the baby in Leila's womb. He said they wished to give thanks and live in the goodness of God.

Leila and Matthew beamed at each other as the priest held his hands over their little family group and intoned a blessing. Shelly felt tears pricking her eyes to see the love that was flowing around her daughter. It was a beautiful moment.

Once that was done, the congregation began to shuffle in their seats, sensing that the ceremony was almost over. As Leila carried Ollie back towards her seat, the priest called her name softly, and she looked around in surprise.

'Leila, can I have you back at the altar for a moment, please? If you could give baby Ollie to someone to hold.'

Leila looked puzzled, but quickly turned to Jake and handed Ollie to him. He took him with delight, nuzzling his little face. Watching him, Fee felt a hundred emotions spill through her at once. That's what I want, she thought with a clarity that took her breath away. She hadn't known it till this very moment, but the sense of longing that overtook her was unmistakable.

Leila walked back to the altar, where the priest and Matthew were still standing. There were whispers behind her as people wondered what was going on. Matthew took her hand and led her up the red-carpeted stairs. The priest took a few steps backwards, leaving them standing alone.

Leila was looking from the priest to Matthew in confusion. Matthew smiled at her, then dropped to one knee and gazed up at her. Leila's hand flew to her mouth.

'Leila Dillon,' Matthew said, as twenty different cameras

clicked and flashed from the pews, 'would you do me the very great honour of becoming my wife?'

There was an expectant silence, then Leila stroked his cheek softly and said, 'Matthew, my darling, I couldn't think of anything I'd like more.' As she kissed him and told him she loved him, the congregation exploded in whoops and clapping and laughter. Shelly and Fee hugged each other, crying at first, then laughing as their mascara got steadily worse with their tears. Jake walked up to their pew with Ollie, and Shelly kissed her son and grandson. Fee smiled shyly at him.

At the altar, Leila and Matthew were still locked in a tight embrace, laughing and crying and looking impossibly happy.

Eventually the delighted and emotional group left the church and made their way out into the lemony sunshine of the square. Valentina brought trays of bubbly and delicious tapas for them to enjoy. There was a wonderful sense of utter joy. Everyone was smiling and laughing, touched by the sight of Leila and Matthew's happiness. They had been through the mill, with Gerry's death and Ollie's illness, but today was all about coming out the other side. It was about life.

When the happy couple emerged from the church a short while after their friends, a huge cheer went up. News had quickly spread of the dramatic proposal, and the locals had gathered and were enjoying the atmosphere too.

Leila ran to Shelly and hugged her.

'I had no idea,' she said, laughing through her tears. 'Oh God, I'm so happy.'

'You look the very picture of newly engaged bliss,' Shelly said, holding her tight.

They both stopped suddenly and looked over at Fee. There was a horribly awkward moment, but before either of them could start apologising, Fee wrapped her arms around them both.

'You do,' she said, working hard to cover her emotions. 'You look beautiful and happy and I'm so, so delighted for you. Isn't Matthew a dark horse, an old romantic at heart! That was just wonderful.'

'Thank you,' Leila whispered.

'Okay,' Shelly called out. 'Let's charge our glasses and toast this wonderful news.'

Chapter 43

THE PARTY IN THE SQUARE WAS MAGICAL. THE shops and houses turned on their fiesta lights, the delicious food kept coming, and some of the locals set up an impromptu session, playing and singing as the daylight faded and more and more people got caught up in the Dillon family celebrations.

Now that Fee was here in front of him, Jake felt terrified of talking to her. As long as he kept his distance, he could imagine her response being all he wanted it to be. But he knew that as soon as he actually spoke to her, he might hear a whole lot of things that would break his heart. He couldn't get the image of that smarmy doctor out of his head. Sure, he'd said Fee wasn't remotely interested in him, but it did mean she'd agreed to go on a date. And that was bad news for Jake.

Of course, he'd gone on a date too, and the only thing it had done was to tell him that Fee was the one he really wanted. Perhaps Fee's date had done the same for her? He didn't dare hope.

They skirted each other for two hours, talking to different people, glancing over at each other constantly, but neither of them making a move. Jake couldn't stop looking at her. She looked beautiful in an elegant floor-length powder-blue maxi dress with a matching floaty wrap.

He was trying to concentrate on his conversation with Matthew, but his mind was racing. Eventually Matthew smiled at him.

'Don't you think you should put yourself out of your misery and go over and talk to her?'

Jake looked at him. 'I want to,' he said. 'But I'm afraid of what she might say.'

Matthew put his hand on Jake's arm. 'The way she's looking at you, I wouldn't be worried at all.'

'You really think so?'

Matthew nodded. 'Yeah. She looks just like you – dying to come over but afraid to.'

Jake took a deep breath. 'Wish me luck,' he said, looking like a man going to the electric chair.

He walked directly over to Fee and touched her arm. She turned round and they looked at one another in silence.

'Can we talk?' Jake said. 'On our own.'

'I'd like that,' Fee said.

They walked to the far end of the square, the noise of the crowd receding behind them, and sat in the shadow of a leafy tree, side by side on a bench.

'I'm so sorry,' Jake said. All the polished phrases he'd prepared deserted him. Her body next to his, the smell of her perfume: the whole realness of her was intoxicating. He didn't want to talk, he just wanted to hold her.

'I am too,' Fee said. 'Jake . . .'

He turned to face her, looking deep into her eyes. 'Yes?'

'I miss you.'

That was all it took. It was like a dam bursting inside him: all the pent-up emotion of these past weeks flooded out, engulfing him. A sob escaped his throat as they moved together at the same moment, their bodies clashing in an embrace that was also a homecoming. They held onto each other tightly, crying. When they were calmer, Jake held her face in his hands and kissed her, putting his life and soul into it, telling her through it all the things he couldn't say.

When they pulled apart, they were both breathless, wide-eyed, astounded at the force of the emotion between them. He held her hand, not letting go.

'I went to the hospital to try to talk to you,' he said. 'I met some arrogant dickhead who told me that you were a cold fish and all he got was a snog in exchange for a gin and tonic.'

Fee blushed and looked immediately furious.

'He is a dickhead,' she agreed. 'I met him for a drink. I thought it was a good idea, that I was finished with you . . . He was all over me like a rash. *And* the horrible sleaze-bag told me he has children with his partner and they're still together.' She shuddered.

'I went on a date, too,' Jake admitted.

'And?' She looked at him, anxiety in her eyes.

'It was an unmitigated disaster. I wanted you.'

She let out the breath she'd been nervously holding. 'So where do we go from here?'

'I thought I didn't want to be a pilot any more. I thought I didn't want to work hard and fulfil all the dreams we'd talked about. I mistook a broken heart for a change of heart.' He looked stricken for a moment. 'I think the bottle of wine was self-sabotage. Some part of me knew what I was doing and didn't care. I was tempting fate.'

Fee nodded. 'And I've realised that killing myself doing extra shifts and having no life outside of my career is a waste of time. None of it is any use without you.'

'I want to be with you,' he said, taking her in his arms again.

'That's all I want in the world,' Fee agreed, kissing him.

'Well in that case,' he said, smiling at her, 'I think we need a fresh start, don't you?'

She nodded, still wiping tears from her eyes.

Jake slid off the bench and down onto one knee. From his pocket he took a ring box that Fee knew only too well.

'I realise that Matthew has stolen my thunder,' he said, grinning at her, 'but Fee, my love, will you marry me?' He placed the ring back on her finger.

'Yes, I will,' she said. 'But . . . there is a condition.'

'Really?' Jake said, his heart sinking.

'Yes,' she said, leaning forward to whisper in his ear. 'You must take me to my room right now to consummate our union.'

Jake bowed his head and shook with laughter, then looked up at her.

'That is my kind of condition,' he said, getting to his feet and pulling her up with him. He kissed her fervently. 'Let's go.'

Hand in hand, they practically ran to Café del Sol, slipped inside and skipped up the stairs to the first floor. Once in Fee's room, they were out of their clothes and into each other's arms in seconds. As the crowd sang below the window and the musicians' melodies filled the air, Fee and Jake melted into each other.

All too soon, Fee sat up and tapped Jake on the leg.

'Come on, darling, we'd better go back downstairs. Leila and Matthew might notice we're not there.'

Reluctantly they dressed and went back down to the

party. They joined the table where Leila, Shelly and Matthew were sitting, and Leila immediately noticed the ring sparkling on Fee's finger.

'Oh my God,' she squealed. 'Have you two made up?'

Fee nodded, hugging Leila tightly, then going over to hug Shelly. It was all too much for Shelly, who was crying freely now, a crazy mix of love and happiness and grief.

Matthew and Jake shook hands and slapped each other on the back, and the cry went up for more champagne. Leila and Fee took a photo of their hands together on the table, both rings sparkling, and Leila uploaded it to Facebook, with a caption: *My sister-in-law-to-be rocks!*

'So, Shelly,' Fee said, 'could we get a good rate if we book Casa Maria for the wedding? If Jake doesn't mind, of course.'

'Great minds think alike,' Jake said with a grin. 'I thought of that ages ago!'

'I'll see if we can fit you in!' Shelly said, laughing. 'Of course you're to have it here. Nothing would make me happier. And do you think your parents will travel to Spain, Fee?'

'Hopefully not,' Jake whispered.

Fee giggled and told Shelly that she would offer to pay for her parents to come down, and after that it was up to them.

'It's all about you and me from here on in,' she said to Jake as she hugged him tightly.

Chapter 44

THE NEXT MORNING, SHELLY WAS FIRST UP, AS THE others enjoyed a lie-in after the celebrations of the night before. She made herself a strong coffee and went and sat in the garden, trying to work through her emotions. She was exhausted from feeling so much. She'd given in last night and taken a sleeping pill, but she didn't wake up feeling refreshed. She felt low and mixed up.

She was thrilled for Leila and Matthew and baby Ollie. They were a wonderful little family. She was equally over the moon that Jake and Fee were engaged once more, and that her son had seen sense at last. But nothing could stop her feeling utterly alone without Gerry. It was almost worse when good things were happening.

As she sat there, she heard the calls of the men arriving at work, greeting each other. They were working long days now in order to meet the deadline. Gerry would've loved all of this, she thought sadly. He'd be in his hard hat, flitting from one room to the next, absorbing the excitement of it all. He'd probably drive the men nuts, but he'd mean well and would be in his element.

Without even thinking about it, she got up and started walking, leaving the hacienda and meandering towards Señora Garza's house. She knew she could potentially be taking her life into her hands by cold-calling, but she couldn't stop herself. She felt compelled to share her feelings with someone, and she didn't want to upset her children by talking to them.

She'd knocked on the door before she knew it. Doubt crept over her, and for a crazy second she considered fleeing, like the games of knick-knack she used to play in her youth.

The door opened a crack.

'Señora Garza, it's me, Shelly. I'm sorry to come unannounced. I needed someone to talk to. I can go if you'd prefer.'

The door opened fully and the other woman beckoned her inside. Shelly was astounded by how beautifully groomed she was. For someone who had no intention of going out and wasn't expecting visitors, she looked stunning. Today she was wearing long jersey palazzo pants in charcoal grey with a crisp white shirt. The pale pink pashmina she'd draped over her shoulders softened her angular frame. In spite of her height, she wore platform shoes and walked holding herself erect and with incredible grace.

'Would you like tea?' she asked.

As Shelly nodded, she realised she hadn't even managed to wipe the tears from her face.

'I won't be long. I'm sorry to see you so sad, Shelly. Stick with it. Tea won't mend your heart, but I'm glad you came to me.'

She indicated for Shelly to wait in the living room. Minutes later, a perfectly set tray appeared, and they sat down opposite one another. Señora Garza poured and offered a plate of biscuits. Shelly refused a biscuit and cradled her cup and saucer.

'What has happened?' Señora Garza said after a few moments.

'I don't know . . . Nothing really,' Shelly said. Instead of feeling ashamed or worried, she felt relief at being able to cry like a baby. 'I couldn't let my children see my crying yesterday. I wanted to . . .'

'To die?' Señora Garza supplied.

Shelly nodded. 'Is that dreadful? I wanted to be with Gerry, no matter what it took.'

'I understand that feeling,' the older lady said, looking into the middle distance. 'It's horrible.'

'Yesterday was lovely in so many ways,' Shelly said. 'I'm happier than I can express for my children. I longed for Jake and Fee to get back together, and they have. I'm so content that Leila and Matthew and Ollie are a family bound by God.'

'But?' Señora Garza prompted.

'I stood in the middle of the commotion at Casa Maria just now and felt more alone than I've ever been in my entire life.'

'I used to feel that way,' said Señora Garza. 'It was usually within a crowd too. It's almost easier to swallow grief when alone. People assume that company makes for an easier time. But it's quite the opposite.'

'Do you still miss your husband?' Shelly asked.

'Yes, of course,' Señora Garza said matter-of-factly. 'I miss him each time I look at Alejandro. He was a good and kind man, just like his son.'

'So there is no way I'll wake up one morning and feel as if I'm fine again?'

'Perhaps you will, Shelly,' Señora Garza said, leaning forward. 'I'm sure you've guessed that I suffer with depression. That's why I don't go out much. But there's no reason why you won't make a new life for yourself.'

'I'll try,' Shelly said bravely.

'You deserve to,' Señora Garza said. 'You're a wonderful woman. You are the first person who has managed to get under the hard coat of armour I have wrapped myself in for years. Would it be all right if I called you my friend?'

'Of course you can, Señora Garza,' Shelly said.

'Please,' the old lady said, 'my name is Giselle. I would be honoured if you would use it.'

'What a beautiful name. It suits you so well, too. It's elegant and graceful and pretty.'

For the first time since they had met, Señora Garza laughed. When she did, Shelly was stunned by her beauty.

'Perhaps we could try and do things together?' Shelly suggested. 'Like meeting for a coffee in the square?'

'I'd like that,' Giselle said.

By the time they'd finished their tea, Shelly felt a whole lot better. They parted company, with Señora Garza saying she could call any time she felt like it. Shelly knew she'd be back soon.

Not wanting to hang about at Casa Maria while the work was going on, Shelly walked back towards Café del Sol.

'Mum!'

She turned to see Leila rushing towards her with Ollie in the pram. 'There you are! I've been searching for you.'

They fell into step, and Leila told her that she'd checked the website and there were four new bookings for weddings in August and September.

'It's happening, Mum! You're creating a business!'

As they approached the square, Shelly looked over at Leila. 'What's wrong?' she asked.

'Oh, it's nothing,' Leila said.

'I'm your mother, Leila, you can't fool me.'

'The hospital rang,' she said. 'I've to take Ollie for some tests when we fly home to Dublin.'

'What sort of tests?'

'They want to see if he has any after-effects from the meningitis. Apparently it's not easy to tell just yet, but they want to start with his hearing.'

Shelly hugged her and stroked Ollie's little round cheek. He looked so happy and content that it was hard to believe he'd been in such grave danger so recently.

She hoped with all her heart that he would be okay.

Chapter 45

JAKE HAD ENJOYED EVERY SECOND OF HIS TIME IN Rondilla with his fiancée. It felt so good to be able to say that again. The day after the christening, he had gone to Casa Maria to put the final coat of varnish on the stairs. He worked slowly and methodically, knowing this was the final step and wanting to get it perfectly right.

Finally he stood up, straightened his back and looked at his handiwork. He was so proud of what he'd achieved. He had started out thinking he wouldn't be able to do it, but he had proved himself wrong. He looked at the lovingly restored balusters and knew they were his gift to Casa Maria, and to Shelly.

She had allowed him to keep Gerry's scribbled notes, which he kept folded carefully in his wallet. Now that the stairs were done, he felt like a weight had lifted from him. He realised that once he had seen Gerry's suggestion about asking him to work on the wood, he had been gripped by a burning need to do it. Nothing else had mattered until it was completed to his satisfaction. But as he accepted that the work was finished, it was as if that need had let him go. He had done what was asked of him; now he was free to do as he wished.

He brought Fee to see his work later that day, and enjoyed how impressed and surprised she was at his level of skill. He tried to explain about how he had had to do this, how it had mattered so much, and she had kissed him and understood.

'It's a catalyst,' she said, smiling at him. 'It's the final thing Gerry asked of you, and that's why you had to do it. And you're feeling lighter now because you've made the transition from needing to do it to having it done. I hope it frees you up inside.'

After a couple of wonderful days with the family, Fee and Jake had caught a flight back to Dublin. It felt good to organise his overnight bag and set his uniform out again. He had contacted the airline and said he felt ready to end his leave of absence early. He could tell they were shocked by just how little time he'd taken. But it was true – he did feel ready. Thankfully, the schedules were incredibly busy, so they had agreed to cancel the rest of his leave and let him come back to work. Tomorrow he would be Jake Dillon, pilot, once again.

Fee had flown back with him and was at work now. Jake made time to buy food for dinner and picked up some candles and a few flowers. When she arrived home, their kitchen certainly looked a lot messier than it had before.

'Wow, you've been busy,' she said with a grin. 'It smells gorgeous.'

'It's only spaghetti bolognese with garlic bread,' he said, 'but at least it's home-cooked.'

They enjoyed their meal, even though Fee could barely see Jake over the flowers and candles. She figured it wouldn't be a good idea to complain about them, though, so she craned her neck instead. They had an early night, although Jake knew he'd struggle to sleep with excitement. It was as if he was starting from scratch, a brand-new job.

He was awake before his alarm went off, and used the spare room to get ready. As he was about to go downstairs, Fee appeared.

'You weren't leaving without saying goodbye, were you?'

'I didn't want to wake you,' he said, stepping over to hug her.

'I'm on the early shift, in case you didn't remember! I've to get up now anyway.'

At the front door, they kissed goodbye and Fee straightened his tie and told him Gerry would be with him today, and that she would miss him, and that she loved him.

As he made his way through the airport a short while later, Jake nodded his head at passengers and felt as if he was walking on air. Jim was in the flight lounge, and they sat and had a coffee together.

'Thanks again for vouching for me, Jim. I won't let you down. I'm actually delighted to be back.'

'I never doubted you for a second,' Jim said.

'And about that good news . . .'

'Oh yes?' Jim said, his eyes widening. 'Any progress on that?'

Jake grinned at him. 'I asked Fee all over again to be my wife, and she has accepted. The ring is back on her finger and the wedding plans are in the pipeline, which means you're back on the rota for best man duties.'

Jim smiled in delight. 'That's the very best news you could have given me. Congratulations. I'm made up for you.'

Jake explained that he and Fee were planning their wedding in Casa Maria during the summer.

'Mum is peppering for you to visit, so at least I can do

her the favour of ensuring you finally get there. You know, she's really struggling without Dad. I felt so sorry for her on the day of the christening. She put on a brave face, but I could tell she was dying inside.'

'I wish I could have been there,' Jim said. 'Leila invited me, of course, but I couldn't swing the time off at short notice.'

'I think it was the hardest day for Mum since the funeral, to be honest.'

'I feel her pain,' Jim said. 'When Martha died, I honestly didn't know how I would survive without her. When you've been married to the same person for thirty-eight years, it's such a shock to have to go it alone.'

'How did you cope?' Jake asked. 'Is there anything I can do to ease the pain for Mum?'

Jim smiled sadly. 'Would you believe, your parents were my saviours during the first year. Shelly was so thoughtful. If you recall, I spent Christmas at your house last year. None of us knew it would be Gerry's last Christmas.'

'No, we didn't,' said Jake. 'I remember Dad sitting with you by the fire after dinner, chatting about the days before he had kids.'

'Your mother introduced me to Martha, as it happened.'

'That's right,' Jake said, nodding.

'You and Leila were almost like our children in a way. The fact that we never had any of our own meant you and your sister were very special to us.'

'Our friends were always envious of the presents you gave us for birthdays and Christmas. You spoiled us rotten!'

'Believe me, it was our pleasure. Martha would've loved children and it broke her heart that we couldn't have any. You and Leila did more for us than you'll ever know,' Jim said. 'So I'm delighted that I can be here for you now that your dad is gone. And I'll be at Casa Maria in my best togs for your wedding. I'm looking forward to it. I think I'll make a week of it, really get to know the place.'

Jake checked his watch and said his goodbyes to Jim. He wanted to be on the aircraft well ahead of time, to get his bearings again and ensure he did everything perfectly. He knew his superiors would be watching, and he'd give them every reason to trust him.

As he made the take-off announcement a short while later, introducing himself to the passengers and giving the usual flight information over the tannoy, he felt as if so many things were finally falling into place. The future was looking bright.

Seeing as Jake was away, Fee figured it was a good opportunity to visit her parents. Knowing she probably wouldn't make it at bang on six o'clock, and that therefore their tea would be held up, she said she'd drop by afterwards.

'I can do a plate for you and keep it under cling film,' Deirdre said. 'Your father bought a microwave and it's brilliant. We heat all sorts of things in it, from croissants to soup.'

Fee had been telling them for twenty years to get a microwave, but they'd insisted they wouldn't use one. Now it was as if they'd invented the darn thing.

When she arrived at the house at six thirty, there was great excitement: they were melting chocolate in the microwave.

'It's the quickest way of making hot chocolate sauce to go over ice cream,' Dermot said.

'Since when do you two have hot chocolate sauce?' Fee asked in confusion.

'Since Mary next door's daughter, Melissa, started teaching cookery,' Deirdre said.

'I see,' said Fee. 'Where does she do the classes?'

'In Mary's kitchen. She moved the table over near the window and we all brought chairs. It was a bit of a squash and Mrs Crowley's budgie made a racket at the start, but he soon calmed down and we learned loads.'

'Why was Mrs Crowley's budgie there?' Fee asked.

'Because he's old now and she doesn't like leaving him; he tends to fret and peck his own feathers out. Melissa was very understanding and said he was more than welcome and he didn't need to pay.'

'How much did it cost?' Fee asked.

'Two euros each,' said Deirdre, 'but we all got to taste things and there was a cup of tea included in the price. Melissa said she was trying to spread the word and that she was relying on us to do a bit of advertising for her.'

The last time Fee had seen Melissa, she was almost as wide as she was tall and she kept telling anyone who would listen that she had a food allergy, which was why she was 'rotund'.

'She did some dishes that I didn't like,' said Dermot. 'Quinoa and other things that were more like animal feed.'

'Yes, with pretend chicken that's meant to be like the real thing. She kept saying that it tasted just like chicken, so your father put his hand up and asked could she not just bite the bullet and use chicken. But that didn't go down too well.'

'Her body is a temple apparently,' Dermot said.

Fee nodded. She didn't want to be unkind, but from

what she recalled, Melissa's body was more like a bowling ball than a temple.

'Our favourite thing that she showed us was ice-cream sundaes. We have the proper glasses and everything,' Dermot said.

'So you're not interested in any of the healthy stuff, then?' Fee asked.

'No, not if it makes you miserable.' Dermot shuddered. 'The thought of having a bowl of that frog-spawn stuff with manufactured fake chicken on top . . . Ugh, I'd rather die of furry arteries.'

Which was exactly where they were headed, Fee mused as she saw the amount of chocolate they were eagerly stirring.

'You add some of this golden syrup and a bit of butter . . .'

'Wow, not exactly nutritious, is it?' She winced.

'Oh, it's home-made,' Deirdre said airily as she scooped ice cream into the sundae glasses.

'No, Deirdre, you've to wait until I drizzle a spoonful of sauce into the dish first.'

The two of them argued like cats until the desserts were assembled. But as they sat at the table with their newly acquired long spoons to match the dishes, they were thrilled.

'It's great fun. We mix it up, as Melissa suggested,' Dermot said through a mouthful of ice cream.

'Last night,' Deirdre said, 'I bashed up a Crunchie bar with the rolling pin and we distributed that through the sundae. It was delicious.'

Fee moved the conversation to sunny climates, and how wonderful it would be for them to take their new-found ice-cream interest elsewhere.

'We were thinking about a bus tour to Wales, now that you mention it,' Deirdre said.

'How about Spain? In June, for my wedding?' Fee said. 'I'll pay your fares, and Shelly knows a lovely guest house where I have a room put by for you.'

They stopped eating their sundaes and stared at her as if she'd just suggested a month at the Playboy Mansion.

'But we assumed you'd get married here, Fiona. In a proper church, with a real priest.'

'We're not planning on having a church wedding no matter where we go,' Fee said. 'And Jake's family are starting a new business. We want to support it and we also happen to love the area. It's stunning, and I know you'd both love it.'

Deirdre looked over at Dermot and sighed.

'You always have to make things so complicated, Fiona,' she said sadly. 'But your happiness is what we crave. So of course we'll go to Spain if you think that's what you want.'

'Really?' Fee said, shoving her chair back and standing to hug her mother. 'I'm thrilled, Mum, thank you.'

'And you reckon they have a decent selection of ice cream there?' her father said, staring down at his quickly emptied sundae dish like a true addict.

'I promise you there are entire shops at the port of Marbella that sell nothing but ice cream. It's only a short drive from Rondilla and I'll take you there myself.'

Fee showed them photographs of Casa Maria from her phone, as well as the pretty square and narrow cobbled streets of Rondilla.

'I'll book everything and accompany you there,' she said.

Delighted with her night's work, she drove home feeling more relaxed than she had in years. She called Shelly and firmed up a date, and said she'd let Jake know that the fourth of June was in the book.

Just as she was settling down in bed, Jake rang. She filled him in on the new ice-cream obsession and how easy it had been to convince her folks to come to Spain.

'That's amazing. I'm relieved,' he said. 'I honestly thought it was going to be a Mexican stand-off.'

'I know, me too,' she said.

For the next ten days, it was business as usual for Jake and Fee. They spoke on the phone daily, and the wedding plans were going ahead full tilt.

It so happened that Jake ended up stepping in for a collegue and taking an unexpected flight to Malaga, with a one-night stopover. Thrilled at the chance to pay a visit, he took a taxi up to Rondilla. Alejandro greeted him as he walked into Casa Maria.

'Jake, *hola*!' he said, banging him on the back. 'Come and I will show you. We have many things done now.'

He wasn't lying. The kitchen had been refitted with new cupboards, the old stove was fired up and working, and Jake could see that the back garden had been tamed and there were plenty of newly planted things. There were even tables and chairs on the freshly laid patio. In the large dining room, the floors had been cleaned and sanded and re-waxed. There was a man on a dangerously high ladder, hooking up drapes.

'Wow, this is amazing,' he said. 'I can't believe how much you've done in ten days.'

'Your mama asked me to bring more men because she need to finish quickly. She ask and I do,' Alejandro said. 'You walk about. I need to go to work now.'

Jake thanked him and continued through the hallway to the large front reception room. It had new curtains and a couple of large coloured rugs. It was all set and waiting for the furniture. The room was freshly painted and looked so grand, yet so welcoming.

The two small reception rooms had been redesigned, one as an office area and the other as a library. Shelly had thought of having a quiet reading room, which was a lovely idea. It had been lined with shelves, and already there were an astonishing number of books in place. Jake smiled. Both his parents were avid readers and they'd had many heated discussions about the books they'd read. He felt overcome with emotion as he gazed at some of the titles that had been Gerry's. He'd been a great man for thrillers, and it was lovely to see so many of them here for others to enjoy.

There was a man polishing the banisters as he moved upstairs. The steps had been re-varnished and the golden-coloured carpet running up the middle was secured by pretty brass bars. Another man was hanging picture hooks.

The first two bedrooms had been carpeted, with sweeping drapes hung and wardrobes and dressing tables delivered. As he made his way into a third bedroom, he caught up with the carpet layer. The slightly eggy smell of fresh wool filled the air. Mixed in with the paint, it made for exciting stuff.

'Hello, Jake!' Shelly said, rushing to hug him. 'Isn't this like Santa's workshop? I can't get over how swiftly Alejandro has turned the place around.'

'It's quite astonishing,' Jake agreed. 'It's so inviting and homely, Mum.'

'Did you see my library? I had all our books shipped

over. They arrived yesterday and I arranged them this morning.'

'I saw,' Jake said with a watery smile. 'I'm thrilled to see all Dad's favourites there too.'

'I feel as if he's now a part of Casa Maria,' she said. 'I'm hoping we'll end up with some foreign titles as time rolls by.'

'You're brilliant, Mum, do you know that?' he said.

Before they could talk any further, the beeping sound of a reversing van outside caught their attention. Jake walked to the window and grinned.

'Looks as if half the furniture shop has just arrived.'

'Already?' Shelly joined him. 'Cripes, it wasn't supposed to be delivered for another two weeks. Seems they do things instantly around here.'

Alejandro was calling Shelly's name, so they both descended to the hallway, where one of the furniture delivery men was handing over a pile of paperwork.

'You can check this for me?' he asked, handing the wad to Jake. 'Are the bedrooms finished with the carpet?' he asked Shelly.

'I think the last one is being done right now.'

'Bravo!' he said. 'We can keep one or two things in the hall. The rest, I will ask the men to put in the correct rooms. Did you pay for the assembly?' he asked, looking worried for a moment.

'I don't know,' Shelly said. 'Does it make much difference?'

'Yes,' said both men together.

'It's a bloody disaster if you haven't,' said Jake. 'I tried to put a TV stand together recently, and even that was almost beyond me.'

'I think I mentioned it to the lady on the phone, but I can't be sure,' Shelly said, biting her lip.

Alejandro searched the paperwork and couldn't find any record of it. A loud arm-waving conversation ensued as several men scurried from the huge delivery van. Alejandro shot off outside to ask someone else, and returned smiling, saying the company made a point of assembling all their furniture.

'They say it make *big* problemas if they leave the boxes. So we are all happy-clappy, yes?'

'All happy-clappy,' Shelly said with a laugh.

Jake brought his bag out to the mews. The last time he'd been here, the carpets were being done and it was in chaos. Now it was cosy, neat and welcoming. Only some of the walls were painted, but there were two young lads lashing away at high speed to get the place finished. He said hello to them and changed into a tracksuit before returning to help with the furniture.

He couldn't stop grinning. It was coming together. It was really happening.

Chapter 46

LEILA HAD BROUGHT OLLIE FOR SOME TESTS AT the children's hospital in Dublin. They reiterated what the doctors in Spain had said: that it would take a while for them to establish whether there was any lasting damage. It was a wait-and-see game, unfortunately for Leila and Matthew. Only time would tell.

She spent the rest of the week in Dublin getting the boxes unpacked at the house. It was tough work, especially when she was pregnancy tired and had Ollie to mind all day long, but she did her best and the house began to look more settled and homely.

At the end of the week, she decided to give herself a break and go back to the mother-and-baby group.

'Leila!' Nina said, rushing to say hello as she walked through the door. 'We thought we'd frightened you off last time. How are you getting on?'

Leila sat down with Ollie on her lap and told them all about the dreadful time she'd had. 'But things took a turn for the better. We christened Ollie, and Matthew proposed!'

The women were so lovely, and even though she barely knew them, they were full of congratulations. Like the time before, she thoroughly enjoyed the morning and promised to come back again soon. Feeling as if she'd had a therapy session, she went home happy and bolstered.

The next day she was flying back to Rondilla, as Matthew was on a junket to Japan to see the Lexus people. She couldn't wait to get back to Casa Maria again.

As the aircraft taxied down the runway, she couldn't help feeling terrified. She worried that Ollie would become ill again. She felt ill herself with anxiety, but thankfully it all went off without a hitch and she made it to Casa Maria safely.

Shelly was thrilled to see them again. She immediately picked Ollie up and took him for a walk around the garden, talking to him non-stop, cuddling him close. It made Leila smile to see Ollie's effect on her.

Leila left her bags in the mews, then took her iPad outside to the new swing seat in the garden and logged on to check the Casa Maria accounts. She updated the Twitter feed, taking a photo of the view from the seat she was reclining on and uploading it. Her phone buzzed with a text from Matthew, promising to try to join them for the weekend. She went back to her iPad, but was interrupted again by her phone. This time it was an email from the children's hospital, stating that they had an appointment available for Ollie with a renowned ear specialist. Apparently a cancellation had created a gap in the schedule and they felt it would be a good idea to have this consultant review Ollie's case. Leila wrote back thanking them and accepting the appointment.

She reluctantly left the comfort of the swing seat and went to find Shelly, to tell her the news.

'I thought you needed to wait a few months?' Shelly said.

'I thought so too, but the hospital are telling me that this specialist is the main man for paediatric ear problems. I want the best for Ollie, so I figure it won't do any harm to let him have a look.'

'Of course,' Shelly agreed. 'When is the appointment?'

'At the end of June. So once the wedding is over, we'll have to face the music.'

'I've a good feeling about it,' Shelly said, gazing adoringly at Ollie. 'He seems so bright in himself, doesn't he?'

'Yes, but we won't know for sure.'

She texted Matthew, to keep him in the loop. He replied saying he was glad she was with Shelly and apologising for not being there with her to support her.

Her heart went out to him. She reassured him how proud she was of him and that she knew it was hard on him to have to go from country to country working crazy hours.

They both agreed that it would be worth it in the end.

'Everything okay?' Shelly asked as Leila put her phone away.

'Yes,' Leila said brightly. 'Poor Matthew is just missing us – and this place.'

'He's such a hard worker,' Shelly said. 'Now there's something I want to broach with you, and please don't take it as me interfering.'

'Okay,' Leila said. 'What is it?'

'I would feel better if you had a gynaecologist here in Spain, just in case. You're spending a lot of time here, so I think it's sensible to have a trusted care option here too.'

Leila nodded. 'It hadn't occurred to me,' she admitted, 'but now that you say it, it is a good idea.'

'Great,' Shelly said, obviously relieved. 'I asked Valentina, and she recommended a female doctor in Marbella. Here's the number.'

Leila took the number and rang immediately. The receptionist was able to give her an appointment the next day.

That evening, Leila and Shelly enjoyed a casual cold supper in the mews and caught up on everything. They talked until midnight over a glass of wine, although Leila had to settle for an alcohol-free version that didn't exactly float her boat. But it was just so good to have Shelly to herself for a few hours and to talk about their lives.

The following day, they took a taxi down to Marbella for the appointment. To Leila's relief, the gynaecologist spoke fluent English, and she was so warm and friendly that Leila felt certain she would be very happy to have her involved in the birth of her baby, should it come to it.

To their surprise, she had an ultrasound machine in her rooms, which was a routine part of every appointment. Leila felt the usual flutter of nerves as the doctor moved the wand over her stomach, but they all heard it clearly: the unmistakable beats of a little heart. The screen showed the tiny growing baby floating in the darkness of Leila's womb.

'Oh Leila, look!' Shelly said, holding her hand. 'I can't believe there's another little mite joining our family soon.'

'Can you tell the sex?' Leila asked.

'Let me see,' said the doctor. With a few more clicks and zooms, she nodded her head and asked if they wanted to know.

'Ooh, I don't know if I *do* want to know,' Shelly said. 'In my day, nobody knew and it was a wonderful surprise.'

'But now that equipment has changed and we *can* know, I think it's nice to be able to prepare,' Leila argued.

'Does Matthew want to know?' Shelly asked.

Leila nodded.

The doctor smiled at them. 'It looks like you're having a girl!'

Shelly and Leila both started to cry.

'Oh Leila, you'll have one of each. How gorgeous is that?'

After the excitement of the check-up, they stopped for a cool drink at a portside bar, then hailed a taxi to take them home.

Chapter 47

AS THEIR TAXI PULLED UP AT THE GATE, A VERY TALL, distinguished-looking lady was approaching the entrance.

'Who's that?' Leila asked.

'Señora Garza, Alejandro's mother,' Shelly said.

They walked over to her, and Shelly introduced her to Leila and baby Ollie.

'Come in, Giselle!' she continued. 'What a lovely surprise.'

Señora Garza looked utterly stunning in a red silk blouse tied with a floppy pussy bow, paired with flowing dark navy trousers. She was so elegant, she could be on her way to a smart luncheon.

'I'm delighted to see you,' Shelly said as she led her into Casa Maria. 'I hope you like the changes since you were here last. Alejandro and his men have done Trojan work, as you can see.'

'May I see the finishing touches to Charlotte's room?'

'Of course,' Shelly said. 'Follow me. I hope you like it.'

Moments later, Señora Garza perched on the edge of the newly delivered chaise longue and gazed slowly around the room. She closed her eyes, as if hearing the voices she remembered.

'I can't believe it's sixty years since Charlotte died.'

'Is her anniversary around now?' Shelly asked, as she leaned against the chest of drawers and folded her arms.

'It's today,' she replied. 'But as I sit here, I feel as if it could have been last year. Time is a strange thing, Shelly. When I allow my mind to wander back over the years, I comprehend that it is a lifetime ago. But in here,' she said, patting her heart, 'it could have been yesterday.'

'You really miss Charlotte still, don't you? She must have been a wonderful person to work for.'

'Don't you see?' Señora Garza said, with tears shining in her eyes. 'She was more than my boss. She was my friend and my companion.'

'I understand,' Shelly said. 'I'm sure you were a great support for her.'

Señora Garza rocked gently back and forth. Her mind seemed to have gone to another place altogether. Shelly waited, knowing how distancing grief could be.

'I think I relied on Charlotte more than she relied on me,' the old lady said. 'Once I was widowed, I substituted her for my husband. I made Casa Maria my home and I thought that I would always have a place where I belonged.'

'So when Charlotte died and Casa Maria was closed up, you felt destitute?'

'Yes,' said Giselle. 'As the years rolled by and this house began to crumble, so too did my happiness and my ability to derive the best from life. I know that will sound utterly pathetic to you. But since you've come along, so much hope has sprung forth.'

'Thank you,' Shelly said. 'I'm glad Casa Maria is working her charm on all of us. She's helping to heal so many broken hearts.'

Señora Garza walked across the room and leaned the heels of her hands on the sash window, looking out at the valley below.

'You are doing superb work in the garden,' Señora Garza said. 'Could we take a walk around and you can show me the progress?'

'I'd be delighted to,' Shelly said warmly.

As they came down the stairs, Alejandro was standing there, looking astonished.

'Mama?'

'*Hola*, Alejandro,' she said. 'I came to see. You have done a wonderful thing here.'

Shelly watched as a smile lit Alejandro's face, a smile she'd never seen before. Mother and son looked at each other intently, and she knew this was something new for them.

'Thank you, Mama,' he managed to say. 'This means very much to me.'

Señora Garza nodded. 'Shelly is going to take me around the garden. I want to see all of your work.'

Alejandro looked as if he might burst with pride. 'So you stay here for a little while?' he asked.

'Yes,' she said. 'I will not outstay my welcome, of course, but I am very interested in everything.'

'I must run an errand,' Alejandro said, 'but I bring you home then, okay?'

With that, he turned on his heel and dashed outside, towards the driveway.

Shelly laughed. 'He's the hardest-working man I've ever met. Come, I'll show you outside.'

Leila let Shelly and Señora Garza go ahead. She knew Ollie needed a nappy change, so she walked back to the mews to clean him up and change him. She was fascinated by the regal Señora Garza and wanted to talk to her, maybe even hear some of her stories about Casa Maria.

As soon as Ollie was fit for public viewing again, she

hurried out into the garden to find the two women. When she caught up, they were in the rose arbour, discussing the varieties Alejandro had chosen to plant.

'There you are,' Shelly said, reaching out to take Ollie. 'You smell fresh as a daisy, little man.'

'He is a beautiful child,' Señora Garza said. 'Is he easy to mind, or one of the tough ones?'

Leila laughed. 'I love it when a mother says it like it is,' she said. 'He's tough when it comes to sleeping, so I'm usually exhausted, but he's wonderful in everything else, so I guess I can't really complain.'

Señora Garza nodded. 'He will grow into his sleep, then he will be perfect all over.'

'Leila is expecting her second child,' Shelly said, handing Ollie back to her daughter. 'She had a scan this morning, in fact, and we were told it is a girl.'

Señora Garza clapped her hands. 'Wonderful news. Many congratulations, Leila. We used to call this a gentleman's family.'

They all laughed at the description.

'I'll have to remember to tell Matthew that,' Leila said.

They walked slowly back towards the house, stopping often to examine plants, enjoying the view of the revamped facade.

As they passed under the shade of a carob tree, Señora Garza tapped the bark with her walking stick and tutted.

'I hate to see graffiti in trees. I never understand it.'

She walked on, Leila at her side, but Shelly stopped, curious about what she had meant. She hadn't noticed graffiti on any of the trees. She stepped closer to the bark, and then she saw it. Just above her head, a crude heart and arrow had been carved into the trunk. The initials inside the hearts were SD + GD.

She gasped and put her hand out to steady herself. She stared, uncomprehending at first, then slowly her brain worked out that Gerry must have done this. It was a joke between them. After an argument one day, he had apologised by carving their names on a tree in their garden back in Dublin. It had made her laugh, which ended the argument. And over the years, it always made her smile whenever she looked at it.

And now here it was, the same carving, in Casa Maria.

'Oh Gerry, you old romantic,' she said, reaching up to touch the roughly hewn initials.

She began to laugh. It was simply too wonderful. For him to have thought of it, to have done it, and now for it to be uncovered like this. She shook her head in disbelief. The amazing thing was, she wasn't crying. Yes, her heart heaved in her chest, but just as in the Dublin garden, the sight made her smile. It made her happy. She felt as if he had transferred here with her, bringing a little of their old home with him but at the same time making a new home. That was exactly what she had done too. The sense of connection, in spite of death, was overwhelming. It was as if he had reached out through time and space to stroke her cheek.

Still a little stunned, Shelly remembered her guest and began to make her way towards the house again to find Leila and Señora Garza. As she approached the front door, she was puzzled to see Alejandro and Valentina walking quickly up the driveway towards her. Valentina looked grey in the face, as if something awful had happened.

'What's wrong?' Shelly asked, fearing their answer.

'Is Mama still here?' Alejandro asked tersely.

'Yes, I think she must be inside.'

'We need your help,' Valentina said. 'We hope you don't mind us taking liberties, but we need to have a meeting . . .'

'With Mama,' Alejandro added.

'Okay,' Shelly said, 'and how can I help?'

'It's one that we've waited ten years to have,' Valentina said.

'I don't understand,' Shelly said in confusion.

'We think Señora Garza will take very badly what we have to say. If you are there, it might be more pleasant.'

'But if it's something serious, which it appears to be, don't you want to talk in private?' Shelly asked. 'I'm not sure Señora Garza would appreciate me sitting in the middle of you.'

'I would be delighted.'

They turned to see the old lady standing in the doorway, looking as stoic as ever, leaning on her perfectly polished walking stick. Leila was standing beside her with Ollie in her arms, looking intrigued.

'Shall we go into the drawing room?' Shelly asked.

In silence, they made their way inside. As she entered the room, Señora Garza gasped.

'You have made it more beautiful than I've ever seen it. Congratulations, Shelly. You have a great eye for colour. Most people, in my experience, have horrible taste. Not you, however.'

'Thank you, Giselle,' she said, delighted. 'Please sit down, everybody.'

She had no idea what was going on, but she reckoned she'd better play hostess for this unusual meeting. She brought tea and biscuits, and they made a great charade of pouring and passing round.

'All right,' interjected Señora Garza. 'Let's try and get to the point. So you two want to tell me something?' She raised an eyebrow.

Shelly and Leila exchanged a look.

'Yes. We want to ask for your blessing on our relationship,' Alejandro said, taking Valentina's hand in his own.

'No way!' Leila said. 'Valentina, you're a dark horse. That's wonderful news! When did this all come about? Wow, I'd never have guessed in a million years!'

Valentina blushed and nodded, dropping her gaze to the floor.

'Well your powers of observation clearly aren't up to much,' said Señora Garza.

'Mine mustn't be either,' said Shelly, in defence of Leila.

'I guess you managed to fool some of us, then,' Señora Garza snorted.

'There is something we must tell you,' Alejandro said.

'Let me guess,' said Señora Garza. 'You are moving away to some foreign land where you can conduct your affair away from prying eyes.'

'No,' Valentina said. 'Nothing like that.'

'We recently discovered that Valentina is expecting my child,' Alejandro said.

Señora Garza nodded.

'But why is any of this such a serious topic?' Shelly asked. 'You're both adults. Isn't this a happy time?'

'It's being perceived as a problem, Shelly, because they came to me ten years ago and said they wanted to be together. But I forbade it.'

'Why?' Leila asked.

'Because she didn't believe I was good enough for Alejandro,' Valentina said.

Shelly and Leila looked at the old lady in confusion.

'With all due respect, Señora Garza,' Leila said, 'you can't tell your son who to fall in love with.'

Shelly smiled inwardly. In terms of blunt delivery, Señora Garza might just have met her match.

Señora Garza eyed Leila silently for a moment, then sighed. 'No. And I should've known better. When I married Alejandro's father, the entire village took against me. They said he was too old and that no good would come of it.'

'So surely you should've encouraged Alejandro to grab love with both hands?' Leila said.

'I thought I was protecting him from a grave mistake,' the older woman replied sadly. 'Alejandro is thirty years older than Valentina.' She looked at Valentina. 'I never thought you weren't good enough, my dear. I'm sorry that you believed that. It was more that I didn't want to see history repeating itself. I didn't want you to end up alone, like I did.'

'So you spoiled their chance of being happy together?' Shelly said.

'I'm sorry,' Señora Garza said. 'I was living in the shadow of sorrow for so long. It has taken Shelly's friendship and her bravery at being widowed to make me see that. I have begun to take medication for depression.'

'So you will give us your blessing?' Alejandro asked hesitantly.

'Not only that, but I would like to beg for your forgiveness too. Both of you.'

Valentina looked over at Alejandro and nodded as tears filled her eyes.

'Where will you live?' Señora Garza asked.

'We were hoping to turn the rooms above Café del Sol into an apartment.'

'I can carry out the work,' Alejandro said.

Señora Garza looked genuinely happy as she asked them all about their plans.

'*Gracias, Señora Garza. Estoy muy agradecida,*' said Valentina.

'I know you are grateful,' said Señora Garza. 'You have Shelly here to thank for my change of heart. She has made me see that we are all entitled to happiness and that we should make the most of it when it crosses our path.'

'Thank you, Shelly,' Alejandro said, beaming across at her. 'I never dare to believe my mama would be happy for us!'

It seemed that a huge mountain had been climbed that day. The conversation moved on, and Alejandro told his mother that they had in fact sought the help of the fertility clinic to have their baby.

'We endured three rounds of IVF,' he said.

Valentina nodded as she smiled bravely and took Alejandro's hand.

Señora Garza looked genuinely shocked. 'I am so sorry,' she said. 'I feel dreadfully ashamed that you went through such heartache and difficulty and I didn't know. I should have supported you; I should have been there to help.'

'I came to your house eighteen months ago,' Valentina said. 'I wanted to speak with you so I could tell you about our plans. We didn't want to do anything behind your back.'

'I sent you away,' Señora Garza said, her voice strained.

'But you told me there was a man looking to buy Casa Maria. You didn't say anything about Alejandro . . .'

'You not allow her,' said Alejandro. 'As soon as she mention Casa Maria, you were crazy. You shout and yell and tell her she must go.'

'I cannot tell you how much I regret behaving that way. I hope with time that you will forgive me.'

Valentina nodded and looked to Alejandro as if she'd just won the lottery.

'We very much want for our baby to have a grandmother,' Alejandro said.

'This will be the most wonderful adventure for you, Giselle,' Shelly said. 'Speaking from experience, there is nothing more wonderful than having a grandchild. It breathes new life into everybody's world.'

'Yes,' said Señora Garza. 'The future looks hopeful.'

The others were too caught up in the moment, but Shelly noticed the sadness in the old lady's eyes. She recognised it because she felt the same way. Perhaps one day they would both find a new spark to warm their hearts once again. Shelly knew it was far too soon for her, but Señora Garza had waited almost a lifetime to feel loved. If all were right with the world, she would come alive again before it was too late.

Alejandro hugged Valentina and said he needed to get back to work, which made Shelly smile.

'Nobody could ever accuse your son of being lazy,' she said to Señora Garza.

'He's a good man,' she agreed. 'Valentina is a lovely girl, too. I'm happy for them. Truly. And now I think I am ready to go home. I need some rest after such an eventful day.'

They put Ollie in his stroller and the three women walked

the short distance to Señora Garza's house. She didn't invite them in, and Shelly didn't ask. She knew her friend was worn out from the emotions of the day. She saw her to the door, then returned to Leila and Ollie.

Leila grinned. 'My God, who'd have thought Rondilla would have its very own Charles and Camilla?'

'You bold thing,' Shelly said, as the two of them dissolved into laughter.

In the back of her mind, she was seeing the love heart on the tree trunk. It was like a talisman to ward off worry and fear. It was Gerry reaching out to tell her she had made the right decision, and that everything was going to be just fine.

Chapter 48

IT WAS MID MAY, AND WITH CASA MARIA PRACTI-cally ready for its debut wedding season, Shelly decided to make a return trip to Ireland while she still had time.

She wanted to get an outfit for Jake and Fee's wedding, and to see friends. Leila was back home with Ollie, and they hadn't seen one another for a whole month. She knew the baby was due to have a series of tests and that Leila was being amazingly strong, but she was worried that they were keeping things from her because she was in Spain.

In addition, the estate agent had called Jake to let him know that the sale of their family home was ready for final signing. Plus she wanted to pay a visit to Jen, the photographer.

'Come and stay with us,' Leila said.

Shelly was delighted to have the company, and the fact that it was around the corner from Jake and Fee meant she'd be able to see them easily too.

They had eighty people confirmed for their wedding, and Shelly knew it was going to be a wonderful day. All the guest houses in Rondilla were grateful to Shelly for the plentiful bookings, and as a result, many of the owners had come to chat to her and introduce themselves.

As she sat in Leila's house waiting for two of her oldest

friends to call over, she realised with a jolt that these days she almost knew more people in Rondilla than in Dublin.

The oven pinged, and she got the oven gloves to take the sponge cake out and set it on a wire tray. The mews at Casa Maria wasn't properly equipped for baking yet, so this was a pleasure she missed.

'Hello, girls!' she called out as she opened the door a few moments later. It was brilliant to catch up with her friends and hear all the local gossip.

'You're so brown!' Sue said. 'Is that fake tan or the real thing?'

'No, it's real,' Shelly said. 'I've been pottering in the garden in Spain and I suppose all the bits of sun count.'

As she filled the cake with jam and whipped cream, they sat down in the good room to the side of Leila's kitchen.

'This is a fine house, isn't it?' said Jane. 'I'm delighted for Leila.'

Shelly told them about her daughter's second pregnancy, and the ladies nearly choked on their cake.

'I know, no wasting time, eh?' Shelly laughed. 'But now that we've all got over the shock, we're really excited. How is Michael?' she asked Jane.

Silence descended for a moment, and Shelly suddenly realised that Jane looked utterly weary.

'I don't want to trouble you with my tales of woe,' she said.

'Why? What's happened?'

Shelly sat and listened as Jane poured her heart out. Her husband Michael had been diagnosed with Alzheimer's the year before. He'd been put on a new type of medication and it had helped hugely. But since Gerry's death and

Shelly's move to Spain, she and Jane hadn't been in regular contact.

'So things are really bad now,' Jane finished. 'I only get out one afternoon a week.'

'I've tried to relieve her at times,' Sue said. 'But Michael gets really nervous when she isn't there. He can become a bit violent, so it's not worth it.'

'What about the boys?' Shelly asked. 'Aren't they pulling their weight?'

'Michael Junior has gone to Perth in Australia and is engaged to be married. David lives up north, in Belfast. He comes down every second weekend, but his children are ten and twelve now, so they have sport and all sorts of things happening. It really doesn't suit for him to be shooting off to us.'

'I had no idea things were so bad,' Shelly said. 'I'm sorry I've been of no support to you.'

'You've had your own troubles, Shelly,' Jane said. 'I didn't come here today to dump my problems on you. That wasn't my intention at all. I only wanted to see you.'

'Hey, I've been a useless enough friend without you feeling you can't talk to me,' Shelly said.

'I know you'll understand, but I won't make it to Jake's wedding. I didn't want to send a refusal without explaining myself first.'

'Of course,' Shelly said. 'Maybe you can come down to Spain another time?'

They changed the subject after that, but Shelly could tell that Jane had enjoyed the chat. By the time her guests were leaving, the three of them had made a pact that they would have a week in Casa Maria as soon as they could. While

Jane was in the bathroom, Sue divulged that Michael was in the latter stages of his illness.

'The doctors have said weeks rather than months,' she said.

'Oh no,' Shelly said. 'Poor Jane.'

'I know this sounds callous, and I don't mean it to, but the thought of a trip to Casa Maria when everything is over will be so important for her.'

Once Jane and Sue had gone, Shelly decided to walk around to the graveyard to pay her respects to Gerry. Yet as she stood at the neatly kept grave, she felt nothing. Oddly enough, his presence was much stronger at Casa Maria.

Today's visit with Jane and Sue had really opened her eyes. Gerry's death had been the most horrendous shock, but now that she thought about it, perhaps it was preferable that he'd gone this way. Jane's situation with Michael was the pits. Watching someone you loved wasting away and being eaten up by a horrible disease was unthinkable.

Shelly left the graveyard with a comforting sense that Gerry wasn't in that cold, hard soil. Rather, he was in the warm breeze that wafted around Casa Maria. He was there, not here.

Norah and Fee arrived at half nine the following morning, ready for a day of wedding dress shopping. Shelly had been looking forward to this most of all. It was a good way for the Dillon women to bond.

Matthew had offered to take Ollie for the day, so that Leila could go along. By the time Norah and Fee rang the doorbell, Shelly and Leila were dressed, bags at the ready, champing at the bit to get going.

As Leila drove them into town, Norah teased Fee for not having picked out her dress yet.

'You haven't even chosen it?' Leila shrieked. 'What have you been doing?'

'Exactly,' said Norah, sounding satisfied to find someone who agreed with her so wholeheartedly. 'I've tried to drag her shopping a million times, but she won't go. She's either working or tearing around doing stuff for Jake!'

'Right then, we are women on a mission today,' Leila stated. 'We are finding Fee her dress come hell or high water.'

'Now that's my kind of shopping trip,' Norah said, high-fiving Leila from the passenger seat.

In the back, Shelly and Fee rolled their eyes and giggled.

Leila managed to get a space not far from Fee's first-choice shop. They walked down an iron staircase and into a cellar. Inside, it was beautiful and intimate, with lilies scenting the air and fairy lights festooning the mirrors.

They were offered a glass of champagne, and Norah elbowed Leila when she began to say she was pregnant.

'Give it to me,' she hissed.

Leila slapped her hand to her forehead. 'What was I thinking? Of course you want two glasses. I mean, it is ten twenty in the morning after all.'

The two of them giggled like schoolgirls as the owner of the shop looked down at her nose at them disapprovingly.

They kicked back on the cream sofa, waiting for the catwalk to begin, while Fee was whisked off to a dressing area, her arms laden down with dresses.

'So is this going to be a double wedding?' Norah asked innocently.

'If another person says that to me . . .' Leila said, shaking her head. 'No, it's not. Would I seriously want all my wedding photos to be me with a bulging belly standing next to skinny-malink Fee in a slinky gown? I think bloody not.'

Norah threw back her head and laughed. 'Yeah, when you put it like that . . .'

The curtain parted and out stepped Fee, looking angelic. First up was an empire-line soft chiffon dress with a layer of blush pink over the top. Emer, the shop owner, was pushing this as 'the one', and Fee, who was clearly feeling emotional, looked as though she was being swayed. The ladies on the sofa weren't saying much.

Just then, the bell on the door tinkled and they looked up to see Deirdre in the doorway.

'Mum!' Fee said in surprise. 'You came!'

Shelly had met Deirdre once or twice over the years, but they'd never had much to chat about. Knowing this was a perfect occasion to bond, she stood to greet her.

'I hope that's not in contention?' Deirdre said, staring contemptuously at the dress Fee was wearing. 'It looks like it's made from a soggy tea bag, don't you think, Shelly?'

'I can't say I would've described it as that,' Shelly said, as Leila giggled.

Fee tried everything from ball gowns to one-shouldered taffeta gowns, but none of them seemed to hit the right note.

'Look at this one,' Leila said. 'I would *love* to be able to get into this if I didn't have a bulging belly.'

The dress wasn't one that any of them might have imagined would be Fee's choice. It was strapless, with lots of bling across the boned bodice, a wide sash and a ballet-length tulle skirt with tiny twinkling crystals dispersed throughout.

Emer appeared with a tiara and matching veil, along with an exquisite pair of pointed satin kitten heels.

'They are divine,' said Leila. 'With my puffy pregnancy ankles I would look like a dressed-up baby hippo. I *need* you to try them for me.'

'I would wear those in a flash,' Norah agreed. 'They are totally wow!'

Fee laughed, until she saw the price tag.

'They're outrageously expensive!' she gasped. 'There's no way I can justify spending this.'

'Humour us,' Shelly said, enjoying the spectacle so much she was actually clapping.

'Now that's all lovely,' said Deirdre. 'Not a hippo in sight.'

'That's about as good as I'm going to get,' Fee said with a giggle. As she turned on the plinth and looked in the full-length mirror, she began to cry. 'Oh my goodness,' she said, dabbing daintily with the tissue Deirdre had handed her. 'I look like a bride.'

'When is your wedding?' Emer asked.

'June the fourth.'

'Next year?' Emer said with a smile.

'No, this year,' they all said in unison.

'But brides order their dresses eighteen months or two years in advance. I don't think I can get this made on time.'

'What's wrong with this exact dress?' Fee asked. 'It fits me like a glove.'

'But that's not the way it works,' Emer said, looking distressed.

'Why not?' Deirdre said. 'Either you want to sell it or you don't. I think you need your head examined.'

Feeling the pressure, Emer said she'd sell Fee everything. She even gave her a discount because the dress had been tried on.

As Fee emerged from the dressing room and went to the till to pay, Emer pointed at Shelly. 'It's all been taken care of,' she said.

With tears of disbelief, Fee hugged Shelly. 'You didn't need to do that. Thank you.'

'I wanted to,' Shelly said. 'You and Jake are such a wonderful couple, and I'm so happy you're joining our family.'

'Can you be my mother-in-law too?' Norah asked. 'Have you any more sons you haven't told us about?'

Shelly laughed. 'Jake's taken, so unless you can get Leila to fall for you, there's no more openings, I'm afraid.'

Leila, Norah and Fee burst out laughing, but Deirdre pursed her lips and looked very miffed at Shelly's joke.

Next it was the turn of the bridesmaids, which wasn't going to be easy seeing as Leila hated the fact that she'd have a bump at the wedding. She and Norah tried on dress after dress, bickering good-naturedly all the while. Just when they were about to move on to another shop, Emer came out from the storeroom with a dress that caught both Norah and Leila's attention. It was made of pale lemon chiffon over a simple floor-length satin sheath.

'There are two versions, as you can see. The more fitted version will flatter Norah, while the Grecian style will adapt beautifully to Leila's shape.'

When they came out from behind the curtain, Fee gave them the thumbs-up.

'I think we have found your dress, ladies.'

Norah was happy because it was slimming and sexy, while Leila was relieved that it made her bump look neater.

'I don't look like Tweetie Pie with my big belly, do I?' she asked as she turned sideways.

'No, you don't,' Shelly laughed. 'And I adore the delicate line of sparkles at the neckline. It's lifting you both. That colour will be so pretty in the sunshine, too.'

'I could get away with sandals and not look like a monk,' said Leila.

'And I can wear sky-high sparkly numbers and look like a vamp,' said Norah. 'I have to advertise myself at this wedding. We're not all off the market.'

'What will you be advertising?' Deirdre asked, looking confused.

'My ass—' Fee widened her eyes and shook her head fervently at Norah, so she changed tack. 'My assertion that I am actively seeking a husband.'

'Oh, so it'll be like an old-fashioned coming-out,' said Deirdre. 'I like the old traditions and I'm delighted that Fiona has such a sensible and grounded bridesmaid.' Fee elbowed Shelly, who stifled a giggle.

With the shopping out of the way, they all went to the Shelburne Hotel and had the most opulent afternoon tea imaginable. The array of tiny sandwiches and savouries, followed by miniature cakes that were total works of art, blew them away.

'I had no idea it was possible to make a sandwich look like that,' Deirdre said, examining hers closely.

They talked about the wedding and what had still to be done, and Shelly told Norah and Deirdre that she couldn't wait to welcome them to her new home.

Then they raised their teacups in a toast: 'To the fourth of June.'

Chapter 49

WHEN SHE WOKE ON THE MORNING OF HER wedding, it took Fee a few seconds to remember where she was. Jake had been sent to stay in the guest house that her parents were in. As she gazed around the pretty bedroom at the mews, which was decorated simply in neutral grey and cream tones, she felt calm and content.

Leila knocked on the door and came in with Shelly trailing behind.

'We thought we'd bring you coffee in bed,' she said, grinning at her. 'Your last coffee as a single woman, so relish it!'

Fee laughed. 'Are you trying to make me have second thoughts?'

Leila shook her head. 'Matthew has gone with Ollie to find your father and Jake. They're all off to the barber for a cut-throat shave and haircut. Ollie will observe, naturally!'

'Your mum is on her way,' Shelly said as Norah joined them. 'We'll have a nice girlie time.'

'This is all very civilised,' Norah said, yawning. 'The last wedding I did the honours at, the bride and her mother were half cut by ten a.m.'

Shelly looked horrified. 'That certainly won't be happening today,' she said.

The wedding wasn't until four in the afternoon, as it was too hot before then, and they wanted the celebrations to carry on into the night.

Deirdre arrived with her outfit in a suit carrier and surprised them all by bringing matching pink dressing gowns with crystal writing on the back of each one.

'Mine says *Mother of the Bride*,' she said with a giggle. She handed Fee hers, with *Bride* on it, Norah and Leila got *Bridesmaid* and *Maid of Honour* and Shelly got *Mother of the Groom*.

'I hope mine goes around my tummy,' Leila said. 'I'll be the fattest bridesmaid in history.'

'Ah, that's fine,' said Deirdre. 'It's better than having you look like a movie star and Fiona looking like an old boot.'

'Mum!' Fee said, wide-eyed.

'Well it's true,' she said. 'I only picked Aine Murphy to be my bridesmaid because she had terrible acne and a dose of alopecia at the time.'

Fee looked mortified as Shelly, Leila and Norah stifled their giggles.

'No offence to you, Norah love. You're a fine-looking girl. I wouldn't have chosen you myself. I think Fiona is being brave to have you trotting around. But as you explained, you're on a mission to avoid being left on the shelf, though mind you don't extend that search to married men.'

'No, that wasn't my plan,' said Norah, laughing.

'I don't know why you're single, though. I've seen some of the guests who are coming today and they have fine men with them. They're nothing short of—'

'Mum!' Fee said. 'Let's try and have positive and kind talk, okay?'

Thankfully, the hair and make-up girls arrived just then. They'd come from Marbella – after the disaster of Ollie's christening day, Shelly had decided to reach further afield – and they were brilliant. They made each of them look their best, and as Shelly went to pay them, she promised to pass on prospective clients in the future.

'We not take all money today,' one of the girls said. 'You will give us more client and we only charge you half price.'

'Oh no, I couldn't do that,' Shelly said. 'It wouldn't be right. You've worked so hard.'

But the girls insisted, and Shelly shook their hands and assured them they would be the first names she'd recommend to her wedding guests.

Leila looked radiant in her dress. The pale shade of lemon they'd chosen was really becoming, and since the dress had been made to fit her properly, it flattered her blooming tummy. She looked so pretty with the matching tiny flowers the girls had entwined in her hair. Norah's dress had turned out just as she'd wanted it, too. It hugged her figure and made her feel every bit as sexy as she'd hoped.

Deirdre looked like the cat that got the cream as she emerged in her pale salmon-pink shift dress with matching cardigan. Her fascinator, encrusted with pearls, matched her demure stud earrings and her make-up flattered her alabaster skin.

'I think we all scrub up quite nicely,' said Shelly as she appeared in the pale green dress with matching shawl that she'd picked up in Marbella.

'You look very smart,' said Deirdre.

When Fee walked into the room, they were all silenced.

'Oh no,' she said. 'Do I not look right?'

'You look like an angel,' Shelly said.

'You really do, Fiona,' her mother said.

'I want to cry looking at your tiny waist,' Leila said. 'Jake is one lucky dude to be marrying you.'

'You're an advert for brides,' said Norah. 'You look amazing, Fee.'

Fee's smile could've lit the entire square as she made her way to the front of Casa Maria. Shelly had organised for a beautiful little horse-drawn cart to take her to the church. Dermot was sitting in it, looking delighted.

'Dad! Look at you in your suit. You're incredibly smart!'

'I'm beginning to melt, if the truth be told, Fiona. But your mother warned me against taking my jacket off. She said she'd smash my sundae glass.'

'Mum!' Fee laughed. 'That's a bit harsh.'

'You know what your father's like,' Deirdre said, sniffing. 'He'd be sitting there in his shirt with the sleeves rolled up, making a show of us. I had to hit him where it hurts.'

The ladies kissed Fee and said they'd see her in the square.

As they tottered slowly across the cobbles, with Leila reminding the others that it was much harder for her not to topple over on account of her bump, they were delighted with the scene that met them.

'The bride is on her way,' Shelly announced.

Deirdre waited for Fee and Dermot, with her camera poised. Leila found Matthew and Ollie, and Shelly stood hoping she'd manage to remain calm.

'Hello, Shelly.'

She turned to see Jim standing there.

'Hello, Jim,' she said, embracing him warmly. 'I'm so glad to see you.'

'I'm honoured to be here. I was blown away when Jake asked me to be his best man. An old codger like me.'

Shelly smiled. 'It was really important to Jake that you share in this day, and I'm so glad he chose you. Come on,' she said, slipping her arm through his, 'the bride is on her way.'

Jake appeared by their side. 'Hello, you two,' he said. 'Can we do a quick little salute? To Dad and to Martha. We all wish that both of them were here today.'

'I've got a feeling they're here in spirit,' Jim said.

Murmurings and a flutter of excitement let them know the bride had arrived. The horse and cart stopped just around the corner so Fee and Dermot could make their grand entrance.

The couple had decided on a church wedding after all. The christening had been so personal, and Fee knew it would mean the world to her parents. The compromise was that they would have a humanist ceremony but the priest had been gracious about allowing them to use the church, saying he would like to give them a final blessing. Both agreed that they would love that idea.

Jake and Jim quickly made their way to their position at the altar, while Shelly took up her place in the front pew. She looked to her right, where Gerry should have been sitting. *I miss you,* she said inwardly. *But I'm going to try hard not to be sad today. Help me to do that.*

Leila and Norah walked ahead, bursting with excitement. At the door of the church, they turned so they could see Fee's face.

'Oh my!' Fee said, smiling in delight as she drank in the scene in the square.

Valentina and Alejandro, directed by Señora Garza, who

was honouring them with her presence here today, had wound fairy lights around every pillar and post in sight. The square looked like a scene from fairyland. It continued inside the church, with extravagant flower displays that matched the flowers worn in the girls' hair and in Jake's buttonhole. The whole effect was incredibly romantic and special.

Fee made her way slowly down the aisle, looking like the happiest woman in the world. Jake was bowled over by how beautiful she was. When Dermot placed Fee's hand into his, he looked at her with shining eyes.

'Hi,' he said quietly.

'Hi,' she replied, smiling at him.

'You look incredibly beautiful,' he said, squeezing her hand.

'And I'd like to jump your bones too,' she deadpanned, making his shoulders shake with silent laughter.

'And that,' he said as the celebrant came towards him, 'is why I'm marrying you, you gorgeous woman.'

The humanist ceremony was well thought out and went off without a hitch. It was followed by the civil marriage ceremony and the blessing by the local priest. Finally, it was time for Jake to kiss his wife, which he did with a relish that made the whole congregation laugh and clap.

Afterwards they all made their way outside into the warm summer sunshine. Their joy filled the whole square and the atmosphere was fantastic.

Valentina and the team at Café del Sol had produced a delicious fancy picnic. Freshly sliced Parma ham with shavings of sweet nutty Parmesan cheese, spitting garlicky prawns *al pil pil*, and great big dishes of divine paella were enjoyed with warm, straight-from-the-oven crusty breads. There was no formality – Fee had no time for top tables or any of the other traditions. Instead, guests helped themselves liberally from trestle tables spread with food, taking their plates to the small tables and chairs outside, to the wall of the fountain, or to the benches that were dotted around the square.

The wedding cake was made up of layers of different flavours. The largest was chocolate biscuit, followed by lemon curd and topped off with rich carrot cake. It was unorthodox, but that was just how Fee and Jake had wanted it.

Purely for Deirdre and Dermot, Fee had also added a sundae course, made with summer berries and topped with home-made almond praline. They agreed it was as good as, if not better than, the Crunchie one they made at home. Fee caught Valentina's eye and gave her a thumbs-up. Her parents were a hard couple to please, but Valentina's stupendous cooking had managed to overcome their pickiness. In fact, Fee noticed they even had seconds of everything.

The guests mingled, ate and toasted the happy couple over and over again. The fact that the wedding meal was outside made it feel much more fun and free. People wandered around, chatting to each other and to the locals, enjoying themselves immensely.

As the sun started to dip down into the valley, Jake stood on the wall of the fountain and shouted above the din, inviting the guests to follow the bunting flags up the hill to Casa Maria.

'What's going on?' Fee asked. 'I thought we were having dancing here in the square?'

'All in good time,' he said. 'I'm using the opportunity of having eighty people here to advertise by word of mouth.'

'Good thinking,' she said with a grin, and they set off, leading the whole entourage out of the square and towards the hacienda.

Jim offered Shelly his arm and they walked together.

'It's been great having you by my side today,' she said. 'I don't know how I'd have managed without you.'

'I still find it incredibly hard,' he admitted. 'It's difficult to break the habit of a lifetime. We were both married for so long. It's a shock to be suddenly alone.'

'That's exactly it,' Shelly said, nodding. 'Will I get used to it?' she asked hopefully.

Jim smiled. 'Maybe. But I won't lie, it's one of the hardest things about being on your own. You suddenly realise you're minus a plus-one, and it changes everything. People think twice before inviting you to things because you unbalance the numbers. You've been occupying a world made for two, and you fitted it so perfectly, you didn't even realise that was what it was.'

Shelly nodded sadly. 'I suppose that's true. At least I've made some new friends. I think people who didn't know you as part of a couple tend to find it easier to go with the flow.'

Jim looked thoughtful. 'Yes, that makes sense,' he admitted. 'Maybe that's been my mistake, treading in the same old waters.' He nodded at her. 'You're right, Shelly. I need to take a leaf out of your book and get out more, meet new people on my own terms.'

As they walked into Casa Maria, Jim was silenced by the sight that greeted him. Expecting an unprepossessing old pile, he was wildly impressed by the newly revitalised hacienda. Shelly proudly described the work they had done, how they had rescued the garden, the sheer level of graft that had gone into making it look as it looked today.

'Gerry would be so, so proud of you,' Jim said, taking it all in.

'Thank you,' Shelly said, emotion clear in her voice. 'It means everything to me that you would think that.'

They made their way to the wonderful champagne reception held in the living room, hall and dining room. Jim fetched a flute of bubbly for Shelly, then fell into his best man duty, making sure everyone was being looked after. Once every guest had a glass in their hand, Jake proposed a toast to his beautiful wife, and then Fee did the same to her handsome husband.

When Jim took to the stairs to deliver his speech to the people thronged below, he silenced the place.

'I'm an odd choice for a best man,' he began. 'Because I was also best man at Shelly and Gerry's wedding over thirty-five years ago.'

There was a ripple of ah's around the rooms.

'But sadly, my own wife, Martha, and Jake's beloved dad Gerry are no longer with us. So it's my great honour to be here today. I think it's fitting that I should stand up and speak about Jake, seeing as I've known him all his life.'

The speech was wonderful. Jim talked about how Gerry had reacted to having a son, and how proud he'd been of him. He also talked about Shelly and Leila, 'the first two women in Jake's life', then moved seamlessly to Fee and said that he was officially handing him over to her care on behalf of Gerry and Shelly.

'I've no doubt that Fee can handle Jake. If he misbehaves, she could always cut off a finger, or even a limb.'

By the time his speech was over, everyone had laughed and cried. Although it wasn't the usual type where a fellow young man tried to make a fool of the groom, everyone agreed it was the best speech ever.

As the mood lifted and it was clear that lots of people wanted to dance, Jake let them know that the band were ready to get going back in the square.

Most of the revellers left quickly, but Shelly, Jim, Giselle, Deirdre, Dermot and a few others stayed behind, choosing to sit in the living room with a last glass of champagne before bed.

'We can't get over the food and the atmosphere,' said Deirdre. 'We would definitely come back here again.'

'Yes, and we haven't even been to the ice-cream parlour yet,' Dermot said.

'I'm so glad you like it here,' said Shelly. 'We'll go and explore the bullring and the museum tomorrow. I think you'll find it really interesting.'

Giselle told stories about the days gone by, and how Charlotte and José had entertained famous matadors.

'Casa Maria was *the* place to be,' she said. 'And now, thanks to Shelly, it will be again.'

'A toast to Shelly,' Jim said.

They all raised their glasses, and Shelly felt the warmth of their regard, and their friendship. It was a wonderful feeling.

Through the open windows, the faint sound of music reached them from the square. There, Jake and a now barefoot Fee swayed in rhythm, holding each other close, never letting go. Around them, their friends danced and laughed and celebrated.

'What a wonderful day,' Fee murmured into Jake's ear.

'And it's just the first of many,' he said, kissing her gently.

Chapter 50

THE NEXT DAY STARTED QUIETLY AS EVERYONE slept off the effects of their late night, but Fee was up early, determined to take her parents on the promised special trip to Marbella. Jake groaned when her alarm clock woke them, but she pushed him out of bed, laughing at his protestations. It didn't take long for them to get showered, dressed for the beautifully warm morning and ready to go.

When they reached the square, Deirdre and Dermot were sitting stiffly side by side on a bench, looking for all the world like two strangers waiting for a bus.

'Look at them,' Fee said, shaking her head and smiling. 'What are they like?'

Jake had organised a hire car, and he drove them to the affluent port, where they strolled along ogling the yachts belonging to the rich and famous.

'I'm shocked by the girls in skimpy bikinis lolling around and prancing on the decks of those boats,' Deirdre said. 'Have they no shame?'

'I think they're rather proud of the fact that they're on those boats in the first place,' Dermot said.

Jake asked Dermot if he'd like to join him for a coffee, and Dermot readily accepted. Fee cast a longing look as they sat themselves outside a pretty café and she was marched off to go shopping with Deirdre. She'd thought Deirdre would enjoy seeing the high-end boutiques of Marbella, but as soon as they walked in the door of the first one, she regretted the decision.

Her mother was dressed in Bermuda shorts with a vest top and her ancient strappy brown leather sandals that she'd owned since the year dot. The shops were full of designer goods, most of them were either leopard print, or sparkly, or both.

'Who on earth would want to go around in that?' Deirdre asked, pulling a white dress with Swarovski crystals from the rail. 'You have a grand figure on you, Fiona, but you'd be like a lady of the night in that.'

'Can I help you?' the assistant asked, looking like she already thought they required far more help than she could ever give.

'Definitely not,' said Deirdre, utterly oblivious to the saleswoman's snootiness. 'Have you any normal clothes in here?' she asked. 'I shop in Marks and Spencer, and they have the most beautiful selection of things. Every colour you could want. This place has about ten things. Don't you get bored looking at them?'

'This store stocks only couture label with magnificent cut,' the lady said, looking Deirdre up and down with disdain.

'Oh look, Fiona,' Deirdre said, laughing suddenly. 'Put your hand out again, love,' she said to the assistant. 'Show my daughter your nails. They are a gas. I've never seen nails as long as those. Are they meant to be dogs on there?'

'This,' said the horrified woman, 'is nail art, and they are also couture.'

'That's hilarious,' said Deirdre. 'Wait until I tell the neighbours about this. They won't believe it. I'll bet you don't do much cleaning with those yokes stuck to your fingers.'

'Come on, Mum, we'd better go,' said Fee, who was just about ready to drag her out physically.

'Bye now, love,' Deirdre said to the sales assistant, who looked like she was about to call the police. 'If you get a chance to go to Marks' any time, I think you'd love it.'

They walked to the end of the promenade and met up with the men. Fee had done her research, and she led them towards the place she hoped they would love. Nothing, though, could have prepared her for the hysteria that followed.

'I can't believe it,' Deirdre said in awe. 'Look at it, Dermot.'

They spent the next ten minutes swapping phones and taking photographs on each one – and that was just for the outside of the ice-cream parlour. As they shot inside and pressed their faces against the cool glass of the display cases, Fee was terrified they'd lose the run of themselves altogether.

'Let's sit and look at the menus,' she suggested, corralling them into a corner seat.

Fee ordered a coffee while her parents laboured over the decision of which sundae they'd go for. Their excitement was infectious, and Fee and Jake figured a good feed of ice cream would be the perfect cure for their hangovers.

'I'd never have thought of coming here ordinarily,' Fee admitted. 'But I cannot tell you how much I'm enjoying this. I had no idea that Ferrero Rocher ice cream would be so amazing.'

'Mine is out of this world,' said Jake. 'I think we've found a new place to come.'

Deirdre and Dermot were beaming as they left.

'Have we converted you both to sundaes?' Deirdre asked. 'Can you understand why we were so taken with Melissa now?'

When they drove back up to Rondilla, lots of the wedding guests were wandering about. Some were eating at the various restaurants and cafés and others were at the bullring museum.

Shelly had issued an open invitation for a buffet supper at Casa Maria that evening. Jake and Fee spent some more time in bed, then around five o'clock they showered and changed and walked hand in hand up to Casa Maria.

When they arrived, the food on display was mouth-watering. Everything from fresh squid to large colourful platters of delicious salads was on offer. At the edge of the garden two chefs, complete with tall hats and striped aprons, were tending to a pig on a spit.

'Mum, this is incredible,' Jake said. 'I had no idea you were putting on such a spread.'

'Well, we couldn't expect your guests to come such a long way and not feed them properly. Besides,' she said, looking impish, 'I wanted to make sure these hog-roast fellows are worth their salt. One of my wedding bookings is using them.'

'Ah,' said Jake, 'so we're the guinea pigs!'

The evening was balmy, and even by nine thirty there was still enough heat in the sun for people to sit comfortably outside. With citronella candles spiked into the ground, the garden looked stunning.

Leila and Matthew made a little announcement that their

wedding gift to the happy couple was ready to go, and everyone turned as a traditional Spanish band began to play flamenco music.

A wooden dance floor had been erected, and two dancers in full flamenco dress appeared. When their castanet-twirling dance finished, they pulled the merry guests onto the floor and an impromptu lesson took place. Everyone from Fee's parents to the bride and groom's friends joined in.

When the party was in full swing, Shelly went over to Jake and Fee for a quiet word. They smiled and nodded at what she said to them, then split up to round up the others. Five minutes later, the whole family was gathered in front of the carob tree – Jake, Fee, Shelly, Leila, Matthew and Ollie. Shelly had asked the photographer to do a special family portrait beside Gerry's tree. He lined them up and took a number of shots, before releasing them back to the dancing.

'Thank you so much,' Shelly said to the young man. 'When will you have the photos ready, do you think?'

'I bring them in two days, okay?' he said.

He was a very personable young man, and Shelly knew he was eager to impress her and become the recommended photographer for her wedding packages.

'That would be perfect,' she said, smiling. 'And will that include the other photo I talked to you about?'

'Oh yes,' he said, nodding. 'I look at that last night and this will be no problem. I can do as you requested.'

Shelly clapped her hands in delight. 'Wonderful. Thank you so much for all your hard work today.'

'*De nada*,' he said, smiling shyly.

* * *

Leila and baby Ollie were the first to sneak away to bed, while everyone else was still dancing.

'Sorry to be a lightweight,' she said to Shelly and Matthew. 'But I'm beat.'

'I don't know how those young people do it,' Shelly said, looking at the dance floor in awe. 'They've been going for hours.'

'I know,' Matthew said, 'and the thing is, the band and dancers were only paid for a couple of hours' service. I've told them several times that they can go, but they keep saying they're having too much fun! I think I've done my bit for Spanish–Irish relations.'

Leila laughed. 'Well you've certainly taught them that Irish people can't dance! Right, I'm off before I sit down and stay another hour. This little man needs to be tucked up in bed. Goodnight, you two.'

'Night,' chorused Matthew and Shelly.

'I think we can safely say the hog roast has been a roaring success,' Shelly said to Matthew, pointing to the plates of meat sandwiches doing the rounds. 'It fed the whole party, and look, there's still enough left over for a midnight snack.'

'Great value,' Matthew said. 'You know, if you ever want help with the figures, like working out the margins and where you're making and losing money, I'd be delighted to help. I've never had the best head for maths, but I've had to learn on the job, so I might be of some use.'

Shelly looked at him gratefully. 'That would actually be fantastic, Matthew,' she said. 'In fact, could we do it over the next few days? It would be very instructive to work out the costs associated with this wedding and extrapolate from that.'

'Absolutely,' Matthew said. 'I was hoping I could have a role here, so bookkeeper will suit me fine.'

Shelly laughed. 'It's a proper family business, isn't it?' she said.

'In the very best sense of the term, yes,' Matthew agreed.

Chapter 51

TWO DAYS LATER, JAKE AND FEE HEADED OFF ON A driving tour for their honeymoon, promising to be back a week later. Leila and Matthew had to return to Dublin as well, and Shelly sadly said goodbye to them and baby Ollie. The wedding guests were very reluctant to leave, but once Jake and Fee were gone, that signalled the exodus. By the time the last of them had left Rondilla, Shelly had a couple of days' grace before her first paying customers arrived.

Jim was staying on a whole week, using some of the many holiday days he had built up. He hadn't been bothered with holidays since Martha had died, but Shelly could see that Rondilla was working its magical effect on him. She smiled to herself as she watched him relax into a slower pace, reckoning he might well be a regular visitor from now on.

Over breakfast a few days later, he broached a subject that had been bothering him.

'You need a car, Shelly. You're far too dependent on taxis and it makes no sense.'

She smiled; it was exactly what Gerry would've said. 'I also need to learn more Spanish. I know enough to greet people and get by. I mean, I wouldn't starve or die of thirst. But I need to be able to do orders for the business and converse with the locals.'

'I saw a Smart car for sale when I was passing a large garage on the way into the port,' Jim said. 'It would be ideal, and easy to manage.'

'Sounds good,' she said as she swiped away on her iPad. 'Hey, there's a language school that sounds as if it's close to the garage you're talking about. Would you come with me, and I'll try to sign up for some classes?'

'I'd be delighted to,' said Jim.

By the time a taxi arrived, they'd both almost lost patience with the idea of going anywhere.

'You could've been there and had yourself organised by now if you had a car,' Jim said grumpily.

'I know,' Shelly said. 'I think I needed to get to this point, though. Where I can't bear it any longer.'

Sure enough, the Smart car was perfect for Shelly's needs. She took it for a little drive and came back smiling.

'Will I shake hands with him now and call it a deal?' she asked Jim.

'You certainly will not,' he said, puffing out his chest. 'It's a nice enough car, but it's too expensive. We'll look around. Pity, though,' he said, kicking a tyre. 'It's almost a good little buy.'

'How much you will pay me?' the salesman asked, looking terrified at the thought that they might walk away.

Jim offered him eight hundred euros less than the asking price. 'I can't pay a cent more,' he said.

The salesman glanced from one to the other. Shelly was sweating and wishing the whole ordeal could be over.

'Okay, sir. You can have car for your wife. She is beautiful lady.'

Shelly laughed out loud when he said that. 'Thank you,' she said, kissing Jim's cheek.

They stood and stared at one another awkwardly for a minute.

'Thank you,' she whispered.

She paid the man and they walked amicably towards the language school. There were posters in the window, and instantly Shelly pointed to one.

'Look, there's a beginners' class starting this Thursday,' she said. Suddenly nerves overtook her. 'Oh, I don't know if it's such a wise idea now that I'm here,' she said. 'What if I'm the only one who hasn't a breeze?'

'You won't be,' said an English voice from behind them.

They turned to see a woman who looked to be of similar age to Shelly.

'I'm Anna. I've just moved here to live with my sister. I lost my husband two years ago and found England with no family of my own far too lonesome. I can't understand a single word the locals say and I'm fed up with myself.'

Shelly smiled at her bluntness. 'I'm Shelly,' she said. 'I moved to Rondilla recently following *my* husband's death.'

'Well then,' said Anna. 'We'll egg each other on. Although you clearly don't waste time.' She looked Jim up and down.

'Oh, Jim is an old friend, that's all,' Shelly said. 'He's here visiting because my son just got married.'

'Pleased to meet you,' said Anna. As she sidled over to Jim, Shelly noticed him jump.

The two women signed up and even swapped phone numbers, while Jim waited outside.

'I'm so pleased to have met you,' Anna said. 'I feel that I rely on my sister hugely, and it would be wonderful to have a friend of my own!'

'Likewise,' Shelly said.

They chatted easily for another few moments before Anna glanced at her watch and realised she was late for a hairdresser's appointment.

'See you on Thursday. See you too, Jim,' she said, and winked at him.

As Anna walked away, Jim took Shelly's arm and rushed her in the other direction.

'She seemed like fun,' said Shelly.

'She pinched my bottom,' Jim said, looking utterly shocked.

Shelly stared at him for a moment, then burst out laughing.

'It's not funny,' he said, looking mortified. 'I'm not used to being treated as an . . . an object . . .'

As soon as he said it, the two of them fell about laughing.

They walked on towards the port. The sun was shining and it was absolutely scorching, so they decided to sit inside for lunch and enjoy the view of the water from a cooler spot.

'It's been a pretty productive day so far,' Shelly said. 'I'm really excited about my little car. And I think the Spanish classes will be fun, especially now that I've met Anna. You won't have to worry about her, seeing as you'll be up in the sky!'

'I'm actually considering winding my hours down, Shelly,' he said. 'I'm getting too old to tear about the world. What am I doing it for? *Who* am I doing it for?'

'It's a totally different pace of life here,' said Shelly. 'I know Gerry would've loved it. It makes me sad that he never got to enjoy his retirement. He worked so hard for so many years. I wonder if he's sitting on a deckchair somewhere with a cold beer.'

'I'll bet he is,' Jim said. 'Do you reckon Martha is sitting beside him, helping him the way I'm trying to help you?'

'Do you know what? I hope she is,' Shelly said, as she put her hand out.

He placed his hand on top and smiled.

'It's so unfair that you're not allowed to have this time with him. I know I'm only a trailing second choice, but you've been so amazing to me since I lost Martha. I'd never have survived without you and Gerry during the first dark days. I never dreamed I'd be returning the favour.'

'You're not a trailing anything,' Shelly said. 'I've needed you more over the last few days than you'll ever realise.'

'I'm glad I could be here. For you and for Jake. He's a credit to you and Gerry. Fee is a fabulous girl; I think they'll be very happy together.'

'I certainly hope so,' said Shelly.

After they had ordered, they sat in companionable silence, both of them deep in thought.

'I know it's far too soon for you to even entertain the thought of finding someone else,' Jim said hesitantly. 'I don't know if we could ever be anything more than friends.'

'What are you saying, Jim?' she asked, looking shocked.

'I just want to put it out there . . . Any time you need a plus-one, I'd be honoured. No strings attached.'

She smiled at him, and nodded. 'We've spent a lot of time in each other's company over the years, haven't we?'

'Yes, it's just that there used to be four of us, and we're all that's left now.'

There was no awkwardness between them. Shelly appreciated Jim's offer. She felt no pressure in any way and she knew that she would happily ask him to accompany her should the situation arise.

'For what it's worth, I'm available for you as a plus-one too.'

'With or without strings?' he asked.

She laughed. 'Without for now. I still love Gerry so much, it physically hurts. I don't know if that will ever change. But if it does, you'll be the first to know.'

'That'll do nicely,' he said.

They smiled at each other in easy understanding. What Shelly had said was true: she still loved Gerry with an intensity that she feared might never ease. In her heart, she felt she had had her great love and there would be no one else. But then the last twelve months had held more change than the previous ten years, so she didn't dare make any vows to herself. Life was constantly shifting: that was one thing her time on earth had taught her. Things mightn't change all that much, but they certainly never stayed the same.

Epilogue

SHELLY WAS SO PLEASED THAT EVERYONE COULD gather again, just as she'd hoped. It was Gerry's first anniversary, just ten days after the wedding, and she had wanted the whole family together in Rondilla to mark the day. Jake and Fee were due back from their driving trip anyway, but she hadn't been sure about Leila and her family. Thankfully, they were able to come and were on their way right now. They were due to arrive in the afternoon, which should coincide nicely with Jake and Fee's arrival.

Shelly was sitting out under the carob tree, allowing herself to remember. It had been the strangest year of her life in many ways, starting with devastation, then slowly becoming a story of renewal and acceptance. She still couldn't quite believe this was her life now, but she had plotted it out and Casa Maria was her new home. Probably for a long time, she thought as she looked up at the love heart carved into the trunk of the tree.

She was sitting at a table that was spread with photos. The wedding photographer had been as good as his word, and the pictures he had delivered were marvellous. The day had been captured beautifully in a fly-on-the-wall manner that made her relive it all so clearly. She would most certainly be putting all the business she could his way. She was delighted with the work he had done for her, and today was the day to deliver it. Hopefully it would be well received.

She slid a large black-and-white photo into a stiff envelope, leaving the rest behind, and set off down the driveway of Casa Maria. Outside the gate, she turned right, making her way towards Señora Garza's house.

When the front door opened, Giselle's face broke into a smile. 'Shelly, what a lovely surprise. Come in, I'm so pleased to see you.'

They sat in the meticulously tidy kitchen, enjoying a cup of English breakfast tea. After some minutes catching up, Shelly produced the envelope and slid it across the table. 'This is for you. A gift. I hope you like it.'

Giselle looked taken aback, then curious. She picked up the envelope and opened the seal, peering inside at the contents. When she pulled out the photograph and looked at it, she gasped, then held it close, examining every millimetre of it. She looked over at Shelly, unable to speak, as tears rolled down her cheeks.

'I don't understand,' she said in a choked voice. 'Where . . . how did you get this?'

Shelly smiled. 'I hope it isn't a shock for you. I saw it among Alejandro's photos, and after a while, I noticed that there was a woman in it. When you showed me your photograph of Charlotte, I realised it was the same woman.'

'But I've never seen this before,' Giselle said, transfixed by the image of Charlotte curled up in the armchair in Casa Maria, lost in a book.

'Yes, you have,' Shelly said. 'It was among your photos, but it was very hard to make out the figure. I had a local photographer work on it, and thanks to modern technology, he was able to blow it up so you could see her like this.'

'My God,' Giselle said, touching the photograph as if it was Charlotte's cheek she was stroking.

'It's amazing, isn't it?' Shelly said. 'I couldn't believe it worked so well myself. And I love the fact that she's so casual and at ease with herself. The photograph you have is very stiff and formal, so I thought you'd enjoy having one like this, where she's more like herself.'

'Shelly,' Giselle said, and it came out as a gasp. 'I can never, ever thank you enough. This is the most precious thing I've ever received. I'm just so . . . so overwhelmed.'

Shelly put her hand over Giselle's.

'When people are gone, photographs truly are precious,' she said. 'I'm so glad I was able to retrieve this for you.'

They embraced, and Giselle kissed her cheek, which really took Shelly by surprise. She took her leave, smiling to herself about the sea change in Giselle's life these past months, as much as in her own.

Back at Casa Maria, she returned to the photos on the table. The album had arrived from Jen in Dublin, and it was to be her anniversary gift to her children – eighteen photos that summed up Gerry's *joie de vivre* and his love for all three of them. Her fiftieth birthday seemed like a lifetime ago. It was amazing how much things could change in just twelve short months.

The album was not complete yet, though. Jen had done a superb job on it, but there was still something missing. She sifted through and selected a stunning photo of the family gathered under the carob tree. She gazed at it and smiled. Her beautiful family. Yes, it was missing a hugely important person, but this was its new make-up, and that needed to be celebrated now too. In the photo, Leila had smoothed down her dress so that her bump was clearly visible – the next chapter in their lives was well under way. Shelly would never stop missing Gerry, but she knew now that she could live without him, and that was a lot more than she'd once thought possible.

Carefully she glued the recent family photo into the last page of the album, which Jen had left free, as requested. Then she folded down the clear flap, to keep it safe.

Now it was complete.

She wrapped the album tastefully, finishing it with an oversized red bow. She would present it to Jake and Leila today, on the anniversary of the day Gerry had left them. It would make them laugh and cry in equal measure, but that was just how life was, she supposed. Looking up at the trunk of the carob tree, she blew a kiss to her husband, the love of her life.

'We'll spend the whole day talking about you, my darling,' she whispered into the air. 'We'll remember and never forget.'

Hearing the sound of a car door shutting, Shelly stepped out onto the path, and saw that they had all arrived. Jake and Fee, Leila and Matthew and Ollie were laughing together in front of the entrance to Casa Maria, kissing and hugging and talking loudly. She watched them for a moment, happy that they were here with her. As she gazed proudly at them, she realised that this was their home now, as much as hers. And more than that, these people she cherished would always be there for each other. That was truly the one thing that mattered most of all.

'Hello, you lot,' she called as she walked towards them, arms outstretched. 'Welcome home.'

Emma Hannigan

The Wedding Promise

Bonus Material

engage with me on Facebook (Author Emma Hannigan) and Twitter (@MsEmmaHannigan) or via my website (www.emmahannigan.com).

The Wedding Promise was my companion at a time when I was in so much pain that I couldn't get out of bed, sometimes for days on end. The characters became my world and what happened to them truly mattered to me. I sincerely hope my cherished readers will connect with my fictitious friends and enjoy the story as it unfolds. Its setting is based on the stunning Ronda high above Marbella in Spain and I hope you will get a sense of this special place.

As I sign off on this book, I am so grateful for the opportunity to share another story with you. Without my writing and the ability to use my imagination to take me away from the sickness I've been enduring, I honestly don't know how I might have coped. Writing is my job and I take that very seriously. But it is also my hobby and my favourite form of escapism. I know I am very lucky to have found this path in life.

Thank you for reading *The Wedding Promise* and I really hope you enjoy connecting with the characters as much as I did.

Wishing you all health and happiness, love and light
Emma x

Acknowledgements

AS ALWAYS, I AM INCREDIBLY GRATEFUL TO everyone who helped me get this book to print. Sending a new novel into the world takes a team effort and I am so lucky to have the greatest people with me.

Huge thanks to my editors Ciara Doorley and Sherise Hobbs of Hachette Books Ireland and Headline respectively. Together you nurture my writing and bring out the best in my stories.

Thanks to Rachel Pierce for her amazing copyediting skills. Her attention to detail and fabulous suggestions were so gratefully received.

Thanks to team Hachette Books Ireland (Ciara, Breda, Jim, Ruth, Joanna, Siobhan and Bernard) for all that you do. Special thanks to Ruth Shern for taking me to bookshops up and down the land of Ireland to do signings. Thanks to Susie Cronin for her PR skills and general kindness.

Thanks to team Headline, especially Sherise Hobbs, Jo Liddiard, Fran Gough and Emily Gowers for all your hard work and for minding me so carefully when I come to London.

Massive thanks to my agent Sheila Crowley at Curtis Brown, who is always there to champion me, counsel me, chat to me and keep me afloat! Thanks also to her lovely assistant Abbie Greaves at Curtis Brown for all the wonderful help.

The past year has been one of the toughest of my life health-wise. I've been in more pain than I ever thought possible. My cancer returned for a phenomenal tenth time and on this occasion the battle was fierce. It invaded my neck, shoulders and skull and it wasn't pretty. But thanks to my astonishing medical team at Blackrock clinic, led by Dr David Fennelly, I am slowly bouncing back. I am so lucky to have such a dedicated group of clever and caring people looking after me. I owe them my life and cannot ever thank them for what they do each day.

I wouldn't have stayed sane without my family over the past year. My husband Cian and our children Sacha and Kim have been troopers. My parents Philip and Denise have carried me like never before. Our cat Tom and dog Herbie have helped with lots of furry snuggles. I wish this hideous disease would get the hint and leave us all alone. I despise the fact that cancer has invaded our lives and caused so much stress. All I can say is thank you all for being here with me. It's a horrible journey and I wish I didn't have to drag you all through it too. I would be nothing without you all. Thank you seems weak and meaningless in return for what you do, but I hope I can show you how grateful I am in the coming months when I rise from the ashes and start to have fun again.

I have wonderful friends. I am so aware of the love and support you all show me. Thank you from the bottom of my heart.

My readers constantly send me messages of support and those nuggets of divine human kindness lift my spirits higher than the clouds above. Please continue to chat and

My special memory of Ronda

WHERE MY NOVELS ARE SET IS OF HUGE IMPORTANCE to me. I have written about rural places and cities and my books are predominantly set in Ireland. So this time I wanted to take my readers to another country. Spain is a place I adore. I spent time there as an exchange student in my teens and like so many others I've had many wonderful holidays there, and so Rondilla where Casa Maria exists is based on memories of a trip to the beautiful Ronda.

That particular visit has always stayed in my mind. Cian and I were newly married and we'd gone on a holiday to Marbella with a large group of friends. Most of the group were either unattached or with their current squeeze (some of whom disappeared into the woodwork soon after that time!)

Cian and I were the first of our friends to get married and at the time of that holiday we were in our twenties. Needless to say, the holiday involved plenty of sangria and beer for everyone but me. I was six months pregnant with our son!

I thoroughly enjoyed the holiday and our friends were incredibly kind to me but there were moments when I felt like the boring one in the corner, with the big bump and the swollen ankles.

On one of the days we decided to take a day trip to the stunningly picturesque Ronda. As usual, I was the designated driver, which I didn't mind. But as we trooped around, with the relentless heat of the sun beating down on us, the group decided to stop for cool drinks. They ordered chilled white wine and iced bottles of beer. I asked for a sparkling water. Not exactly exciting but it was all I could think of.

As the alcoholic beverages were served, I know I was gazing at them longingly! I distinctly recall rubbing my belly and smiling as I concentrated on the fact that our baby's health was far more important than the cool glass of wine I was craving!

Once all the other drinks had been served, the waitress, who was full of smiles from the moment we sat down, approached with a small round tray thrust high above her head. Ceremoniously she placed a tall tulip-shaped glass in front of me. She had threaded fresh fruit on to a pretty cocktail umbrella and coated the rim of the glass with sugar.

'I thought you would be happier with something more exciting than water. No alcohol, just fruit,' she said. 'My gift to you, Mama.'

It was the first time I'd been called *Mama* and it was such a lovely surprise that I promptly began to blub! This is really unusual for me, as I am not a crier. Never have been and probably never will be. So Cian and all our friends got great mileage out of seeing me swatting my hands around my face as I made a complete fool of myself!

I'm placing part of the blame on baby hormones and secondly I wholeheartedly acknowledge that the kindness and thoughtfulness of a complete stranger totally knocked me for six.

So Ronda has a very special place in my heart. It's a

place that makes me smile when I think of it. That lovely gesture from a total stranger has always stayed with me.

When I began writing about Casa Maria and the village, I had this warm fuzzy memory in my mind. I hope my readers will fall in love with this place the way I did with Ronda.

Our son is now in his late teens and while we were on holiday in Marbella recently, I told him the story. He made me laugh out loud when he said that he would've preferred the beer to a fruit cocktail! While I don't mind him having a cool beer now that he's older, I certainly wouldn't have given it to him while he was still a mere bump!

I hope you enjoy discovering Ronda through my eyes in *The Wedding Promise*.

Unwrap this captivating story about hope, love and the special bond between mothers and daughters.

Happy Birthday, darling girl . . .

Ever since she can remember, Roisin has received a birthday card in the post. Signed with love from the birth mother she has never met.

Brought up by her adoptive parents, Keeley and Doug, Roisin has wanted for nothing. But on her thirtieth birthday a letter comes that shakes her world. For Keeley, who's raised Roisin as her own, the letter reminds her of a guilty secret she's been holding for thirty years.

And for Nell, keeping watch in the lighthouse, the past is a place she rarely goes. Until a young runaway arrives seeking shelter, and unwraps the gift of hope for them all . . .

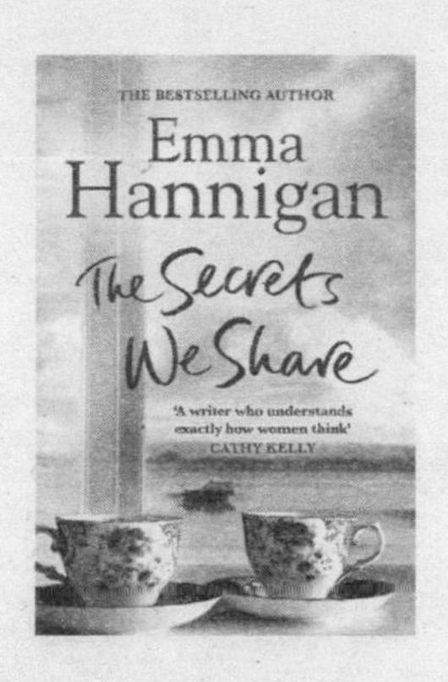

Don't miss this beautiful moving story of heart and home . . .

Devastated after a tragedy, Nathalie Conway finds herself on a plane to Ireland. She is on her way to stay with her grandmother Clara. The grandmother who, up until now, Nathalie had no idea existed . . .

As Clara awaits her granddaughter's arrival, she is filled with a new sense of hope. She has spent the last twenty years praying her son Max would come back into her life. Perhaps now he can find a way to forgive her for the past. And her granddaughter may be the thread to stitch the pieces of her beloved family back together.

Uncover the magical secrets of Caracove in Emma Hannigan's glorious novel

A little magic is about to come to sleepy Caracove Bay . . .

Lexie and her husband Sam have spent years lovingly restoring No. 3 Cashel Square to its former glory. So imagine Lexie's delight when a stranger knocks on the door, asking to see the house she was born in over sixty years ago.

Kathleen is visiting from America, longing to see her childhood home . . . and longing for distraction from the grief of losing her husband.

And as Lexie and Sam battle over whether or not to have a baby and Kathleen struggles with her loss, the two women realise their unexpected friendship will touch them in ways neither could have imagined.

A heartwarming novel of love, friendship and coming home from this bestselling author . . .

When actress Jodi Ludlum returns to the Dublin village of Bakers Valley to raise her young son, she's determined to shield him from the media glare that follows her in LA. But coming home means leaving her husband behind – and waking old ghosts.

Francine Hennessy was born and raised in Bakers Valley. To all appearances, she is the model wife, mother, home-maker and career woman. But, behind closed doors, Francine's life is crumbling around her.

As Jodi struggles to conceal her secrets and Francine faces some shocking news, the two become unlikely confidantes. Suddenly having the perfect life seems less important than finding friendship, and the perfect place to belong . . .